A Summe[illegible]

Also by Elise Darcy

The Living Apart Together series

Living Apart Together

It Takes 2 to Tango

Dear John

Love on the Rooftop

Standalone books

Lola & The Man

A Mallorcan Affair

The Villa in Sicily

We'll Meet Again

The Sunrise Coast series

New Beginnings at the Harbour Inn

The Secret of the Summerhouse

The Cottage by the Sea

The Guesthouse at Shingle Cove

The Houseboat by the Quay

Return to Willow Tree Cottage

The Bookshop of Memories

The Beach House

A Summer to Remember

A Novel

ELISE DARCY

Penny Lane Press

ISBN 978-1-913147-24-2

"We must get rid of the life we've planned, so as to have the life that is waiting for us."— Joseph Campbell

1

Lorna closed the front door after her last music lesson. She'd stood at the front door of her Oxford home, watching her young student, Olive, walk down the short front garden path towards her mum, who was waiting in her car. She'd given a little wave before retreating inside and closing the door. Olive would not be returning as a student, she was not interested in continuing her lessons. She reminded Lorna of her own daughter at that age.

Lorna smiled. Like Olive, she was also taking a break from lessons, although not indefinitely. She'd decided that she was taking a sabbatical from teaching. She'd organised the break both from her job teaching music in a high school and from her private tutoring commitments. The only person who didn't know yet was her husband.

Lorna stood for a moment, still smiling, thinking about her plans. She would be turning forty soon, at the end of October. Although she had intended to spend the long summer holiday doing something special to celebrate prior to her birthday, that plan had been put on hold. Her daughter, Briony, had graduated, and Lorna had found herself hanging on, putting her only child first, as always, waiting to attend Briony's graduation. Briony had achieved a first-class honours degree in biology and was on her way to achieve her dream of becoming a marine biologist, even though Lorna had tried to discourage her at every turn.

Lorna wished that Briony hadn't had such a fascination with the sea and marine life. Her smile slipped. She felt so guilty about not encouraging her daughter's passion. It was all because of what had happened in her own past, which her daughter knew absolutely nothing about – and never would. She'd made sure of that by cutting off all contact with Briony's maternal grandmother.

After putting her own plans on hold to focus on Briony's graduation, she'd then hung on to see her daughter off on a trip of a lifetime in the autumn; she got a coveted place on a research trip to the Galapagos Islands.

Lorna was so proud of her. She knew it would be a wrench for her, leaving her boyfriend, Freddie, behind to go on her trip, but as Lorna had said to her, *Sometimes in a relationship you just have to put yourself first for a change.*

Lorna was doing that now. Her thoughts turned to Andrew. After meeting him at university, starting a family while they were still undergraduate students, and then spending twenty-two years with him, she felt it was about time she put herself first for a change.

Her daughter had finally flown the nest. On her return from the trip, she'd be moving in with Freddie. He had mentioned their plans to her, but it had been the first she'd heard of it. She was surprised that Briony hadn't told her.

Her daughter had lived at home during her undergraduate studies but had moved into the small one-bedroomed apartment on the top floor of the house. It had originally belonged to Lorna's father, Edwin – he'd converted the attic many years earlier for himself. The location of the house had always been convenient; it was within walking distance of Oxford University, where he lectured, but he hadn't needed a family home anymore. Back when Lorna graduated, she'd known he was hoping that she and Andrew would live in the house and raise a family there. That was why he had gifted them the house, even though he was still living there in the attic. It was unconventional, still living with a parent under the same roof, but Andrew had no problem moving in with Lorna *and* her father in her lovely childhood home.

Edwin had also been a wonderful grandfather, and babysitter, for Briony up until she was nine, when he'd left his position at Oxford University – rather abruptly, Lorna had thought at the time – and had just upped sticks and moved to America, where he'd got a position in the history department at Stanford University. They'd head-hunted him, which hadn't surprised Lorna. What had surprised her, though, had been his decision to go.

And so, nine years later, when Briony had started university, she'd moved upstairs to the apartment.

Lorna cast her eyes heavenward as she walked down the hallway. Now the apartment was Angel's home. Angel was Briony's best friend from university, and she had graduated the same year. Briony had offered the attic room to Angel, which had enabled her to remain in Oxford and take up a research assistant post at the university while she studied for a doctorate.

Angel's job wasn't well paid, and Briony knew her parents never charged a great deal when renting out the attic. They'd taken in lodgers in the past at below-market rents after Edwin had left for America. Mostly they were visiting lecturers or overseas postgraduate students. Lorna guessed that her daughter had thought they might do that again, when she left, so she'd offered Angel first dibs on the apartment.

Lorna had become accustomed to only having family in the house, the way it had been when her father had lived upstairs. Although each lodger who had rented the attic had become good friends, almost like family, Lorna had known for a while that once her daughter left, she wouldn't feel as though she wanted another lodger. However, she had also known that the house would feel empty as soon as Briony walked out of the door with her suitcases. She hadn't been looking forward to empty nest syndrome. It would have been just her and Andrew if Angel hadn't moved straight in when Briony had left a week earlier.

Lorna sighed. Her situation wasn't like that of other couples who were parents, who perhaps looked forward to a time reminiscent of their youth, before they'd started a family, when it had just been the two of them. For her, there had always been the three of them – apart from the months when she was pregnant, early on in their relationship.

And whose fault was that? thought Lorna. Briony had never been a mistake – that was not how Lorna had ever thought of her only child – but she had been an accident. Who would choose to spend what was meant to be the best time of their lives at university – going to parties and enjoying themselves – raising a child instead?

Andrew had made sacrifices too, but he'd never complained. At eighteen, he'd stepped up to his responsibilities. Soon after Briony was born, in their first year of university, they'd married.

Perhaps that was another reason that Briony had thought it would be a good idea if someone else moved into the attic. She knew her parents would feel her absence tremendously. She had told them that they should go back to renting out the top floor; they were used to having people around. And Angel wasn't exactly a stranger. She was Briony's best friend, and a friend of the family too.

Angel's background was quite different to Briony's. She was an up-north girl from Toxteth, Liverpool, with four siblings, whilst Briony was an only child. But they'd met on their course, and although their career aspirations were quite different – Angel wanted to be a medical researcher and discover a cure for cancer, which had taken her beloved grandmother when she was ten – they'd become inseparable. Their closeness made it all the more confounding that, when Lorna had asked Angel if she'd heard from Briony since she'd left on her trip a week earlier, Angel had said no.

Lorna stood, staring up the stairs. Angel had been upset when Briony had left, which was understandable; her best friend's life was moving on. Lorna hoped that her daughter stayed in touch with Angel and her other friends while she was away. Briony had said it might be difficult to text or WhatsApp, but when she had time, and there was internet available, she'd send emails.

So far, an email hadn't materialised, although she was only seven days into her eight-week trip. Perhaps Briony had managed to contact Angel today? Lorna thought she'd nip upstairs and ask.

Angel was the most talkative, outgoing, fun-loving person anyone could hope to meet. Although it hadn't been Lorna's intention to get another lodger, she'd been more than happy for

Angel to stay, imagining she'd join them for dinner, and they'd have long conversations about her work at Oxford University, where both Lorna and her husband had studied too.

But surprisingly, this had not happened. Since she'd moved in on the day Briony had left for her trip, Angel had not joined them for dinner once. She was often out, and when she was indoors, she barely said hello before whipping upstairs and locking her door.

It was all very strange – so strange, in fact, that Lorna had decided she'd just come right out with it and ask Angel if she wasn't happy there. They hadn't drawn up a contract or rental agreement, although Lorna would do that, if that was what Angel wanted. Perhaps that was the problem. Maybe she didn't feel secure.

Lorna hoped that Angel would join them for dinner that evening; she intended to tell her that she'd draw up a contract for however long Angel wanted – at the same below-market rent, of course, for the entire duration. She wanted Angel to feel relaxed staying in her house, and treat it as if it were her own home.

'Dinner's nearly ready!' Lorna heard Andrew call out in a sing-song voice from the kitchen.

Lorna strode down the hall and poked her head around the door. 'I'm just going to nip upstairs and ask Angel if she'd like to join us for dinner.'

'Good luck with that.'

Lorna frowned at him. 'Yeah, I know. I just can't help feeling that something is up. I'd like to get to the bottom of it.'

'Perhaps it's just boyfriend trouble. Not a lot you can do about that, I'm afraid.'

'She hasn't got a boyfriend.'

'Girlfriend then?'

Lorna looked at him. Perhaps that was the problem. If she'd met someone, perhaps she wasn't sure whether she could bring them home or whether they could stay overnight. That was silly. Lorna had assumed that Angel knew she could treat the apartment as if it were her own home, where she was free to do as she pleased. She had her own front door key.

On her way up the stairs, Lorna wondered whether she should have made the situation clear. She hadn't needed to with the other lodgers. Obviously, they would prefer that Angel didn't hold parties and invite all and sundry home. But she couldn't imagine Angel would do that. She enjoyed going out and clubbing, but she wasn't the type to roll up drunk after a night out. Lorna knew that for a fact because of the number of times Angel had stayed over with Briony after a night out. They might have had a few drinks, and been a bit loud, and quite giggly, but they certainly weren't embarrassingly drunk when they got home.

Lorna intended to put her at ease about everything, and then perhaps she'd join them for dinner. Lorna couldn't wait to find out any details Angel could tell her about Briony's trip.

She took the second flight of stairs that led straight up to the attic door. Lorna was about to knock when she overheard Angel talking. *She must be on the phone*, thought Lorna. She lingered outside her door. *Is she on the phone to Briony?* Lorna desperately wanted to know.

She heard Angel say, 'Thanks for letting me know that she's arrived safely, Freddie.'

Lorna put her ear closer to the door, feeling ever so guilty for listening in on Angel's private conversation. If it wasn't for the fact that Angel must be talking about her daughter, she'd have walked back down the stairs as soon as she realised Angel was on the phone.

'No, I haven't heard from her.'

Lorna nodded to herself. She guessed it made sense that Briony had contacted Freddie first.

'Yeah, all right, it's true – we have had a falling-out.'

Lorna raised her eyebrows. That might explain why she was avoiding them; maybe the falling-out had made her feel awkward around them. Lorna was a bit surprised to hear it, though. Briony and Angel never fell out.

'Well, there's a first time for everything, Freddie.'

Lorna thought that Freddie must have just said exactly what she was thinking. By the tone of her response, Angel didn't sound happy about it. Lorna wasn't surprised. They were best friends, after all. She hoped their argument had nothing to do with Angel staying there. She couldn't imagine that was the case – after all, it had been Briony's idea.

'No, I don't want to talk about it, if you don't mind.'

Angel did sound upset. That was probably another reason she was avoiding them, and retreating to her attic room when she returned after work. What a shame that she and Briony had fallen out just before Briony's trip. They would be thousands of miles apart for several weeks, and there would be little opportunity to patch things up.

'No, I don't want you to come round.'

There was a pause. Lorna wished she knew what Freddie was saying.

Angel said, 'No, I'm sure Briony's parents are fine with me having friends round. They're so kind and caring, really laid back. Considering I am living in someone's home, although it is perfectly self-contained, I couldn't have asked for a nicer couple to live with. Briony's parents are lovely people.'

Lorna smiled at that. At least it answered her questions and concerns about how Angel really felt about living there.

Her smile faded. She knew that Angel wouldn't feel the same way if she discovered her standing right outside her door, listening into her private conversation.

'We'll meet up, Freddie, I promise. I just wish Briony had—'

Lorna noticed she'd stopped dead. Whatever she was going to say, or wanted to say, she abruptly changed her mind.

'Look, I've got to go now. I've got a mountain of reading to do this evening … No, I'm not brushing you off.'

It sounded like it to Lorna. She heard Angel say, 'Is Briony all right, though? Is … everything going okay?'

Lorna pressed her ear to the door, holding her breath, hoping her daughter was all right. As the days had ticked by, and had turned into a whole week without any word, it had been bothering her more and more, and was starting to give her sleepless nights.

Andrew kept reminding her that their daughter was an adult now, off in her own life, and they couldn't expect her to check in with her parents all the time. Lorna had been annoyed with that comment; she didn't want her to check in with them all the time. Once would have been nice, though.

'Oh, good. I'm glad to hear everything's fine.'

Lorna heard Angel's reply and let out an audible sigh of relief. She clamped her hand over her mouth, praying Angel hadn't heard.

'Yeah, I was surprised she'd changed her mind too, but you know, things happen.'

Lorna stared at the door. *What an odd thing to say*, she thought. *Changed her mind about what?* She shook her head, thinking it was probably something of no consequence. Maybe it was something they'd arranged to do, the three of them, before she went away on her trip. She had thought that Briony was going out for a meal with Freddie before she left, but that hadn't happened. Perhaps Angel was talking about that.

'Well, I'd better go.'

Lorna looked at the door and thought the same thing. If she knocked and asked Angel to join them for dinner now, Angel might wonder how long she'd been standing outside her door and whether she'd been eavesdropping on her conversation.

Lorna turned around, hoping she didn't step on a creaky floorboard. *So far, so good*, she thought as she started down the stairs. That was the trouble with old Victorian houses; everything seemed to creak. As Lorna made her way down the stairs, she chose her footing carefully.

She knew every inch of the house, every creak of a floorboard. She should do – she'd grown up there. Her parents had split up when she was eighteen. She'd stayed there in the family home, with her father, and had studied music at Oxford University, in one of the most prestigious music schools in the country. She was glad she'd brought up her own daughter there too.

She thought of Briony again as she reached the bottom of the stairs. Although her daughter had had the odd weekend away with Freddie, and had taken family trips to see her grandfather, Edwin, in America during summer holidays, she'd never been abroad, away from friends and family, for any length of time.

Lorna paused at the bottom of the stairs and smiled. Of

course Briony would get in touch with her friends first. Lorna imagined she'd be in contact with her family soon enough. Her daughter's trip had galvanised Lorna into thinking how much she wanted a change, an adventure, of her own. She was planning a life-changing trip herself with her husband for her fortieth – he just didn't know it yet.

She smiled. She still couldn't quite believe that her daughter was thousands of miles away in the Galapagos Islands. She'd had to look it up on a world map to see exactly where it was. It still didn't feel real, and she imagined it wouldn't until she'd heard from Briony.

2

'Ah, there you are,' said Andrew, glancing over his shoulder when Lorna walked into the kitchen. 'Dinner was ready a few minutes ago. I was wondering where you were.' He was dishing up spaghetti bolognese onto two plates. 'I guess Angel won't be joining us.'

'Oh, I didn't ask,' Lorna said.

'I thought that's what you were nipping upstairs to do before I dished up – to ask her if she was going to join us?' He turned from the kitchen countertop with two plates in his hands and looked at her. 'Why are you grinning like a Cheshire cat?'

'Briony is fine.'

'I'm relieved to hear it.' He grinned too as he walked over and put the plates on the table as Lorna pulled out a chair. 'You got an email, then? Or did she manage to text?'

Lorna chewed her bottom lip as she took a chair.

Andrew sat at the table opposite her. He raised his eyebrows. 'She phoned you, then?' He frowned. 'She didn't call me.'

Lorna shook her head. 'No, um … she didn't email, text or call.'

Andrew picked up his knife and fork and paused before he

dug into his meal. 'So, how do you know that Briony is fine?' He stopped abruptly. 'Ah, Angel told you.'

'Not exactly.'

'Little wonder you forgot to ask her to dinner after you'd heard the good news.' Andrew was just swirling some spaghetti around his fork when he stopped and looked at her. 'Sorry, what did you mean when you said *not exactly*?'

'I haven't spoken with Angel.'

Andrew was about to put the forkful of spaghetti into his mouth when he stopped. 'You haven't spoken to her? But you just said—'

'I overheard Angel on the phone when I walked up the stairs.'

'You overheard her?'

Lorna nodded.

Andrew frowned. 'You mean that you were standing outside her door, listening in on her private conversation?'

'Well, no, not intentionally. I overheard Angel mention Briony's name, so of course I just wanted to know she was okay.'

'So, why didn't you come downstairs and wait until she got off the phone, and ask her?'

Lorna stared at Andrew across the table as he put the forkful of spaghetti into his mouth. She'd thought he'd be pleased to hear that Briony was all right, even though she had only contacted her friends. She had not expected his tone to be accusatory, as though she'd done something wrong.

Andrew shook his head as he ate. 'Really, Lorna. First you steal Briony's personal mail, and bin it, now you are spying on her friends.'

Lorna had just picked up the napkin to put on her lap. She slammed it down on the table and was about to remind Andrew why she'd had to steal the letter her mother had written to Briony – not that he knew the details; he never would. But even so, she was about to remind him that she was estranged from her mother and didn't want her having any contact with Briony when she was interrupted by a knock on the kitchen door.

Lorna could feel her face flush with embarrassment, wondering how much Angel had heard while standing outside the kitchen door before she knocked. *Serves me right*, thought Lorna, *for eavesdropping.*

'Oh, hi Angel,' Lorna said, as soon as she opened the door. 'Everything all right?'

'Sorry, was I interrupting something?'

Lorna looked at the napkin. 'Um, I thought I saw a fly.' She made a show of gingerly lifting the napkin. 'I was trying to swat it, but by the looks of it, I didn't.' She exchanged a glance with Andrew. The look on his face said he wasn't amused that she had lied to Angel.

Andrew rolled his eyes at Lorna, and said, 'Not at all, Angel. Come in and join us for dinner, why don't you? Lorna was going to nip upstairs and ask you to join us, but …'

Lorna glared at him.

Andrew continued, 'She got a bit waylaid with … something.'

Lorna turned to Angel, eyeing her hovering in the doorway, hoping to goodness she had not been privy to their whole conversation. The look on her face suggested she had not.

Andrew added, 'You don't have to knock in future. Just because the attic room is self-contained, we don't want you to feel that you can't come down and join us. Or just sit in the lounge or dining room for a change, or use the house kitchen. Really, we want you to feel at home.'

Lorna vigorously nodded her head in agreement.

'Thank you,' said Angel.

Andrew got out of his seat and pulled out a chair. 'Do you like spaghetti bolognese? I've cooked loads. I always seem to overdo it.'

'Um … I've got a work thing tonight. We're having a meal too, so …' Angel trailed off.

Andrew pushed the chair back under the table. 'Another time, then?' he asked, hopefully.

Lorna caught that inflection in his voice. He missed Briony too, and the trouble was that Angel had not proved the welcome distraction that either they, or their daughter in her absence, had hoped for.

It was playing on Lorna's mind that Briony and Angel had, from what she'd overheard, had a falling-out. She stole a glance at Andrew and thought that after what he'd said, perhaps she wouldn't divulge any more of Angel's private conversation.

Lorna said, 'Have you heard from Briony?' Of course, she knew that Freddie had, and that he'd told Angel; she just wanted to see what more Angel might divulge. Out of the corner of her eye, she caught Andrew shaking his head at her.

Lorna ignored him and focused on Angel, anticipating some more details. 'No,' Angel said. Lorna was surprised at the abrupt answer. She glanced at Andrew, who looked as surprised as she did. 'Ah, so … has, um, Freddie heard from her, do you think?'

Angel shrugged. 'I guess, maybe. Look, I've got to go. I'll catch you later.' She slunk out of the door.

Lorna stared across the table at Andrew, miming *what the hell?* Angel had just told a bare-faced lie. Granted, Lorna knew that she shouldn't have even been aware that Briony had been in contact with Freddie. But why had Angel lied about it? Lorna spoke her thoughts.

Andrew said, 'How do I know? Maybe there's something going on with Briony's friends that we don't know about.'

Lorna breathed a sigh. 'Actually, Angel and Briony have had a falling-out.'

'Really? That's unusual. That might explain why she's lied, though – maybe she just doesn't want to talk about Briony. Did she say what it was about?'

Lorna chewed her lower lip again, avoiding eye contact.

'Lorna, how much of her conversation did you overhear?'

'Well, not enough, apparently,' Lorna said indignantly, now wishing she hadn't been so quick to retreat down the stairs.

Andrew looked at his dinner. 'I wish Briony would get in contact with us. I don't like that she's abroad, miles away.'

'Neither do I. Look, I was thinking I might contact the company who runs the expeditions. I don't even know whereabouts in the Galapagos Islands she's based.'

'It's on a research ship, though, isn't it?'

Lorna silently berated herself for not asking more about the trip. After years of discouraging her daughter from heading down the marine biology route, Lorna had finally come to accept that it was her daughter's passion and that nothing, not even Freddie, would stand in the way of her dreams.

The research trip was the culmination of those dreams, and Lorna had been so excited about Briony securing a place that she'd forgotten to ask her for the details. Lorna had assumed she'd contact her and let her know. And another reason she hadn't really asked was that her departure, along with Angel's arrival, had all been quite sudden. Somebody had dropped out of the trip at the last minute, and that was how Briony had secured a place. It had seemed as though there had barely been time for Briony even to pack before the biggest adventure of her life.

'I want an adventure,' Lorna mumbled under her breath.

'What was that, dear?' Andrew asked.

After their earlier words about listening in on Angel's conversation, Lorna didn't think that it was quite the right time to bring up what she was planning for her fortieth. She'd save that, and the fact that she'd taken a sabbatical from work, until later.

Instead, she said, 'I'm sure there's a leaflet or an itinerary lying around somewhere about Briony's trip. Perhaps there's a contact number for the company that runs the expedition. They would be able to tell us how her trip is going.'

Andrew finished his spaghetti bolognese and mopped the sauce off his plate with a slice of garlic bread.

Lorna had also finished her meal. She put her knife and fork together on her empty plate. 'Did Briony talk to you about her trip – I mean specifically about the company running it?'

Andrew looked up and shook his head. 'If Briony has left any details behind, they'll be upstairs in her room.'

They both raised their eyes to the ceiling. Andrew said, 'Lorna, don't even think about going upstairs to Angel's room to find out.'

Lorna looked at her husband, keeping her expression neutral. She decided that she wouldn't go up there straight away, while Andrew was in. After revealing that she'd been eavesdropping outside Angel's door, he'd no doubt be watching her every move.

'Lorna ...' Andrew's voice held a warning note.

She lowered her eyes. 'What? I'm not going up to her room.'

Not yet, anyway. She did have a spare key in case Angel locked the door and lost the key.

She knew she was worrying out of hand, but Lorna had already decided that if she hadn't heard from Briony soon, she would go upstairs another time when Angel was out and have a little root around. If she could just find out the name of the company running the expedition then she could phone the organisers, and ask them to check in with the research vessel – surely they had a satellite phone or something – just to put her mind at ease that her daughter was okay.

The question was: how long would she give it?

3

'Is everything all right?'

Briony turned around at the sound of Reggie's voice. She looked at the violin in her hands. She was meant to be putting it back in the music shop window. She'd got as far as the window display, but her attention had been drawn to the little shop across Cobblers Yard, which was run by a man in his thirties called Joss.

'You're thinking about the appointment with Joss tomorrow, aren't you?'

'Yes.' It was lucky for her that Joss had decided to open his legal practice, which offered free legal advice, on a Saturday that week. She had her appointment with him on her mind, and a lot more besides. She carefully placed the violin, which she'd just dusted, back in the window display. Reggie had kept the shop open later than usual that Friday evening while Briony worked on the window display, cleaning all the instruments.

Besides the appointment with Joss, Briony was also thinking about her parents and the lie she'd spun that had brought her to the Suffolk Coast unbeknown to them. She thought back to a week earlier, when her mum had excitedly helped her pack for the research trip that she was meant to be going on. She had already known she was not joining. She wasn't off to the Galapagos Islands, as they thought, but she couldn't tell them that – especially her mum, for two reasons.

She had been so excited that she'd been offered a place on an eight-week research trip to the Galapagos Islands. Her boyfriend Freddie had been less excited. He'd just proposed to her, and was hoping for an answer, and to be able to set a date. She hadn't been able to answer him. She'd needed time to think – about everything.

Whilst Freddie hadn't really wanted her to go away, when he'd discovered that she'd changed her mind about the trip, he'd been equally stunned. He'd surprised her by encouraging her to join the trip and not change her mind.

The problem was that Freddie had no clue as to why she'd changed her mind. She'd told him a half-truth. She'd recently received a letter from her maternal grandmother, whom she'd never met in her life. Her mum and grandmother were estranged, and her mum wouldn't talk about it. Briony hadn't even known where her grandmother lived. But she'd discovered that her grandmother had recently sent her a letter.

Freddie had dropped her off for her journey down to Suffolk, still confused as to why she had changed her mind about the Galapagos Islands. She'd told him she was visiting her grandmother instead. He'd wondered why she'd needed to cancel her trip to go; she could have gone any time – unless her grandmother was at death's door.

Briony didn't know whether that was the case. Her main reason for going to see her grandmother straight away rather than holding on until after the research trip was actually that she had discovered that she was pregnant. She didn't want to risk travelling to a remote area, and she wasn't ready to tell Freddie just yet – or her parents.

Briony's parents had had her young, and she just knew that her mum would be disappointed when she discovered her daughter was pregnant before she'd got married and before she'd even got her longed-for career in marine biology off the ground. Briony still had a master's to do. And as for Freddie's proposal – although Briony imagined that it was the dream of many girls to walk down the aisle, she wasn't sure she was ready for that quite yet either.

She had confided in her best friend, Angel, that she was pregnant, and also that she'd found the letter from her grandmother. Briony's mum was not in her good books, to say the least. The letter had been delayed in the post, and when it had arrived, her mum had intercepted it. Briony might not have even discovered that her grandmother had written to her if it hadn't been for her well-timed arrival home one day. She'd overheard her parents arguing – and they never argued. She'd discovered that her mum had binned a letter addressed to her from her grandmother. She'd rescued her letter from the bin without her mum knowing.

The letter had turned out to be the perfect excuse to visit her grandmother instead; to get away and stay with a relative who had no idea about the other trip she should have been on for the next few weeks. She hadn't confronted her mum, because the last thing she needed was for her mum to put a stop to her seeing her grandmother, or to find out the reason she had changed her plans so dramatically to travel instead to the Suffolk Coast. Besides her unexpected pregnancy, Briony did want to see her grandmother and to find out what had really gone on to cause her mum's and grandmother's estrangement.

Thinking of the past week, and her decision to abscond to Suffolk without her parents' knowledge, Briony knew she still had an email to write. She'd promised her mum she'd stay in touch. So far, she hadn't. She'd said that texting might not happen if there was no signal, and that internet might be sketchy. Of course she had no idea if either of those things were true – how could she? She'd never been to the Galapagos Islands.

Freddie had been in touch, and she'd told him everything was fine – which it wasn't. Briony had not expected to turn up at The Beach House – an aptly named property sitting right on the beach in a Suffolk coastal village called Dunwich Heath – and discover that her grandmother, Blythe, wasn't there.

A week had gone by, and Briony – who fortunately had a key to The Beach House that she'd found in an old shell box belonging to her mother – had been living in The Beach House on her own. Well, not quite on her own. For a start, there was Luna; a wolfdog hybrid who had been left by Blythe at a boarding kennels while she went into hospital for a knee operation.

The kennels were run by a vet – a young lady called Emily, who had been trying to get in contact with Blythe when she had failed to pick Luna up. Emily had phoned The Beach House, and Briony had answered the call.

It had been a fortnight since Blythe had dropped Luna off, but according to Emily's friend, Nate – a doctor at Aldeburgh Cottage Hospital – nobody who'd had a knee op in the recent past had had any complications, and all had been discharged.

Unfortunately for Briony, that had not been helpful; she still had no clue where her grandmother was or why she had failed to pick up Luna. So Briony had visited The Four Paws Guest House and veterinary practice, where she'd met Emily. And somehow, Briony had returned to The Beach House with not one dog, but two, along with two kittens. That had not been the plan, but once there, she'd decided to continue fostering cats and kittens as her grandmother had been doing. Wilbur, the little dachshund sausage dog, who had been left at the pet hotel when his owner had gone to live in a care home, had stolen her heart in a matter of moments. She just hadn't been able to leave the elderly dog behind. And although she was just meant to be fostering him, he had 'foster fail' written all over him. For someone who didn't want any responsibilities, Briony now had four pets on her hands.

She'd left the kittens sleeping at The Beach House while she was at the music shop, but the two dogs had been accompanying her to her new job in Reggie's music shop in Cobblers Yard. Luna was sitting over by Reggie's stool, watching him mend some strings on a guitar at his desk at the back of the shop. Little Wilbur had found a cosy spot on a cushioned chair and was curled up, fast asleep. Briony smiled affectionately at the little sausage dog. Sometimes she thought he had more cat than dog qualities; he'd already found his favourite spot on one of the sofas back in The Beach House.

Wilbur was an old dog, so he slept a lot, which was understandable, but like cats he favoured a spot up high on a chair, sofa, or preferably someone's lap. But Briony didn't have time to sit all day and be that comforting lap for her dog now she had her little part-time job.

When she'd first visited Reggie, after finding out through Emily that he was a friend of her grandmother's, Briony had been hoping he'd know her grandmother's whereabouts. He didn't. But he did have something else for her – this part-time job. It was a far cry from her aspirations to become a marine biologist, but she'd had music lessons for several years; her mum, a music teacher, had insisted that she learn to play some instruments. Even though she didn't enjoy it, she could play the piano, violin and guitar. But what she had enjoyed, in the past, was singing. She had a lovely singing voice.

Briony had been planning to begin her master's degree in the autumn term to further her career aspirations, but first the research trip had come up, and then she'd found out she was pregnant, and now she had found herself working in a music shop.

This isn't forever, Briony reminded herself. *But it could be, if I wanted it to be.* She was thinking of the friends she'd made since arriving there just a week earlier – Reggie at the music shop, Emily, and Emily's friend Clarissa, a reporter and aspiring investigative journalist, who worked for a local newspaper.

She would never have imagined she'd find herself on the beautiful Suffolk Coast that autumn rather than on an adventure in the Galapagos Islands. But this was no less of an adventure – travelling to find her grandmother, and hoping to discover why her mum and grandmother had been estranged all these years. And making new friends along the way. It had given her a glimpse into another life – perhaps a simpler life – that she would never have even envisaged if she hadn't gone there. But what about her career, Freddie, and her life in Oxford?

Briony put all thoughts of her future to one side for now; she was thinking of her mum ripping up the letter she'd been sent by her grandmother. What had happened in the past that was so terrible that she'd never had an opportunity to even meet her maternal grandmother, let alone get to know her? Even now, as an adult, her mum had taken the decision about meeting Blythe out of Briony's hands. Why? Anxiety gnawed away in the pit of her stomach at the thought that perhaps her mum had good reason for them not to meet. Maybe she should have asked her about it before making this trip.

She ought to know where I am right now, Briony thought. She stared out of the shop window and sighed. She stole a glance at her phone again, checking for any texts or missed calls from her best friend, Angel. They had not parted on good terms when she'd left for Suffolk. Briony now wished she had not told her best friend she was pregnant. Angel had disagreed with her decision not to tell Freddie. What if Angel told Freddie herself? What if she told Briony's parents?

She couldn't imagine that Angel would tell her mum and dad. If they discovered Angel knew that Briony was not in the Galapagos Islands, and hadn't told them, while living under their roof, Angel might have to leave.

Her parents were very generous, kind-hearted people, but she couldn't imagine that under those circumstances they'd want Angel to stay on living with them.

4

'I made you a cuppa.'

Briony had been so lost in thought that she jumped at the sound of Reggie's voice behind her. She turned around and smiled at the older man. He looked like an ageing rocker. Whenever she looked at him, The Rolling Stones came to mind.

'You know, it's almost time for elevenses,' added Reggie.

Elevenses. Briony smiled at Reggie. The word brought to mind the first time they'd met. He'd offered her a cuppa and a chocolate digestive. When she'd thanked him, he'd mentioned his neighbours, Marjorie and Mabel – sisters and retired widows who ran the charity shop next door. They were older than Reggie, and it didn't sound as though he had always got along with them, but they did keep him stocked up with biscuits and tea for elevenses.

Briony wouldn't have been surprised if they made sure all the little shops in Cobblers Yard had tea and biscuits for elevenses. Although Reggie had also mentioned that the bookshop in Cobblers Yard had its own coffee machine, and a sofa so that customers could make themselves comfortable with a book. She recalled what he'd said: *You should try it. Their coffee is divine.* It sounded as though if anyone visited one of the shops at this time of day, the shopkeepers in Cobblers Yard would invite them to have a cuppa – which is exactly what had happened to Briony when she'd first set foot in Reggie's shop.

She took the cup of tea. 'Thanks, Reggie.' It was only her second day, and she hoped he didn't regret employing her. She was aware that she'd spent the best part of the morning starting a job he'd asked her to do, then staring off into space, lost in her own thoughts. She didn't want him to let her go. The money was handy, even though she was only working part-time, mornings or afternoons – Reggie said the times might vary, but she didn't mind that, as they were only half-days; she had pets to look after. The kittens could only be left for so long.

Briony joined Reggie at his desk, perching on another stool. There was a more comfortable seat, but Wilbur had bagged that already. She reached out and stroked the sleeping dog for a moment or two before she turned to face Reggie. 'I'm sorry about this morning.'

Reggie had resumed stringing a guitar in between sips of tea. He stopped what he was doing and looked up, blue eyes regarding her above his half-moon glasses, his expression bemused.

'I've been preoccupied.'

'You don't say.'

Briony hadn't known him long, but she was already familiar with his not-so-subtle sarcasm.

He smiled, and she smiled back. He glanced over at the window. 'There's nothing to apologise for, Briony. I understand.' Reggie offered her a chocolate digestive biscuit from a plate on the desk. She took one, eyeing Luna. As always, her grandmother's wolfdog was being a good girl. Her nose popped up, sniffing along the desk towards the plate of biscuits, and she could easily have nabbed one, given her height, but she didn't.

'You've got your grandmother on your mind.' Reggie gave Luna a dog biscuit from a jar on his desk.

Briony dunked her biscuit in her cup of tea. Reggie didn't know that it wasn't all she had on her mind. She'd enjoyed working in the music shop the previous day, even though she'd stayed late after closing time to help Reggie with the window display. And now she had found that the morning had gone quickly, probably because there had been no shortage of customers, as it was a Saturday. However, it was bothering her that she didn't have a car to get to work. There was a bus service, but Reggie had insisted on picking her up from The Beach House. He had said he didn't mind, but she was worried about the cost of petrol; he was going miles out of his way just to collect her from Dunwich Heath and then take her back after work. She'd offered to pay him some petrol money, but he'd said he wouldn't hear of it.

'I feel bad that I just don't see what I've done this morning, and you're paying me for my time, and paying petrol back and forward to Dunwich.' The last thing she wanted was for Reggie to be out of pocket. She said as much.

'Not at all. You've cleaned my entire window display, all the shelving, and polished the violins and guitars in the window – something I've been intending to get around to for months. With the arthritis, I knew I'd have a tough time getting it done. And that's the first thing people see, looking in my window. And look, I've sold two instruments this morning already. All because of my work-shy assistant.'

There it was again – Reggie's well-meaning sarcasm masking

a compliment. 'But seriously, Briony, you are just too hard on yourself.'

Briony smiled shyly at Reggie. She'd known him such a short time and yet already he'd picked up on one of her character traits – or flaws, as Briony often thought of it. She was too hard on herself. But as the only child of two overachieving parents – they both gained first-class degrees in music while raising a child – she felt there was lot of expectation on her shoulders. She felt it even more keenly, knowing that she'd disappointed her mother by not following in her footsteps to study for a music degree. Her dad was a lot more pragmatic and just wanted her to follow her dreams.

Briony had always got the impression that her mum wasn't impressed at all with her chosen career of marine biology. She didn't know why; perhaps she simply had no interest in it. But that didn't mean she shouldn't encourage her only daughter in the pursuit of her passion. In fact, her mum had always seemed to do her best to discourage her.

Trips to the seaside had always been firmly off the menu when it came to family holidays. Briony had never understood; what parent didn't take their child to the beach on a seaside holiday? Perhaps her mum had had a bad experience. It did now make her wonder, though, if it had anything to do with her grandmother and The Beach House. Maybe seaside holidays would have dredged up her mum's memories of her childhood.

Briony had seen the framed photographs in the hallway, and on the grand piano in the double-aspect lounge. There were a lot of photos of her mum growing up. She had spent her holidays, especially her summer holidays, there on the Suffolk Coast. She didn't look unhappy in those photos – not at all; especially on the ones taken outside The Beach House, which Briony had discovered her great-grandparents had built.

She'd found an old photo album with black-and-white photos of a youngish couple. Judging by their clothes and hairstyles, she imagined the photos dated back to the late forties or thereabouts. In one of them, the lady – Briony's great-grandmother, Edith whose name was written on the back of the photo – was holding a baby. That baby was Briony's grandmother, Blythe.

Briony thought of her mum and wondered, as she had done many times, why the happy, fun-filled summers of her mum's childhood, along with her mother's relationship with Blythe, had turned sour. Briony had always been told that the estrangement had happened when Blythe had left her grandfather, Edwin, and her grandparents had divorced. But Briony believed there was more to it than that – much more.

'Lost in thought again?'

Briony apologised. 'Sorry.' She finished her tea. 'Look, I'd be much happier with our arrangement if you docked my wages to pay for the petrol.'

'What about your grandmother's car?'

Briony put her teacup down. 'What did you just say?'

'Blythe's old Morris Minor. I'm sure she wouldn't have driven it to the hospital, knowing she wouldn't be able to drive home. Although to be honest, I wouldn't put it past her to try.' He guffawed.

Briony recalled Emily mentioning an old Morris Minor when she'd asked her if her grandmother had a car, but like Reggie had said, she wouldn't have been able to drive home straight after a knee op. Surely she would have organised someone to drive her to the hospital and back. *So, where is her car?* Briony thought. There wasn't a car on the driveway outside The Beach House.

Briony told Reggie, 'There wasn't an old Morris Minor parked outside The Beach House when I arrived.'

'Well, there wouldn't be.'

Briony frowned. 'What do you mean?'

'She never parks it there. It will be in the car park by the public loos next door to The Beach Café. She leaves it in the car park and walks from there.'

Briony thought that it was the stupidest thing she'd ever heard. What was the point of a car if you didn't drive door to door? Blythe had a big enough driveway to park it on. 'Why wouldn't she park it outside her house?'

'I asked her that once, when I came to tune her piano and thought she was out because her car wasn't there. She said, *It's a jolly old car.* She'd inherited it from her parents. It hadn't let her down, but she wouldn't risk running it up and down that dirt track to the main road. The suspension wasn't brilliant – and neither was her back, apparently; she was worried she'd do herself and the car an injury. So she always left it in the car park.'

Briony tried to think. Had she seen an incredibly old car in the car park when the taxi driver had dropped her off the day she'd arrived?

'If it's in the car park, and you can find a set of keys, then …' he trailed off.

'I can drive myself to your music shop in Cobblers Yard?'

Reggie grinned. 'Absolutely.' He changed the subject. 'So, I guess you haven't been given a specific time to see Joss, apart from being allocated morning or afternoon?'

'That's right – and thank you for letting me finish work

before lunchtime today, Reggie.' Briony had realised that Joss's free legal advice centre operated on a drop-in basis and had thought that if she was one of the last to turn up in the morning, she wouldn't have a long wait to be seen.

Reggie said, 'Well, it *is* only your second day, and I hope you haven't been too bored, working in a shop. I know this kind of work is … how shall I put it … quite different from what you hope to do in the future.'

Briony nodded, recalling how surprised she had been when Reggie had told her that her grandmother talked of her only grandchild whenever he saw her, and how proud she was of her achievements – especially her first-class honours degree. But that hadn't been the only surprise Reggie had had in store when Briony had met him. She'd found out that although her grandmother hadn't had an invitation to her graduation, she had secretly been there. Apparently, for weeks afterwards, she'd talked of nothing else. Briony wondered if that was what had prompted her grandmother to send her a letter, in an attempt to open a channel of communication.

Briony had had no clue that Blythe was at her graduation, and wouldn't have recognised her even if she'd known. She knew that Blythe wouldn't have come forward and introduced herself because Briony's mum was there.

Briony had wondered how Blythe had known about her degree and her graduation, but it hadn't taken her long to figure it out. Briony had surmised that her grandfather, Edwin, had been sending Blythe photos of her over the years; she'd discovered them all in frames in The Beach House. They'd clearly remained in contact with one another, which suggested, contrary to what everyone had told her, that when her grandparents had divorced, they'd remained on good terms.

Her grandfather had never once hinted that he was in contact with Blythe. And he had never told her that he'd been sending her grandmother photos of her and updates about her life.

'I'll be relieved when I've had a chance to speak to Joss,' she said to Reggie.

'I hope things are okay with you.'

'Oh, it's not me – it's my grandmother,' blurted Briony. She looked at Reggie's kindly old face and decided she could trust him. 'It's about The Beach House. The deeds are missing.'

Reggie raised an eyebrow. 'Really?'

'At least I think so. I've looked everywhere for them.' Briony didn't want to go through her grandmother's things, but she felt she had to do something.

'Why are you looking for them?'

Briony had arrived at The Beach House to a stack of letters. Briony breathed an exasperated sigh. 'She keeps getting these official-looking letters from a solicitor, asking to see the deeds. If she can't prove she owns the land, it sounds as though the person who instructed the firm of solicitors is after stealing it from under her.'

Briony hadn't opened the letters. She wouldn't stoop that low and open someone else's mail – unlike her mum – but she had come across some open letters in a kitchen drawer. She wouldn't have read them if it hadn't been for the others she'd discovered on the doormat on her arrival. It was obvious that something was up, and Briony wanted to make sure her grandmother didn't return from wherever she was and find the locks had been changed and she'd lost her beautiful home on the beach to some unscrupulous person or company. After some initial misgivings about living in her grandmother's house without her permission or knowledge, even though the letter she'd received from her had invited her to visit, Briony was now feeling a lot different about her stay. It felt as though it was meant to be – as though she *should* be there, saving The Beach House that her great-grandparents had built.

She didn't know who was hiding behind the firm of solicitors sending those letters, but she hoped that Joss could help.

Reggie said slowly, 'Do you think her disappearance could be linked? It sounds very stressful, getting those demanding letters.'

The conversation wasn't making Briony feel any better. Would her grandmother do that? Just run away somewhere and bury her head in the sand? Briony understood that it must be stressful getting those letters, but it really wasn't the right way to go about dealing with the situation.

'I don't know about you,' continued Reggie, but whoever they're representing sounds like a nasty, land-grabbing son-of-a …' he halted. 'Well, you know what I mean. Hounding an old lady out of her home.'

Briony nodded, trying to picture the sort of person who would do such a thing.

5

She stepped out of the music shop and walked across the yard to Joss's office. There were a surprising number of people still waiting, seated on sofas and easy chairs dotted around the room. She'd imagined he would have got through nearly all his morning clients.

Briony spotted a coffee machine on a trestle table along with milk, sugar, teabags, mugs and a plate of biscuits. She also noticed free newspapers, magazines, and a bookshelf of novels. It rather reminded her of the little church halls where people gathered for a cuppa, a scone, and a chat. She noticed another table with a plate of fruit scones and a large cake on a cake stand. There were disposable plates and forks. She imagined the scones and cake were homemade and that Joss had baked them himself. Emily had mentioned that Joss rather liked baking. She noted that there was no one taking money for the food and drinks and supposed it was all part of the free service.

Briony stood in the doorway, wondering where Joss was.

'Hello, there.' An older lady, very slim, dressed in skinny black jeans and a bright red jumper with sequins approached her. 'You must be Briony.'

'Um, yes.'

'Emily said you were popping along today. I'm Cheryl, Emily's mum. I help out here, looking after Joss's clients and doing some secretarial bits and bobs.'

'Oh, hello. I thought you were retired,' blurted Briony. She looked away, embarrassed. 'Sorry. It's just that when I was chatting to Emily, she mentioned that you ran a guesthouse before you retired.'

Cheryl smiled. 'That's right. It's the reason Emily called her boarding kennels The Four Paws Guest House when she took over the building. And yes, my husband and I did retire after I handed over the guesthouse to Emily, but then I got very bored, and being around my husband all day wasn't helping at all. We'd worked hard all our lives. My husband, Gerald, worked on the fishing vessels. I was so used to being busy all the time, and meeting people, that I was starting to get depressed.'

'Oh, dear. I'm sorry to hear that.' Briony had always imagined that retirement would be blissful; spent just pottering about, doing your own thing. But how do you fill an entire day, a week, a month when you have absolutely nothing to do? She'd been at The Beach House for only a few days, and at first, she'd imagined she'd enjoy just hanging around, spending lazy days reading and going for long walks on the beach. Even if her grandmother had been there as she'd expected, and things had worked out as she'd hoped, she imagined she'd soon have become restless. It was why she'd jumped at the chance to work at the music shop.

Her thoughts turned to years gone by at The Beach House. In the photo album she'd found from when her great-grandparents were still alive, it was obvious that The Beach

House had been quite the social hub, with lots of friends and relations visiting. It made Briony wonder how lonely her grandmother might feel, living in the house all alone, and wondered if that was why she fostered animals. They would give her company, and a purpose, beyond her private piano lessons.

'Retirement is not all it's cracked up to be, I can assure you,' said Cheryl conversationally as she led Briony past the other people sitting in the waiting area. Briony noticed that a bamboo screen had been placed in the deep-recessed front window so that nobody could look in and see who was sitting in the waiting room.

Cheryl continued, 'Don't get me wrong, I love my husband. But I needed to get out of the house and do something different – preferably where I was surrounded by people.'

Briony looked at the full reception area and grinned. 'Well, you're certainly working in the right place. And Joss does all this for free?'

'Yes. Of course. However there are some folks who insist on paying him for his time and expertise. But he only accepts money if people make a charitable donation towards helping Emily feed and rehome rescues.'

Briony nodded. 'Then that's what I'd like to do.'

Cheryl grinned. 'Wonderful – but only give what you can afford. However small the donation might be, Emily would really appreciate it. What with the cost of living going through the roof, Emily has ended up in a bit of a pickle, financially speaking, taking in strays and abandoned pets. She'd never put a healthy animal down, but she isn't a charity, obviously. The money has to come from somewhere. My husband and I help Emily out where we can.'

Cheryl glanced around the waiting room. 'I do love my voluntary job here. There's only so many garden centres you can visit, coffee shops you can waste time in and holidays you can go on before reality sets in.'

Briony nodded.

'It was my husband who voiced how I'd been feeling. He said he was bored, and went out and got a part-time job as a delivery driver, delivering flowers for The Potting Shed across the yard. Their online business has really taken off, and although they could still cope with making up the bouquets, they needed someone to deliver the orders.' She shook her head and smiled wistfully. 'It's funny, because we'd both been feeling like that for some time, unbeknown to each other, but we both felt guilty about it.'

'I think couples need their own jobs, interests, and friends,' said Briony, thinking of Freddie. She hadn't felt guilty about applying to go on that eight-week research trip. In fact, she'd barely thought of him when she'd made the decision to go.

Cheryl smiled. 'I think so too. Now, as you can see, we're quite busy this morning. I think Joss's morning clinic will overrun. But not to worry – Joss will get around to seeing you. We have a little ticket machine. It's first come, first served, I'm afraid.'

'Oh, I see.' Briony wished she'd turned up first thing, instead of waiting until gone eleven. She sighed.

Cheryl must have caught the look on her face. 'Sorry, he can't book specific appointments as he doesn't know how long each client will be. He would never turn anyone away, no matter how long their case takes, or how complex.'

Briony was glad to hear it. She didn't know how long and

drawn out or complex the legal fight to save The Beach House would turn out to be.

Cheryl handed her a ticket. 'Now, take a seat, and have a cuppa and a slice of Joss's delicious homemade cake, or a scone. Help yourself to a magazine or a book, if you like. There's a selection of daily newspapers too.'

Briony looked at her ticket, and then around the crowded room, and said, 'Do you think I'd have time to nip to the bookshop across the yard?'

Cheryl glanced around the room too. 'Oh, I think so. Take your time. Is there anything in particular you're looking for?'

Briony stopped at the door and turned around. *An answer to the question of what's happened to my grandmother*, she thought, although she doubted she'd find that answer in the bookshop.

6

Briony stood in the lovely bookshop, holding an old copy of a classic novel by H. Rider Haggard. It wasn't what she had intended to read, but the lovely old gentleman called Henry, who owned the bookshop, had suggested it.

'It's about as close to an exotic location as I'm going to get,' Briony said to herself, thinking of the adventure story set abroad within the books' pages.

She turned from the counter and thought of the window display she'd paused to look at before stepping into the shop. She'd thought she was walking into a modern bookshop. There were lots of brand-new releases nicely laid out in the window display – a selection of romances, thrillers, good old-fashioned whodunnits, and modern, cosy mysteries by well-known authors. There were also hard-boiled detective novels, police procedurals, and some literary fiction by up-and-coming authors. Any one of the new releases looked interesting, and worth buying. Briony wondered how she had ended up buying a dog-eared copy of an old book.

The window display belied the shop's true nature – it not only sold modern fiction but was stuffed to the rafters with a huge selection of second-hand books. It also had another a twist. There were little bistro tables and chairs outside, along with potted plants and hanging baskets. It would be easy to mistake it for a little café if you didn't look in the shop window or see the name of the shop.

Briony loved that she could help herself to a tea or coffee – much like in Joss's office across the yard – and sit with a cuppa and a biscuit. She thought of Reggie; although there wasn't a café in Cobblers Yard, there appeared to be no shortage of refreshments when you ventured into the shops.

Briony hadn't been long buying her book, so she decided to help herself to a cup of coffee and take a seat on the sofa. An older lady was already sitting there with a cup of tea, reading the morning newspapers. She didn't look as though she'd bought a book and appeared not at all bothered by the fact that she was sitting on the comfy sofa, sipping a free cuppa, and helping herself to the free newspapers without making a purchase.

A young woman appeared from behind a bookcase. 'Mabel – are you still here?'

Briony heard the rustle of a newspaper. She looked over at the older lady called Mabel. She'd lowered her newspaper. 'Shush! Marj thinks I'm out running errands. That's what I told her, Thea.'

'She's not going to hear you from over there in the charity shop.'

Mabel replied, 'Walls have ears.'

Briony glanced at her in amusement.

'Well, these walls are mighty thick,' said Thea. 'Why don't you just tell Marj that you like popping into the bookshop every day for your morning coffee and a chit-chat with us?'

Briony looked at the young woman called Thea, who was holding an armful of books.

'If I tell Marj where I am every morning, do you know what's going to happen?'

Briony saw Thea smile. 'No, Mabel, I have no idea.'

'Marjorie will want to come too. Then we'll have to close the charity shop all morning. You know how I like to savour my morning coffee from my coffee machine.'

'Yes, I do, Mabel, and we do so appreciate you giving us your coffee machine. Have you thought that it might be fair to take it in turns, so Marjorie could come one day, and you the next?'

'Or Marjorie could come in the afternoon,' said Briony, speaking her mind. She immediately wondered if they would be affronted by a stranger butting into the conversation.

Thea smiled. 'Now there's an idea, Mabel.'

'I like things just the way they are, thank you very much,' said Mabel indignantly.

'Ah, you mean you sitting here, and Marjorie doing all the work.'

Mabel returned to reading her newspaper as though she hadn't heard Thea's last comment.

Briony caught Thea smiling and shaking her head before turning her attention to her new customer. 'Hello. I haven't seen you in the bookshop before.'

'It's my first visit. I'm new to the area.' Briony saw the elderly lady lower her paper again, deep-set eyes staring in her direction. *Oh dear*, thought Briony, suddenly remembering what Reggie had said the very first time she'd visited the music shop, about The Gossip Girls, who worked in the charity shop. Mabel must be one half of that duo.

'Welcome to our little piece of heaven, Cobblers Yard,' said Thea. 'Most of our customers live in the area. We hardly have any passing trade. Cobblers Yard is so easy to miss. I'm Thea.' She held out her hand.

'I'm Briony.'

'It's lovely to meet you, Briony. I see you've found a book already.'

Briony looked at her purchase. The man at the counter had packed it carefully into a paper bag emblazoned with the words – *The Bookshop of Memories.* Briony showed her the book. 'It's not exactly what I came in here for, but the old guy—'

'That's my dad, Herny.'

Briony was surprised. She guessed the young woman standing in front of her was in her early thirties. Henry could have been her grandfather. That was probably an exaggeration, but she guessed he was around her grandmother's age, in his early seventies. She realised that having young parents herself probably altered her perspective. 'Oh, I didn't mean to call him *old.*'

Mabel laughed out loud. 'Oh, my dear. I don't think there is anything to apologise for. We're old, there's no getting away from it.'

Briony caught the young woman smiling too. 'My dad was middle-aged when he had me and my sister.'

Briony stared at her, realising that perhaps it wasn't a bad idea being a young parent. It might not be great right now, with all the plans she'd had, but when her child was grown up, she'd only be in her forties. *Not ancient, like Thea's dad.* Briony winced, wishing she'd stop thinking unkind thoughts. He wasn't ancient.

'What were you saying … about the book?'

'Oh, yes,' said Briony in relief, glad she'd changed the subject. 'I hadn't thought of purchasing an old-fashioned adventure story. Exotic location, some romance too – your dad recommended it. He's quite knowledgeable about the author. Has he been running the bookshop for long?'

'Yes, he has.'

'Apart from a little – well, a long – break,' said Mabel under her breath.

Briony heard the comment and wondered what she meant.

Thea must have heard her too, as she felt the need to explain. 'Oh, yes. My dad went away for a while, but … now he's back.'

Briony recalled Reggie mentioning that the bookshop had been closed for years. It was when they'd first met. She'd told him her grandmother was missing. He'd said, *Blimey – not again!* She'd wondered who he'd meant by that comment, although she'd noticed him glancing towards the bookshop across the yard. He hadn't elaborated. All he'd said was, *Someday I'll tell you an incredible story about the bookshop across the yard, which was closed for decades.*

Briony hoped Thea might tell her that story, but was not surprised she didn't. Briony could understand. She didn't want to talk about her personal life with strangers either, even though Thea seemed very nice.

'How did you find the bookshop?'

'Emily brought me here to visit Reggie. I'm working part-time there now.'

'Ah, you're into music?'

Briony eyed the old lady. 'I play, yes. He tunes my grandmother's piano. We got into a conversation about the guy who used to work in the music shop years ago.'

Briony didn't know whether Mr Cribbins had been the previous owner or whether, like Reggie, he'd rented the place. The fact was, she had no idea who owned the music shop now, but she wasn't interested in that. What interested her was someone called Frank who, decades earlier, had written some love letters to her grandmother that Briony had found, unopened, in an old bureau in the outbuilding on her grandmother's property, with the return address as the music shop right there in Cobblers Yard. He must have lived in the flat above the shop at some point. But did the town gossip, Mabel, or her sister, know anything about him?

Mabel eyed her. 'And what is your interest in Mr Cribbins?'

So Mabel did know him – or at least *of* him. Briony suppressed a smile and shrugged nonchalantly instead. But she saw the look on Mabel's face when she did that, and realised Mabel was no fool.

Briony decided to be straight with her. 'I'm not interested in Mr Cribbins, but Frank Cribbins – his son, perhaps?'

Mabel eyed her a long moment before she said, 'Hmm … Frank. I haven't heard that name in a long, long time.'

'So, you knew Frank?' *Of course she did*, thought Briony. She imagined Mabel and her sister had lived in Aldeburgh all their lives.

'Yes, he was Mr Cribbins' son. Mr Cribbins owned the music shop for years, and then I'm not sure who bought it when Mr Cribbins died. It obviously changed hands, but remained as a music shop because Reggie took over the lease. I believe Reggie thought there were more profitable businesses that could have moved into the premises, so he was surprised he was given the option. Perhaps it was pure nostalgia on the owner's part because the shop had always been a music shop, as far as he was aware.'

Mabel was just about to say something when the door to the bookshop opened and someone thundered in, slamming the door behind them, making everyone sitting in the alcove, out of sight of the door, jump. Briony thought it sounded like a customer who wasn't very happy.

'There you are!'

Briony looked up to see a plump older woman who, apart from her weight, did resemble her slim sister. She stood there, hands on hips, her face like thunder.

'Ah, Marjorie. I was just having a quick cuppa before I returned after doing the errands.'

'Were you, now?' Marjorie said sarcastically.

Thea said, 'I'm, er … going to help Dad.'

Briony caught her glancing Marjorie's way and wondered if she had sensed trouble brewing and decided to make a swift exit before the two sisters had a spat.

Briony glanced at Mabel, who didn't seem at all bothered that she'd been found out.

Mabel said, 'I struck up a conversation with Briony here. She's new in town. I couldn't exactly get up and walk out, could I? That would be rude.'

The way Marjorie eyed her sister suggested she wasn't sure she believed her.

'We were just talking about Mr Cribbins – weren't we, dear?'

Briony wished she'd made a quick exit too. 'Um, yeah.'

'Were you, now?' Marjorie folded her arms across her ample chest, eyeing Briony, making her feel rather uncomfortable under her stern gaze.

'Yes Marj. Do you remember him?' asked Mabel.

Marjorie turned to look at her sister. 'Mr Cribbins? I haven't heard that name in years.'

'Me neither,' agreed Mabel. 'Do you recall Frank – his son?'

'Frank Cribbins?' Marjorie pointed at her sister. 'The little boy who used to stand in the middle of Cobblers Yard under that lamppost and sing. Do you remember, Mabel?'

Mabel chuckled. 'Oh, my goodness! I remember now. He knew our bedroom was upstairs in the eaves. He used to serenade us, even though we were young women and he was a little boy of five or six.'

'Bless his little heart,' said Marjorie. 'But didn't he have the most wonderful voice?'

'Oh, yes – voice of an angel.'

Briony stared at the sisters. 'Did you used to live in Cobblers Yard?'

The sisters exchanged a glance. 'We grew up right here.'

'In Cobblers Yard?'

'In this bookshop,' said Mabel. 'My father used to own this shop.'

Briony stared at her. It was little wonder she loved to spend time there, in her former childhood home. Briony looked about her at the cramped but cosy bookshop, and thought she'd probably like to spend every opportunity she could there too; the sofa was comfy, the coffee from Mabel's donated coffee machine was delicious, and the tall bookshelves were crammed with books. It reminded her of the library at Oxford University. The bookshop was obviously tiny in comparison, but Briony thought that its size just added to its old-fashioned charm. She imagined the place hadn't changed much since the sisters' father had owned the place.

She felt she could spend hours lost amongst the bookshelves, perusing the books. Perhaps it was just as well that Henry had suggested a book, otherwise she was pretty sure she would go on to miss her appointment with Joss.

'Didn't he suddenly up and leave, and join the Royal Navy?' commented Mabel. 'Quite a shock for his father, as I remember. Wasn't he sweet on a local girl?'

'A local girl?' Marjorie sat down on the sofa next to Briony. 'I don't remember.'

Briony's head darted from one sister to the other as they sat either side of her.

Marjorie continued, 'We'd both left home by then, got married, hadn't we? But I'd heard he had his heart broken by some lass. Perhaps that's why he never returned to Cobblers Yard.'

'That's right. Then we heard from Father, when he stopped to talk to Mr Cribbins, that the poor man was broken-hearted when his son didn't return. I think he wanted Frank to take over his music shop.'

'Yes, that's right,' agreed Mabel. 'But we always thought he was destined for … well, for bigger things, didn't we, Marj? Not that there's anything wrong with running a shop,' added Mabel. 'Nothing wrong with that at all.'

'You're talking about his singing voice, aren't you?' Briony said. 'When you talked of him being destined for bigger things?'

'Yes. I thought he could have grown up to be an opera singer.'

'Or maybe sing in a boy band,' said Marjorie. 'Not that there was that sort of thing around in those days.'

'What are you talking about?' Mabel scoffed. 'Boy bands

started in the sixties! There were The Beatles and The Monkees, The Jackson 5, The Osmonds, and—'

'All right, Mabel, I see your point.' Marjorie rolled her eyes.

Mabel said, 'It's a shame there weren't things like *The X Factor* and *Britain's Got Talent* though. Oh, he would have surely been a hit on one of those if they had been around in his day.'

'He might still have that wonderful singing voice. He could go on one of those shows. We watch those shows avidly, don't we, Mabel? Can't say I've seen a familiar face, though.'

'How old do you think he'd be now?' Briony asked.

The sisters looked at her thoughtfully. Mabel replied, 'Oh, in his early seventies, wouldn't you say, Marj?'

Her sister nodded. 'Yes, that would be about right. We were in our teens, around fifteen or sixteen years old, when he was born.'

'Remember, Marjorie, when we thought that if he left the Navy, we might recognise him on television or in a West End Show, with a singing voice like that? We thought that perhaps he'd become rich and famous. He might have changed his name, though. I mean you wouldn't want to keep the name Cribbins, would you?'

'I do remember, Marj. Yes we anticipated if he was on the stage or screen he'd change his name. I mean, Cribbins doesn't sound very much like a singer.'

'No, not like Sinatra.'

'And did he?' Briony asked, 'become famous?'

'Frank Cribbins?' Mabel and Marjorie said in unison. They both shook their heads. 'Not as far as we are aware,' said Marjorie. 'Such a waste of a beautiful voice.'

Mabel looked at her sister. 'Yes, and nobody in Cobblers

Yard ever heard from him again once he left home.'

Briony hoped nothing had happened to him when he was in the Navy.

'We heard from his father that Frank was in the Falklands War in the eighties.'

'The Falklands War?'

'Oh, you're far too young to know about that, I expect.'

Briony had, in fact, learned a little about it in a history lesson when she was in school. 'It was when Britain was at war with Argentina.'

Mabel breathed a sigh. 'But he never came back.'

Briony looked at their solemn faces. 'You mean, he was …' she swallowed, 'a casualty of the war?'

'Quite possibly. Perhaps he died in the war. I remember there were casualties on both sides. Mr Cribbins never spoke of his son after that.'

Briony's heart sank. And there she was, thinking she could find him and reunite her grandmother with her lost love.

'All we know,' continued Marjorie, 'is that Mr Cribbins told us his son never returned from the war. Perhaps Frank decided there was nothing to come back for.'

Mabel looked at her sister thoughtfully. 'Do you know the name of the girl he was sweet on?'

They were both shaking their heads, when Briony said, 'Blythe. Her name was Blythe.'

Mabel and Marjorie looked surprised. Briony expected it made a change for someone new in town to know something they didn't.

7

Thea popped her head around the bookcase. 'Did you just say *Blythe*? Sorry, I was rearranging some bookshelves when I overheard. She's been one of our regular customers since the bookshop opened. Always pops in if she's in town and buys a novel. Romances mostly.'

Briony knew Blythe's taste in books already from what Reggie had said, along with the bookcase full of romance novels in the lounge back at The Beach House. It made her feel so sad to think of all those novels, and the possibility that her grandmother might still love Frank.

Reggie was right; there were no second chances if a person was gone. And by the sound of what The Gossip Girls had said, it was most likely the case. Either that, or he'd stayed in South America after the war and had made his home there. Maybe he'd married, had children, and put his past, and his first love Blythe, behind him.

But had Blythe put her past, and him, behind her?

Briony realised it had been the stupidest idea to think they might be reunited. He was mostly likely either living thousands of miles away, having had a good life, or he'd died in the war.

Either way, Briony's fantasy of a second chance romance was just that – like something out of the books lining her grandmother's bookshelves.

Reggie was right in what he'd said: *Life doesn't always play out like the stories we read in books.* She expected Reggie's guess as to Blythe's whereabouts was more likely to be the case – she was just recuperating after her knee op with a friend, who was waiting on her hand and foot, and hadn't contacted Emily about Luna because she felt guilty that she'd rather stay with her friend than collect her dog. Perhaps her friend didn't want Luna around; the size and appearance of a wolfdog hybrid could be intimidating.

It wasn't *really* a convincing explanation, though, of why her grandmother hadn't just picked up the phone and got in touch with Emily. Briony knew that Emily would have been quite happy to keep Luna for a little while longer. It made Briony wonder whether her grandmother simply hadn't been in touch because she couldn't afford any more boarding fees. Perhaps she'd decided to abandon her dog.

She wouldn't do that – would she? It occurred to Briony that she didn't know her grandmother. Was she capable of doing that?

Thea asked, 'Are you all right, Briony?' Her eyes roved to Mabel and Marjorie. 'Well, you two are quiet, all of a sudden.'

Mabel said, 'Briony, how on earth did you know her name was Blythe?'

Briony sighed. She realised that she might as well tell them. 'Blythe is my grandmother.'

'Your grandmother? The lady who comes in here and always buys romance novels. Well, isn't it a small world?'

'She wasn't a local girl when she met Frank,' said Briony. 'My great-grandparents owned a holiday home in Dunwich. She spent her summers here, and I guess that's how she met Frank.'

'You guess?' Mabel raised an eyebrow. 'Didn't she tell you?'

'Really, Mabel. Perhaps it's not something you'd want to discuss – a lost love – with your grandchildren.' Marjorie raised her eyebrows knowingly at Mabel. Something unspoken passed between the sisters; something they weren't about to share with a stranger, Briony guessed.

Marjorie turned to Briony. 'You knew about Blythe and Frank – how?' she asked.

Thea stood there, a couple of books to hand, listening.

'I found a stack of letters written by Frank to Blythe.' Briony opened her bag and took out one of the letters that had a date on the top right-hand corner. 'Actually, the dates on these letters are several years prior to The Falklands War, so he sent them before he joined the Navy, I guess …'

'She didn't reply to him,' said Mabel flatly, 'did she? That's why he left.'

Briony thought of all the unopened letters. At first, she'd thought that perhaps Blythe hadn't loved him, and had chosen not to open them. But then another possibility had occurred to her. Frank had said in one letter that Briony had read that he was going to better himself, prove he was worthy of her – whatever that meant.

'I think that Blythe's parents, my great-grandparents, hid the letters, so she never got them.' Briony had wondered why they hadn't just destroyed the letters. But she guessed that maybe the guilt of keeping them from Blythe would be made even worse by destroying them completely.

Briony frowned when she thought of her mum destroying the letter that had been sent to her by her own grandmother. The stack of letters suddenly made her wonder how many letters her mother had kept from her over the years. Had her grandmother sent Christmas and birthday cards and other letters that she'd never seen?

Briony wanted to ask her mother, but she couldn't – not yet.

'Well, that's just terrible,' said Mabel, cutting across her thoughts, 'keeping someone else's letters from them.'

Marjorie and Thea readily agreed.

Briony didn't want to talk about that.

The room fell silent.

Mabel picked up her newspaper, held it up, leafed through the pages, and started to read.

Marjorie stood up and frowned at her sister. 'I know you're rather settled in here at the bookshop, but we've still got a shop to run, you know.'

Mabel didn't look up from her paper.

Briony caught Thea smiling at the sisters. She guessed this wasn't unusual, the little spats and squabbles between them. It made Briony rather aware of the fact that she didn't have siblings. What would it have been like, arguing, fighting, competing for her parents' affections? Thinking of it that way, she was rather glad she was an only child. Except that now she was getting older, she thought it would be nice to have a sibling to share her life's journey with. Perhaps she'd have confided in them first that she was pregnant.

Suddenly, out of nowhere, Briony resolved to have two children close together. It was a ridiculous thought, when she didn't even feel ready for one child, let alone two. *Perhaps I'll have twins.* But that was not at all what she wanted. Coping with one baby at a time would be enough.

Briony caught Marjorie make a big show of looking at her watch. 'Isn't it time we got going, Mabel?'

Briony jumped at the mention of the time. 'Oh, goodness! If I don't get going I'll miss my appointment with Joss.'

'Joss,' said Mabel, lowering her newspaper. The mention of his name had caught her attention. 'Nothing the matter – I hope?' She leaned forward in her seat.

Briony chose not to mention the missing deeds, or her missing grandmother to one of The Gossip Girls. If there was a chance, however slim, that the information might get back to whoever was after The Beach House, she didn't want to risk it.

'Mabel, put your nose back in the newspaper,' said Thea light-heartedly.

Marjorie said, 'I'd rather she didn't!' She grabbed the newspaper out of Mabel's hands and thrust it at Thea. 'Here – take this. Coffee morning is over. Mabel, come on!'

Briony picked up her bag while the sisters were still squabbling. Someone had to have the last word, but Briony would not be there to find out who that was.

'I'm sure I saw a customer walk into the charity shop,' said Thea, glancing out of the window.

Marjorie turned around. 'Really?'

'You didn't lock the door?' Mabel said incredulously, standing up and barging past Thea. Marjorie quickly followed.

Briony was about to follow when Thea whispered, 'Well, that got them moving, didn't it?' Briony looked at Thea. They both grinned. Thea shrugged unapologetically. 'Well, it's only fair that other customers get a look-in with the sofa, coffee machine, and free biscuits.'

It occurred to Briony that Thea might know something

about her grandmother, seeing as she was a customer. 'My grandmother didn't happen to mention that she was going into hospital for a minor op, did she?' Briony wondered if she might have also mentioned whether she was intending to stay with a friend for a while afterwards.

Disappointingly, Thea shook her head. She touched Briony's arm. 'I hope it went well, and she's okay.'

Briony hoped so too. She didn't want to get into a conversation just then about the fact that she had no idea where her grandmother actually was, although she did say, 'Look, my grandmother might be in a bit of trouble …' Briony didn't mind mentioning this to Thea. She wasn't one of the Gossip Girls. 'I know she came in here a lot to buy books. She wouldn't have happened to mention anything to you about The Beach House, and some letters from a solicitor she's been getting?'

Thea looked at her thoughtfully and shook her head. 'I'm afraid not.'

'What about your dad?'

They both looked over at Henry, who was busy organising some notebooks and pens for sale on the counter. Briony knew his name because he had a large name badge on the lapel of his jacket. She looked at Thea, wondering why she was hesitating.

Thea sighed. 'Look, my dad's memory is … not what it was.'

'Even if he remembered something, anything, it might help. I'll go ask him.'

'NO!'

Briony stopped in her tracks, surprised by Thea's tone. She'd been so kind and helpful up until that point. Briony didn't understand what the harm would be in asking.

Thea touched her arm, obviously realising that she had been

quite rude and abrupt. 'Sorry.' She appeared to struggle with what to say next. But there was clearly something on her mind. 'Any friend of Emily's is a friend of mine. I like to think that our little community in Cobblers Yard treats strangers just like the locals – as friends. You're no exception, Briony. It's just that I don't necessarily want to share my dad's condition with … everybody.'

'Condition? I didn't realise he wasn't well.'

'Oh, he's perfectly fine when he's in the shop, surrounded by books, and his memories of living and working in the bookshop. He just doesn't cope well with … anything else.'

'He lives in the past?'

'He has to. It's the only way he can function now.'

Briony didn't understand. Her bemused expression gave her away.

'He has dementia.'

Briony looked at her dumbfounded. 'But he recommended I buy this book, and told me all about the author, and … and I paid for it, and he packed it in this bag – no problem.'

Thea stood there smiling. 'I'm sure there would be no problem. But ask him to go and buy a pint of milk from the Co-op around the corner, and you'd have to send out a search party to find him. He'd be lost the moment he stepped foot out of Cobblers Yard.'

'I am so sorry.'

'Don't be. We're just happy that he's back.'

'He's back – what do you mean?'

'Thea?'

Thea turned around at the sound of her dad's voice. 'Yes, Dad?'

'Are you still playing with your friends? I thought you were helping me out in the shop. You won't get your pocket money.'

Briony stared at Thea.

Thea just kept smiling. She lowered her voice. 'See what I mean?' She looked over her shoulder. 'I'm coming, Dad!'

'Good girl.'

Briony stepped out of the shop and closed the door behind her, thinking about what Reggie had said about The Bookshop of Memories. *Someday I'll tell you an incredible story about the bookshop across the yard, which was closed for decades.*

Whatever had happened, she was sure one of her new friends, Thea, Emily – or most likely her new reporter friend, Clarissa – would get around to telling her. But just then, Briony was focused on making sure she didn't miss her appointment across the yard with Joss.

8

Briony had her ticket to hand as she crossed the cobbled yard. Cheryl had said that she had time to go and browse in the bookshop while she waited to see Joss, but it felt like she'd been an age. She stole another glance at her watch. It was lunchtime. She was a morning slot. What if Joss had gone to lunch? As she crossed the yard and approached the old shop front, she couldn't hear any voices. There was no longer anyone waiting inside. The place was deserted. 'Oh, no.' Briony sighed heavily. She'd missed the morning session. Now she'd have to wait until after lunch.

'Hello.' A young man stepped out of a door at the far end of the room, putting a jacket on.

She looked him up and down, relieved that someone was still there. He must have just had an appointment with Joss. He looked like a surfer dude who'd just stepped off the beach, with his three-quarter-length shorts, open-toed sandals, and old AC/DC t-shirt. He also had a faint tan and blond windswept hair that looked as though it needed a cut.

Briony looked at her ticket. 'What number are you? I'm hoping I haven't missed my slot.' Maybe, if someone was just leaving and there was nobody else waiting, she'd just made it.

She caught the young man looking at her, bemused. 'I, um … haven't got a ticket.'

'Oh, did you just walk in?' She assumed he must have. She looked at her ticket. 'You must have taken my slot.'

The young man grinned. 'Ah, I think we are talking at cross purposes. I'm not here to see Joss.'

'You're not?' Briony looked past him at the door he'd just closed behind him.

'No, because I am Joss.'

Briony took a step back in surprise.

He clearly guessed what she was thinking. 'I don't like wearing starchy suits, and I'm sure my clients don't want me to, either. I think it's just more comfortable all round. Puts people at their ease. I like to keep things informal.'

'I'll say!' blurted Briony. She looked away, embarrassed. 'Look, if I'm too late for the morning slot—'

'Not at all. You're Briony – right?'

Briony smiled. 'That's me.'

'The thing is, Briony, my morning session sort of overran, although there's nothing unusual there.'

'Oh, I see.'

'It's lunchtime, and I'm starving. Sometimes I like to go for a takeaway fish and chips or get a filled roll and a cup of coffee in the town. Wasn't Emily meeting you to run you home after our appointment?'

'Oh, goodness – yes. I'd forgotten.'

'That's all right. Sometimes Emily and I meet up in Aldeburgh for lunch if she's not too busy. Would you like to join us?' He quickly added, 'Then you can come back to the office, and we can go over your case.'

Your case. Briony had expected it would be a one-off appointment. She hadn't thought that he'd be taking her on, like a client, until her issues were resolved. 'I hope it won't inconvenience Emily that I haven't even had my appointment with you yet.'

Joss waved her worries away. 'Nah, I'm sure it will be fine.'

'Actually, I am hungry,' commented Briony, feeling her stomach rumbling. She hadn't had much to eat for breakfast; she had been far too preoccupied with what answers she might glean about her missing grandparent.

She stepped outside, still feeling embarrassed about assuming he was a surfer who'd popped in for legal advice. She watched him lock the door and thought about how looks could be deceiving.

As he joined her in the cobbled yard, falling in step as they walked down the little lane between the shops into the high street, Briony apologised again. 'Look, I'm really sorry for mistaking you for one of your clients.'

Joss said cheerfully, 'No harm done. We do have clients who are dressed in suits, and I have had some interesting reactions from them when they meet me, but they soon look past my lack of dress code when my legal skills are front and centre. I'm pretty good at what I do.'

Briony hoped so.

'The truth is, I feel more comfortable dressing like this. I could never go back to wearing a suit – that's not my life anymore.'

Briony understood. He'd left corporate law behind. *If you can't be who you are, working for yourself, then when can you?* she thought.

'To be honest, if it wasn't for Emily's business, I'd quite happily welcome my clients into our home. But with so many animals, and the noise sometimes, it just wouldn't work. Besides, not everyone likes animals, no matter how cute they are. And we are quite off the beaten track. You can't get a bus to where we live, it would have to be a taxi or a car, so straight away it excludes anyone with transport issues, who might not be able to afford a car or a taxi. At least in Aldeburgh you can get a bus to see me.'

'Yes, I visited to collect my grandmother's dog, and two rescue kittens, and I agree that you definitely need a car to get there.'

'Well, I hope you like my premises.'

Briony hadn't been in his office, but she said, 'I love Cobblers Yard, and your reception is like no other reception I've been in.'

Joss smiled. 'That's good to hear, especially as the theme extends to my office at the back. We don't sit at desks, we sit on sofas, share a cuppa, eat a biscuit, and have a chat. Then I write up my notes on my iPad afterwards.'

'Sounds great,' said Briony, looking forward to her chat with Joss. She just hoped he could help.

Briony felt the hairs on the nape of her neck stand up – someone was watching her. She cast a glance behind her before they left Cobblers Yard. There was no one at the window in the bookshop, nor the charity shop, where she half-expected one of the sisters, probably Mabel, to be standing by the window, watching her walk out of the yard with Joss. But she did see Reggie, who was standing at his window with a violin in his hands. He was passing it over to his client, who must have turned up to collect it. Reggie wasn't paying attention to the violin, or to his customer.

His attention was firmly fixed on her, she noticed.

Briony paused for a moment, raising her hand to give him a friendly wave.

He offered a perfunctory wave in return, quickly looking away, turning his attention back to his customer.

'Everything all right?' Joss asked, noticing she'd paused at the entrance to Cobblers Yard.

Briony was still staring at Reggie. He'd been perfectly friendly in the music shop, letting her go early that morning for her appointment with Joss, but perhaps he hoped she'd pop back to the shop afterwards. I think I might need to pop into Reggie's music shop.' She wasn't sure why she'd need to let him know that she was going for lunch with Joss and Emily. After all, he didn't expect her back after her appointment.

'Did you forget something?'

She turned to Joss. She didn't want to miss out on lunch if she got into a conversation with Reggie. She looked at the paper bag in her hand from the bookshop and thought of the letters in her handbag. 'No, I've got everything.'

'Good, let's go then.'

They walked out of Cobblers Yard. Emily was sitting in her car. She wound the window down. 'Oh, hi Briony. How did it go?'

Briony bit her lower lip. 'Actually, I haven't had my appointment yet.'

Emily looked at Joss crossly. 'Why haven't you seen Briony?'

'My morning appointments overran – you know what it's like.'

Briony noticed that he didn't mention the fact that she had been late. It occurred to her that he might have been sitting in his office waiting for her to arrive but was too polite to say.

Joss said, 'How about we all go to lunch? Then Briony can be my first afternoon appointment.'

'If that's all right with you, Emily,' Briony added, conscious of the fact that Emily might not want to hang around Aldeburgh after lunch. Although it was Saturday, she still had a vet practice to run, and might have some appointments. There were also the pets staying at her boarding kennels, not to mention all the lost, abandoned and surrendered ones she had ended up taking in.

Joss and Emily were a lovely couple. If it hadn't been for them, Briony knew she wouldn't be there, meeting the lovely people in Cobblers Yard.

Emily got out of the car and smiled. 'Of course it's all right with me. However, I do have some vet appointments booked in this afternoon.'

Briony had thought that might be the case. 'I could come and see Joss another day, if you wouldn't mind running me home after lunch? Sorry.'

'I've got a better idea.' She put an affectionate hand on Joss's shoulder. 'If you don't mind doing a house call, Joss, we could grab some lunch to go and head back to The Beach House. We can have lunch there while you chat to Briony and have a look at the letters.'

Emily turned Briony. 'If that's all right with you.'

'Oh, that would be perfect, if you have the time, Joss.'

Joss smiled. 'I can do that. It's one of the perks of working for yourself – you do get to have an extended lunch break, if it's not too busy, although that is a rarity, and it will be a working lunch while I'm seeing my first client this afternoon – that's you, Briony.'

'What about your office?' Briony asked, concerned that people would turn up and it would be closed.

'Ah, that's not a problem. Cheryl will be back soon. She'll open up the office.'

Emily turned to Joss. 'It's settled, then.' She gave him a kiss and took his hand. 'Come on, sweetheart, let's get some lunch.'

Briony followed them down the high street, watching them walk hand in hand. Emily pulled Joss close, hugging his arm, smiling as they chatted. Joss was attentively hanging on her every word. Briony looked at Joss and thought of Freddie. *He loves me just the way Joss is in love with Emily*. Briony knew he'd do anything for her, just the way she imagined Joss would for his fiancée. *So, why didn't I give an answer to Freddie's proposal? It doesn't make any sense. We should be engaged now. I should have no qualms about saying yes.*

Emily glanced over her shoulder, released Joss's hand, and joined Briony. 'Sorry, Briony, didn't mean to ignore you.'

'You're in love – I get it,' said Briony, smiling. Joss quickened his pace, aiming for a queue outside a café up ahead.

'I imagine Freddie is missing you *so* much.'

For a moment, Briony wondered how she knew about Freddie, until she recalled her first visit to Emily's, when she'd picked up the dogs and the kittens. Troy – a young man whom she'd met when he'd turned up at The Beach House to start some work that her grandmother had arranged, renovating the outbuilding – had given her a lift, and Emily had assumed they were a couple. Briony had only just met Troy. Briony had set the record straight with Emily; she had told her that her boyfriend, Freddie, was back in Oxford.

'Such a shame he can't be here with you,' continued Emily. 'I bet you desperately wanted him to come.'

Briony just nodded and smiled. She hated lying to her new friends. But she didn't feel like telling them that she didn't want Freddie to visit her there at all.

9

As they approached a café called The Two Magpies Bakery, the queue had shortened. Arriving at the café counter, they chose homemade filled rolls. Joss got a coffee to go, insisting on footing the bill.

When they returned to the car, Briony said, 'Would you mind stopping by the car park in Dunwich before we head to The Beach House?'

'Not at all,' Emily said. 'Here, sit up front with me.'

Briony got in the passenger seat next to her. Joss climbed in the back, putting the filled rolls beside him on the back seat.

As Emily started the car, she said, 'Has Troy started work on the outbuilding?'

'Yes, he started last Monday after you and Clarissa were so kind as to help me clear it out. He's working today too.'

'But it's Saturday.'

Briony smiled. 'I know. He's so dedicated, isn't he? Working six days a week like that.'

'He's obviously enjoying the job …' Emily paused to look at Briony. 'Or the company.'

Briony ignored that comment. She was thinking about how it

had all come about. She'd come across the plans that her grandmother had drawn up to renovate the old outbuilding by the seashore in the grounds of The Beach House. The plans had been on the kitchen table when she'd first arrived. Her grandmother's plan was to turn it into a summerhouse with large floor-to-ceiling glass windows fronting the sea, a woodburning stove for the colder months, a lovely, vaulted ceiling and warm pine panelling for the walls, making it feel like a lodge.

Troy, whom Briony had not met before, had turned up along with his little half-sister, Willow, to inspect the outbuilding, clearly with a view to starting the job. Briony realised he had no clue that her grandmother, who'd obviously employed him to do the job, was missing.

She's not necessarily missing, Briony told herself. Reggie had suggested that Blythe was probably staying with a friend after her knee op. Who, then, was that friend, and where were they? Briony hoped her grandmother would return soon. In the meantime, she'd decided to let Troy get on with renovating the outbuilding. The plans had been drawn up, she obviously wanted it done, and as an added bonus, Briony intended to pay for it herself out of the savings that were intended for her trip to the Galapagos Islands.

There was just one thing bothering her a little about the renovations. Troy. It wasn't that she didn't have confidence in his ability. From what she'd seen over the past week, he was working hard and doing an amazing job. The problem was that she didn't want him to finish the job and leave. The previous Tuesday, when Briony had been unable to sleep, she'd decided to take Reggie's advice and watch a sunrise – she'd discovered that the Suffolk Coast wasn't called The Sunrise Coast for nothing. It was gorgeous, but it had been made all the more special by the unexpected company on that beautiful morning – Troy had turned up on the beach at an ungodly hour, saying that he couldn't sleep either. He obviously had things on his mind, about which he wouldn't elaborate.

Fair play, Briony had thought. He wasn't the only one keeping his problems to himself. Her grandmother was on her mind.

The only people, so far, who knew Blythe was missing were Reggie, Emily and Clarissa. It was Clarissa who had suggested that perhaps Briony ought to declare her a missing person and contact the police. Briony was still holding out for her grandmother to return, hoping Reggie was right and she was just staying with a friend. Otherwise, if she was considering involving the police in a missing person case, she really would have to contact her mum and her grandfather first and find out if they knew her whereabouts. Her grandfather might, given that he'd stayed in contact with her grandmother.

Briony really didn't want to contact her grandfather; he'd be so shocked to discover she wasn't on the research ship but was instead in Suffolk. However, as time went on, she realised that if she couldn't find her grandmother pretty soon, she would have to contact him. She'd already been in Suffolk for a week. The longer it went on, the more concerned she was becoming that something had happened to Blythe.

She hadn't told Troy, though. He was aware that her grandmother wasn't around, obviously, but she hadn't actually told him that Blythe was missing – just that she was away. For some reason, he'd seemed to accept that – no questions asked. It wasn't that she didn't trust him with the information. It was just that she didn't really know him. *That just isn't true*, Briony silently berated herself. You knew him well enough to hold hands while watching the sunrise that morning. If Luna hadn't intervened, worming her way in between them for attention, they might have even kissed.

Briony still couldn't believe that had nearly happened, although it was clear that they were attracted to each other, even though they'd only met a few days earlier. She couldn't believe she'd been with Freddie for almost three years, and yet she had been able to fall for someone else so quickly.

In that moment, as they'd watched the sunrise together, Troy had asked her to stay, and Briony had convinced herself that it was what she wanted – for herself, for her child. Not that Troy was aware she was pregnant. She had yet to tell him that. Perhaps that was why she'd been avoiding him since, and had just let him get on with the work on the outbuilding.

Her job at Reggie's shop was proving a distraction – some of the time, at least. He might be out of sight, but Troy certainly wasn't out of her mind.

'Briony? You seem lost in thought,' commented Emily, glancing at her as she drove.

Briony apologised. 'Sorry, I've just got so much on my mind.' Some of it she hadn't shared with her new friends, like her personal predicament, and how she had come to be in Suffolk. She *had* shared with Emily the news that she was pregnant, and it had turned out that Emily was too. Neither had yet told the fathers – Emily was waiting for the right moment, aware that although she was engaged to Joss, they still hadn't set a date. Briony didn't see that as a problem; in fact, she expected that Joss would see it as a great excuse to speed up the wedding, if they could.

Briony imagined that Freddie would react in a similar way as soon as she told him, telling her that now she had to accept his proposal and get on with planning the wedding. *But why do I have to do that?* Briony thought to herself. She knew what Freddie would say to that. It was obvious – at least to him – *because we love each other.*

Inevitably, Briony's thoughts turned to Troy once more.

'You're thinking about him – aren't you?' whispered Emily.

Briony bit her lower lip and nodded. They both knew who she was talking about. Especially after Emily had turned up that day to help her in the outbuilding and discovered her and Troy together. It hadn't been exactly how it had looked. Briony had got into difficulty while going for a dip in the sea, and Troy had appeared unexpectedly and waded into the sea to save her. Emily had happened upon them at the very moment Troy was carrying her in his arms, laying her down on her towel. It was ever so awkward, and even now, exactly one week later, Briony was still embarrassed just thinking about it.

Emily smiled wistfully, glancing in the rear-view mirror at the man she loved.

Briony glanced over her shoulder and wished her life was as uncomplicated and carefree as theirs. She thought of Troy. Was he in a relationship that he wasn't sure was right for him too? She had no clue. She really knew next to nothing about him, apart from the fact that they were the same age, and he had a little half-sister, Willow, who was five years old. He looked after her while their father worked away as a deep-sat diver for weeks at a time. Briony hadn't heard of deep-sat diving before, until she'd Googled it and discovered that 'sat' meant 'saturation'. It was a specialised from of diving that enabled divers to stay submerged for lengthy periods, working in pressurised underwater environments – often hundreds, if not thousands, of feet below the surface. It didn't sound like a job for the faint-hearted.

Their father was due home soon, apparently.

She did know one other thing, though; it sounded as though their father and grandfather had fallen out. She had no clue what it was about, but although Willow and Troy were welcome to stay with their grandfather – according to Willow, her grandfather was quite well-off and lived in a big house – their father insisted they stay in his small cottage – Coastguard Cottage – where he and Willow lived. When he wasn't looking after Willow, Troy lived with his grandfather.

Perhaps I should ask Willow, next time I see her, whether her brother has a girlfriend. She wondered what little Willow would say.

Emily commented, 'I'm so glad we managed to get the outbuilding cleared for Troy to start.'

'Yes, me too.' The previous Saturday, when Emily had brought along her friend, Clarissa, a journalist and good friend, to help her out clearing the outbuilding, Briony hadn't voiced her reservations about whether she should really be taking it upon herself to clear it out. After all, none of the stuff in there belonged to her.

Should she even be touching it, let alone sorting through and deciding which items to keep, and which to get rid of? Would her grandmother be angry with her when she found out she'd done that – and that she'd even roped in new friends to lend a hand? Even Willow had got involved; they'd made a game of it. Their first task as the Wolf Girls Club – a name Willow had come up with, as the club included Luna too – was to clear the outbuilding.

Their next mission, according to Clarissa, was to find out where the key fitted that Willow had found in an old shell box that belonged to her father. Clarissa wasn't serious about finding which lock fitted that key; it was just a mission she'd invented for Willow's benefit.

Briony hadn't mentioned at the time that she knew exactly which lock that key fitted. The shell box was identical to one belonging to Briony's mother, which Briony had brought with her. Willow's key was a replica of the one Briony had found in her mother's shell box, and Briony just knew it was another key to The Beach House; she'd used her mother's key to get in when she'd arrived. She wanted to find out why Willow and Troy's father had a key before she told anyone, though. Briony's mother's box also contained a necklace with a wolf pendant that was one of a pair – and Briony had noticed Troy wearing the other half.

'So, shall I drop you and Joss off at The Beach House, and park in the car park?'

Briony furrowed her brow, and looked at Emily. 'Why?'

'Well, you asked me to drive to the car park. There's no point all of us traipsing along the coastal path to The Beach House. It's a bit of a walk, I imagine.'

'It is,' Briony agreed. 'But you can park at The Beach House.'

'Won't Troy's truck be there?'

'Yes, but there's still space to park.'

Briony caught Emily raising an eyebrow. She realised it was an odd request, asking to stop at the car park first. She explained. 'I know I can walk to the car park later, but Reggie mentioned my grandmother's car and said that she always parks in the car park. I can't wait to see if it's there.'

She knew she'd recognise it; Blythe had told Reggie it was the same car her parents had owned; the one she'd learned to drive in. Briony didn't know what colour the car was because the photos she'd seen of it were black and white, but she imagined there weren't many of those cars on the road today.

'Blythe's car? It's a little Morris Minor in vintage green.'

'Vintage green,' repeated Briony.

'You think it's in the car park?' Emily glanced at her as she drove through Dunwich village.

Briony nodded. 'Reggie said it cropped up in conversation one day, when he'd arrived to tune her piano, and thought she wasn't in, because her car wasn't parked outside The Beach House. Turns out that she doesn't like driving Missy – that's the car's name, apparently – down the track in case she gets a flat and ruins the car's suspension, which is pretty non-existent anyway. And it wouldn't do her back any favours either.'

'Have you come across some car keys?' Emily asked.

'No, I haven't. But I wasn't exactly looking for car keys.'

'But mightn't she have them in her handbag?'

Briony frowned. That was a good point. She had not thought of that.

Joss, who had been drinking his takeaway coffee sitting behind Emily, waded into the conversation. 'Yeah, I agree with Em. She's probably got her car keys in her handbag, even though she hasn't been using her car.'

Briony sighed. 'Never mind. It was only a thought.'

'I can still stop off at the car park anyway, if you like,' said Emily.

'I guess.' Briony knew that it wouldn't take them too much out of their way.

'I don't remember seeing it when I arrived by taxi. The taxi driver parked in the car park, but I wasn't really looking at the other cars when we arrived.'

'And if it's not there ...' said Emily.

Briony shrugged. 'Then I guess she drove herself to hospital for her op.'

'And organised a friend to collect her and her car,' said Joss.

Briony sighed. If a friend had collected Blythe, and her car, she was still no nearer to finding her.

10

Briony left Joss sitting in the lounge, looking through the solicitor's letters addressed to her grandmother and making a big fuss of her grandmother's wolfdog, Luna, and her own soon-to-be foster fail, Wilbur.

Briony had fallen in love with the little smooth-coated black and brown dachshund the moment she'd set eyes on him at Emily's. The little sausage dog was normally quite chilled and laid back, so his reaction when he'd realised that she was leaving without him to go to work in Reggie's music shop that morning had surprised her.

When she'd opened the front door to leave, she'd been surprised that it wasn't Luna who raced to the door, but Wilbur. Of the two dogs, it was Luna who was the needy one – always following her around, wanting to join in with whatever she was doing. Wilbur, on the other hand, was quite content to spend the days lazing on his favourite sofa. But today, he had obviously heard her open the front door and didn't want to be left on his own in the house.

He'd kicked up quite the fuss, whining, barking, and even grabbing her trouser leg between his jaws, pulling and growling like they were having a game of tug of war, trying to stop her leaving.

Luna, on the other hand, had simply raised her head from her paws – she'd been in the kitchen, keeping a watchful eye on the kittens, her mothering instincts front and centre – when Briony had patted her head and said she'd see her at lunchtime.

Although Reggie had insisted she could take the dogs with her to work, which she had been doing, on that particular morning Briony didn't think it would be fair to assume she could leave them with Reggie while she popped across the yard to see Joss. She imagined that Reggie probably wouldn't have minded, but Briony didn't know how long she'd be. If Reggie had a customer who wasn't keen on the dogs – especially Luna, who could be a bit intimidating on first sight – then Briony would not be there to take the dogs into the back room.

She had decided it was better to leave the dogs at home. She'd just hoped they would be okay. It would only be for the morning, but it was the first time she'd left them home alone. Her resolve to leave them had nearly dissolved when Wilbur had started whining and lying by her feet, his drooping ears and sad eyes pulling at her heart strings.

She knew that if she had bent down and picked him up, she'd have had to take him with her. And then she'd have had to take Luna too, because she'd feel guilty taking one and not the other. But it was Luna who saved her from an indecisive few minutes spent standing at the front door, wondering what to do.

Luna had obviously heard Wilbur whining, because she had walked out of the kitchen and down the hall and had lain down beside Wilbur, licking his face as though she was giving him lots of reassuring kisses. It was lovely to watch Luna caring for one of her pack, as Briony liked to think of them; all of them, including herself.

Although Luna only had a miniscule bit of wolf DNA, the more time Briony spent with her, the more she recognised what appeared to be wolf-like behaviour. She was no animal expert, but she had caught an interesting snippet of a programme on wolves in the wild a few evenings earlier – with no internet, it was quite the novelty to watch something on terrestrial television.

When Briony came home after her morning's work, she was worried what she might find – a chewed sofa, or one of the animals, most likely Wilbur, having had an accident on the carpet. But all had been calm and serene. Wilbur was sleeping on his favourite spot on the sofa, and Luna was still in the kitchen.

She saw Wilbur through the window before she unlocked the door and guessed Luna had been keeping a watchful eye over the kittens while she was gone. As soon as she walked in, Wilbur ran out of the lounge and Luna appeared from the kitchen, both dogs making a beeline for her, smothering her in doggie kisses as she knelt down to greet them. They were so excited to see her, as though she'd been gone for days.

Not having had a dog before, she was a little surprised by their over-the-top reaction to her return, although it was a lovely feeling to walk in to greet such sweet-natured dogs. They were just so happy to see her.

Briony walked into the kitchen and guessed the kittens had been up and about, playing, in the morning – the toys she'd left for them were now strewn all over the kitchen floor. She cleared away the toys and glanced at the sleeping kittens in their plush, cosy, calming cat bed.

She picked up the cat bed with the kittens still fast asleep inside and carefully placed it in a corner where the sun was streaming through, casting a warm window-shaped square of sunshine.

One of the kittens stretched, looking as though he was about to wake up. Briony winced. She'd rather they stayed asleep. She did not want two playful kittens on her hands while she chatted with Joss.

Emily joined her in the kitchen. 'Well, Luna and Wilbur appear to have settled in.'

Briony smiled. 'To be honest, I know I've only been here a week, but although I had my own self-contained little apartment in the attic in my parents' house, I'm not used to living alone – I never have. I don't think I'd manage without them for company.'

Emily smiled. 'Oh, I know the feeling, having grown up in a terribly busy guesthouse. Sometimes I just wanted everyone to go away so I could have the house all to myself. Well, I'll tell you, just after my parents moved out, I started the process of setting up the vet practice and pet hotel, and Joss had his pro bono legal work in Cobblers Yard off to a flying start. I remember the first time he went out to work, leaving me in the big old house all on my own. I should have been overjoyed. My wish had come true. But it was awful. Just awful. I hated the silence, the sheer loneliness.'

Briony recalled a similar silence when she'd walked into The Beach House.

Emily cast her gaze around the kitchen. 'Blythe has done an amazing job of renovating The Beach House, but honestly, after seeing those photographs of all your family from years ago, gathered in the house, playing board games, frolicking on the beach, and just laughing and clearly having a whale of a time together, she must look back on those times and … well … feel quite lonely in this house.'

Yes, but things could have been so different, thought Briony, *if only I'd been allowed to come and visit with mum and dad during the school holidays, and we'd all spent time together.*

Briony remembered something her grandfather liked to say: *There's no good in crying over spilt milk*. But she still felt sad over what might have been.

Briony looked at Emily. 'At least my grandmother has Luna, and her foster cats and kittens. I don't know what I'd do if I didn't have them. Probably go home.' *And face the music when they found out I'm not in the Galapagos Islands*, she thought.

'Well, you can't go home now, unless you take all the animals with you. And besides, Willow still has visitation rights. You've got to honour those.'

Briony offered her a wisp of a smile. She remembered when Troy and Willow had given her a lift to collect Luna from Emily's on the day she'd arrived at The Beach House. When she'd agreed to foster a kitten, Willow had wanted one too. Troy wouldn't allow it, saying it wasn't up to him; it was up to their dad whether she could have one. And since their father was away working, Briony had come up with a compromise: she would foster two kittens. One would be for Willow, with the idea being that Willow could come round and visit her foster kitten. Willow had been at school over the past week, and Briony had missed her.

Briony had wondered whether Troy would bring Willow to work with him that day, as it was the weekend, but she guessed Willow must be spending the day with her grandfather.

'And you have Troy,' commented Emily.

They both turned to the kitchen window to look outside.

Although the summer was long gone, October had turned out to be unseasonably warm, and according to the weather forecast, a mini heatwave was on the horizon. The day felt like a precursor to the rising temperatures, with blue skies and a shirtless young man in and out of the outbuilding.

'Nice view,' said Emily.

Joss walked in the kitchen at that moment and overheard Emily. 'Yes, it's great seeing the ocean. This house has amazing views.'

Emily sniggered.

'Oh. Oh, I see.' He narrowed his eyes, staring at Troy as he walked by carrying two plastic bin liners full of the things that Briony had decided to throw out. They'd been left outside for Troy to dump. Blythe wouldn't miss broken pots and pans, a trunkful of old moth-eaten clothing from yesteryear, and old curtains and net curtains that had once hung in the house before she had renovated the place. Briony recognised the heavy curtains from the photos. Like the clothes, they were damp, moth-eaten, and completely unsalvageable.

'Would you look at those abs?' said Emily.

Briony was trying not to, but she was having trouble averting her gaze as Troy walked by.

'Now you're just winding me up,' said Joss.

Emily turned to him. 'Are you sure?'

'Perhaps I'll take my shirt off and parade up and down.'

'You don't have to do that, Joss. You have amazing abs.'

'Yes, I do, for a guy in his mid-thirties, but I'm not twenty-odd anymore.'

Briony caught him frowning. The light-hearted banter had gone. He wasn't joking any more. Briony got a feeling that he might have some insecurities over the ten-year age gap between himself and Emily.

Emily looked at him adoringly, all the same.

Briony wanted to tell him that he had nothing to worry about. She wanted to tell him how excited Emily was to have his baby, and how lucky he was to have found someone who loved and adored him just as much as he did her.

Briony really, really wished Freddie hadn't popped into her mind at that moment, along with guilt over the fact that she didn't feel quite the same way about Freddie. *So tell him!* she thought. *I'll break his heart, and I can't do that.* But she knew she owed it to him, and to herself, to be honest.

Briony was just trying to shut the door on that internal conversation, wishing that little voice would leave her alone, when there was a knock on the kitchen door. She walked over and opened it. 'Hi, Troy.'

Briony glanced at Joss. He was looking crestfallen. As well he might. Unfortunately, Troy, sweat dripping down his toned torso, dark hair plastered to his angular face, looked drop-dead gorgeous.

'Ahem, do you want a glass or water – or some juice? Or a slice of cake?' She didn't want to be one of those people who treated workmen with disdain, and wouldn't even offer them a cup of tea or coffee. And anyway, he wasn't just someone she'd employed. He was more than that – potentially much more.

She had invited him to join them for lunch, but perhaps it was just as well he'd declined, choosing to sit on the beach and eat his packed lunch, because she was meant to be chatting with Joss about her grandmother and The Beach House over lunch.

He shook his head. 'I've got a bottle of water.'

Briony looked at Emily and Joss and thought that perhaps he'd feel uncomfortable sitting having lunch with strangers. *Or perhaps he'd much rather just have lunch with me.* She looked away, embarrassed, when she thought of them sitting on the beach together, holding hands, watching the sunrise.

She silently berated herself. *I am not single*, she said to herself. But even so, she couldn't fail to notice that the moment Troy had seen Joss – when they'd all first arrived at The Beach House – he'd called her outside on the pretext of checking with her that she wanted him to dispose of the black sacks. He already knew that she did. He'd seemed more interested in who Joss was.

She'd told him he was Emily's fiancé, and they were friends who'd come round for lunch. She chose not to mention the reason for the visit – some free legal advice.

'I've seen him somewhere before,' Troy had said, 'although for the life of me, I can't think where.'

Briony didn't want to ask if he'd visited Joss for some legal advice.

Troy cocked his head to one side, gorgeous brown eyes regarding her. 'Anything the matter?'

Plenty, thought Briony staring back at him. She was beginning to wish she'd not asked him to renovate the outbuilding. Perhaps she should ask him to put his shirt on.

'Um, nothing. Do you need anything?' She was still wondering why he'd come to the door. She noticed his eyes rove to Joss.

'I need a hand moving that bureau.'

'Oh, the bureau.' Briony had nearly forgotten about it. 'I want to keep that.'

'I suggest it's brought indoors now, as we'll be cracking on with the inside renovations.'

'We?'

'I can't do it all myself, so I've enlisted some help. Just some guy I know who works in the building trade.'

'Okay, great.' Briony tried not to show her disappointment. The more people there were working on the outbuilding, the quicker it would be completed. She knew why she didn't like the thought of that. As she'd confided in Emily, she was lonely. She had got used to Troy coming round each day. No, it was more than that. She looked forward to it.

'So, you're happy for the bureau to be brought into the house now?'

'Fine by me.' Briony looked about her, wondering where it could go. She had an idea. 'Could you put it in the second bedroom – the single bedroom – under the window?'

'Yeah – sure. But I'll need a hand. The other guy isn't starting work here until tomorrow, and there's some things I wanted to get done, so it's all prepared.'

Now, she knew why he was looking at Joss.

'I'll help,' said Joss. He started unbuttoning his casual checked shirt until Emily shook her head from side to side as if to say, *That's totally unnecessary, Joss, you've got nothing to prove.*

Joss caught Emily's expression and rolled up his shirt sleeves instead. 'Let's do this,' he said before turning to Briony. 'You don't mind if I help Troy first, then we can have a chat about …' he glanced at Troy, '… things.'

Briony nodded. She understood that he was talking in code in front of Troy. 'Okay.' She caught Troy staring at her for a moment before heading across the sand to the outbuilding.

'So …'

Briony turned around to find Emily staring at her. 'Yes?' She caught Emily's gaze shift to the window.

'How're things with you and Troy?'

Briony pursed her lips. Emily was aware that she already had a boyfriend. Perhaps she should tell Troy that. 'There is no me and Troy.'

'Hmm.' Emily regarded her for a long moment before her gaze shifted to the window. 'Oh, they're coming with the desk.'

A few minutes later, Joss and Troy had managed to carry the heavy oak bureau up the stairs and position it under the window in the second bedroom. 'It needs a bit of work,' said Troy, 'but if you applied some good wax, well, I can't say it would look brand-new, but it would certainly be an improvement.'

'It's a nice desk,' commented Joss. 'Do you want to sell it?'

'It's not mine to sell,' said Briony.

'Oh, yes, of course it isn't. I forgot it's your grandmother's.'

Troy stood there looking from one to the other.

Briony nodded. 'Yes, and even if it was mine to sell, I wouldn't do it. I love it.'

Joss clapped his hands together and rolled his shirt sleeves down. 'Right, that's my good deed done for the day.'

Troy said, 'Sounds like you do a hell of a lot of good deeds in a day.'

Joss smiled. 'Thank you, Troy. I try my best.'

Briony looked at Joss, annoyed. She didn't know why she was getting irritated that he must have chatted to Troy as they were shifting the bureau and mentioned his free legal advice practice. She knew that Joss would not have told him that he was there to give Briony legal advice over lunch.

Troy said, 'I'd better crack on.'

'Me too,' said Joss.

Briony wished Joss hadn't said that. She caught Troy raising a questioning eyebrow and glancing her way before the two of them walked out of the bedroom.

Emily ran her fingers along the bureau. 'It's gorgeous. I'm so glad you found the key.'

Briony nodded, watching her turn the little key in the lock and carefully lower the bureau's drop-down flap, turning the lovely piece of furniture into a desk and revealing little drawers and cubby holes in which to store notepaper, pens, and letters.

Emily brought over a chair from the corner of the room and placed it in front of the bureau. She took a seat. 'This is perfect. Just look at the view.'

Briony stood at the desk behind Emily and looked at the view out to sea. The calm, sparkling turquoise water would not have been out of place in the Caribbean.

'Makes you feel like writing a letter, doesn't it?' Emily turned in her seat to look at Briony. 'No one seems to write personal letters anymore. It's all texts and emails, and social media. Such a shame.'

Briony agreed. She looked at the bureau and thought of sitting down and writing Freddie a letter. Perhaps she'd get a letter back, like the ones Frank had written to Blythe decades earlier, professing his undying love for her.

'And love letters are so romantic – don't you agree?'

Briony nodded, guessing that Emily was also thinking of those love letters from Frank that they'd discovered in the bureau.

Her thoughts turned again to the other letters – the ones she wished her grandmother hadn't received through the post, and the reason for her meeting with Joss. 'I'd better go and speak to Joss.'

Emily turned around in her seat and caught her hand. 'Briony, are you okay about not finding your grandmother's car? We haven't really spoken about it.'

'There's nothing to talk about.' Briony was disappointed when they'd arrived at the car park and discovered the little Morris Minor wasn't there.

Briony was sticking with her theory that Blythe had driven herself to hospital and a friend had collected her, driving Blythe's car to their own house.

Briony thought about who might have collected her from hospital. Oh, how she wished her friend, whoever it might be, had decided to stay with her at The Beach House instead.

'I wonder if my grandmother is with this person called Frank, from those letters?' Reggie had dismissed that idea – Blythe had been living on her own all these years, as far as he was aware, so why would Frank turn up now? Unless, after hearing nothing from either her daughter or granddaughter, Blythe had, in fact, managed to find Frank.

Briony liked to hold on to that thought. It made her feel so much better, imagining that Blythe was with a good friend.

Emily smiled. 'Oh, how romantic if she's found her lost love after all those years! I wish there was some way we could find out if that's who she's with.'

'Me too. I just don't know where to start.'

'Start with Joss – get to the bottom of those nasty solicitor's letters first. That will be one thing off your mind.'

Briony agreed.

Emily said, 'Do you want me to close the bureau?'

'No. I might want to write a letter.'

'To Freddie?'

Briony glanced out of the window. Troy was in and out of the outbuilding. 'Yes, to Freddie.'

'A love letter. How romantic.'

Briony glanced at Emily, who was sitting at the desk, staring dreamily out of the window.

Emily turned in her seat. 'I see the way you look at Troy.'

Briony pursed her lips, avoiding eye contact. 'Emily, I don't know what you mean.'

'Don't you?' Emily sighed. 'Perhaps you should tell Freddie how you *really* feel.' Emily turned in her seat to look out of the window again. Briony followed her gaze, and frowned. She thought, *Will someone please tell him to put his shirt on.*

11

'So, I've looked through these letters,' said Joss. Briony took a seat in the sofa chair opposite him in the lounge and picked up her filled roll. They'd left Emily in the kitchen, eating her lunch and making a cuppa.

Luna remained asleep by Joss's feet. Briony had noticed that for some reason Luna seemed to gravitate to guys, even though her grandmother had had the wolfdog since she was a puppy. Luna had lived with Blythe almost all her life. Her early puppyhood seemed to be a bit of a mystery – at least that was how Emily had made it sound; apparently Blythe wouldn't divulge where the pup had come from.

Wilbur, on the other hand, was not asleep. He had jumped up on Briony's lap the second she'd sat down. She stroked the little dog's silky soft ears, taking a moment to watch as his eyes closed. As an elderly dog, he slept a lot, which made her realise he'd be no trouble when she took him home, as long as she didn't leave him home alone too much. He was definitely her dog now.

Briony looked across at Joss. 'What I don't understand is why someone thinks they can pressure my grandmother to sell, and send threatening letters demanding that she produce the deeds, otherwise they'll go after the land. At least that's what it sounds like to me.'

Joss pushed the letters to one side and leaned forward in his seat. 'I think the way to end all this is to do exactly what they want.'

Briony looked at him in surprise. 'Pardon me?'

'Just show them the deeds.' He rubbed his forehead. 'What I don't understand is why Blythe didn't just produce the deeds after the first letter landed on her doormat. That would have saved all this—' he gestured at the pile of letters, '— aggro.'

Briony did see his point. 'Yes, I get that. Unless they're missing.'

'That would not be ideal.'

Briony thought that this was putting it mildly.

'However, it's not unusual. Deeds do go missing, if they are not held by a bank, often if there's no mortgage on a property. I'm pretty sure that will be the case here.'

'My great-grandparents built it.'

Joss picked up a photo album from the box that Briony had found in the outbuilding when she had been sorting through all the stuff stored in it. 'Hope you don't mind, but while I was waiting for you, I had a leaf through one of the photo albums.'

'Not at all.'

He held up the photo album and grinned. 'This is just the kind of thing that can provide proof of ownership.'

'Really?'

'Oh, yes. You see, there are other ways to prove ownership of a property if there are no deeds. For example, around three quarters of property house deeds are registered with the Land

Registry in England. Which means if your deeds go missing, then the Land Registry has seen the physical copy and created a digital copy which you can get from them. They just charge a small fee.'

'Great – let's do that then!' Briony was so relieved this was going to turn out so much simpler than she thought. While she was trying to find her grandmother, she could sort all this out for her, and finally stop these letters coming.

She looked at Joss. Her face fell when she guessed a big *but* was coming.

'But …'

Briony sighed. *Here we go.*

'I think if things were that simple, and the deeds were missing, as I suspect they are, she would have done that already.' Joss sighed. 'I mean why would you let all this aggravation go on, if you didn't have to?'

'Perhaps she didn't know she could do that, get a copy from the Land Registry.'

'Then I wish she'd come to me, and I would have sorted this out weeks, months, ago.' Joss looked at the letters. 'I will check when I get back to the office, as I guess your grandmother doesn't have internet here.'

Briony shook her head. 'Nope, no internet, and patchy mobile phone reception. The place does have electricity and a phone line, but without the internet, it feels a bit off-grid.'

'I'll say,' said Joss. 'But it is an amazing place.'

Briony got the impression that Joss would quite enjoy living off-grid. 'You were saying there's a way around the missing deeds, even if it's not registered with the Land Registry?'

'Ah yes.' Joss picked up the photo album. 'Now, this is quite interesting.' He flicked back to the beginning of the photo album.

'See here …'

Briony gently lifted Wilbur off her lap, stood up and put him on his favourite sofa chair. Wilbur curled up in a ball and fell asleep again. She looked at him and thought, not for the first time, that he was more like a cat than a dog.

Briony sat down next to Joss. She happened to glance out of the window on to the beach as she sat down, and caught Troy at the window looking in. *That's odd*, thought Briony. *What is he doing?* He quickly passed by the window as soon as she spotted him, but she knew he must have seen her shifting to sit next to Joss.

'So, look here,' Joss was saying, pointing at the photo album on his lap. 'This series of photos shows your great-grandparents on site with workmen building this property. Was it their holiday home?'

'Yes, I think it was. My great-grandparents lived in Oxford, but I know the house in Oxford was passed to my grandparents when they married. That's where my mum was raised. So my great-grandparents must have moved into The Beach House.'

'So, when they passed on, they left The Beach House to Blythe?'

'Yes. Like my mum, she was an only child.' Briony had been through the photo albums, and it was obvious that Blythe was an only child whose parents doted on her.

'So, your grandmother kept the property as a holiday home, until she moved in permanently.'

'Yes. My grandparents divorced just before I was born, so my grandmother came to live here.'

'Well, at least you had a lovely place to come for your holidays.'

Briony breathed a heavy sigh. If Joss was going to help her

out, although she didn't quite see it as relevant, she felt she really must tell him the truth – all of it. 'Actually, no, that wasn't the case. You see, my mum and grandmother are estranged – have been all my life. This is the first time I have visited The Beach House.'

Joss looked at her, surprised. 'Oh, sorry. I just assumed …'

'Yeah, it makes no sense, does it? I would have loved to spend my school holidays here, but it was not to be.'

'What brings you here now?' Joss asked. 'Have they patched things up, your mother and grandmother?'

Briony shook her head. 'Nope. I got a letter out of the blue from my grandmother to meet her here.' Briony left out the part about her mum opening and reading her letter, and binning it, despite still being upset with her mum for doing that.

But that did make her think. 'Could I be in trouble for reading my grandmother's letters?'

Joss shook his head. 'In these circumstances, with your grandmother missing, and the official nature of the letters, I should think not.' He paused. 'What I don't understand is that if your grandmother wrote to you to come and see her, why isn't she here?'

'My letter got lost in the post, and only resurfaced a few days ago.' *In the bin.* Briony tried to sweep that thought aside.

'I see. So, it sounds to me as though she wanted to see you before her op.' He tapped his chin with his forefinger. 'I wonder …'

'What is it?' Briony asked, studying his thoughtful expression.

'May I ask why she wrote to you? What did the letter say, exactly, if you don't mind me asking?'

She shrugged. 'Not at all.' Briony didn't need to go and fetch the letter from her handbag. She'd read it enough times. 'She said she had something she wanted to give me, and that there was something she wanted to tell me; something important that she didn't want to tell me over the phone or in a letter. It had to be in person. She wanted me to meet her here.'

Joss rubbed his chin. 'Hmm, go on.'

Briony had told him the gist of it, but he had rightly got the impression that there was more. In the spirit of telling him almost everything, bar the fact that her mother had read her letter first, she told him the rest. 'She mentioned that she'd also sent a letter to my mum asking her to come and look after the house while she was in hospital for a minor operation.'

'I take it your mum didn't come.'

'No, she didn't.' Briony frowned, realising that if her mum had done as she was asked, her grandmother would most likely have recuperated at home, maybe even mending bridges with her daughter while she did so. And she would not have gone missing.

Briony stood up and returned to her seat opposite Joss. She sighed. 'There's more.' She remembered reading the final sentences in the letter, which warned her not to accompany her mother to The Beach House. Blythe had also said that if Briony's mum did do as Blythe had asked, she suspected she would not tell Briony about her trip, and certainly wouldn't want Briony to join her. But it was the last sentence that had sent a chill down Briony's spine – and still did.

On no account tell her about this letter or your trip to see me, if you choose to come.

Joss sat back in his chair and regarded her for a long moment after she had told him this.

Briony finally said, 'What are you thinking?'

Joss let out a sigh. 'I might have an idea what it's all about.'

'Really?'

'I have come across these sorts of scenarios before – unfortunately, all too often.'

Briony looked at him, wondering what he meant by *these sorts of scenarios.*

'Look, what I'm thinking is, although your grandmother's op was routine, she isn't getting any younger …'

Briony recalled what her cheeky best friend, Angel, had said. She'd encouraged Briony to go and see her grandmother, if for no other reason than the possibility that she was including her in her will.

Joss continued, 'I'm not saying your grandmother is going to pass away imminently; I mean, she's only in her early seventies. But it's possible the thought of going into hospital perhaps brought her mortality home to her. No operation is without its risks, and she'd probably considered the possibility, even though its miniscule, that things might go wrong on the operating table.'

'You're saying she wanted to see me because she intended to change her will. I'd already thought of that.'

'Or make a will.' Joss added, 'You'd be shocked how many people die intestate – without a will – and leave behind a right mess for their poor relations to pick up in their wake.' Joss stopped. 'Did I just say 'wake'?' He shook his head. 'Um, excuse the pun.'

'You're excused.' Briony smiled. 'My best friend suggested the same when I told her that I'd received a letter out of the blue from my grandmother – that perhaps she was leaving The Beach House to me.'

Joss nodded. 'It's highly probable. If she's been estranged

from her daughter for years, and they are still not on speaking terms, it would make sense for her to leave the place to you. And it would explain why she told you not to mention the letter or the trip to see her.'

'In case it caused a rift between me and my mum, if she found out Blythe had cut her out of her will, in favour of me?'

Joss breathed a heavy sigh. 'Let's put it this way: I would never advise people to avoid dealing with their personal issues by simply writing someone out of their will. It's better to try and resolve things while you are still alive than effectively making a sweeping statement through your will that can never be undone, after you're gone, leaving things basically … unsaid. Unresolved.'

Briony stared at Joss. She was getting a bit more out of this meeting than she'd bargained for.

'I think any conversations around your grandmother's will should include your mum. Whatever has happened between Blythe and your mother, the last thing you want is for that to affect you and your mum.' Joss shifted in his seat. 'Sorry, but I take it you are on good terms with your mum?'

Briony nodded. Apart from the fact that her mum had never really supported her decision to become a marine biologist, they'd always got on well.

'Then I think when you find your grandmother, you need to let your mum know about the letter she sent you.'

But she already knows! Briony didn't quite know how to tell him about her mum intercepting her letter. For whatever reason, her mum was determined that she would never meet her grandmother.

Joss noticed that she was subdued. 'Of course, until you find her, I can only surmise what your grandmother wants to see you about. I could be barking up the wrong tree, and it's something else entirely.'

That didn't make Briony feel any better. If the letter wasn't about being a beneficiary of her will, then she couldn't imagine what it was about, and it was making her anxious – especially in light of what Angel had said before Briony left for Suffolk. Angel had warned her about opening Pandora's Box, saying that there might be a good reason why her mum didn't want her to have any contact with her grandmother. Angel had even gone so far as to suggest her mum had withheld the letter to protect her.

But from what? Briony had met some lovely people since she'd arrived on the Suffolk Coast, and nobody who knew or had met her grandmother appeared to dislike her. They didn't have a bad word to say about her. On the contrary, it sounded as though she was well-liked. Her grandmother fostered kittens, for goodness' sake. And she'd taken on a wolfdog puppy. She clearly wasn't an ogre.

'Briony? Are you all right? I haven't upset you – have I?'

'No, no – of course not.' Perhaps Joss was right: it was time that three adults, her mum, grandmother, and herself, sat down and talked.

12

'Briony, have you looked for a will? If you found one, and discovered you are the sole beneficiary, it might clear up why she summoned you here.'

Briony looked at Joss with interest. She hadn't thought of that. 'No, but I *have* been looking for the deeds, and haven't come across anything like that while I was looking.'

'All right, so we've established that it's most likely not in the house. That's probably quite sensible anyway. That means if she *has* made one, it's probably lodged with a solicitor.'

Briony had a sudden eureka moment. 'And the deeds might be with the will?' she said excitedly.

Joss nodded. 'They could be. Or they could be stored with the courts and tribunal service, or the probate office. I can do a search and find out if your grandmother has lodged a will.'

Briony stared at him. She wasn't sure she wanted him to do that. She'd rather speak to her grandmother. 'Can't we just see if we can find the missing deeds first? I think I'd rather speak to my grandmother before I find her will. It's not what I'm here for.'

At least, I hope not. My grandmother is safe and sound somewhere, I just know it.

'All right. I'll start with an electronic search at the Land Registry, and see what turns up. But this is good …' He tapped the photo album with his finger. 'If it turns out the deeds are lost, and unregistered, then if all else fails at least we have some proof that your great-grandparents built this property.'

Briony glanced at the old photo album on his lap and nodded. Her eyes roved to the outbuilding through the large window in the double-aspect room. Perhaps it was fortuitous that she'd given Troy the go-ahead to renovate the outbuilding in her grandmother's absence. If it wasn't for that, she would not have ventured in there, with all the cobwebs and spiders. While sorting it out, she'd rescued precious family heirlooms, like the old bureau, but was also glad she'd found the photo albums. And she was especially glad she'd found the unread love letters that she suspected Blythe knew nothing about.

'As well as these photos, there will be evidence of who has possession of the property right now – your grandmother through utility bills. Of course, her parents might have had a will showing that your grandmother inherited the property, which in turn explains why she should be in possession of the deeds. But that's assuming there were some originally. Sometimes a property is just passed down the generations with no deeds.'

Joss caught the look on Briony's face. 'But let's assume, for simplicity's sake, that there was an original paper copy of the deeds. Then it just comes down to explaining the circumstances around how they came to be lost, and the lengths she has gone to in order to find them. This is called reconstitution of the title. That means we provide the Land Registry with as much information as we can about the property and its background, and they decide whether they are happy that enough information has been provided in order to register the property.'

Briony nodded. It could be reasonably straightforward – if Blythe, when she was found, had the missing information.

'Now, not to get you worried or anything, but if in those circumstances they do register the property, it will be called a possessory title, as opposed to an absolute title. Basically, you haven't got the same legal protection that an absolute title gives you, so it's still possible for someone to dispute your right to the property or the land it sits on.'

Briony gaped at him. 'That means we might be back to square one, after all that.'

Joss sighed. 'Quite possibly.' He glanced at the solicitor's letters. 'It depends on what lengths someone is prepared to go to in order to get their hands on this place.'

Briony didn't know what to say.

'And to rub salt into the wound, when you've provided all the evidence, the Land Registry will write to any interested parties who may dispute your grandmother's right to the property or the land it sits on.'

Briony sighed heavily. She knew Joss was doing his best, but she just felt she was going around in circles.

'Or you can find the bast … er, I mean the person hiding behind their solicitor, and take them out.'

'I'm sorry – what did you just say?'

Joss looked at her, wide-eyed. 'I've got a terrible sense of humour. Emily will vouch for that. I can come out with unbelievably bad jokes.' He looked at her apologetically. 'Sorry. Not very professional of me.'

Briony managed a smile. 'Actually, that's not a bad idea.'

'I thought so.' He smiled too. 'But seriously, what I should have said was that you could find out who this person is and see what their game is. Blythe's lived here for decades without any issues.' He glanced at the letters. 'I'm not sure why all this has suddenly reared its head.'

Briony didn't have a clue either. She stared at Joss. 'Can you do that? Find out who this solicitor's client is?'

'It's tricky. You see, they're not legally obliged to divulge who it is. So as a solicitor, there's nothing I can do. But I might know someone who—'

'Clarissa!'

Joss smiled. 'Ah, you've met Emily's friend. She's a very good budding investigative journalist.'

Briony guessed he meant she was particularly good at finding out other people's business.

'I'll have a word with her and see what she can dig up for you, Briony.'

Briony had a thought. 'About the deeds. How do you turn a possessory title into an absolute one?'

'That's a good question. Obviously, let's hope the real deeds, along with your grandmother, resurface soon, but in answer to your question – it might be done pretty quickly if we can prove she's lived in the property for twelve years uncontested, which I assume she has.'

Briony thought that this was the first piece of good news she'd heard during the conversation.

'But—'

'Seriously!' Briony blurted. 'There's another *but*?'

'I'm afraid so. Say we sorted the possessory title, and an absolute title was granted by the Land Registry. If the deeds were to subsequently surface, and there are rights or covenants on the original deeds that we weren't aware of, or your grandmother wasn't, for that matter …'

Briony stared at him. 'Then they could still contest it.' Briony rubbed her temples with her fingertips. She realised she'd just entered a minefield.

'It's a minefield,' Joss said, as if reading her thoughts.

'Do you think that this person, whoever they are, knows something?' Briony asked.

Joss furrowed his brow. 'How do you mean?'

'Oh, I don't know. I've just got this feeling that there's more to this, but I can't put my finger on it.'

'You know, I have the same feeling.'

They sat there, staring at each other.

'Well, you two are getting mighty cosy in here. Should I be worried?'

Briony turned to look at Emily, standing in the lounge doorway, holding two cups of coffee. She could smell the coffee from where she was sitting. Briony quickly got up from where she was sitting, right beside Joss, and moved back to the sofa chair across from him.

Joss rolled his eyes. 'Ignore her, she's just pulling your leg. And what are you doing, interrupting my client's appointment?' he said light-heartedly.

'Sorry, was I interrupting?'

'Nah, we'd just finished, actually.' His tone changed. 'Where were you? I thought you were making a coffee. That was, like, half an hour ago. Surely, it doesn't take that long to boil a kettle!'

Emily looked at Briony. 'He gets irritable if you don't top him up with coffee frequently.'

'I do not!'

'There you go.' Emily smiled affectionately at her fiancé. 'Sorry, sweetheart, I got a bit sidetracked.'

'Looking out of the window at the good-looking, bare-chested guy, no doubt,' Joss said miserably.

'Not at all. The kittens woke up.'

Briony smiled. Of course. Who wouldn't get sidetracked by the cute kittens? She imagined Emily had spent the last half an hour cross-legged on the floor, playing with them.

'Here you go, sweetie.' Emily handed Briony a cup of decaf coffee.

Briony took the mug and suddenly felt terribly homesick. Despite the company of her new friends, she was missing home dreadfully. She missed her mum calling upstairs and asking her if she wanted a cuppa.

'Can I join you guys?' Emily asked.

Briony smiled. 'Of course.'

'I'll just fetch my drink.' Emily walked out of the lounge. Briony watched her go, wondering when she was going to tell Joss that she was pregnant. Perhaps she already had.

'Oh, my goodness!' exclaimed Joss. 'I've seen this car!'

'Well, yes,' said Briony. 'It's Blythe's car, so you will have seen it around Aldeburgh or even at home when Blythe has been to see Emily.'

'Yes, I've seen Blythe driving it to ours. I've even helped her with some of her foster cats, carrying the crates over to her car. But that's not what I meant.'

'Then what did you mean?'

'That I've seen it recently.'

'Recently? As in, just-the-other-day recently?'

Joss nodded his head vigorously.

'Where?'

Joss fell silent.

'Joss?'

He closed the photo album. 'I'm just trying to rack my brain and remember exactly where it was.'

Briony fell silent, not wanting to interrupt his thoughts – if only he could remember.

'I was visiting Nate – yes, that was it. We had a coffee around the corner from where he works at Aldeburgh Hospital. I swear I saw it in the hospital car park. I don't know why I didn't think of it when you and Emily were talking about your grandmother's car.'

Briony stared at him. It meant one of two things. Either Blythe had driven herself to the hospital and whoever had picked her up had done so in their own car. Or—

Joss said, 'What if your grandmother isn't missing at all?'

Briony swallowed. 'You mean she's been in the hospital the whole time?'

13

'I still don't understand,' said Emily as she drove down the high street towards Aldeburgh Hospital. 'Nate said that although he couldn't divulge individual patients' personal information, all the patients who'd had an operation on the day your grandmother went in were discharged with no post-surgery complications.'

Briony sat anxiously beside her. They'd just dropped Joss off so he could return to his office for the afternoon. He'd promised that as soon as he had a spare moment, he'd look into the issue of the deeds and whether the Land Registry held an electronic record. And he'd contact Clarissa to see what she might unearth regarding who was behind the solicitor's letters, and why they were intent on getting their hands on Blythe's property.

Briony had thanked Joss, but her mind had been elsewhere – namely on the car in the hospital car park.

Before they'd left, she'd hunted around for the car key, or a spare, but she hadn't been able to find one.

The one thing she still didn't understand was why Blythe would just leave her car in the hospital car park. Why hadn't she had a friend take her to hospital for her op?

Joss's theory was they'd left it there for her to pick up when she was fit to drive again. But that could take weeks. Would she really have left it there for that length of time?

She voiced her thoughts to Emily as they turned up the side street. The small, single-storey red-brick cottage hospital was up ahead.

'Hospital car parks aren't free. It would cost quite a bit to do that.'

Briony nodded, her stomach churning. Something didn't feel right.

'Something isn't right,' said Emily. 'Sorry, I shouldn't have said that. Doesn't help.'

'It's all right, Emily. I feel that way too.'

They pulled into the car park. Briony scanned it, searching for a vintage green Morris Minor. 'I don't see it,' she said, relieved. Perhaps Joss had got the days confused, and it was some weeks ago that he'd spotted it in the car park.

'No, me neither,' said Emily. They parked and got out of the car to look around. They were just getting back into the car, believing the Morris Minor wasn't there, when another car entered the car park and drove towards the last parking space between two SUVs.

'That's odd,' said Briony, noticing the driver not taking the parking space. As the driver backed up, he wound his window down, asking, 'Are you leaving?'

Emily turned around. 'Isn't there a space up there?'

'No, I thought there was, but there's some tiny old car parked in there. Couldn't see it as I drove in. The two SUVs parked either side hide it from view.'

Emily and Briony exchanged a glance. Emily said, 'No, we're not leaving.' Emily shut the driver's door and they crossed the car park. Sure enough, there between the two massive cars was the green vintage Morris Minor.

Briony walked up to the classic two-door car. The first thing she noticed was how pristine the little car was. The paintwork was like new; there was no rust as she'd imagined there would be. She looked inside at the red seats, which looked equally spotless.

'Oh, my goodness,' exclaimed Emily. 'Look at all these parking tickets!'

Briony walked to the front of the car. There were several parking tickets in little polythene bags, stuck to the front windscreen.

'I don't get it,' said Emily. 'I would have come and collected the car and parked it at my house, no problem, if only she'd asked. I know she does like to keep herself to herself, but Aldeburgh, and especially Cobblers Yard, are a friendly, supportive bunch.' She shook her head.

Briony was listening as she looked through the driver's side window. She tried the car door. 'It's open!' She looked at the ignition. 'They keys are still in the ignition!'

'Why would Blythe leave her car all these weeks in a pay and display car park without sending someone to collect her car? Unless—' Emily turned around and stared at the hospital entrance.

Briony followed her gaze, guessing what she was thinking. 'But you said she wouldn't still be in hospital! Otherwise it would have been the first place I looked.'

'I don't know what's going on,' said Emily, staring at the car. 'Come on. Let's go and find Nate. I hope he's working in A&E today. There's got to be a logical explanation.'

Briony hoped so. She reached inside, took the keys out of

the ignition, and then noticed a letter on the floor of the passenger footwell.

'Come on, Briony.'

She grabbed the letter and stuffed it in her bag before shutting the car door and locking it. Not that she imagined anyone would steal the car. After all, it had been sitting there all that time with the key in the ignition.

As they crossed the car park to the hospital entrance, Emily said, 'At least the car hasn't been clamped. I checked.' She had a thought. 'You drive, don't you?'

Briony nodded.

'Great. At least you can drive it back to The Beach House.'

Briony wasn't sure that was a good idea. She hadn't driven for quite some time, and she wondered how she would get on driving a really old car. She shrugged. 'At least then it wouldn't get any more parking tickets.'

'That's if it starts,' said Emily. 'I imagine an old car such as this might need a regular run at least once a week to keep it in working order.'

Briony sighed. Emily had a point.

'But not to worry. I've got some jack leads in the car, and if we can't figure out how to get it started, I'll call my dad.' They walked inside. Emily said to the receptionist, 'Is Nate working today?'

Briony noticed Emily didn't give his surname, and guessed the hospital was so small that everyone knew everyone.

'Oh, hi Emily. Hold on, I'll just have a look.'

Briony expected her to look at her computer. Instead she got up and walked through some double doors, under a sign reading *Minor Injuries Unit.*

'Oh, good – she's going to have a look for him.' Emily turned to Briony. 'She's an old friend from school.'

Briony nodded.

A moment later, the receptionist reappeared with a tall young man dressed smartly in a pair of chinos and a shirt. He had a lanyard around his neck with the word *doctor* on it and a hospital identity badge clipped to it. 'Hi, Emily. What's up?'

'Can you spare a minute?'

'Just about.' He smiled. 'Everything okay?'

'This is Briony. Remember I asked you if all the patients who had knee surgery around a fortnight ago were discharged with no complications?'

'Yes, and that was the case.'

'Well, Briony's grandmother, Blythe, had a knee op, but we've just discovered that her car is still in the hospital car park.'

'With a load of parking tickets,' Briony added.

Nate raised an eyebrow. 'She didn't let you know what her plans were for after her surgery? She obviously drove here, then, but someone would have had to collect her and take her home. We won't do the surgery unless that's arranged.'

'Do you know who agreed to collect her?'

'Hold on.' Nate turned to the receptionist. 'Can I borrow your computer?'

The young woman smiled at Nate. 'Of course.' She got out of her seat.

Nate perched on the office chair, and was about to type something when he looked at Briony. 'You're her granddaughter?'

'Yes, I am.'

'Okay, that's fine.' He proceeded to type something in. He looked up again. 'And her address?'

Briony gave him the address. She waited with bated breath.

'Okay, so on her patient notes we have her daughter as next of kin.'

'That will be my mum, Lorna.'

'Yes. She was named as the person who would be picking her up and staying with her overnight after her surgery.'

Briony looked at the computer and frowned. 'Really? Because I know for a fact my mum was doing nothing of the sort.'

'Ah, I see. So, you're saying she never came?'

Briony nodded. She was so angry with her mum for ignoring her grandmother when she needed her.

'So, she was discharged, and she intended to drive herself home, then.' Nate frowned, shaking his head from side to side.

The last thing Briony wanted to do was get her grandmother in trouble. 'Look, my mum should have come.'

'But she didn't,' said Nate matter-of-factly.

'She did not drive herself home,' said Emily. 'Her car is right here, and she's not at home. Briony can vouch for that.'

Briony nodded her head.

'How strange.' Nate rubbed his chin. 'The only other possibility is …' he trailed off, reading something on the computer screen – her medical notes, Briony presumed. She saw his expression darken.

Briony felt her heart beating in her chest.

He breathed a heavy sigh, and looked up from the computer. He stood up and walked around the desk.

Briony stared at him. The look on his face said it was bad news. 'Let's take a seat over here.'

Oh, no. Something definitely happened, thought Briony.

Briony and Emily followed him over to the small reception area, which was empty. Briony took a seat next to Emily. Nate sat opposite them. He put his hands together. 'So, like I told you, Emily, there were no surgery complications with any of the patients that came in around the time Blythe did. However …'

Briony tried to prepare herself for what was coming next.

'I wasn't working here in A&E on the day she had her operation. So I didn't know what happened next. It turns out your grandmother was discharged, and then a member of the public found her collapsed in her car outside in the car park. It was lucky that they pulled up beside her car just as she was getting in. When they were waiting to get out of their car, they noticed something … amiss. I'm afraid she had a stroke, so she was brought straight back in. She's still on a ward.'

Briony felt Emily take her hand and give it a reassuring squeeze, imagining that she wanted to tell her, *Don't worry, she's in capable hands. Everything is going to be all right.*

'She's here – in the hospital? Alive?'

Nate smiled. 'Yes. She's right here.'

Briony turned to Emily. 'Did you hear that? We've found her! I can't wait to see her, speak to her.'

'Um, you can see her, but speaking with her …' Nate trailed off.

Briony's smiled faded. 'She's not okay, is she?'

Nate stood up. 'Let's go and see her on the ward, and I'll explain on the way.'

A mobile phone rang.

'Oh, sorry – it's my phone,' said Emily, standing up. She looked at her phone. 'I've got a vet appointment booked in after lunch. I completely forgot the time. I bet they've arrived and they're phoning me, wondering where I am.'

Briony placed a hand on her arm. 'Go, Emily. You've gone out of your way to help me, as always, and I'm keeping you from sick animals in need of your care. I know you're super busy.'

'I feel bad just leaving you here on your own.'

'She's not on her own,' said Nate. 'I'm here. I'll look after your friend. Don't worry.'

'All right.' Emily turned to Briony. 'You must let me know how she is.'

'I will. Now go!'

Emily smiled at Briony and answered her phone as she rushed out of the hospital. Briony heard her say, 'Yes, sorry – I'm on my way. I'll be right there.'

Briony turned at the bleeping sound of a pager. She saw Nate take the pager from his trouser waistband. 'Oh, I've got to run.' He looked at Briony apologetically before saying to the receptionist, 'Can you show Briony to the ward to see her grandmother – Blythe?'

'That's not a problem, Nate.'

He turned to Briony. 'I'll come and see you on the ward when I get a spare moment – I promise.' He turned and rushed through the doors to the Minor Injuries Unit.

'I'll show you to the ward.' She looked at the computer. 'Ah, here she is. Your grandmother is in a little side room.'

Briony managed a smile. At least her grandmother had her own room. 'Okay.'

As they walked together down the corridor, the receptionist said, 'Would you like a tea or coffee, or a hot chocolate? I'm afraid we've only got vending machines, but the drinks are quite nice.'

'Yes, I'd like a drink, thank you.' Briony started to look in her bag for her purse.

The receptionist caught her arm. 'Oh, don't worry about that.'

Briony stopped fishing for her purse. Why was it never on hand when she needed it? 'Are you sure? I've got some change, if I could just find my—'

'It's fine. So, what would you like?'

'I'd love a hot chocolate, thank you.'

'Okay, I'll fetch you one in a moment.'

Briony followed the receptionist to a nurses' station outside the ward. The young receptionist told them that Briony was visiting her grandmother.

'Oh, it's so lovely for Blythe to have a visitor,' said one of the nurses. 'It will do her the world of good.'

'She hasn't had any visitors?' Briony asked. 'Not one?'

The nurse slowly shook her head. 'I'm afraid not. We tried to get hold of her next of kin – her daughter. Is that your mum? The mobile phone number we have must be out of date.'

Briony wasn't surprised. Her grandmother must have her mum's old mobile phone number. She recalled that her mum had recently got a new mobile phone. But they were estranged; her mum wouldn't have passed on her new mobile number. And did she even know that she was listed as Blythe's next of kin at the hospital? Somehow, Briony doubted it.

The nurse said, 'When we have time, we do sit with her and chat.'

'That's so kind of you,' said Briony, feeling a little overwhelmed at how kind and caring everyone she'd met at the hospital so far had been.

The receptionist added, 'It's such a shame I wasn't aware that the lady in the side room was known to Emily, otherwise I would have contacted her. I know Emily and Joss would have visited.'

They stepped on to the ward. 'Wait!' Briony stopped. 'I should get some flowers first. I wonder what she likes …' Briony caught the nurse and receptionist exchange a glance. The nurse said, 'Why don't you see her now, and go and buy some flowers later. I'm sure whatever you get will be just perfect, and brighten up her room.'

'All right.'

The receptionist said, 'I'll go and get your hot chocolate. Nurse will show you to the room.'

'Okay.' Briony turned to the nurse who smiled at her reassuringly. 'It's lovely to meet Blythe's grandchild. I can see the family resemblance!'

Briony smiled. So could she when she looked through the family photos. Her mum looked just like her grandmother when she was younger. In fact, if you put photos of her mum and grandmother as teenagers side-by-side, you'd think they were the same person.

Briony knew that if she'd added a photo of herself to the family photo album, nobody would have failed to notice the striking similarities between the three generations of women. Briony knew that she looked just like her mum. She wondered whether, if she had a daughter, she'd take after the maternal side of the family like she had.

Her dad had once told her that when they'd had her, he'd wanted Briony to take after her mother. He'd said that Lorna had the looks.

As she followed the nurse through the ward to the far end,

almost tiptoeing because the patients on the ward were elderly, and mostly sleeping, Briony thought of her lovely dad. He might be right that he'd never have made it as a model or member of a boy band – she was thinking of the bare-chested Troy at this point, and wishing he hadn't come to mind – but her dad was a very good musician, and a first-rate dad. *Her* dad. She was lucky.

She was beginning to wish that she'd told her parents where she was. *But I'm not ready to tell them, or Freddie, why I'm really here.* She had been surprised that Freddie had just accepted her decision not to go, without questioning it further. But later, she had guessed why. He had just been relieved that they wouldn't be apart for two months, envisaging that as she was just going to Suffolk, she'd be back soon.

And he was probably right. She couldn't stay away forever – that had never been the plan. At least, it hadn't been the plan until she'd arrived there, met some lovely people, stayed in her grandmother's gorgeous house, and sat with Troy, watching the stunning sunrise.

'Briony?'

The nurse had stopped in a doorway at the far end of the room, and Briony had nearly walked into her. 'Sorry. I was lost in thought.'

The nurse regarded her for a long moment. 'You look a little peaky. Are you getting enough sleep?'

Briony sighed. At first, she'd slept well at The Beach House, but it hadn't been long before she was waking far too early and having trouble getting back to sleep. 'I've got a lot on my mind. But at least I've found my grandmother. I am so looking forward to talking to her.'

'That's wonderful,' said the nurse. 'I think it may help hugely if she hears a familiar voice.'

'A familiar voice?' Briony's face fell. 'Help – how?'

'Patients who've had strokes, and are in a coma, have been known to wake up when they hear their friends and relations. That's why it's wonderful you're here.'

Briony looked at her, shocked. 'Wait, did you just say she's in a coma—?'

The nurse gaped at her. 'Oh, I am so sorry. I thought you knew.'

Briony shook her head vehemently. It wasn't Nate's fault. He had said he'd come and speak to her as soon as he had a chance, but Briony wished he'd told her so that she'd been prepared. He'd probably assumed the nurse would tell her.

Briony looked at her miserably. *Well, she's told me now*, she thought.

The nurse stepped to one side and motioned for Briony to enter the room ahead of her. They stood either side of the bed.

Briony looked down at her grandmother, wishing her first sight of her could be in different circumstances.

'Here, take a seat.' The nurse pulled over a comfortable, cushioned, high-backed chair close to the bed.

Briony sat down. Her first impression was that Blythe didn't look her age. She had a smooth, supple complexion with high cheekbones, just like her daughter and granddaughter. There were some crow's feet around her eyes, and a little dimpling around her chin, but she'd obviously taken care of herself over the years.

Her silvery-grey hair, about shoulder length, was surprisingly glossy, as though it hadn't lost its lustre even when her natural hair colour had faded.

Briony looked up at the nurse. 'She looks as though she's sleeping.'

The nurse nodded. 'Yes.'

'May I take her hand?'

'Of course.'

Briony gently took her hand. 'Hi … Grandma.' Briony had to pause to think what she'd call her – the grandmother she'd only just met. She felt a little self-conscious with the nurse there.

'How long has she been like this?' Briony asked.

'Two weeks now.'

'When will she wake up?'

'We would hope she'd be in a comatose state for no more than four weeks. Then there's still a chance of a good recovery, all going well.'

'So, I've got, like, a week to get her to wake up.'

The nurse breathed a heavy sigh.

Briony guessed she was being naïve. 'That was a dumb thing to say, wasn't it?'

'With stroke-induced comas, I'm afraid it's anyone's guess when – or whether – they'll wake up.'

Briony got the picture. It could be today, or next week, next month – or never. And she expected that the longer Blythe was like this, the less chance she had of making a good recovery.

'What caused it, do you think?'

The nurse said, 'There are so many factors that could be involved, I'm afraid, that we can't pinpoint the exact cause.'

Briony had her own theory about the cause.

The nurse checked Blythe's monitors. 'I have to go and check on the other patients. If there's anything you need, just let me know.'

Briony nodded, but her mind was elsewhere. She was thinking of the opened letter in her handbag that she'd picked up out of the footwell in the car. She didn't want to get it out of her handbag just then and read it. She had guessed what was inside; she recognised the envelope. It was another one of those letters from the solicitor – someone still after Blythe's beloved house.

Briony looked at her grandmother and imagined her getting in her car after her knee op, ready to drive home, and opening the letter that she'd probably picked up from the doormat and put in her bag before leaving for the hospital.

Briony thought of her earlier conversation with Joss. She gently squeezed her grandmother's hand and whispered, 'I'm going to find the person who is sending those letters, I swear. And when I do …' Briony trailed off. She didn't know what she was going to do, but she felt she knew one thing; they'd caused this – her grandmother's stroke.

The nurse popped her head round the door. 'I forgot to ask. Can you give me your mum's new phone number? I must update Blythe's next of kin contact number.'

Even as she reeled off her mum's mobile phone number, watching the nurse jotting it down, Briony thought, *Don't bother.* Would her mum come and visit even if she knew Blythe was at death's door?

There was one way to find out – she could phone her mum and let her know what was going on. *She's not at death's door.* Briony silently berated herself for the thought. *She's just sleeping, and all I need to do is find a way to get her to wake up.* But she knew that really, she had no idea whether her grandmother would recover.

She decided to be positive, and smiled to herself. She already had an idea. She looked at her grandmother, gently squeezed her hand again, and said, 'I've got something amazing to tell you.'

14

Déjà vu – that was the feeling that came to mind when Briony stepped outside. She was wearing a shawl she'd found in her grandmother's wardrobe wrapped around her shoulders. She shivered. It was colder than it had been on the last morning she'd stepped out on to the beach in the dark, anticipating the sunrise.

Apart from the cooler temperature, this morning was different in another way too. This time she wouldn't be surprised by the sight of a stranger sitting on the beach, who had turned out to be Troy. This time, they'd planned to watch the sunrise together.

She looked up and down the beach, expecting he'd be there already. But he was nowhere in sight. Not that she could see much. It was quite dark, but not completely – the bright moon hung low over the water, casting an ethereal glow over the gentle surf rippling on to the shore.

She pulled the shawl tighter around her shoulders and was about to step back inside the house to wait for Troy when she noticed Luna's body go rigid.

Luna sniffed the air, barked, and took off down the beach. That could only mean one thing. Briony smiled. He was on his way. She could see a figure walking along the beach towards her. She wondered why he had parked in the car park by the café and walked there rather than parking outside The Beach House as he'd done the last time he'd turned up at the crack of dawn. On that occasion, she hadn't heard Troy arrive, as she'd been listening to music on her phone. This time, she'd kept an ear out for his arrival.

She looked down the beach at the familiar figure heading her way. She knew it was him because she could see Luna's outline jumping up at him, getting a fuss.

Briony thought back to the last time they'd sat together, watching the sunrise. There was a reason she'd considered leaving Luna in the house this time – although that would have been difficult; she was a big dog, and the moment Briony had appeared in the kitchen, switching on the light in the early hours, Luna had been awake and up, wondering what was going on.

The two kittens had been asleep in the kitchen. She'd popped her head into the lounge and discovered that Wilbur was still asleep on his favourite sofa. But she'd let Luna out, and unless she went back inside herself, Luna was staying put on the beach – with Troy.

Briony frowned. When she'd sat next to Troy on the beach watching the sunrise, Luna, wanting all his attention, had wormed herself in between them and put a stop to what had nearly happened. They'd leaned in close, and had nearly kissed.

She watched an excited Luna following Troy down the beach towards her, thinking that perhaps, after all, it was just as well she'd let Luna join them. She suddenly got cold feet. Maybe this wasn't a good idea – meeting him like this. Last time, it had just been a coincidence, but this time, they'd planned to meet up, and she was intending to cook him some breakfast too. And it was Sunday.

She swallowed. Why hadn't it crossed her mind earlier that this would feel like a date? She guessed why that was – they were going to spend some time going over the plans. At least, that was her excuse for seeing him on a Sunday. They could easily have planned to do that on Monday morning, when he would be working on the outbuilding, but Troy had readily agreed.

They had originally agreed to meet at a sensible hour, but Briony had woken up in the dead of night, thinking about her grandmother, and hadn't been able to get back to sleep. Then she'd got a text from Troy to see whether, by chance, she was awake. He had been unable to sleep either. And now they were about to watch the sunrise together again.

Despite the feeling in the pit of her stomach that this was wrong – she had the baby and Freddie at the forefront of her mind – she couldn't help herself. They sat down on the beach together. This time, Luna sat the other side of Troy.

Briony held out a corner of her shawl. Troy gratefully took it and wrapped it around his shoulders too. They sat close. Too close. Briony turned to look at his profile. *When are you going to tell him the truth – about Freddie, about the baby?* she asked herself. She didn't want to think about the reality of her situation.

As the sun started to peek over the horizon, casting an orangey yellow glow on the rippling water, Troy's hand reached for hers. She didn't pull away. *Can't I just enjoy this moment?* she asked herself.

'It's the most beautiful thing I've ever seen,' she said, enjoying the sunrise.

'Yes, it is,' Troy echoed her sentiments, but when she glanced at him, he wasn't looking at the deserted sandy beach and the azure sea bathed in sunlight. He was looking right at her.

Briony knew she should have let go of his hand, got to her feet, and put an end to it. She had a partner, responsibilities on the way, a huge, huge change in her life – and Troy had no clue. She owed it to him, to her, Freddie, to everyone, to be honest. And it should start right there.

'Troy, I'm—'

'Hey, Troy! There you are!'

Briony, startled, turned to look over her shoulder and see who else had arrived on the beach at this hour.

A young guy, around their age, dressed in paint-splattered, knee-length cargo shorts and a t-shirt walked towards them from the direction of the house.

Luna spotted him too. She scrambled off Troy's lap and stood, alert. Troy patted her head. 'It's okay, Luna. It's only Sam.'

'Sam?' Briony looked at Troy questioningly.

'You said an early start, mate, so I got here early. I was waiting for you in my van, but I thought I'd walk over and have a look at the outbuilding before you arrived. I didn't expect you would be here already …'

The blond-haired young man, who had blue-green eyes, a ready smile, and a tattoo on his left arm, let the sentence hang, looking from Troy to Briony, and back again. His smiled faded. 'What's going on?'

'Nothing.' Troy quickly got up from the sand and brushed himself down.

Nothing? Briony stared at him as he got to his feet. She'd thought they were watching the sunrise together.

Troy said, 'I parked in the village car park so you had enough room for your van, otherwise turning to get out of the drive would be difficult.'

Sam nodded. 'Thanks.'

'You brought all the materials I asked for?'

'Yep, just like you said.'

'Good.'

Briony, who was still sitting on the sand, wondered when Troy was going to introduce her. Not that she expected to meet any of his friends or work colleagues. She threw Troy a questioning look. He hadn't mentioned that someone else was going to turn up. Was he working today? She had thought he wasn't and that it would just be the two of them.

Briony stook up. There was an awkward pause, when Briony anticipated that Troy would introduce her. He didn't. She gave him a questioning look, and he turned to Sam.

'This is Briony,' he said. 'She's the granddaughter of The Beach House's owner.'

'I see.' He turned from Troy to greet her. 'Hi, I'm Sam.' She noticed that any traces of his initial smile had vanished.

'So, you work with Troy in his business?'

'*His* business?'

'Yes, renovating places.'

'Oh, right. Yeah, sure.'

Briony looked at him. He didn't seem sure. She turned to Troy with a question. 'It's Sunday. I know you said you'd come and look over the plans—'

'What plans?' Sam interrupted.

Briony replied, 'The plans that Troy's company drew up for the outbuilding.'

'Oh, yeah. Right.'

Perhaps Sam just wasn't a morning person, or had had a late night out with his friends the previous night. But to Briony, he just didn't seem to be quite with it.

Briony asked Troy, 'Are you both working here today?'

He shook his head. 'Sam was just dropping off some materials for me. He's working on another job, so he's helping out when he can. I just didn't expect him here so early.'

'So, what are *you* doing here this early?' asked Sam.

'As I said, I was going over the plans before tomorrow.'

'Oh right,' Sam said flatly. He glanced at the sand where they'd just been sitting.

Briony guessed what he was thinking – it was a funny place to be checking the plans. And there were no plans in sight, anyway. And why so early?

'Why not just go over them tomorrow morning, then?' asked Sam.

Briony looked from Troy to Sam, wondering what his problem was. Perhaps Sam thought Troy had stayed the night. She didn't see why Troy had to explain himself even if he had. Unless there was something Sam knew about Troy, that she didn't. Maybe he was already in a relationship. Maybe that was why she had caught Sam looking her way disapprovingly on more than one occasion in their brief conversation.

Whatever was going on – and she knew there was something – she didn't fancy talking to Troy about it in front of Sam. If she was going to come clean about her own predicament, then she expected Troy to do the same. But not there, in front of someone she didn't know – even if he was Troy's colleague or very good friend.

Although she didn't know much about Troy's personal life,

she already knew something was going on. Why couldn't he sleep? Was it because of his father's dangerous job? She couldn't imagine that working as a deep-sat diver was a walk in the park. She had Googled it on her phone in the music shop, where Reggie had internet. She remembered Troy's little sister, Willow, mentioning that he worked away for four weeks at a time, but that he then had at least four weeks off before he went back.

Briony recalled thinking that it didn't sound like a bad job. But there was a reason that divers were paid very well and had so many weeks off in between work period – it sounded like dangerous work. Briony dismissed the idea that it was the cause of Troy's sleepless nights, though. After all, if his father had been doing the job for years, surely he was used to it by now.

There was another awkward silence, with Sam staring at Troy, and Troy looking uncomfortably at his feet, avoiding Sam's gaze. Briony had it on the tip of her tongue to ask what was going on, but thought she'd save the question until she was alone with Troy.

'Well, the sun's up, so I'm going to make a cup of coffee. Would you guys like one? Or breakfast?' Although she had been looking forward to having breakfast with Troy, now that Sam was there, she felt compelled to ask him to join them, out of politeness, even though she didn't want to.

Briony had stopped off and bought some shopping at the local Co-op in Aldeburgh the previous day on the way back from the hospital. She had soon discovered that the old Morris Minor had no mod cons; the lack of power steering in particular had made parking tricky. But at least the car had started, and after some crunching of gears and stalling, she had got the hang of it. It was so much easier to drive herself and not rely on lifts.

Conscious of the fact that she wasn't insured to drive her

grandmother's car, and she'd be breaking the law if she did, Briony had used her phone to purchase car insurance, downloading the documents before she got behind the wheel of the car.

Sam said, 'Breakfast? Would it be cooked, as in bacon and scrambled eggs?'

'Yes, I can do that.' She looked at Troy, about to ask him if he'd like to join his friend, and caught him shaking his head and casting a dark look in Sam's direction. Sam caught it too.

'Actually,' said Sam, looking at Troy, 'On second thoughts, I think I'll pass on breakfast. But I will have some coffee.'

'Okay,' Briony said slowly. 'Troy? Would you like breakfast or just coffee?' She had already guessed his response.

'Coffee is fine, thanks.'

Briony pursed her lips. So much for having breakfast together, as she'd suggested by text. In front of Sam, his demeanour towards her had completely changed. She thought she knew why – it wasn't very professional of him, especially as he was the boss, to be too friendly with his clients. Either that, or he had a jealous streak and didn't want Sam getting chummy with her.

She decided it might be a bit of both – or perhaps it was something else entirely. But it wasn't the time to try to find out. She said, 'Two coffees coming up.'

As she walked towards the house, she could see little Wilbur standing at the back door. She checked that the kittens were still asleep and were not hiding behind Wilbur, waiting to escape.

Briony opened the door and picked Wilbur up, giving him a fuss and a kiss. She put him down on the beach and went to collect some poo bags from the pantry.

A few minutes later, after Luna had said good morning to Wilbur and he'd been out to do his business, Briony returned to the kitchen with a bag of poo held out in front of her and Wilbur trotting behind her. She held her nose, deposited the plastic bag in the pedal bin, and sprayed some air freshener around the kitchen. As she did so, she heard the kittens mewing. The kittens were awake and doing their business in the cat litter tray. At least that was something, and they weren't doing it over the floor, which had been the case just yesterday.

Briony sighed. That still meant she'd have to clean out the litter tray. The chores seemed never-ending. *Wait until you've got a baby*, she thought. *Then all this will seem like a dream by comparison.*

She turned to the kitchen counter and flicked on the kettle to make three cups of coffee. On the kitchen table were the plans for the outbuilding. Briony had left them there in case Troy needed to refer to them. She hadn't been using the kitchen table, choosing to eat her evening meals on a tea tray in the lounge.

Her eyes drifted to Troy, who was talking to Sam outside. She couldn't hear what they were saying, but she could tell by the way that Sam was gesticulating at Troy, pointing at the house and throwing his hands in the air, that something was definitely up. Perhaps Troy was inundated with work, and Sam was annoyed that he'd taken on this project too.

As she made coffee, her thoughts turned to the writing bureau upstairs and the letter she needed to write to Freddie. But before that, she was going to visit her grandmother. She was looking forward to it, convinced she had the magic formula to get her to wake up.

15

'Is everything alright, Mrs— I mean, Lorna?'

Lorna smiled at Angel. Finally, Angel had called her by her first name. Lorna lowered her mobile phone. She'd just got in from the shops with a large bag full of brochures, all in aid of the adventure she wanted to go on with her husband. Then she'd received a text from a number she didn't recognise and was about to read it when Angel had appeared at the top of the stairs. She had obviously caught Lorna's bemused expression.

'Fine, thank you. I just got a text from an unknown number. No matter.' Lorna paused. 'Don't suppose we can tempt you to join us for Sunday lunch? Andrew is cooking a roast dinner. It's a bit traditional, I know.'

'Oh, I love traditional. Mum always cooks a roast.'

'Ah – are you off to Liverpool to see your parents today?' Lorna had noticed the bulky rucksack she was carrying down the stairs. She'd imagined Angel would have said something if she was planning to go home for a few days, or even for one night. Obviously, Angel wasn't her daughter, but even so, she had known her for three years and she was her daughter's best friend. And even if she'd been a less familiar lodger, Lorna knew she would worry if Angel went out one day and didn't tell either herself or Andrew that she was going away.

Angel stopped at the front door and took the bag off her shoulder. 'Er, no. I'm not going anywhere. It's just some stuff I don't need, like old college clothes I don't wear any more, now I'm at work and I've got some new outfits. My parents were due to collect me this weekend on the way back from a break away, so I'm going to give them my old clothes. I don't know what they'll do with them. I'm thinking my younger siblings might like a look at the stuff before it goes to a charity shop.'

'Where are you meeting them?'

'Oh, outside. They're turning up in a minute.'

'I see.' Lorna looked at her bulging bag.

Angel followed her gaze. 'You think I should keep hold of these clothes?'

Lorna shook her head. 'No, not at all. I'd definitely get rid of them. It's just reminded me that I was going to have a bit of a clear-out myself.'

In the spirit of doing some different things with her life, *creating a new post-forty me*, thought Lorna, she was starting small – with her wardrobe. She didn't have the money to throw everything out and completely change her wardrobe, but she felt that it was time to move on, away from those starchy skirts and shirts she'd been wearing for what seemed like aeons – since, like Angel, she'd left university and had known it was time to ditch the teen clothes and enter the grown-up world of work.

Thinking of work, Lorna reflected on the fact that she was taking a sabbatical, although she hadn't told her husband her plans yet. She desperately wanted to do something different to mark turning forty; to have some new experiences, go travelling with her husband. She hadn't stopped work completely – who could, at forty, unless they won the lottery or inherited money? The job would be waiting for her after Christmas, and so would her side hustle – the music lessons.

She did enjoy the music lessons, and teaching most of the time. But with her daughter off exploring the world, standing on her own two feet, she was now free from some of her responsibilities.

She recalled standing at the school gate, a young mum in her early twenties, her child already starting school. A grandparent doing school pick-up had said to her, *Just wait – the next few years will fly by. Before you know it, she'll have left school and flown the nest. Perhaps she'll be off to university.*

Her child had not flown the nest at eighteen, but three years on, she was gone. Lorna felt it was her time now. She smiled. 'I feel like a new me, too.'

Angel stared at her. 'Um, okay.'

Lorna inwardly sighed. The way Angel was looking at her, she guessed what she was thinking – *You're nearly forty – isn't it a bit late for that?* Besides, Lorna knew she had a nice house and a pleasant, easy-going husband. What more could she ask for?

Lorna didn't know. All she knew was that she felt there was something missing from her life. She always had. Perhaps it had something to do with having had the responsibility of raising a child, setting down roots – all those sorts of real, adult responsibilities – so, so young in life. She had barely been an adult herself, and hadn't had any of the freedoms that other young people had enjoyed – to travel, explore, find themselves, put themselves first.

It was why she didn't want her daughter to end up on the

same treadmill at such a tender age. It worried her that Briony had met Freddie so young. When a lot of Briony's friends had found their first boyfriends in high school, Briony had not, which had pleased Lorna no end. And then at freshers' week, barely a few days into her first term at university, it had happened. She'd fallen in love.

Andrew had been over the moon when they'd met Freddie. Lorna, less so. There was nothing wrong with Freddie – not at all. She could tell he was totally smitten with Briony, and would do anything for her. But Lorna would have felt lukewarm about anybody her daughter had met, just simply because she wanted her daughter to make her own choices and live a little before she married and had a family.

Lorna smiled to herself. She had really thought that Briony would give up her adventure in the Galapagos Islands because of Freddie. Lorna could tell he didn't want her to go – which was totally understandable. Two months was a long time to be separated from your love. But she was so proud of her daughter for standing firm and following her dreams. She couldn't wait to hear from her and hear all about her adventure.

She was hoping that she'd soon have an adventure to talk about herself, albeit in the planning stage. She did not want to slide into middle age with regrets over the things she could have done while she was still relatively young, like join her husband for a cruise, and then go on an adventure together. Travel. He was self-employed. It was easier for him to take time out. But a niggling thought kept popping up whenever she thought about surprising him with her plans: what if he didn't want to do something together with her? What if she had to do it on her own? Would Andrew be like Freddie, and not want to let her go, be away from her for any length of time?

She frowned at the thought. He seemed to have no problem going off on those cruises for weeks at a time. But then again, she had no problem with him going. He earned good money. But that wasn't the point. What sort of relationship was it when they actually enjoyed not spending time in each other's company?

But this is what I want to change, thought Lorna. It was the point of planning an extended trip together, to rekindle their relationship, to get to know one another as husband and wife, not Mum and Dad. Their lives had revolved around Briony since almost the beginning. They'd never been together as a couple, not properly, even when Lorna was pregnant. Their relationship, their marriage, what they talked about, thought about, was and always had been Briony. What would happen when she was gone and in her own life? Would they drift apart? Had that happened already?

Lorna had put a pause on her work, on her life, to find this out. She wasn't being selfish; she was thinking about Andrew too – about both of them. She just hoped he saw it that way. This wasn't just about an extended holiday, an adventure; it was about working out how they saw the rest of their lives now that it was just the two of them.

Lorna heard a car pull up outside the house.

Angel said, 'I think that will be my parents. I'll just give them this.' She picked up her bag.

Lorna opened the front door and saw the older couple in the car, looking up at the house. 'Aren't they going to come in and see where you live?'

Angel shook her head. 'They probably want to head off on their journey back to Liverpool.'

'They're more than welcome to come in, Angel.' Lorna saw Angel's dad get out of the car and wave. He opened the front gate and walked up the path.

'Hi, Dad. This is Lorna, my best friend's mum, and my landlady.'

Lorna smiled at the older guy, guessing he was in his early fifties. He shook her hand enthusiastically. 'Fantastic to meet you.'

'Please come in and have a look around.' Lorna opened the front door wide. 'I'd want to see where my Briony was living if she'd moved out.'

It occurred to Lorna that this was the first time her own daughter had left home, and yet she hadn't seen where she was living. Briony still hadn't been in touch, and despite Lorna's habit of dropping subtle hints whenever she saw Angel, Briony's best friend still hadn't mentioned whether she'd heard from her. Lorna had considered asking her directly, but she had already done so once, and Angel had concealed the fact that Briony had been in touch with Freddie.

'Can I go and get my wife, so we can both see Angela's room?'

'Dad, really, you don't have to come in. I sent you photos on WhatsApp.'

Lorna looked at Angel, wondering why she wasn't keen on her parents seeing her little flat upstairs in the attic.

'You've got a long journey ahead of you, back to Liverpool, remember?'

'Yes, I know, sweetheart, but we've been looking forward to seeing you.'

Lorna looked at Angel's dad and had an idea. She was sure

Andrew wouldn't mind. 'You could stay for some lunch. Andrew, my husband, is cooking a roast. It's nearly done.'

Angel's dad was already shaking his head. 'Oh, we couldn't impose.'

'Why don't we go for a pizza – or something, before you set off on the journey home?' suggested Angel.

Lorna frowned. 'Pizza? You don't have to eat elsewhere.'

'You heard my dad – he doesn't want to impose.'

Lorna smiled. 'Not at all. Andrew always cooks far too much.' She knew why that was. She hadn't the heart to tell him that he was still cooking for three, out of habit, and that he'd always cooked far too much even when Briony was home. There were always loads of leftovers because Angel still refused to join them for meals, always coming up with some excuse or other.

Lorna understood that she had her own life, and just because she was living under their roof, she didn't expect her to socialise with them – or, heaven forbid, be a surrogate daughter. That was not what she was there for. But it would have been lovely if she'd just sat with them over one meal. She still felt Angel was avoiding them. She guessed why – for whatever reason, Angel didn't want to talk about Briony.

This was the perfect excuse to have dinner together. And with Angel's parents there, if Lorna steered the conversation to Briony, perhaps Angel might divulge that she'd been in contact and what she knew about her trip.

Lorna said, 'You must stay for Sunday lunch. I insist.' She felt a little guilty that she had an ulterior motive, but Andrew did cook the most amazing Sunday roasts.

'Dinner will be on the table in a sec,' said Andrew, appearing at the kitchen door, wiping his hands on a tea towel.

Lorna smiled. Andrew's timing was spot-on.

'Oh, hello,' said Andrew, spotting a stranger standing in his hallway.

'Andrew, this is Angel's dad. They've come to pick up some things of Angel's on their way home from a holiday. I've invited them to say for dinner.'

Angel's dad stepped forward. 'I'm Trevor. Me and the wife don't want to impose.'

'Not at all, the more the merrier. As usual I've cooked far too much food.' He looked down at his expanding waistline. 'You'll save me from overeating. I keep saying I need to lose weight. Not the best time of year with Christmas approaching.'

Lorna rolled her eyes. 'Andrew, Christmas is weeks away.'

'Yes, I know. But I do like to be prepared. You know what I'm like.'

Yes, Lorna did. She knew it was not going to go down well when he found out she'd taken a sabbatical from her job and music lessons. He wouldn't be prepared for that. The problem was that Lorna didn't want to wait until Andrew was ready. She wanted to do something with her life right away.

She started to wonder what the sudden desire to do something different was really all about. Was it just a desire for an extended break, or was it something else? Was she after a more permanent change? And what did that even mean? Lorna glanced at Andrew.

'I'd better fetch the wife.' Trevor cut across Lorna's thoughts. He turned to the door.

'I'll go get her,' said Angel, suddenly shoving past her dad.

'Do you need help with that bag?' offered Lorna. 'It looks heavy.'

'No thanks.'

'So, Trevor, what do you do for a living?' said Andrew, steering his guest towards the kitchen.

Lorna stood at the open doorway, watching Angel lug her heavy bag towards the car. Angel's mum was a tall, striking woman with thick, glossy, dark hair. She was Mediterranean in appearance, with olive skin, and she was wearing the sort of gorgeous dress that Lorna would have loved to be able to carry off, but knew she didn't have the height.

Lorna watched Angel greet her mum, throwing her arms around her. She felt a lump in her throat at the thought that she couldn't throw her arms around Briony and give her a hug. But she did smile at the thought that the time would come when Briony arrived back from her trip and told her all about her adventure.

Perhaps she'd hear some news about Briony from Angel if she could get her talking at the dinner table. So far, Lorna had not been in touch with the company who ran the expedition. But if she didn't hear anything soon, from Briony or Angel, Lorna had decided she would call them.

Standing at the door, watching Angel with her mum, she felt sure something was going on. She just wished she knew whether it had anything to do with Briony.

She'd been waiting by the door, expecting Angel to leave the bag in the car and return with her mum immediately. She didn't. Lorna noticed them deep in conversation, Angel's mum looking at her daughter, nodding, and throwing furtive glances her way.

Lorna waved. She would have loved to know what they were discussing. Perhaps she was just being paranoid, and it was nothing to do her daughter. But what if it was?

Lorna had an idea. She glanced over her shoulder and called out, 'Trevor, do you like wine?'

His head popped around the kitchen door. 'Oh yes.'

Lorna smiled. 'Andrew, can you open a bottle of wine – or two?' If Angel had confided in her mum something about Briony that she did not want to share with Lorna, then if Angel or her mum weren't going to divulge what that was, perhaps easy-going Trevor, who clearly liked a tipple, would – assuming Angel had spoken to her mum on the phone at some point about Briony, and Trevor knew about it.

Lorna watched Angel and her mum start up the path towards her. 'I don't like secrets,' Lorna muttered to herself. 'But I'm a fine one to talk,' she said under her breath.

'Sorry, I didn't catch that,' said Angel as she approached.

Lorna smiled. 'No matter.' Her eyes settled on Angel's mum. 'Well, hello there. Welcome. I'm Briony's mum, Lorna.'

'I'm Martina.'

'It's so wonderful to meet you.'

Taking Andrew's lead, Lorna put a friendly arm around Martina's shoulders and steered her towards the dining room.

Angel said, 'I was going to take Mum upstairs to show her the apartment.'

Lorna noted she looked a bit flustered. She smiled. 'All in good time. First I'd like to get to know my new guests.'

'But what about that text you received earlier? Don't you want to read it?'

Is it my imagination, thought Lorna, *or is Angel stalling?*

Lorna wasn't interested in reading that text from the unknown number just then. It had probably been sent to her phone by mistake anyway.

'It was just a number I don't recognise. I'll deal with it later.'

She turned to Angel's mum. 'I bet we've got lots to chat about.'

Lorna glanced again at Angel, who was hovering by the stairs, looking worried. Lorna smiled at Martina. She knew one of them would be driving, but she couldn't help herself. 'Now, tell me, do you like wine?'

16

'Are you all right?' Briony felt a little silly, talking to Luna. She kept glancing at her in the front seat as she drove her grandmother's car back to the hospital. She would really rather Luna was not sick in the car on the way there.

She also hoped that she didn't pass a police car. Was there a law against dogs sitting in the front seat of a car, especially if they weren't secured by a seat belt? She imagined there was. Would a police officer believe her if they pulled her over and she told them that she had put Luna in the back of the car, but she'd squeezed between the two front seats to sit up front? *You try making a wolfdog hybrid sit where they don't want to sit,* Briony would tell them.

Luna whined.

'Look, we're not going to the vets, or the pet hotel, I promise you – if that's what you're worried about.' Luna had not wanted to go with her; she'd had to ask Troy to help her get Luna in the car. Briony didn't know whether Luna's only trips in the car were to Emily's. Maybe she associated the car with either going to the vets or being left with Emily. Or maybe that wasn't it at all. Maybe she just didn't like being forced to leave Troy for the afternoon. It occurred to Briony that Luna wasn't the only one who would rather have stayed home and close to Troy. She tried to put him out of her mind and focus on her surroundings instead.

She drove along the high street in Aldeburgh. Luna had been as good as gold, thankfully. She hadn't been sick, and she'd sat quite still, which was just as well in the confines of the small car. And as an added bonus, there had been no police cars in sight.

She parked, bought a ticket, and stepped up to the hospital entrance with Luna. It was a pity, in this situation, that her grandmother didn't have a small dog, like Wilbur. Then she might have picked him up and tucked him under her arm, or even let the little dog trot beside her down the hospital corridor. It was just possible that he would have gone unnoticed.

Briony looked at Luna and sighed. She was not going to go unnoticed; not unless the staff were too busy, and didn't see them go in. Briony had another thought: hospitals allowed patients who weren't very well at all, and might not make it, to see their pets – didn't they?

'But my grandmother *is* going to make it,' Briony said under her breath. 'And you are going to help me,' she said to Luna, 'along with something else I have here in my bag.' Briony smiled. She had a plan. But first, she had to find a way to get Luna past the receptionist and the nurses' station without being seen.

She whispered, 'Come on, Luna. Now, no funny business, do you hear? And for goodness' sake, no howling or any other weird sounds I know you wolfdogs make.'

Luna opened her jaws.

Briony looked at her, wide-eyed. 'Oh, no.'

Luna yawned.

Briony stifled a yawn herself. She felt more tired than normal and knew that being up at dawn was catching up with her. She'd had some coffee that morning, but it had been decaf, and she'd only had one cup, because she'd heard that avoiding caffeine was advisable during pregnancy. At the back of Briony's mind was the thought that she should see somebody – register with a local GP practice temporarily and, as Emily had suggested, go to an antenatal appointment. Then she wouldn't have to keep Googling all this stuff about being pregnant.

But for the time being, her focus was on getting her grandmother to wake up.

Briony looked through the double doors and noticed that the receptionist was away from her desk. 'Right, come on – let's go!'

She quickly scooted past reception, unfortunately capturing the attention of a little boy who was sitting with his mother in the waiting area. 'Look, it's a wolf!' Before his mother could stop him, the boy was in front of Luna and Briony, blocking their way. The boy wiped tears away from his cheeks and said, 'Can I stroke him?'

'It's a her.'

'What's her name?'

'Luna.'

The boy's mum jumped out of her seat. 'Don't touch strange dogs. What have I told you?'

Briony said to her, 'It's okay – Luna is very gentle.'

As if to prove it, Luna lay down with her legs in the air.

'Oh look, Mummy! She's so sweet.'

'I think she wants a belly rub,' said Briony as she looked about her, praying that the receptionist didn't return just then.

The little boy knelt down and rubbed Luna's belly. Then,

when Luna sat up, he stroked her long snout. He smiled up at his mother. 'Can I have a wolf?'

'She's not a wolf, really,' said Briony. 'She's a wolfdog hybrid; part wolf, mostly dog.'

Briony had assumed that the young mum would be quite cross about the fact she'd brought a dog into the hospital and was surprised when she said, 'Thank you for the distraction. He's having an ear examination and a hearing aid fitted. He's quite upset about coming to the hospital, even though the staff here are quite lovely. You've taken his mind off it.'

'Oh, you're welcome,' Briony replied, taken aback. 'I'd better go now. I'm taking her to see my grandmother.'

'Well, I'm sure she's going to love to see her.'

'I hope so.'

Briony left reception. She could hear the little boy talking about Luna and his mum asking him if he'd like to go to the zoo to see some real wolves. Briony smiled. She whispered to Luna as they stole down the empty hospital corridor, 'There, look – you've done your good deed for the day.'

She held up her finger. 'Please don't respond.' Briony was aware after living with Luna that she could be quite vocal when you spoke to her, as though she was actually having a conversation with you. Briony found it quite funny, and endearing. Today, though, she just wanted Luna to keep her jaws shut.

Up ahead, the nurses' station was empty. She stopped to peer around the door frame into the ward. She had to walk through the ward to get to her grandmother's private side room at the far end. Luna sat behind her legs, out of sight.

A nurse who was tending to one of the patients must have

sensed someone staring at her. She whirled around.

Briony immediately put her hand behind her back so that the dog's lead was out of sight. It occurred to her that it would be more polite to ask permission to bring Luna to see her grandmother. It was a hospital, after all. But what if the decision had to go higher, and she had to wait to hear whether the dog would be allowed in? How long would that take?

Briony didn't want red tape to hold up her plan. Time was of the essence; her grandmother needed to wake up soon, otherwise … Briony didn't want to think about the possibility that she would never get to have a conversation with her grandmother, never get to know her.

Technically, Briony thought, Luna wouldn't be on a ward. That was the beauty of her grandmother having a private room. Luna wouldn't disturb anyone.

Briony waved at the nurse. 'Ah, hello. Is it okay if we … if I … see my grandmother, Blythe?'

The nurse glanced at the clock on the wall. 'Visiting hours aren't for another hour, but seeing as you're here, come on through.'

Briony hesitated. *Would she be that willing to let me in if she knew about Luna?* The nurse smiled and turned her back and continued to tend to the patient. Briony took the opportunity to quickly walk through the ward. She caught patients sitting up further in their beds, looking at Luna and smiling.

Briony pointed at the nurse, and held up her finger to her lips. *Please don't give the game away and tell on me,* she thought, raising her eyebrows. She hadn't thought that Luna would cause quite such a stir – but then she should have, recalling the reaction of the little boy as soon as he spotted Luna.

Luna suddenly pulled on the lead. Before Briony could stop her, she was sitting beside a bed, getting a pat on the head from one of the patients. Then another wanted to pet her too. Before she knew it, she was going from bed to bed.

The nurse is going to turn around any minute and catch us.

But she didn't.

Briony had just got to the room, making sure that Luna was inside, behind the door, when the nurse turned around and exclaimed, 'Well, I never!'

Briony thought they'd been spotted.

She heard another nurse who'd walked in pushing a trolley, exclaim, 'I didn't expect you'd all be awake, sitting up, ready for your meds.'

Briony smiled as she closed Blythe's door. She patted Luna on the head and whispered, 'I think you've made quite an impression.' She sat down on the chair next to Blythe. Now it was her grandmother's turn. 'Time to work your magic, Luna. Come and see Blythe. She's missed you.'

Luna stole up to the bed, her muzzle working along the bedclothes, sniffing Blythe's hand, then licking it and nuzzling it for a fuss.

Briony held her breath, staring at her grandmother, looking for any sign of movement. Suddenly, Blythe's little finger moved.

'She's waking up!'

Briony jumped out of her chair and ran out of the room. 'Nurse! Nurse! My grandmother, Blythe, is waking up!'

The nurse rushed in, around the other side of the bed. 'Blythe. Can you hear me?'

Briony stared at her expectantly. 'I saw her little finger move – I swear.'

The nurse stopped and looked at Briony, shaking her head. 'I'm so sorry, but your grandmother hasn't woken up, if that's what you're hoping.'

Briony stared at the nurse, trying to keep her emotions in check. For a brief moment there, she'd been so happy at the thought that she would be able to speak with her grandmother.

The nurse suddenly jumped back from the bed, her eyes wide. 'What on earth is that?' She pointed at Luna.

Briony looked at Luna, her muzzle resting on the bed, on Blythe's hand.

Oh, no! Briony had been so excited at the thought that her grandmother was waking up, she'd forgotten about Luna.

Briony put her hand on Luna's head. 'This is Luna, my grandmother's dog.'

'But she's a … a …'

'No, she's only a little bit wolf, mostly dog. And she's a very gentle girl.'

The nurse seemed to relax a little. 'Have you got permission to bring Luna into the hospital?'

It sounded like dogs *were* permitted; otherwise the nurse would have told her there and then that Luna had to leave. Briony chose her words carefully. 'Not exactly.'

'Hmm. Meaning you haven't.'

Briony winced. 'No. But the thing is, I thought bringing Luna to see my grandmother might wake her up.'

The nurse smiled. 'I see. Look, I understand. I'll have a word with my supervisor, but I suspect that unless Luna is registered as a therapy dog, she won't be able to visit again.'

Briony looked downcast until she had a thought. 'How do I get her registered as a therapy dog?'

The nurse looked at her thoughtfully. 'I'm not sure. Perhaps ask a vet's practice? They might know.'

'Oh, okay.' Briony brightened for a moment. 'I know an amazing vet. I'll ask her.' But she knew it didn't change the fact that Luna wouldn't be coming again.

The nurse was about to leave the room. She stopped at the door, and turned around. 'Did you and Luna visit any other patients before coming in here?'

Briony breathed a sigh. There was no point lying about it. One of the patients in the ward outside her grandmother's room was bound to say something. 'Well, not intentionally.' Briony winced as she explained what happened.

The nurse pointed. 'So Luna said hello to the patients on the ward?'

'Look, I'm really sorry about that.'

'No, no. There's no need to apologise. I've never seen my patients so happy, not to mention willing to cooperate with their meds today. I was wondering what had got into them all. Nobody wants to be stuck in hospital, do they? Especially at their age, wondering if they'll ever go home.'

Briony looked down at her grandmother.

'Now, I'm just wondering if there's a possibility that while Luna is applying for her credentials as a certified therapy dog …'

'… She can be a therapy dog in training – like on probation?' Briony asked, hoping that was what the nurse was suggesting.

The nurse nodded, and grinned. 'You have to get your foot in the door and gain some experience.'

Briony nodded. 'Oh, yes.'

'I'd have to check with matron. Have we got your phone number?'

'No.' Briony frowned. They had her mum's contact number as next of kin, although it had been Lorna's old number they'd had on record, which was why they'd been unable to contact her when Blythe went into hospital. Briony was now regretting giving the other nurse her mum's new mobile phone number, though. What if the hospital contacted her mum? She didn't know why it hadn't occurred to her at the time she'd handed it over. She quickly dismissed that thought. Perhaps the nurses would assume she'd contacted her mum herself and let her know about Blythe. Besides, the nurse had said they needed it just to update their records. They'd be far too busy to give her mum a call, surely.

'I can give you my mobile number.'

The nurse got out a pen and small notepad. 'Okay. Are you her next of kin?'

'Yes, you can put me down as her next of kin.' *Might as well*, thought Briony, as her mum wanted nothing to do with Blythe. And it would hopefully stop them from contacting Lorna.

'Great.'

Briony glanced at Luna. 'Do I have to leave?'

The nurse thought for a moment. 'Well, you're here now. You might as well stay. Besides, I can keep an eye on Luna.'

Briony's eyes lit up. 'Sort of like an informal interview for the position?'

The nursed beamed. 'I suppose you could call it that. We can't have any howling, or barking, or any funny business. We can only have her here if she's calm, with a kind, gentle disposition.'

Briony grinned. 'Oh, that's Luna all over.'

'Well, let's still see how she does in a hospital environment.' The nurse stopped at the door on her way out and looked at Luna, who was still sitting quietly by the bed, muzzle resting on

Blythe's hand. 'So far, so good,' she said.

When she left the room, Briony said, 'Do you hear that, Luna? I think you'll make the grade.'

Luna turned her head to look at Briony.

'You are such a good dog. Oh, excuse me, wolfdog!' Briony was extremely disappointed that her plan for Luna to visit and for Blythe to miraculously wake up hadn't worked. But she had something else up her sleeve – or more to the point, in her handbag.

'Okay. Let's try Plan B.' Briony reached for her handbag. 'Grandma, there's something you should know.'

17

Briony found the letters in her handbag. One dropped to the floor. She picked it up and frowned. 'I don't think you want this one.' She tucked the letter she'd written to Freddie that morning back into her bag.

She had ended up leaving Troy and Sam in the kitchen, looking over the plans to the outbuilding. She'd taken her coffee upstairs and had sat down at the old bureau to write her letter to Freddie.

She knew that she could have got a stamp at the post office and posted the letter on the way to the hospital, but for some reason, she hadn't. *I couldn't leave Luna in the car on her own, or take her into the post office, though.* She knew that neither of these excuses were really true.

Briony tucked the letter back in her handbag and looked at the others she'd spread out on the bed. 'These are for you, Blythe.' Briony still wasn't sure what to call her. But it had sounded right when she'd said *grandma.* 'Shall I call you Grandma?' Briony nodded, deciding that was what she'd do.

'I found them in the old bureau in the outbuilding. I know you've never read them, weren't even aware of them.'

When Briony had ventured into the outbuilding, and discovered the bureau, it had been locked, and at first she hadn't been able to find the key. It was a sheer fluke that she'd been sorting through boxes of old clothes that she'd presumed had belonged to her great-grandmother and had come across the little key in the pocket of a pinafore dress.

The key had unlocked the drop-leaf bureau, revealing little drawers and cubby holes. That was where she'd made a discovery – love letters addressed to Blythe, written decades earlier when her grandmother was in her teens, with a return address on the back – the music shop in Cobblers Yard. Only one letter had been opened. She suspected Blythe's parents had opened it and hidden the rest.

She looked at her grandmother and sighed. 'I don't know why your parents wanted to keep you and Frank apart.'

Briony thought of Freddie. How would she feel if her parents disliked the man she was with and tried to keep them apart? Troy came to mind next. A question crossed her mind – would her parents like Troy as much as they liked Freddie?

Briony dismissed that thought. She didn't even know if Troy was single. And even if he was, she was pregnant with another man's child. Things were just too complicated. She had to put a stop to—

To what, thought Briony. *To my feelings?*

Briony looked at the letters and thought, *I am being so selfish. This isn't about me. It's about my grandmother getting well again.* Yesterday, when she'd first visited, the nurse had said she might respond to a familiar voice. *I think I sound like my mum*, thought Briony. *What if Blythe has that locked-in syndrome, where she can hear everything but can't respond?*

Briony had no idea. But she thought it was worth a try: reading aloud the letters that her grandmother probably never knew had been sent by her first love – a man called Frank.

Briony had felt a little guilty for opening the letters, but her grandmother couldn't read them herself, and besides, she had good reason. Perhaps this would help her grandmother wake up.

The letters were dated. 'I'm going to read them in order, if that's okay.'

She didn't expect a response. Luna turned around and put her muzzle on Briony's lap. Briony looked down at Luna. 'Well, I've got *your* attention, at least.'

Briony picked up a letter. This would be the first time she had read them. She looked over at her grandmother and sighed. 'This is stupid. You can't hear me, can you?' Her grandmother had no idea she was there with Luna.

She was about to pack all the letters away when she saw, out of the corner of her eye, Blythe's little finger move again.

Luna suddenly shifted her head, moving back to the side of the bed.

'You saw it too, didn't you?' Briony stared at her grandmother. It was a sign – it had to be.

'All right. I'll begin at the beginning, with the first letter Frank sent you.' Briony took a deep breath, wishing she could find Frank, and have him read the letters to her in person.

She lowered the letter for a moment, thinking about Emily's friend, Clarissa, the journalist. Joss said that he'd enlist Clarissa's help to find the person who was after Blythe's house. Clarissa had already offered Briony her help. Perhaps she'd help her find Frank too? Briony made a mental note to ask her the next time she saw her.

Her thoughts turned to Reggie. He had told her all he could about the previous owner of the music shop, Mr Cribbins, and his son Frank. The Gossip Girls, Mabel and Marjorie, whom she'd bumped into in the bookshop, had been much more enlightening. They had known Frank as a child when they'd lived in the bookshop with their father.

Apparently, Frank had had his heart broken, and had gone off and joined the Navy. As far as they were aware, he'd never returned to Cobblers Yard. They'd even said he might not have returned from South America, where he'd been posted during The Falklands War back in the early 1980s.

Briony sighed. She might as well read the letters. Unfortunately, unless Clarissa could work miracles, she imagined the chances of finding Frank were pretty slim.

She held up the letter and started reading the first of many love letters that it seemed her grandmother, aged fifteen, had never received from the sixteen-year-old Frank. As she read the beautiful, heartfelt notes, she was struck by the maturity of one so young.

There was no doubt in her mind how in love this boy, Frank, had been with her grandmother.

Frank's father, Mr Cribbins, had apparently been the person who tuned the old piano in The Beach House. In one letter, Frank had talked of the very first time he and Blythe had met. She had been five, he had been six, and they'd struck up a friendship that had, over the course of ten summers, developed into love.

Briony guessed they had needed to meet in secret. In his letters, Frank mentioned his father's little caravan in the caravan park on the road leading to Dunwich Heath, not far from the village. Briony imagined that was where Frank had spent his holidays while he was growing up. Although not far from Aldeburgh, it was a change of scenery – walks in wild heathland and a beautiful sandy beach with sand dunes. It must have been a lovely break from the flat where they lived above the shop in Cobblers Yard.

Even so, it was a far cry from Blythe's parents' holiday home right on the beach. But Frank mentioned in one of his letters how fond he knew Blythe was of the little caravan. She had found visiting it such an adventure. When they were both sixteen, Frank's father had bought him a Vespa – they had been all the rage in the sixties. It sounded as though they'd had to meet at the beach car park, where they'd then take the short drive out of the village and down the single-track road to the caravan park. Not far away, they could take clifftop walks on the heath.

Briony read the last letter, in which Frank begged her to write to him. For some reason, Blythe must have not spent that summer at The Beach House. 'Oh, no!' Briony said, interrupting her flow. She'd read that he'd decided it was his last letter. He was leaving for the Navy if she didn't write and ask him to stay. He must have thought she'd moved on, and didn't love him.

Tears rolled down Briony's face. Luna started licking her face, and putting her paw on to Briony's lap, whining, clearly wondering why she was so upset.

'It's all right, Luna. I'm okay. It's just sad, isn't it?' Briony put the last letter down and sat there, thinking. So it was true, what Mabel and Marjorie believed; Frank's heart had been broken, and that was when he'd enlisted in the Navy, leaving to travel the world and perhaps try to forget Blythe.

She wondered if he'd succeeded.

She took a tissue from an open box on the little table next to her grandmother's bed, wiped her face, and blew her nose. In her handbag was another pile of letters. These were addressed to Frank, unopened. She'd found these in the bureau too.

Her grandmother had written dozens of letters to him, obviously waiting for a reply that never came. But despite the stamps, there were no postmarks. Whether she'd posted them herself, or left it to her parents, the fact was that somehow they'd been intercepted and had never been sent.

Briony hadn't opened these. She knew Frank's were private too, but she'd opened them for a reason, to read them to her grandmother. These, though, belonged to her grandmother. They were tantamount to reading her diary. Briony hoped that one day, if she found Frank, she could give him these letters addressed to him, and he could read them himself.

Briony looked at them. 'He didn't get your letters, Grandma not one of them.' She stared at her grandmother's little finger, hoping for a sign that Blythe had heard what she'd just said.

'Briony?'

She turned at the sound of the nurse's voice and found her standing in the doorway.

'Everything all right?'

'I thought if I read the letters …' she trailed off.

'Letters?'

Briony shook her head. She didn't feel in the mood to explain what this was all about.

'I spoke with the matron and put in a good word. You can bring Luna again, if you wish.'

'Thank you so much.' Briony stroked Luna's soft fur. 'I thought Luna—'

'I know,' the nurse said softly. 'Give it time. Perhaps bring along her favourite book next time and read to her.'

Her favourite book? Briony looked at the nurse miserably. *How on earth do I know what that is? I don't know her!* Briony heaved a sigh and realised that was the problem. She looked at her grandmother. *You don't know me.*

Briony suddenly stood up. 'I can't do this!'

The nurse stepped in the room and put a gentle hand on her shoulder. 'I sense things are not … straightforward between you and your grandmother. But whatever is going on, don't give up on her. I suspect you're all she has.'

Briony slowly sat back down in the chair.

'You and Luna.'

Briony stared at the nurse.

'Would you like a cup of tea?'

'Yes please.'

'All right.' She paused at the door. 'The other patients in the ward outside are asking if they can see Luna again before you leave. If that's all right with you?'

Briony nodded. 'I'm sure Luna will like that too.'

18

'Well, at least something came out of that visit,' said Briony, walking down the road towards Cobblers Yard. It was Monday. She'd visited the hospital again, this time bringing along a book she'd picked at random from her grandmother's extensive collection of romance paperbacks on the bookshelves in the alcove of her lounge.

She had sat and read to her grandmother, as the nurse had suggested, but it hadn't done any good. Luna had sat attentively by the bed, watching Blythe. Briony had no doubt that Luna would have alerted her if there was any movement, any twitch at all.

She smiled at Luna, who was walking by her side, getting a lot of looks from people on the high street. They were probably wondering what type of dog she was.

'Well, haven't you made a lot of new friends?' she said to Luna, thinking of all the fusses and cuddles the wolfdog had got from the older ladies on the ward, yet again. Word had spread of the new therapy dog, even though Luna wasn't officially registered. Even the nurses had asked if she wouldn't mind visiting the Children's Day Unit and the Children's Ward.

Briony hadn't been sure at first. Unlike Wilbur, Luna was a big dog. Would the children, especially the younger children, be afraid of such a big dog? Especially one that looked like a wolf. And would Luna mind having inquisitive little fingers poking and prodding her?

Briony realised that she needn't have worried. The little boy they'd bumped into on their first visit together had proved that Luna was good with children, and they in turn were fascinated, getting up close with a real wolf. That was what the children on the ward believed she was.

Although Briony had corrected them, and tried to explain that she was a wolfdog hybrid, the mention of the word wolf was all it took. Briony smiled. Why were children so fascinated with wolves?

Briony was on her way to The Bookshop of Memories to see if she could find a children's book about wolves so she could share some interesting facts about them and perhaps learn a little herself about Luna's wolf ancestry.

She'd had to promise all the patients at the hospital that she'd be back with Luna to visit them. And she'd made another promise before leaving, to one lady in particular – her grandmother. She'd whispered in her ear, 'I'm going to find Frank, if it's the last thing I do.'

Briony turned down the lane between the shops into Cobblers Yard. Although she wanted to visit the bookshop, there was something she needed to do first. She headed straight for Joss's little office. She didn't have an appointment, but she hoped he would have time to see her.

Although she was friends with Joss and Emily, Briony wasn't expecting to jump the queue. She'd just get a ticket and wait her turn. She glanced at the bookshop across the yard and decided that this time she wouldn't risk missing her turn by making a visit there.

She happened to see Mabel, who was crossing the yard towards the bookshop, and waved. Mabel smiled and waved back, pausing at the bookshop door, Briony noticed, to watch her walk inside Joss's office.

The waiting room wasn't as busy as it had been the first time she'd visited. Cheryl wasn't there either, so Briony took a ticket from the dispenser machine and made herself a cup of tea. There was hot water in two large thermos flasks, milk, sugar, and biscuits – obviously the type Luna liked, because she discovered that Luna had whipped a digestive off the plate while she wasn't looking. Briony was surprised; Luna had been so polite around biscuits previously.

'Luna!'

She took a seat as far away as possible from the other people who were waiting and tried to keep Luna in check. Luna was acting like a Labrador. If she wasn't after more biscuits, she pulled on her lead to go and say *hello* to other people.

'I thought you were a good dog!' Briony whispered, feeling annoyed. She thought of her grandmother, keeping herself to herself, fostering kittens, doing private piano lessons at The Beach House, and realised that Luna had probably led quite a sheltered life. Apart from her stint at Emily's pet hotel, this was probably the most she'd ever got out and about, meeting other people.

Briony realised that Luna, getting used to all the attention, was coming out of her shell.

'Luna!' The dog pulled so hard, that the lead dropped from

her grasp. Briony realised her mistake in allowing Luna to meet all those ladies and the children on the wards. Now, she thought she could do the same here. Not everyone liked dogs. And the size of her could be intimidating.

Briony got out of her seat to fetch the dog from across the room, apologising to everyone for bringing her along. 'I'll take her outside.' She'd have to take her back to the car.

To Briony's surprise, everybody wanted Luna to stay. The waiting room had been silent when she had first walked in, with people looking downcast, lost in their own thoughts and problems. Then the atmosphere had changed, with people smiling as they petted Luna and asking questions about her breed as she walked freely around the waiting room. She even got offered a biscuit or two.

'Now you're all spoiling her,' said Briony, smiling.

A door opened at the far end of the room. Briony wasn't surprised when Luna ran over to Joss. 'Hey, girl. What are you doing here?'

Briony waved from her seat, and said, 'I didn't know whether to come. You might not have any … news.' Briony glanced around the room at the strangers. They appeared nice people, but she didn't know who was trying to hound her grandmother out of her house, so she didn't want to say anything about why she was there.

She couldn't imagine the person behind the solicitor's letters was local. Everyone she'd met since she'd arrived in Suffolk seemed so friendly and welcoming.

It was some big developer, she imagined, who'd stumbled on this beautiful part of the world and thought they'd take advantage of an old lady, and take her land. It really was reprehensible. She hoped Joss had discovered something.

Joss gave the excited dog a fuss. Luna then barged passed Joss into his office.

'For goodness' sake, Luna.' Briony rolled her eyes. What had happened to Luna's manners? Briony got out of her seat at the same time as an older man stood up.

The older man said, 'Oh, I thought it was my turn.'

'Yes it is. I just have to get the dog.'

'I don't mind if she sits in with me. Actually, I'd quite like it.'

'That's okay with me,' said Joss. 'If you don't mind, Briony.'

Actually, Briony didn't. Perhaps Luna would get up to less mischief in the office, where there were fewer distractions, and hopefully no biscuits in plain sight.

The older man said with a straight face, 'As long as she has been trained in lawyer client confidentiality.'

Briony stared at him, and then smiled when he winked, realising it was a joke.

'Can she sit in on my meeting too?' another client asked.

By the time Joss opened his door, and the last of the people waiting in the waiting room with Briony had left, Luna had sat in with every one of Joss's clients. In fact, Briony found it rather funny that every time Joss opened the door, and the next person got out of their seat, Luna went over to fetch them, leading the way back to Joss.

Luna came running over. 'Well, long time no see,' commented Briony as she stood up. There was no one else still waiting to see Joss that morning. 'I see you've made more friends.'

'She's been fantastic,' said Joss, standing by his door. 'People come into my office, often quite unhappy, weighed down by their problems, and quite apprehensive about the appointment and whether I can help them. Well, I've never seen so many smiles this morning. She's quite the calming influence. She just puts people at ease, and I'm sure as a consequence they find it easier to open up and talk. I might have to hire her services, you know, take her on as a … well I don't know – legal assistant?'

Briony laughed. 'Well, you'll have to get in line. She's already been quite the hit at the hospital. I've promised the staff and patients I'll take her back.'

'You took her to see your grandmother? How is she?'

Briony's smile faded. 'She's still not awake.' She didn't want to use the word *coma*, or even entertain the possibility that Blythe might not wake up. That just wouldn't be right; not when she'd only just found her, and hadn't had the chance to get to know her.

Briony followed Luna into Joss's office while he put the 'Closed' sign in the window. 'Feels like déjà vu – doesn't it?' he commented as he walked into the office and closed the door.

Briony thought so too. This was about the time she'd seen Joss on her last visit – just when he was about to close for lunch. She probably shouldn't have popped in again. It was only Monday, and she'd barely given him any time to look into the case of the missing deeds.

'Do you want to go for lunch?' Briony asked. She glanced at Luna and thought of trying to leave her outside the café, and how she would howl to be let in when she caught sight of all those people she'd want to make friends with.

Joss shook his head. 'I think we're better off talking in my office this time.'

This time. Did that mean he'd found something? She hoped it was good news.

19

Briony took a seat in Joss's office. It was like no office she'd been in before. There was no desk or office chairs. Instead, there were two couches, positioned opposite one another, with a coffee table in between. The wooden floor was covered with a woven rug in an Aztec style, and there were many paintings on the walls – watercolours of the coastline. She glanced at the full bookcase lining one wall. There were ornaments on the bookshelves as well as books; the sort of souvenirs picked up when travelling abroad to exotic locations.

For some reason, she had an idea that perhaps Joss had dropped out of practising law for a time and had just gone travelling around the world. The only inkling that it was a law office were the legal books on the bookshelves and the laptop on the coffee table.

Joss leaned forward in his seat and put his hands together. 'Now, about the deeds to The Beach House.'

'Yes?'

'Unfortunately I discovered that there are no electronic records of the deeds.'

Briony had expected as much.

'So, the next best thing, as I explained before, is to do a reconstitution of the title.'

Briony sat back in her seat. She had thought she'd walk into Joss's office to some dramatic news – maybe that Clarissa had discovered the identity of the nasty person who wanted her grandmother's property.

'But at least there's one bit of good news.'

'There is?' Briony leaned forward in her seat. 'What's that?'

'Well, that you found your grandmother.'

Briony sat back in her chair, deflated. Of course she was happy that she had found Blythe, but it had been a bittersweet discovery.

'I'm so sorry. I have a lot of cases, and there's only so much I can do.'

Briony understood. She'd seen the amount of people in and out of his office.

'But I'll get a file together to pass over to the Land Registry in respect of the title deeds and see what they are prepared to do. In the meantime, put together as much evidence as you can regarding how long your grandmother has lived there, like utility bills, council tax, photographic evidence.'

'You mean those in the old photo albums?'

'Indeed. Then I can start the process of sorting out the application with the Land Registry.'

'Thank you.' Briony was about to get out of her seat, when she realised Joss had something more to say.

'Look, something you said when we spoke at The Beach House has been playing on my mind.'

Briony couldn't imagine what it was. They had talked at length, but she couldn't remember the conversation verbatim.

'I have a photographic memory. That's why I can type up all my notes after the sessions, in case anyone else, like the police or courts, needs to know what has been discussed.'

'Okay, so what was it that I said that's been playing on your mind?' asked Briony, intrigued.

'You said, *Do you think that this person, whoever they are, knows something?* I asked you, *How do you mean?*'

Briony nodded. 'Yes, that's right. I remember.'

Joss continued, 'And you replied that you just had this feeling there was more to this, but you couldn't put your finger on it.'

'Yes, I still feel that way about the whole business with my grandmother's house. I just can't explain why.'

'I feel the same. Call it lawyer's intuition.'

Briony had a thought. 'What about Clarissa? Did you manage to speak to her? Has she found out anything about the person who's after The Beach House?'

'Yes that's the other thing I was going to tell you. There are other beachside properties further along the coastal path. As far as Clarissa has ascertained, none of those have received letters asking them, or pressuring them, to sell.'

Briony frowned. 'Perhaps it's because my grandmother can't prove ownership of the property.'

'We don't know that she can't. Not for sure, not until she … wakes up.'

Briony fell silent.

'What are you thinking?' asked Joss.

'I'm thinking if she could prove that she had a copy of the deeds, surely she'd have, you know, responded to those letters.'

'Maybe she's just stubborn, and thinks she doesn't have to prove anything.'

Briony thought of the sheer number of letters Blythe had received. It certainly felt like the person responsible knew something. 'Do you think they did a search of the Land Registry, to find information about the property, and discovered there were no title deeds of the property electronically registered?'

'I thought of that. The Land Registry does record any searches that have been done on properties. No such search was carried out.'

Briony sighed. That wasn't helpful.

'So, in light of that, I suggest that apart from myself, Emily and Clarissa, you tell no one else that your grandmother is not well until we get to the bottom of what is going on.'

Briony raised her eyebrows. 'You think it's someone local?'

Joss shook his head. 'I don't know. But if it isn't, it's possible they have a contact locally. But the fact that no searches were done through the Land Registry suggests to me that whatever is going on might be … personal.'

Briony had become convinced that some big-shot property developer had targeted the property and wanted to get their hands on The Beach House for the land, so that they could build a massive house there and make a lot of money. But what if it wasn't a developer targeting The Beach House at all, but someone targeting her grandmother personally? What if they were trying to get back at her for something by evicting her from her home?

Briony stared at Joss. A scary thought came out of nowhere. 'So, wait, you're saying that my grandmother might have an enemy?'

'I wouldn't exactly put it like that.'

'Someone with a grudge, then.'

'I suppose it's always a possibility that someone might be bearing a grudge, for some reason.'

Briony stared at Joss, nervously chewing her fingernail.

Joss said, 'Do you have any idea who that might be?'

Briony didn't want to acknowledge the thought that had just popped into her head. 'I wish I had the letters with me. I'd like to know when they started.'

'You mean from the solicitor?'

Briony nodded.

Joss tapped his temple. 'I have that information right here.' Joss reeled off the date that he recalled seeing on the very first official letter that Blythe had received.

Briony stared at him.

'Briony?'

'I'd better go.' She grabbed her handbag and stood up abruptly. She almost ran to the door.

20

'Briony!'

She whirled around. 'What is it?'

Joss held up the dog lead. 'I think you've forgotten something.'

Briony rolled her eyes at Luna, who was still sitting by Joss's feet. 'Luna – come here, girl.'

Luna was still misbehaving. She didn't budge.

Joss said, 'Luna – go on, girl.'

Luna stood up immediately, turned to Joss and got a goodbye fuss, then slowly walked towards Briony.

Briony grabbed her lead. She was about to walk out of the door, when Joss said, 'Are you sure you don't want to tell me what's on your mind? It helps to get things off your chest.'

Briony didn't want to voice what she'd just thought. Saying it out loud might make it seem a lot more plausible, and she did not want that. Briony had just discovered that the first solicitor's letter that Blythe had received had been sent soon after her mum had discovered that Blythe had sent Briony a letter, asking for her granddaughter to come and see her, and stating that she had something to give her.

Does my mum think that Blythe is going to leave The Beach House to me? If there was one person who might know the situation regarding the deeds of the property, it would be someone who had close links to The Beach House; someone related to Blythe. Her own daughter.

Even though they'd been estranged for years, would her mum really do that – try and get hold of The Beach House, her own mother's home? Briony thought of the lovely house. Who wouldn't want to inherit it themselves? How would it feel to discover that the person you assumed would leave it to you might change their will in favour of someone else?

Joss stood up too. He crossed the room to where she was standing. 'Briony, I just wanted to say something.' He appeared to be choosing his words carefully. 'I'm sorry I haven't got any further, yet, with your case. I don't want to muddy the waters, but all this might have nothing to do with your grandmother.'

'What do you mean?'

'Perhaps your great-grandparents had a falling-out with someone years ago over the property, or possibly the land.'

'You think this might be something to do with my great-grandparents?' The idea didn't seem to make sense. 'But – but they've been gone years! Why would someone be doing this now?'

'You'd be surprised how many people I come across who bear grudges, or have been on the receiving end of them, going back generations.'

Briony stared at him. She nervously chewed her bottom lip, thinking of her mother and grandmother, and said, 'No, I wouldn't be surprised.' But she was thinking about how awful it would be to carry around resentment like that for years. 'Do you think that's it then – what this is all about, some grudge?'

'I don't know. I'm only speculating, based on my experience.'

Briony was glad he had raised the possibility. What if it were true – that it was a grudge going back to her great-grandparents' day? She actually hoped that was the case; then it wouldn't have anything to do with the rift between her mum and grandmother. Of course, she could clear it up straight away if she chose to. She could phone her mum and ask if she had anything to do with the letters.

'Clarissa will be doing her best to find out who is behind this, and what exactly is going on. I'm sure she'll be in touch soon for a catch-up with the results of her investigations.'

'I was thinking of having another Wolf Girls Club meeting, so I'll see her there.'

'A what?'

Briony grinned. 'Oh, um, it's just something us girls thought up – just an excuse to get together, really. Luna's in the club too, aren't you, girl?' Which reminded Briony that she needed to ask Troy to bring Willow along, perhaps the next weekend. Briony missed Troy's little five-year-old half-sister with the blonde pigtails and large brown eyes.

The last time she'd seen her was just over a week earlier, the Saturday before last. Briony hadn't see her the Saturday just gone because she'd been working at Reggie's shop.

The Wolf Girls Club had been created as a bit of fun. Willow, Emily, and Clarissa were all sworn to secrecy over whatever they talked about together. That meant Willow too – she'd found out about Briony's pregnancy. One slip and it would all be out there.

A part of Briony wished that Willow would slip up and tell

her brother what she'd heard. But knowing Willow, who had taken their Wolf Girls Club very seriously, she wouldn't repeat a word that the members of the Wolf Girls Club had said.

Thinking of Willow brought to mind Troy. She didn't know how long Troy was working that day, and whether, when she arrived back at The Beach House, he would have finished work for the day and left.

She hoped that wouldn't be the case. Briony had left him working in the outbuilding after another really early start, watching the sunrise together. They'd joked that they ought to get some help for their insomnia. Of course, they knew it really was no laughing matter, and that it was an excuse to spend some time together. But Briony's insomnia was real – she felt as though she had an awful lot on her plate, and a lot of it was of her own making.

She knew what would stop the sleepless nights – telling her parents where she really was, for starters. *I can't do that – not yet!* she thought to herself.

She remembered the letter in her pocket addressed to Freddie that she had yet to post – at least that would be a start.

She didn't know what Troy's excuse was for being awake so early. Perhaps he really didn't have any issues and he was just getting up at the crack of dawn to see her – although the dark rings under his eyes suggested otherwise.

Then ask him what's going on. The problem with doing that was then it would spoil the moment. Briony would much rather they didn't talk about their problems – especially hers – during a beautiful sunrise. Although the previous morning, when Sam had turned up, it had been on the tip of her tongue to tell Troy she was pregnant. The moment had been lost. Now, she had to summon the courage to tell him all over again.

She felt Luna's wet nose nuzzling her hand and smiled. It was as though Luna sensed she was sad. Briony stroked her soft fur as she asked Joss, 'Do you think Emily might be free at the weekend?'

'I'll certainly ask.'

'I'll text her anyway, and Clarissa too.'

He said, 'You'll let me know if Clarissa mentions she has come up with anything? Sometimes, I get pretty busy, so if you hear anything first …' he trailed off.

Briony understood. He had so many clients, but he was trying his best.

She glanced over at the door. Briony could hear people coming into the reception area, and Emily's mum, Cheryl, in her friendly sing-song voice directing people to get a ticket and help themselves to tea, coffee, biscuits, and homemade cake. She hadn't seen Cheryl on her way in, but guessed she didn't work all day, every day. She realised that the afternoon session must be starting soon.

Joss took out a shop-bought sandwich from a plastic carrier bag and started undoing the wrapper. 'Just going to grab a bite to eat.' He looked at Briony.

'And remember, best to keep the fact that your grandmother is in hospital, and in a … and not well, under your hat.'

'Of course – it's just between you, me and the Wolf Girls Club.'

Joss smiled. 'Good.'

Briony appreciated that he hadn't used the word *coma.* It just made it sound so serious. In fact, she was relieved that her grandmother didn't have internet at The Beach House, otherwise she probably would have found herself Googling to find out.

Joss put the sandwich down, walked around the coffee table and surprised her by leaning forward and giving her a hug. 'I'm a bit of a hugger. Hope you don't mind.'

Briony felt tears in her eyes. Apart from Troy putting his arm around her shoulders and pulling her close, keeping warm while they watched the sunrise together, she missed physical human contact. Her dad was a hugger too. Her mum not so much, nor Freddie.

Briony thought of the letter she'd written to Freddie. She had a feeling she was going to put off posting it. Perhaps it wasn't the right thing to do, to say what she needed to say in a letter. *But if we were face to face, could I tell him?* She doubted it.

Joss put his hand on the doorknob. 'I will write to the solicitors and ask them to desist from sending any more letters, and that I am acting on her granddaughter's behalf as you are looking after the property while your grandmother is away.'

Briony nodded. 'Sounds good to me.'

'Obviously, you'll keep me posted regarding your grandmother because if … *when* she wakes up, if she does have the deeds, and can tell you where they are, then we can just get them registered and there will be a digital copy. So if anyone does a search with the Land Registry in future, she's covered.'

Briony was back to thinking what else she could possibly do to try and get Blythe to wake up. *Phone your mum, let her know what's going on. Perhaps if Blythe hears her daughter's voice …*

'Are you all right?'

Briony guessed he'd caught her downcast expression at the thought of phoning her mum. She knew she had to, quite soon, in case … Briony didn't want to think about that. *I just want one more week, to see if there's something I can do that will wake her up.*

She looked at Joss, wondering if he'd have any suggestions, but he was doing enough already. She sighed.

Joss gave her another hug. 'Everything is going to turn out all right in the end. Just you wait and see.'

Although she appreciated his kind, reassuring words, Briony felt her bottom lip tremble. She hoped he was right. She knew she was a glass-half-empty kind of person.

'Now, I'll be sure to ask Emily if she's free at the weekend so you girls can get together. What did you say the name of your club was?'

That brought a smile to Briony's lips. She glanced at Luna. 'The Wolf Girls Club.'

'Remember what I said? Everything we've discussed is between you and me.'

'And the Wolf Girls Club.'

'Who is in that club again?'

'Oh, just me, Emily and Clarissa.' Briony didn't mention Willow. She was just a child.

'That's all right then.' Joss opened the door to the office. 'We'll speak soon.'

21

Briony walked out into the crowded reception room.

Cheryl spotted her almost immediately, but turned her back. It surprised and upset Briony to not even get a hello. She had thought Cheryl liked her.

Briony looked down and discovered Luna was no longer by her side. 'Luna!' She was working the room again, meeting new people, getting lots of fuss and plenty of exclamations of, 'Ooh, aren't you a lovely dog,' as she did her rounds, cheering people up and taking their minds off their problems.

'Briony!' Cheryl turned from the coffee and tea counter. She crossed the room towards her, smiling. 'Well, hello. I've got something for you.' She held out her hands. 'It's a nice big lump of cake that Joss baked yesterday evening. I spotted you and thought, I bet you haven't had a slice, so I wanted to quickly cut you some. This is for you to take with you.'

Briony took the cake. 'Oh, thank you.'

'It's chocolate cake. You can't leave without a slice – and one of these.' Cheryl was a hugger too; she put her arms around Briony's shoulders. 'There. I can always tell when someone needs a hug.'

Briony smiled at her affectionately. 'You and my dad would get on really well. He's a hugger too.'

'Well, I would like to meet your parents one day. Do they visit your grandmother often?'

Briony pursed her lips. 'No. But I'm hoping to change that.'

'Well, good for you. Family is important. The most important thing in the world. When all is said and done, it's the people you can depend on, family and close friends.'

Briony raised her eyebrows. Yes, that was what she needed to do – work out how to bring about a reconciliation between her mum and grandmother. But Briony knew she was at a disadvantage. She thought that it might be an idea if she could find out the reason they'd become estranged in the first place. *Oh, if only she'd wake up! Then she could tell me.*

Briony walked out into Cobblers Yard, carrying her generous slice of cake wrapped in a serviette. Luna sniffed along her arm, trying to get near her cake. 'Luna! That's *my* cake.' She raised her hands and happened to glance across the yard. She spotted Reggie in the music shop, picking a musical instrument out of the window.

Briony saw him look up, see her, and wave.

She tentatively waved back. Before she'd spoken to Joss, she had planned to nip across the yard afterwards and tell Reggie the good news – that she'd found her grandmother, although she was still in hospital, and had yet to wake up.

Instead, Briony almost ran out of the yard in case Reggie came to the door and asked after her grandmother. Fortunately, she didn't drop her cake.

She felt bad, and very silly. After all, she'd be seeing Reggie the next morning when she was working in the music shop. At least she'd have some time to think through what to say, though. As she cast a glance over her shoulder, before she exited the lane into the high street, she had a feeling she might just ignore Joss's advice to tell no one. Reggie was her grandmother's friend. He deserved to know where she was. Perhaps if he paid her a visit, a friend's familiar voice might help.

Briony emerged into the high street and left Luna with her lead tied to a post outside the Co-op. She went inside, emerging a few minutes later with a book of stamps. Up ahead, she spotted a post box.

Someone passed by, carrying some flowers. She looked at the stamps in her hand. 'I'll post it later,' Briony said to herself as she retraced her steps into Cobblers Yard. Reggie was no longer standing in the window of his shop.

Briony nipped into the shop next door, The Potting Shed, to buy a bunch of fresh flowers. A lovely lady called Lili, serving in the shop, helped her pick some bright flowers and then wrapped them in pretty purple cellophane.

'Are they for yourself, or someone else?'

'They're for my grandmother. She's in hospital.' Briony silent cursed herself as she thought what Joss had told her. She looked at Lili and thought that surely Joss hadn't meant her to include the nice people in Cobblers Yard in his advice to tell no one. Although she'd only just met them, and she really didn't know them, she couldn't imagine any of them would be involved in the threatening letters. What would Thea and her father in The Bookshop of Memories have to gain, or the two sisters from the charity shop, or Reggie? She couldn't imagine.

Briony walked out of the shop, smelling the sweet scent of the flowers as she carried them back towards the hospital.

When Lili had asked who they were for, and Briony had let slip that they were for her grandmother in hospital, Lili had offered to give her a little card to go with the flowers. Briony had readily agreed.

What if her grandmother woke up and she wasn't there? Then at least she'd see the card in the flowers and know that her granddaughter had visited.

She smiled as she walked straight through the hospital entrance, no longer worried about taking Luna inside. What was on her mind was what to write in the little card.

'Those flowers are gorgeous,' commented the nurse, who recognised her from her earlier visits.

'I thought they would brighten up her room.'

'They most certainly will. And she'll know then that she's had a visitor, if she wakes up.'

Briony ignored the *if* word.

'Have you got a card to say who they're from, in case I'm not here?'

Briony held up the little card. 'Have you got a pen I can borrow?' Briony kept hold of Luna's lead, even though she was pulling to get on to the ward.

Briony stood at the nurse's desk, wrote, *Dear* – and then stopped, wondering if she should write, *Blythe, Grandma, Grandmother*? She'd settled during her first visit on *Grandma*, but she had no clue how her grandmother would like to be addressed by her granddaughter. She looked at the nurse.

'Is there a problem?' the nurse asked.

'It's so silly, but I don't know how to address the card. What to call her.'

'What you always have.'

Briony frowned. She'd forgotten that the nurse had no clue she'd only just met her grandmother. She decided she'd stick with what had felt right when she'd first visited.

Dear Grandma, I hope you get well very soon. I will visit every day. Lots of love, Your granddaughter, Briony xoxo

There wasn't a lot of space to write a long message, but Briony preferred it that way. She looked at the *xoxo* and wondered if her grandmother would even know what that meant – kisses and hugs. She didn't want to cross it out and make the little card look untidy. Instead, Briony added the words love and hugs.

'I'll take those, and the note,' said the nurse.

'It's fine, I can manage.'

'Um, you're outside visiting hours, I'm afraid. However, I suppose it wouldn't hurt if you wanted to pop the flowers in her room. There is a vase. We can fill it with water for you.' She glanced at Luna.

Briony followed her gaze.

'Luna will have to stay out here. She's welcome during visiting hours, but I'm afraid she is going to disturb the patients on the ward. They're having lunch at the moment.'

Briony thought she could smell cooked food. She spotted someone wheeling a trolley with meals on to the ward.

Briony looked at Luna. There was no good asking if the nurse could keep her out there by the desk. She had a feeling Luna wouldn't cooperate. Briony nodded. 'I understand.' She handed over the flowers and the little card.

'I'll pop the card by the vase.'

'Thank you.' She looked towards the ward. 'There's been no change, then. My grandmother is still—'

The nurse shook her head solemnly. 'No change. But please keep visiting. Just hearing a familiar voice could make a world of difference.'

Briony thought of her mum. She was the one who needed to visit. Her voice was familiar. But what about Frank?

Briony looked at the nurse. 'I don't suppose you know of somebody called Frank? He's someone my grandmother used to know, years ago. He used to live in the music shop in Cobblers Yard here in Aldeburgh with his father, Mr Cribbins. I need to find him.'

The nurse looked at her blankly. 'Cobblers Yard? I've been living here for ten years, and I've never heard of the place.'

'Really?' Briony didn't know why she was acting all surprised. It was easy to miss the little narrow side street between the shops, and the signage to Cobblers Yard was poor. Briony explained what, and where, it was.

'Is that where you bought the beautiful flowers?'

Briony nodded. 'It's called The Potting Shed. Lili, the lady who runs it, is lovely. And there's a music shop, which old Mr Cribbins used to own. Next door is a charity shop, and there's also a bookstore that's recently reopened apparently, called The Bookshop of Memories. It's worth a look if you fancy a book.' *Or a natter with one of the ladies from the charity shop who seems to spend all her time there*, she thought. 'There's an arts and crafts shop too, but I haven't been in there. Oh, and a drop-in legal advice centre that's free. If you need help. Not that I'd know anything about that. I mean I don't need help or anything. Neither does my grandmother.' Briony realised she was rambling. She stopped.

'Well, sounds like a lovely little place to browse some shops. I might pick up a novel or two while I'm there.'

Briony was disappointed, but not surprised, that she didn't know of Frank. Still, at least the nurse said she would visit Cobblers Yard, so the shops there would get more customers. 'Will you tell your colleagues and friends about Cobblers Yard?'

'Yes, I will. How amazing that in all the years I've lived in this little seaside town, I've never visited Cobblers Yard. I'll be sure to ask them if they know Frank too.'

'Oh, er … right.' Briony thought of what Joss had told her about keeping things under her hat regarding her grandmother. 'Um, you won't tell them about my grandmother – will you?'

The nurse's expression turned serious. 'Of course not. We don't talk about patients, only in a professional capacity.'

'Sorry.' Briony apologised. Of course they wouldn't.

'Now, I'll take these flowers in to your grandmother.'

'Perhaps I can just wait out here for a moment.'

The nurse smiled. She knew what Briony was waiting for. 'If I'm not back in five minutes, then there's no news regarding your grandmother. Why don't you take a seat?'

Briony looked at the row of plastic chairs by the nurse's station. 'It's fine. I'll wait here.' Briony watched the nurse disappear into the ward with the flowers. She glanced at her watch, paced, and eventually took a seat. Briony found that five minutes when you were clock-watching seemed interminable.

After ten minutes had elapsed, just to be sure the nurse wasn't coming back with news that her grandmother had miraculously woken up, Briony walked out of the hospital. Glancing at Luna, she was reminded that there was something she'd forgotten to do. She headed back to Cobblers Yard to visit the bookshop, hoping there was a children's book about Luna's ancestor – the wolf.

22

Briony parked the car at the car park in Dunwich Heath and decided to walk Luna along the beach to The Beach House. Luna needed a good run, and Briony needed a moment or two to think before she ran into Troy. She still had the letter addressed to Freddie, which she hadn't posted, although she had made progress by sticking a stamp on the envelope.

She walked down to the shore, slipped off her trainers and socks, and walked barefoot in the shallow water. The sea tickled her ankles as the water washed over her feet on to the shore with the tide. The sun was out, and still surprisingly warm for autumn.

She passed mothers sitting with toddlers, who were building sandcastles and writing their names in the wet sand. The unusual weather was encouraging people who were not at work on a Monday to spend the day on the beach.

Luna ran ahead a little way, paws splashing in the surf. Every now and then she stopped to wait for Briony.

Briony kept an eye on Luna too, to make sure she didn't bother anybody. She noted some mothers eyeing Luna cautiously. She wasn't surprised; if she had been sitting with her child on the beach, she'd be doing the same.

Briony smiled at the small children as she passed by, thinking about what her future held. She hadn't really thought about what it would be like, being a mum. She'd never yearned to have children, having been too focused on her education and what career would follow.

Perhaps the lack of yearning was her age. Maybe as she got older, that yearning for motherhood would awaken. Perhaps it was the fact that she'd never particularly liked babies, although perhaps that would change too. *It'd better*, she thought. But seeing little ones playing with buckets and spades on the beach, Briony suddenly saw her future, and she rather liked what she saw, especially there, on a sandy beach on the Suffolk Coast.

She stopped walking and turned to look out to sea, feeling the soft wet sand beneath her feet. 'I'd like to raise my child here,' she said aloud. She gazed out to sea, the turquoise water looking more like something out of the Caribbean rather than the English coast.

'Oh, I'd recommend it,' said a voice behind her.

Briony whirled around to find a young mother, who was carrying a toddler, balanced on her hip. He was in a nappy, and wearing a little white tee-shirt with a blue dolphin motif on the front. 'Sorry, I didn't mean to intrude on your thoughts, but I couldn't help overhearing. I love it here. Imagine bringing your children to the beach after school, and crab-fishing, and swimming. We come here in the not-so-nice weather too. It's just as magical any time of year.'

Briony imagined it was.

'You won't regret moving here.'

'Mummy – where's my swimming costume?'

Briony turned to look at another child, who had shouted out

as she ran down the beach towards them. She caught the young woman rolling her eyes. She said to Briony, 'Could you hold Harry for just one second. That's my daughter.' She raised her eyebrows. 'She loves coming to the beach after nursery school.'

Briony didn't have time to object, even if she had wanted to, before a rather rotund toddler was thrust into her arms. Briony balanced him on her hip, just like his mother had. The toddler stared at her.

Oh, goodness, thought Briony, *please don't cry.*

She smiled at him. To her surprise he gave her the most endearing little smile back, which turned into a big yawn. *Oh, I'm boring him now*. 'Hello, Harry. My name is Briony.' She sucked in a breath. 'Oh, my goodness! You are *so* cute.'

As if to prove the fact, he sucked his fingers and gurgled.

The young woman helped her daughter into her swimming costume. She glanced at Luna, who appeared by Briony's side, her inquisitive nose sniffing the air as she edged closer to Harry's foot.

'Is that your dog?' the young woman asked, her eyes wide as she caught sight of Luna.

'No, she's my grandmother's. She's a gentle dog, wouldn't hurt a fly.' Even so, Briony moved Harry's foot away from Luna's muzzle and gently tapped her nose, *no*, sensing that the young mother would rather such a big dog was not near her child.

Luna whined and lay down on the beach, muzzle on her paws, staring up at Briony and making her feel guilty for not introducing Harry.

'There are a lot of activities for little ones. They run music sessions in the library,' the young woman said conversationally. She peered at Briony. 'Have you got children?'

'Um, not yet.'

'Ah, you're planning to have one?'

'Quite soon, actually. I'm pregnant.'

'Oh, congratulations. When's the baby due?'

Briony looked at her, trying to think how far gone she was.

The young woman touched her arm. 'Don't worry. I was just like that with my first. The midwife told me. I'm sure yours will do the same.'

'I haven't got one,' blurted Briony.

'That's all right. See your GP and they'll sort out your antenatal care for you, book you in to see a midwife.'

Briony looked at the bonny little boy she was bouncing on her hip and smiled.

'Mummy, I want to go paddling,' said her older child.

'All right, hold on.'

Briony watched the young mother slip her daughter's clothes into a bag and sling it over her shoulder. She held out her arms. Briony reluctantly handed Harry back.

'Well, I hope you do get to bring up your child here. Who knows – perhaps we'll bump into each other again.'

Briony looked at Harry, wondering whether, if she stayed, her little one would be in the same nursery as him.

'Bye.'

Briony smiled, waving them off. She stood for a moment, watching them paddling in the sea and thinking, *What am I going to do? Stay with Freddie, for the baby's sake? That's what being a parent is all about – isn't it? Sacrifices? And what do I mean by sacrifice? Freddie loves me to bits, I know, and he's going to be the best dad, and provide a good life for us both.*

But what about love? Real love?

Briony got out the letter that she'd written to Freddie. She thought about what she'd said aloud a little earlier – that she'd like to raise her child in Suffolk. What about that?

Briony glanced at the receding figure of the young woman, who was walking with her two children along the beach. Freddie's work was in Oxford. That was where their life would be. Not in Suffolk. This was not her life. This was somebody else's.

Luna had run off again to chase the waves, but she soon came running over and sat down on the beach beside Briony. Sensing something was up, she put a wet paw on Briony's lap, making Briony's trousers wet. But Briony didn't scold her. Instead, she said, 'Aren't you a good girl? I'm going to miss you when I go back to Oxford.'

She looked along the beach towards where The Beach House was, around the corner of the headland, hoping that Troy had let Wilbur outside at some point. She'd given Troy a key so he could use the bathroom, help himself to a cup of coffee, and lock up if she wasn't back before he left.

She looked at Luna, who put her head on Briony's lap. 'I think, since I arrived, I've been living in some sort of fantasy, with something like a teenage crush on Troy, and visions of never leaving this place. Crazy – huh?' She stroked Luna. For some reason, she was having a reality check. She knew what it was – holding that child. That had been very real indeed. She could have been holding her own child. No – *their* child.

Briony looked at the letter she'd written to Freddie. She held the top of the envelope in her fingertips, about to tear it up and throw it to the wind, when a gust caught the letter and it flew out of her hands, the wind carrying it high into the air, in the direction of the sand dunes.

Briony hurried to her feet, but by the time she'd turned around, intending to chase after it, the letter was gone. She imagined it was lost somewhere in the dunes. She shook her head. She could walk up the beach to the dunes, but she hadn't even seen which exact direction the wind had carried it. She knew it wasn't towards the sea.

Briony shrugged. She decided there was no point searching for it. It wasn't as though she was going to post it now. The letter would no doubt be torn into pieces by the elements and disintegrate.

'Come on, Luna. Let's go and see how much progress Troy has made with the outbuilding today.'

Briony was relieved she'd had a moment of clarity, walking along the beach with her thoughts. 'Thank goodness I didn't post that letter,' she said to Luna.

She stood up, brushed off the sand, and happened to glance up the beach before she set off. It was quite deserted now; people had gone home for lunch, no doubt. Her own stomach was rumbling. Further up the beach, towards the dunes, she saw a man walking a dog. He waved at her.

Briony waved back, one dog walker to another, thinking how friendly she'd found the people, strangers, on the Suffolk Coast.

She started in the direction of The Beach House.

The old man stopped waving as soon as she turned her back. He looked at his hand. 'Darn, she didn't see what was in my hand. I'm too old to chase after her.' He glanced at his dog. 'Shame you can't run over and give her this. I'm sure it's hers.' He looked at the letter in his hand. 'Well, it's got a stamp, so I suppose I could post it. That would be my good deed for the day.'

23

Briony walked along the beach, looking forward to seeing Troy. There was nothing wrong with that, she convinced herself, nothing wrong at all with making new friends, even if one of her new friends was very handsome. Thinking of friends, Angel came to mind. She wished Angel would reply to her texts.

Angel had confided in her once, when she was drunk, that she really liked Freddie. From that, Briony understood that she meant that she fancied him. It didn't stop Angel being good friends with him; with both of them. 'Just like my friendship with Troy,' Briony said to Luna as she trotted beside her. 'There's no harm in that.' She hoped they might have lunch together.

Briony also hoped Sam wasn't there, which she knew was a bit mean, as he was working on the outbuilding with Troy. She got the impression, though, that for some reason he didn't like the easy familiarity between herself and Troy. She imagined that he probably thought it wasn't very professional of his boss.

But there's nothing going on between us. Watching the sunrise together was innocent enough, even if he did have his arm around my shoulder.

Briony slowed her pace as she thought of how having Troy's arm around her had given her goosebumps. Although it had been the perfect start to the day, a little voice in her head that she desperately wanted to ignore said, *Perhaps watching the sunrise together has to stop. And maybe having lunch together isn't a good idea.*

Briony's phone sounded with a text, surprising her. She stopped where she was, aware that she might lose the signal by the time she got to The Beach House. Was it Angel reminding her that she still hadn't contacted her parents?

Briony had promised her parents she'd send them an email when she had a chance, but she'd been putting it off. The issue was the thought of writing them a load of lies about the trip to the Galapagos Islands. Every time she thought of sending an email, she couldn't. And yet she knew she had to, if she was going to stay where she was and keep up the pretence.

Briony looked at her phone. It was Emily. Joss had spoken with her, and she was free the next weekend to meet up for the Wolf Girls Club.

Briony grinned. She texted back, saying that she was looking forward to seeing her, and hoped that Clarissa could make it too. Briony wanted to catch up with Clarissa. Maybe she'd found out who was behind the letters her grandmother had been receiving. Now all she had to do was speak to Troy and hope the last member of their little club could make it too – Willow.

She sent the text, and then sent Angel another one, hoping things were going okay back in Oxford.

Briony sighed and scrolled through all the texts Freddie had sent since she'd left. She had been keeping in touch, but hadn't answered some of them, feeling guilty that he'd been texting how much he missed her, and how he hoped she'd be back soon, and offering to come and pick her up when she was ready to return home.

Briony was about to reply to his latest text when Luna bolted up the beach. 'Luna!' Something, or someone had caught her attention.

Although she knew that Luna was a gentle giant, and wouldn't harm a fly, she preferred for Luna to stay close in case she ran up to a child and scared them – and their parents. Seeing a wolf-like dog approaching at speed would be enough to scare anybody.

As Briony neared The Beach House, she realised that it wasn't some random person on the beach who had caught Luna's attention; it was Troy. But as she drew closer to the house, she noticed that Luna had come to a halt. She caught up with her and realised the man standing with his back to her wasn't Troy after all. She looked at Luna, who had clearly made the same mistake.

Briony noticed that the man was running his hand along the old, beached boat in front of The Beach House. He was clearly lost in thought; he hadn't heard the dog galloping towards him or Briony approaching behind him.

Briony recalled that Clarissa had said she would ask her father to take a look at the beached boat and see if it could be repaired. This guy couldn't be her dad. Although he was older than Troy, perhaps in his late thirties, early forties, he was too young to be Clarissa's dad. Perhaps he'd sent someone else from the boatyard to have a look.

Briony stepped forward. 'Are you here about the boat?'

The slim guy, who was wearing jeans, old-fashioned loafers, a white t-shirt and an unbuttoned checked shirt, whirled around at the sound of her voice. 'Oh, my god!' he exclaimed, staring at her, his knees buckling. He grabbed hold of the boat to steady himself.

Briony rushed forward and grabbed his arm, putting it around her shoulders just as Troy appeared around the side of the house. He looked at Briony, and then at the man next to her, who had sat down, perching on the side of the boat. 'Dad, what's going on?'

Briony looked at Troy. 'This is your dad?'

The guy with his arm around her shoulder said, 'I'm fine. Everything's … um, fine.'

'What happened?' Troy asked, kneeling in front of his dad.

'I think he had a funny turn.' Briony caught Troy's dad staring at her. She couldn't quite see the resemblance to Troy, but he was tall and slim, like Troy, and had close cropped dark hair and piercing blue eyes.

'If you're not up to helping out today, like you said, then don't worry. You've just arrived back from a long stint at work. I didn't think this was a good idea. Sam said he'd try and see if he could fit in coming here later today.'

Troy's father turned to Briony. 'Who *are* you?'

'I'm Briony.' She held out her hand.

He tentatively took it. 'Briony.'

She found the way he was staring at her a little unnerving. She didn't want to be rude, but she rather fancied having her hand back.

'Dad, would you mind giving Briony her hand back?'

'Yes, sorry. I'm Troy's dad.'

Briony smiled. 'Well, pleased to meet you, Troy's dad.'

Troy rolled his eyes. 'My dad's name is Sebastian.'

She said, 'Sebastian,' letting the name roll off her tongue. It was a very distinguished-sounding name. 'Would you both like something to eat? I haven't had lunch yet, so you could join me.'

Troy said, 'Coffee is fine for both of us.'

'Are you sure?'

Troy nodded. 'I went to pick up some more materials and grabbed something for lunch on my way back.'

Briony wasn't surprised. It was long past lunchtime. She looked at Sebastian.

Troy quickly added, 'He's eaten – haven't you?'

Briony got the impression that Troy did not want her to have lunch with his dad. 'Well, two coffees coming up then.'

She went to walk inside The Beach House, but stopped to look through the glass door first to check the kittens were not near the door and wouldn't escape when she opened it. In doing so, she unwittingly overheard what Troy said to his dad.

'What is with you? I know she's really pretty, but for goodness' sake, you're old enough to be her father.'

'Well, not necessarily. I was so very young when you came along.'

'Yes, but even so, she's a client. I only wanted you here as an extra pair of hands. It would be very unprofessional to get involved.'

'Wow, steady on. I only shook her hand,' said Sebastian. He paused. 'You like her.'

Briony looked over at them, walking towards the outbuilding, their backs to her. She guessed because of the way the wind was blowing, their voices carried. She noticed Troy didn't respond to his dad.

'Who is she?' Briony heard Sebastian ask Troy, pausing mid-step to ask the question.

Troy stopped too and turned to his father. 'Briony – she told you. She's the one who hired me to do the work.'

'Since when have you done a day's work in your life?'

'What is that supposed to mean?'

Briony stood at the door staring at them, thinking, *How odd.*

'You know what it means, Troy. Since when have you rolled up your sleeves and actually done some *real* work as opposed to sitting behind a desk all day?'

'Since now.'

Briony raised her eyebrows. So, this wasn't his usual job. If he was normally office-based, perhaps he was the head of the company, or something. When she'd first met him at The Beach House, perhaps she'd caught him on a dress-down Friday, or something, coming to scope out the new job. It was little wonder his friend, Sam, had seemed a bit off when he'd turned up at The Beach House early the previous morning to discover Troy working on the outbuilding. But she wondered why Troy hadn't said anything to her.

She had an idea why. She smiled to herself at the thought that he was doing the work on the outbuilding himself all because he liked her – and clearly wanted to spend time in her company, even if he had to roll up his sleeves and do some *real* work, as his father had put it.

He clearly didn't need to do the work himself.

'So, you *do* like her. It's about time you met someone. I mean, I know you're married to the business, and your family, but you've got to put yourself first for once.'

'Yeah, right – says you, who made sacrifices to bring me up, and then Willow.' They fell silent for a moment.

Briony stepped into the kitchen and closed the door behind her. She filled the kettle, but before she flicked it on, she went to the lounge, where Wilbur's little head popped up from the sofa.

He jumped down and started to yap, excited to see her.

Briony picked the little dog up, gave him a kiss on the top of his head, and said, 'Shush.' She gingerly walked over to the lounge window. Through the slatted shutters, which were open, she could see that Troy and his father were still standing in the same spot on the beach, both with their backs to the house.

Briony felt ever so guilty for eavesdropping. It was beyond rude, but she couldn't help herself. Ever so slowly, she opened the lounge window a crack, hoping that her little sausage dog did not whine, or yap, and give the game away. At least if they did hear Wilbur, and turn around, she was only opening the window for some air. She stroked the dog in her arms as she managed to catch a bit more of their conversation.

'But what I don't understand, Troy, is why Briony is hiring you to do work on the outbuilding? She doesn't live here – does she? I know I haven't been here for years, but I don't remember this place changing hands. I thought Blythe still lived here.'

Briony stared at Sebastian. *He knows my grandmother. How far back did they go? Would he have known Frank?*

Briony shook her head at that thought. He wouldn't even have been born when Frank and Blythe knew each other.

Troy said, 'That's right. She doesn't live here – she's visiting her grandmother.'

'Her grandmother?'

'Yeah.'

'No wonder she looks familiar.'

'Are you saying that you think she looks like her?'

Briony saw Sebastian nodding his head. The last words she heard him say were, 'Briony is the spitting image of her mother.'

24

Briony stirred the coffee, lost in thought. So, he knows my grandmother *and* my mum. Briony had been thinking about the conversation she'd overheard between Troy and his father as she made coffee for them and a sandwich for herself. She was about to pick up the cups of coffee and take them to the outbuilding when one of the kittens ran over and pounced on her shoe.

She looked down at the little kitten, who was playing with her laces, then knelt and picked him up, cradling him in her arms. Jerry, the ginger kitten, was waddling over towards her too. He was always following his brother Tom. She walked over and picked him up as well, cradling both kittens in her arms. They reminded her that she wanted to ask Troy if Willow could come along on Saturday. She expected Willow was missing the kittens.

Briony felt something else by her feet. She knew Luna was outside, with Troy. 'Oh, Wilbur,' Briony exclaimed, looking down. 'How could I have forgotten about you?' Preoccupied, she'd left him in the lounge when she'd gone into the kitchen to make the coffees and her sandwich. He'd been in all morning while she'd visited Joss, and the hospital; she imagined little Wilbur was dying for a wee.

Wilbur put his paws on her legs. 'Ah, you want a cuddle too.' She carefully put the kittens down on the floor, Wilbur sniffing them as she did so, and picked up her little dog instead. 'Good boy. Let's you and me go outside, eh? You've been very good not having any accidents indoors.'

She put Wilbur down and turned to the two cups of coffee. She decided to leave the kittens in the lounge with a few of their toys, a scratching post, and their litter tray, so she wouldn't have to worry about leaving the kitchen door open. She didn't want the inquisitive kittens getting out of the house. 'There. You two play nice.'

Back in the kitchen, Briony found Wilbur waiting by the back door, bouncing from his left legs to his right legs like a child dying to use the loo. As she opened the door, she lowered her voice. 'Now, if you don't bark, perhaps I can be really naughty, and sneak up on the outbuilding, and see if there's anything further of interest I might hear.' Like how exactly Sebastian knew her mother.

Briony set off with the two cups of coffee. Wilbur immediately disappeared around the side of the outbuilding. She smiled. She was used to it now; Wilbur liked privacy when he was doing his business. She made a mental note to clear up after him as soon as she'd delivered the coffees.

Gingerly approaching the outbuilding, she could hear voices – Troy and Sebastian. She couldn't hear what they were saying yet. She quickened her pace and had just reached the outbuilding when the sound of someone behind her, shouting out her name, made her jump.

Sebastian popped his head out of the door. 'Is that our coffee?' He smiled at her as he took a mug inside.

Troy appeared next. 'How long have you been standing out here?'

Briony returned his frown. She didn't like what he was implying, even though he was correct. The fact was that she hadn't had a chance to eavesdrop any further. 'I literally just walked up to the door when I heard somebody call my name. Here.' She shoved the other mug of coffee at Troy, along with a black look, and turned around to see who had called her.

'Briony – is it?' An older man was striding along the beach from the direction of the car park.

'Yes,' Briony replied warily. 'Can I help you?' Her heart sank at the thought that it might be something to do with the hospital. Maybe they couldn't get through to her on her mobile and had sent someone to fetch her. But would an NHS hospital really use their resources to do that? She doubted it.

'I'm Peter,' said the tall man with white hair, a slight stoop, and bright blue eyes.

Briony didn't recognise the name as they shook hands. 'Um, how can I help you?'

'Ah, I think it's more the case that I can help you.'

She didn't understand. 'Sorry, I'm not sure what—'

'I'm here about the boat.'

Briony looked at him blankly, still at a loss.

The older man stooped low, so he was eye-to-eye with Briony. 'My daughter, Clarissa, sent me. Said there was some old boat beached on the shore, and wanted me to do a favour for one of her dear friends.'

'She called me a dear friend?'

'Oh, yes. Quite a compliment. You must have made quite an impression.'

Briony narrowed her eyes, thinking, *Either that, or Troy has.*

'Anyway, she's asked me if I can take a look at the boat.'

Briony grinned and clapped her hands. 'Oh, yes! I really hope it can be fixed up.' What an added delightful surprise that would be for her grandmother.

'It would be great if you could,' said Sebastian, appearing behind her, his voice bizarrely sending shivers down her spine. 'Sorry, couldn't help but overhear.' He stepped forward to introduce himself to Peter. 'I'm helping my son out, renovating the old outbuilding.'

'I see. Do you have any experience with boats?'

'Not fixing them up, no.'

'You sail then?'

'Ah, a long time ago, yes.'

'In this boat?' asked Peter.

Briony looked at Peter.

'Yes, I used to sail it. I've got … fond memories. I'd hate to see the boat have to go for scrap.'

Briony turned around and looked at Sebastian. She was dying to ask him if he'd ever sailed in this boat with her mother. She recalled what she'd overheard him say to Troy – *Briony looks the spitting image of her mother.*

'Well, let me take a look, see what can be done,' said Peter.

Briony stared at Sebastian. When she had first seen Sebastian, he'd been standing beside the boat, lost in thought. She wondered whether he'd been lost in memories from the past – perhaps memories of her mother.

Briony walked behind the two men up the beach towards the boat, listening to their conversation with interest.

'Got a special significance for you, has it?' Peter asked

Sebastian. 'Most boats do, you know.'

'Belonged to my girl's grandparents.'

Peter said, 'Your girl?'

Briony caught Sebastian glance over his shoulder at her before he replied. 'Oh, it was just a teenage crush, a lifetime ago. We used to dive together. We both loved the ocean.'

Briony frowned. He couldn't be talking about her mum. She didn't like the sea, and she certainly couldn't dive – could she? But she knew he must be talking about Lorna; she was an only child.

'I taught her sailing and scuba diving, along with another good friend of ours.'

'Well, perhaps if I can fix this boat, you can use it to go sailing and diving together again next summer.'

Sebastian shook his head. 'No, that's not going to happen.'

Briony stared at Sebastian. She had so many questions about her mother, but she didn't want to break the spell. Sebastian seemed to have forgotten she was there, right behind him, as he walked with Peter, talking about his past.

'We … lost touch.'

'Ah, that's a shame,' said Peter. 'Drifted apart, did you?'

'No, I sent her letters, but never got a reply. We had plans to meet at The Beach House, but even though she gave me a key, she never turned up.' He paused. 'Sorry, not sure why I'm telling you all this.'

Peter said, 'It's good just to get things off your chest.'

'Yeah, you're a good listener. My father … well he'd just tell me to shut up and get on with it.'

'That's not very kind, when you're sharing your innermost thoughts.'

'No, it isn't. That's why sharing in our family is never a good idea. I just hope my son, Troy, doesn't feel that way about me.'

'Oh, I'm sure he doesn't. What about the other … friend you were talking about?'

'She's gone.'

'I'm sorry for your loss.'

'Thank you. She had a child really young, so I stepped in, even though I wasn't the father, and brought up Troy.'

'You must have been really good friends to do that,' commented Peter.

'We were, yes.'

'But you must have only been eighteen,' Briony blurted, followed in quick succession by, 'Does Troy know you're not his real dad?' Briony rolled her eyes, immediately regretting opening her big mouth and voicing her thoughts.

Sebastian slowly turned around. She thought he'd tell her to mind her own business. After all, it really was no concern of hers.

An apology was just on the tip of her tongue, when he said, 'It's true, I was young. And yes, Troy knows.'

'So, he's not Willow's biological half-brother?'

Sebastian's silence said it all.

'Then why—?'

'Willow is too young right now to understand that relationships can be … complicated. I brought up Troy as my son. He *is* my son, although we're not biologically related. Willow will know in time. But right now, all she needs to know is that Troy is her big brother.'

Briony bit her lower lip. She still had so many questions. How on earth had he ended up bringing up someone else's child? There must have been more to it than being good friends, taking on such a huge commitment when he was barely an adult himself.

She had a feeling he was holding something back. But she couldn't bring herself to ask. They barely knew one another. His personal life was none of her business. Although she did say, 'If Peter fixes the boat, will you take me out in it?'

Unfortunately, Troy's timing couldn't have been worse. He must have been walking towards the house with his empty coffee mug when he overheard Briony's question. 'Briony, he hasn't come here to take you out sailing!'

'I'll make time,' said Sebastian. He turned around and smiled at her. 'Perhaps you'd like to learn to dive, too?'

Troy looked at him, exasperated. 'If you saw her swimming, you would not ask her that.'

'You've been swimming in the sea together?'

Briony glared at Troy. Why had he brought *that* up? She said, 'No, we have not. It was just an unfortunate misunderstanding. I went for a dip, and silly Troy here got all flustered and thought I was drowning.'

'I was not flustered.'

'You appeared to be when you carried me out of the water. Which was totally unnecessary, I should add.'

Sebastian looked at Troy. 'You carried her out of the water?'

Peter slapped his knee and suddenly guffawed. 'You two ...' he pointed at Briony and Troy '... remind me of me and the wife when we were young. The silly, petty arguments we used to have. Of course we always made up, and could laugh about it, in hindsight, but they used to be godawful. Like you two, we both stood our ground, convinced we were right.' He smiled. 'You know, if Clarissa was here right now, she'd say you two make the cutest couple.'

'Well, we're not a couple,' Briony said, still angry with Troy for bringing up the swimming incident.

'No? Well, perhaps you should be.'

Briony grabbed the mug out of Troy's hand. 'Give me that!' She stormed off into The Beach House.

Troy turned on his heel and stormed off in the other direction, back to the outbuilding.

'Well, would you look at that?' said Peter.

Sebastian frowned. 'Look at what?'

'Two people in love.'

25

'Can it be fixed, do you think?' Briony asked after she'd composed herself in the kitchen and had checked that Troy was nowhere to be seen before she stepped outside.

'I think so,' replied Peter. 'I can't do it here, though.'

'That's disappointing,' commented Sebastian.

'Yeah, I know, but the hull needs a lot of restoration, and for that it would need to be taken to Southwold boatyard. There's a boat restoration and repair company there that I used to work for.'

Somehow, Briony had imagined that Clarissa's father would come along with a toolbox, and that with a few nails and a hammer, it would all be fixed up, right as rain. Of course, she knew she'd been being wildly optimistic.

'It might even need a new hull.'

'A rebuild, then, as opposed to a repair,' Sebastian commented.

'Quite possibly. Until I get it hoisted up, and we can take a good look, I can't really say for certain the full extent of the work needed.'

Briony's brow creased into a frown. She knew what that

would entail – money, and plenty of it.

She was about to bring it up, when Peter said, 'I don't know what Clarissa has told you, but obviously, as I would need to use the boatyard facilities to repair the boat. I couldn't do it for free.'

Briony nodded. 'No, I understand.'

'But I can take the boat, and give it a proper assessment, see how much time and materials it would take, and then let you know what the cost would be.'

Briony knew that her savings had dwindled considerably.

Peter noticed her hesitate. He added, 'An assessment will cost you nothing.'

Briony stared at the boat, wondering if it was worth even having it assessed. What was the point if she couldn't afford to get it repaired? She realised that she hadn't thought it all through. Briony heaved a sigh. 'What is your honest opinion of the state of it – is it even worth taking a look, or ...' she trailed off.

'She'd be a beauty if I could repair her.'

'She *was* a beauty,' said Sebastian. 'If it's money, I'll buy her and pay for her to be restored. I'd rather that than see her chopped up for firewood.'

'I was going to offer to do that myself,' said Peter, 'if you didn't want to go ahead. Not chop her up for firewood, obviously, but buy the boat and do the repairs myself.'

Briony looked from one to the other. It would be one thing to have the boat renovated, like the outbuilding, for her grandmother's return, but another thing altogether to sell something which was not hers to sell. Briony shook her head. 'It's not mine to sell. It belongs to my grandmother.'

Peter nodded. 'I understand.'

'Sorry, but I think it's probably going to turn out too costly for me to go ahead and have the boat repaired, after all,' admitted Briony. She dropped her eyes from his gaze, embarrassed that Peter had made a special trip for nothing.

'I can secure it with some tarpaulin to protect it from the elements while you ask your grandmother what she'd like to do with it.'

'That's really kind of you, Peter.' Briony sighed. 'The thing is, I can't ask her. Not right now. She's … not well at the moment. I'll just have to wait until she … she's better before I ask if that's what she wants.'

Briony assumed she must have the money because she wouldn't have been planning to spend it on the outbuilding renovations. Whether she wanted to spend it on the boat, though, was another matter.

'It's really kind of you both to offer to buy the boat. I will put that to her too, when I can.'

'I know who wouldn't want to sell it,' Sebastian said under his breath as they both watched Peter examine the boat some more.

Briony stared at him. She decided to be direct. 'Are you talking about my mother?' she asked.

Sebastian turned to Briony. 'I guessed you were Lorna's daughter. Troy confirmed it when he told me you were here staying at your grandmother's place.'

'That's why I gave you quite a shock – when you first saw me. You knew my mum, years ago, and I look just like her.'

'I thought I was seeing a ghost. Your likeness is uncanny.'

'Yes, everyone tells me I take after her. My dad says it's just as well that I didn't take after his ugly mug. Not that he is ugly, or anything.' Briony suddenly felt a lump in her throat. She missed them both, and hated herself for lying to them.

She sat down next to Sebastian on the edge of the wooden hull. 'The thing is, what you said about going sailing and diving with your friends. Were you talking about my mum, Lorna? I can't imagine it. She hates the ocean, and anything to do with sea life.'

Sebastian's dark eyes studied her. 'Well, it wasn't always like that. Although she loved music, her passion was the ocean.'

'Her passion was the ocean. Are you serious?' Briony couldn't believe what she was hearing.

He nodded. 'Oh, yes. We used to spend the summers sailing and snorkelling. Then we both earned our PADI Adventure Diver certification.'

'Okay,' Briony said slowly. She had no idea what that meant.

'And unbeknown to her parents, who would have probably freaked out, we enrolled in the Wreck Diver Speciality course. That meant we could go diving the shipwrecks along the Suffolk Coast too.'

Briony stared at him.

'Those summers when she came here on holiday were … were amazing.'

Briony suddenly thought of the shell box and the key her mum had said was the key to her heart. Briony assumed she had been talking about how much she'd loved The Beach House, but what if she had been talking about somebody she'd known years earlier at The Beach House – somebody who had broken her heart? What if it was Sebastian?

Even if that were true, there was still something playing on Briony's mind. All this talk of sailing, and diving, and the ocean – she still couldn't marry that up with her mum. Briony was wondering if he was mistaken. After all, it was a long time ago. It was as though the young woman he was talking about was a different person.

'Are you sure you're not talking about your best friend, the other girl, Troy's mum?'

Sebastian slowly shook her head. 'No, I know who I'm talking about. I wouldn't forget. How could I forget, when I was in—' he stopped abruptly.

Briony stared at him. Was he going to say, how could he forget when he was in love with her?

She glanced at the outbuilding. Troy's angry face appeared at one of the windows. Not for the first time, she guessed Troy was jealous seeing her in Sebastian's company, chatting.

Briony fixed her attention on Sebastian. 'What happened to Troy's parents? Why did Troy's mum leave you with her baby?'

Sebastian stood up. 'Troy needs help with the outbuilding.'

Briony reached for his hand. 'Sorry. I know it's none of my business.' She wished she hadn't been so direct.

Sebastian looked down at her hand in his. 'I can't believe how much you look like her.'

Briony said, looking up at him, 'I can't believe what you said about my mum. You see, I love biology and marine life, but she always seemed to do her best to discourage me from pursuing marine biology.'

'You want to be a marine biologist?'

'Yes, it's been my dream since I was really little. I've graduated with a degree in biology, and I've got a master's lined up.' Briony's eyes lit up when she talked of her passion.

'Well, that is just so exciting, Briony. Obviously, your mother's early passion rubbed off.'

Yeah, but she didn't want it to, thought Briony.

'You are your mother's daughter – that's for sure.'

Briony looked at him thoughtfully. It had never seemed that way. She wished her mum had told her about her past, what she had been like as a teenager, that they were really so alike. But then she would have had to tell her about Blythe, The Beach House, and the summers she had spent there.

'That was *my* dream once,' said Sebastian, interrupting her thoughts.

'To be a marine biologist?'

'Ah, not exactly. I love marine archaeology. It's what I used to dive for.'

'Sunken treasure?'

'If you'd call shipwrecks *sunken treasure*, then I suppose yes. There are thousands off the coast of Suffolk.'

'Did you find any?'

'None that hadn't already been found.'

'So, you did dive to a wreck?'

'Oh, yes. So did Lorna.'

Briony stared at him. This was a whole other side to her mum she never knew about.

'So, I'm guessing Lorna … your mum … didn't end up working in marine conservation?'

'She was interested in conservation? Wow – that's what I'm interested in doing!' Briony shook her head in response to his question. 'Music, like my grandmother. She became a music teacher.'

'Oh, right. That *does* surprise me.'

'How come? She's pretty good, you know.'

'I know. She was a really good piano player.'

'So, why does it surprise you that she became a music teacher?'

'Because she said she never wanted to be one. Guess something changed her mind.'

'Responsibilities,' commented Briony, realising what it meant to have children young and put your life and your own needs on hold. It suddenly dawned on her just what she was giving up, and quite possibly would never return to, by having this baby. She suddenly saw her future all mapped out for her, working in Reggie's music shop, perhaps even taking over from him, if she could stay living in Suffolk and bring up her child there.

It wouldn't be a bad life – would it? With the lovely community in Cobblers Yard, and all the lovely friends she'd met. But she had to acknowledge, like her mum, like Sebastian, that it wouldn't be what she had always dreamed of.

Was that why her mum had never encouraged her in marine biology – because she was just resentful that her daughter would get to do the things she had never had the chance to do herself? *Well, perhaps she'll be pleased to hear I'm pregnant, and I can't pursue my dream anymore, either.*

'Responsibilities?' echoed Sebastian.

Briony heaved a sigh. 'Yeah, well she got pregnant and got married really young, obviously, so that's bound to affect your decisions, you know.'

'Oh, I know, believe me.' Sebastian cast his gaze over to the outbuilding, where Troy was busy working.

'Troy mentioned that his dad is a deep-sat diver because you can earn good money.'

'Yeah, I'm good at diving. Wasn't quite how I envisaged using my diving experience, but there you have it – life doesn't always turn out how you expect.'

Oh, I know, believe me, thought Briony. She asked Sebastian, 'What was she like, when you knew her?' She wanted to know about the carefree, world-at-her-feet teenage Lorna before she'd become pregnant and got married.

Sebastian's dark eyes lit up. 'She was the life and soul. I mean if you wanted to have fun with a capital F, she was wild.'

'Really?' Once again, she thought that it didn't sound like her mum. She was no fun at all now. Mind you, neither was her dad.

Briony felt so mean for thinking that. But it was true – the only time she saw her dad really animated, cracking jokes, was when he was packing for a cruise.

A funny thought occurred to her. Perhaps if her parents had never got together, her mum might have been more fun. Briony shook her head. *If they hadn't got together, I wouldn't have been born.*

'I guess if you were friends with my mum years ago, visiting The Beach House when she was here during the summer, you met her grandparents, my great-grandparents, before they passed away?'

'Yes.' He looked about him. 'They used to hold the most amazing parties.'

'I've seen the photo albums.' Briony voice her thoughts. 'It just seemed that when my great-grandparents were alive, this place, which I understand used to be their holiday home until they retired here, was just full of people having lots of fun.'

'Oh, yeah. There were always a lot of people, friends and relations, who came to visit. There were beach games, and parties, and everyone got a chance to sail in this boat. Then it all changed when they died.'

'How so?'

'They both went pretty quickly, one after the other. Best way to go, if you ask me. But anyway, that's a bit morbid. That summer was a summer to remember, but for all the wrong reasons – your mother and grandparents came down for the funeral. We met up, me and your mother, as usual, but things had… changed, obviously. We knew things were coming to an end. We were growing up. She was going to Oxford University; I was meant to be going into the family business. We still took the boat out, enjoyed the summer as much as we could. We promised to write. She had to return to Oxford early after the funeral. We promised we'd meet here at the end of the summer. But she never showed up.'

Briony stared at Sebastian. Whatever he felt for her mum, she imagined those feelings would no longer be reciprocated. She'd moved on with her life, to Oxford, and had met Andrew. 'I'm sorry.' For some reason, Briony felt the need to apologise.

'Oh, don't apologise. We were young. I guess I always knew those summers would come to an end, and she'd move on to better … things.'

Briony stared at him, guessing he wasn't only talking about Oxford, but who she'd met there.

'Have you enjoyed your holidays here?' Sebastian asked, changing the subject.

Briony bit her lower lip. 'My mum and grandmother had a huge falling-out before I was born, apparently. They've been estranged ever since. I never knew my maternal grandmother, or this place, until I got a letter asking me to come here.'

'Really? That *is* sad. Such a waste, for you and your grandmother, not having the opportunity to know one another, and for you to spend your summers here at The Beach House.'

Briony thought so too.

'Well, now you're here, I hope things work out for you, with your grandmother.'

Briony hoped so too.

'Will your mother be joining you?' He looked down the beach, as if she'd been joining them any minute.

God, I hope not, thought Briony.

'Sorry to disturb you both, but I've got the tarpaulin.'

They both jumped up from where they had been perched on the boat. Briony had forgotten all about Peter.

'Here, let me help you with that.' said Sebastian.

Briony looked at the tarpaulin. 'You didn't drag that all the way up the beach, did you?'

'That's where the car park is. Didn't have a choice, did I?'

'Actually,' Briony didn't want to tell him, 'there's a single-track lane just before you enter the village that leads to the property. There's a driveway.'

He rolled his eyes. 'Now you tell me!'

The look on Peter's face brought to mind the taxi driver who had driven her there a little over a week earlier. Had it only been that long? It seemed like a lifetime ago – which reminded Briony, once again, that she still hadn't contacted her parents as she'd promised she would.

She vowed to herself that during the week, while she was working in the music shop and had internet access, she would send an email – otherwise her mum might start questioning Angel to see if she'd heard from her, and Angel might drop a clanger and tell her Briony's secrets. It was only Monday. *As long as I do it before the weekend*, thought Briony.

Peter walked around the boat and checked that the tarpaulin

was secure. He stopped in front of Briony. 'When your grandmother is well enough to decide what she wants doing with the boat, just let me know. Then we can get it fixed, if that's what she'd like.'

'Oh, I'm sure she would,' said Briony. 'She's in hospital at the moment, but I'll be sure to let her know, when I can.' Briony frowned. She hadn't meant to say that Blythe was in hospital.

As she said that, Troy walked by and overheard the snippet of conversation. He looked at the boat, at Peter, and then frowned at the sight of Briony, sitting with his dad.

26

Briony stepped out on to the freezing beach, wrapped in a throw. Even Luna, who would normally be around her feet, dying to get out, slunk back from the cold as soon as she opened the kitchen door. She retreated to lie down beside the radiator, next to the kittens, who were snuggled asleep together.

Each morning, for the rest of the week, Briony had hoped that she'd see a familiar silhouette sitting on the beach, awaiting the sunrise. But since Monday, when she'd spent time with Sebastian – and Troy had cheesed her off by bringing up that embarrassing incident when he'd rescued her from the sea – Troy had been avoiding her.

She'd hoped that he might turn up one morning, and they'd watch the sunrise together again, but so far that hadn't happened. And worse, the previous day – Friday – Troy, Sam and Sebastian had put the finishing touches to the outbuilding. The work was finally finished, and that meant Troy's days at The Beach House were over too.

Troy obviously didn't appreciate the friendship she'd struck up with his father – but was it any wonder, given their shared passion for the ocean? She just wished Troy hadn't started avoiding her. Briony had spent the rest of the week working mornings with Reggie at the music shop, visiting her grandmother in hospital, and then spending the rest of each afternoon trying to find any excuse to see Troy, offering to make coffee and supply biscuits to the three guys pulling out all the stops to finish the renovations.

Briony pulled the throw tightly around her and crossed the sand to the outbuilding, barefoot. She was still in her pyjamas. She didn't expect Troy to be on the beach that morning. Even so, she had risen in the early hours, hoping he'd be out there, waiting for her. Perhaps it was just as well that he wasn't. The mornings were a lot cooler now, and she was aware, given her condition, that she shouldn't be hanging around outside in the freezing cold in case she caught a chill.

Briony approached the outbuilding with the key to hand. It hadn't been kept locked previously, but now it had been renovated, Troy had fitted a new door with a lock and had given her the key.

She could see the gorgeous floor-to-ceiling picture window with the sea view through the little glass pane in the wooden door, and the pitched, beamed roof where the mezzanine level was meant to be. She imagined stairs rising to a bedroom, and the en suite in the eaves.

Although Troy had stuck to her grandmother's plans for the outbuilding, leaving Briony's additional ideas for the conversion on the back burner, as they'd discussed, he had applied for planning consent for the mezzanine – if and when Briony and her grandmother wanted the additional work done.

They'd done an amazing job. She loved the little kitchenette Troy had installed, which was in her grandmother's original plans.

After all, you couldn't spend time there without sitting on a sofa with a cuppa to hand, looking out to sea. The building inspector from the local council had signed it all off the previous day.

Briony should have felt like celebrating. It was everything she'd hoped for – and some. What they'd done inside, exposing one of the brick walls, and putting in a chimney and log burner, made the place feel like a barn conversion, rather than an outbuilding conversion. The place had been transformed.

'I'd better get in the party spirit,' she said to herself, thinking of the small party she'd arranged to celebrate the completion of the work. But all she could do was wonder when she'd see Troy again. At least the Wolf Girls Club would be meeting that day before the party, at their new HQ – the outbuilding. She had yet to think up a name for the little summerhouse.

Willow would be coming along to the party too – Briony had checked with Troy yesterday, but he'd been quite standoffish, short-tempered and had said, *Why are you asking me? Ask Sebastian.*

She had asked Sebastian, and had invited him to the little celebration too. Briony had shopped for some party food the previous day – sandwiches, sausage rolls, that sort of thing – hoping the last of the unseasonal warmth would hold just for one day, so they could celebrate on the beach, perhaps play some beach games. It would remind her of the old photographs she'd seen of her great-grandparents and all their friends.

Briony had ordered some old-fashioned stripy deckchairs online from a hire company who would deliver them, so they could all sit together on the beach. She had invited everyone she knew. The members of the Wolf Girls Club would be there, along with Clarissa's dad, Peter, and Reggie, Joss, and Lili from The Potting Shed in Cobblers Yard. Briony didn't know Lili that well, but had thought, *Why not invite her too?*

Briony had popped into The Bookshop of Memories and invited Thea and her dad. Thea doubted that Henry would go, but had accepted the invitation. Briony had also invited Lili and Thea's partners along if they wanted to bring them too. She knew Reggie was single. Mabel had been sitting reading the newspaper, and drinking coffee from her lovely coffee machine, so she and her sister had got an invite as well, even though a part of Briony wondered if it was a good idea to invite The Gossip Girls. What if they asked after her grandmother?

That was the other reason, besides Troy, that Briony felt like cancelling the party now. A few days earlier, when Troy had said the outbuilding would be finished on Friday, she'd impulsively decided to throw the celebratory party and place a ribbon across the door. She had somehow imagined her grandmother would have woken up, and would be back to join in the celebrations and cut the ribbon. That hadn't happened. And now Briony didn't feel like celebrating. It wasn't going to feel right without her, and she wasn't sure she should be throwing a party while her grandmother was still in hospital.

'I can't cancel now,' she said under her breath, taking a moment, before she unlocked the outbuilding door, to stare at bright moon, hovering above the black ocean.

'Why didn't things just go to plan?' she asked herself. She hadn't found Frank. Clarissa had tried, but she'd had no luck either. Briony had texted her, but Clarissa had said she'd found out nothing yet, and she hadn't got to the bottom of who was behind those solicitor's letters. Neither had Joss. She was still bothered by whether it was her mum who was behind those letters, but she was doing her best to ignore that possibility, focusing instead on Joss's theory that it could be a grudge going back a long way.

Briony was disappointed that there was no further news on that front, but her mind was occupied by other matters: what she wanted more than anything was to find Frank. If she did, and he visited Blythe in hospital, she hoped that the sound of his voice, reading those letters of Blythe's she'd found hidden in the old bureau, would wake her up. She was also convinced that if that didn't work, nothing would.

Her grandmother was lost to her, and at some point, if Frank didn't materialise, she knew the outcome would not be good. At the back of her mind was also the looming question of when exactly she was going to contact her mum and let her know what was going on with Blythe.

It made Briony feel terribly guilty about living in her grandmother's house, and taking it upon herself to get the planned work done on the outbuilding in her absence. She had meant it to be a nice surprise, but that was when she'd thought Blythe was just away, staying with a friend. If Blythe didn't wake up, it would have all been for nothing. Briony was just so relieved that she hadn't got carried away and gone ahead with her own plans for the outbuilding in the hope that she could continue living there, with her child, when her grandmother returned. Would her grandmother even want her there? Especially after she'd renovated the outbuilding in Blythe's absence. She had no way of knowing.

Briony sighed heavily. That was beside the point. She hadn't sent Freddie the letter, realising that whatever fantasy was playing in her head – of leaving Freddie and staying there, on the Suffolk Coast, with her new friends, with Troy – it was just that. A fantasy. Perhaps it was just as well that Troy hadn't turned up to watch the sunrise with her. It would only fuel the fantasy. It wasn't going to happen.

Soon, she'd have to face the reality that Freddie would be contacting her to find out when she was coming home and moving in with him. But she still had things to resolve – finding the deeds and waiting for her grandmother to wake up.

She knew she had quite a day ahead of her, preparing and hosting the little beach party. She should go back to bed and get some rest. But she still wanted to watch the sunrise. It was too cold to sit outside on the beach. She could have watched it from her bedroom window, but she'd had a much better idea. The outbuilding, with its huge glass window fronting the sea, would be an amazing place to sit and watch the sunrise. It would be the first of many such summerhouse sunrises.

The first of many? She frowned at that thought. How could it be, unless she didn't go back to Freddie?

Briony looked at the hot cup of tea in a flask mug she'd brought with her from the house. She had nearly brought two, but she'd had a feeling that Troy wouldn't be there. She'd brought her own drink with her because she didn't know whether Troy had left coffee, tea, sugar and milk in the kitchenette. Unfortunately, with the kitchenette installed, there had been no reason for Troy to nip up to The Beach House for a cup of coffee or tea that week as they put the finishing touches to the outbuilding.

Briony hugged the warm flask mug. She knew that she wouldn't have time to get the log burner going in the outbuilding. But there were electric heaters, and the hot drink she'd brought with her. Between them, they would warm her up.

There was a small table and chairs for two, along with a coffee table, a lamp, and a large rug that Briony had chosen from a family furniture store in a nearby town called Woodbridge. Briony had even bought some warm throws for the two armchairs and the small sofa, imagining cosy evenings around the log burner.

The furniture had arrived late on Friday afternoon, in time for Troy, Sam and Sebastian to load it inside, take off all the packaging and arrange it all. She'd chosen the furniture in keeping with what was in The Beach House, hoping that her grandmother would approve.

It made her wonder what her grandmother had been planning to use the outbuilding for, once it was decorated. Perhaps she was intending to move her piano there, by the window, and conduct her music lessons there. Or maybe it was just somewhere she could go for a change of scenery, away from the main house, where it sounded as though she spent most of her time.

Briony thought of the mezzanine level she'd planned, with the bedroom and shower room. If she'd gone ahead with the additions, her grandmother could have got a tenant, or even turned it into a lovely holiday let. She imagined her grandmother would earn a good income from it. That would be the end of the Wolf Girls Club, though. But it probably would be the end of it when she left anyway – unless her grandmother took it over. The thought made her smile. It would be lovely to see her grandmother making new friends.

Briony cast her gaze down the beach one last time and listened out again for Troy's truck arriving on the driveway. She was disappointed, but not surprised, that he hadn't turned up.

She sighed, accepting he most definitely was not coming. *You didn't want him to*, she said to herself. *You said it was for the best*, she reminded herself.

With no sign of Troy, Briony turned the key in the lock and discovered that the outbuilding was already open. She realised that Troy must have forgotten to lock it the previous day before he went home. The lock had only just been fitted, and he wasn't used to locking up before he left.

Briony stepped straight into the little kitchenette from the side door. She turned around and quietly closed the door, unsure why she was creeping around. She could see the place quite well, half-lit in the moonlight coming through the huge glass window. She glanced up at where the mezzanine level might have been, and thought that if she'd gone ahead with her plans, she'd have bought a bed too. Then she might have crawled into it and watched the sunrise from there before snuggling down under a throw and going back to sleep. She suddenly imagined that happening, and oversleeping, and how embarrassing it would be if everyone arrived for the party, only to discover her fast asleep, still in her pyjamas. She smiled. At least there was no fear of that. There was no mezzanine, and no bed. And if she did go back indoors and have a lie-in after the sunrise, she had the kittens, or the dogs, to wake her up.

She put the key down on the wooden countertop. Briony loved the little kitchenette. Although it was exceedingly small, and open to the lounge area, it had everything one would need, from an oven and a hob to a fridge-freezer and a dinky dishwasher. There was even a small space for a washer-dryer in case there were further renovations down the road to make it a proper self-contained little home.

It seemed that her grandmother had thought of everything. Briony wondered if her grandmother had also been considering making further changes at a later date to turn the outbuilding into a guesthouse.

She turned from admiring the kitchen and stood for a moment with her mug of tea to look through the large window. Something caught her eye. She could see the back of the sofa and thought she heard a creak. If Luna had been there, her exceptional hearing would have caught that too, confirming it wasn't her imagination.

Briony stood stock still. She wanted to think she was imagining things, but the hairs on the nape of her neck stood up. Someone was there, in the outbuilding, with her.

At that moment a hand appeared on the back of the sofa. Briony's instinct was to run, but her body just wouldn't move. She was rooted to the spot in fright.

A dark shape sat up on the sofa.

Briony nearly dropped her tea. Then she recognised the outline in the moonlight. 'Troy?'

27

'I thought you weren't talking to me anymore, after I got chatting with your dad?' Briony sat down next to Troy on the sofa.

'Sorry, that was quite childish of me. I was, well, you know …'

'No, I don't know.' Briony wasn't making it easy for him to apologise. But then he had scared her when she'd stepped into the outbuilding. She hadn't realised he'd been there all along, lying on the sofa, asleep.

'I was jealous.'

Briony shook her head at Troy. 'There's no need to be.' She knew she didn't feel physically attracted to Sebastian; not like she was to Troy.

He was still talking about you when I drove him home.'

'He was?'

'Sounds like you've got a lot in common.'

'We both love the ocean. Your dad said he wanted to be a marine archaeologist, but then … life got in the way.'

'You mean, *I* got in the way.'

'My parents had me way too young. I bet they must have

some regrets about that too,' said Briony.

Troy breathed a sigh. He patted the sofa seat next to him. 'Will you join me?'

Briony hesitated.

'Won't be the same, watching the sunrise without you.'

That elicited a smile from Briony. She admitted, 'I came out here hoping to see you on the beach, thinking the exact same thing.'

They cosied up to each other on the sofa, Briony sharing the blanket she'd brought with her from the house, Troy sharing the throw from the sofa, placing it over her legs. 'How long have you been here?'

'Does it matter?'

'I guess not. I couldn't sleep. What's your excuse?'

He nodded. 'The same. Although this sofa is way too comfortable. I fell asleep the moment I sat down.'

She passed him her mug of tea.

'Thanks – it's cold in here without any heating on.'

'We could switch on the heater, or light the fire?' suggested Briony.

'No, I'd rather not.'

'In case the heaters or the fire don't work?'

This time, Troy smiled. 'Of course they'll work. I installed them myself. I just don't want to get up from my cosy spot on the sofa – with you.'

Briony didn't want him to get up either. She asked, 'Who were your parents?'

Troy shifted in his seat to look at her.

She realised she'd thrown him a totally unexpected question. 'Sorry, but your dad said that he adopted you. Sounds as though your mum was one of his best friends when they were young.' *Along with my mum*, thought Briony, but she didn't add that.

He handed back the tea. 'It's nice, you should drink some too.'

Was he avoiding the question? Briony took a few sips. It was still hot. 'I make a lovely cup of tea.'

'Yes, you do.'

Briony eyed him. 'Are you going to answer my question – about your parents?'

'Yeah – sure. I guess it's the least I can do after I treated you quite appallingly this week.'

'Yes, it is,' Briony replied, her lip curling up into a smile, even though it was true. She'd tried to catch his eye and speak to him on several occasions since Monday, but he had acted like a sulky teenager.

'There's not much to tell. She got pregnant young, at seventeen. Her family cut her off. Apparently, her parents wanted her to get rid of it, me. She didn't, obviously, and her boyfriend stuck by her for a bit, but then … she died. And he didn't stick around.'

Briony didn't press him about how she'd died so young.

'Dad and my mum had been best friends. He couldn't stand the thought of her baby going into care, perhaps being lost in the system, lost to him, so he took me on, fostering and then eventually adopting me.'

Briony pursed her lips, thinking that was a massive thing for a teenager to do – take on the responsibility for someone else's child, even if they were best friends. She couldn't help feeling that there was more to it.

'I'm so sorry.'

'Don't be. I've been lucky to be adopted by a lovely guy, and grow up in a great family.'

'How did Sebastian do it, look after you and work? I mean, that is really young to foster a baby. Did your grandparents help out?'

'My paternal grandma died a long time ago. At first, my grandfather, Sebastian's father, did not understand his decision to take on someone else's kid, let alone at the tender age of eighteen. But from what I understand, Grandpa surprised himself and my dad by falling in love with me, the moment he set eyes on me.'

'That's so sweet,' said Briony, hugging his arm.

'I think he saw in me, from a really young age, his successor to the business – something my father never wanted. Although apparently he did warn my father I'd hold him back.'

'From studying marine archaeology?'

'Oh, no, my grandfather never wanted my dad to do that – he was talking about the family business, which my father wanted no part of anyway.'

'Construction?'

'Yeah. Look, about that. I've got a confession to make,' said Troy.

Briony thought she knew what that confession might be; she'd overheard Sebastian saying that Troy had never done a day's work in his life that didn't involve sitting at a desk. It looked to her as though Troy knew what he was doing, working on the outbuilding. But she imagined he was going to tell her anyway that it wasn't something he normally did.

But then she had a confession or two to make herself. For starters, she normally didn't employ people to do up someone else's property. She intended to tell him that her grandmother was in hospital, and that all this was meant to be a surprise for her to return home to when she was well. He hadn't really questioned where her grandmother was. Perhaps he'd just assumed she was away, visiting friends, or on holiday.

But before she got into all that, she had another little confession to make. A rather big one.

'So have I,' said Briony. 'I've got a confession to make too. But can we watch the sunrise together first?' She had a feeling, after what she was about to tell him, about the baby, that it would be their last sunrise together.

28

Willow sniggered into her hand.

Emily looked at Clarissa. 'Well, this is awkward,' she whispered. 'Does this mean we have to admit one more to the Wolf Girls Club?'

Willow overheard, and stamped her foot. 'No boys allowed!'

The couple were snuggled together, holding hands, Briony's head resting on Troy's shoulder. They were fast asleep, unaware of the new arrivals. They started to wake up. Briony opened her eyes first to find Emily, Clarissa, Willow and Luna standing in front of the sofa, looking down at them.

'What are you doing here? What's the time?'

'Party time!' exclaimed Willow, running over to her.

'Willow, the party isn't until later,' Emily reminded her. 'This was meant to be a Wolf Girls Club meeting first, then we were helping out with party prep before everyone else arrived.' She turned to Briony. 'I did explain to her that everyone would probably want to pop into our HQ to see the new outbuilding. I see you're here already.'

'You're still in your pyjamas,' Willow exclaimed as Briony cast the throw aside.

'Is this meant to be a slumber party?' asked Clarissa.

Willow misheard. 'Is this a pyjama party? Can we have pillow fights?'

Troy, still half-asleep, also woke up and echoed Briony's surprise as he sat up. 'What time is it?'

Willow shouted, 'You can't join the Wolf Girls Club because you're a boy!'

He looked at Willow, wide-eyed. 'What's going on? What are you doing here this early?'

'It's not early,' Willow shouted.

Emily said, 'Clarissa, why don't you take Willow over to The Beach House. I'm sure the kittens will be waiting for breakfast.'

Briony caught Clarissa grinning at her as she walked towards the door. Briony wanted to tell her that whatever she was thinking, and however it looked, there was nothing going on between her and Troy.

Troy quickly got up and handed Briony her blanket. He glanced at his watch. 'Oh, hell – is that the time?'

'You said *hell*!' Willow announced. 'That's rude!'

Clarissa grabbed her hand, 'Come on, let's go feed those kittens.' They walked out of the door.

Briony stood up too and turned to Troy. 'You're going to stay for the party – aren't you?'

'Yes, I'll be back for the party. I said I'd pick my father up.' He looked towards the door. 'How did Willow get here?'

Sebastian popped his head around the door at that moment. 'I brought Willow. She said on no account was I to go into the Wolf Girls Club new headquarters.' Sebastian looked him up and down. 'What are you doing here? Willow made it sound as though no boys are allowed.'

Troy nervously put his hand through his hair. 'I'm just doing some last-minute checks.'

'On the outbuilding?'

'Yes, on the outbuilding.'

Sebastian's eyes flicked to Briony as Troy joined him at the door.

Briony saw Sebastian put a fatherly hand on his shoulder as he walked out of the door, whispering something in his ear.

Troy said, 'It's not what it looks like, I can assure you.'

Briony pursed her lips. It *was* kind of what it looked like; they *had* slept together, for a bit. She was just so pleased that Sebastian was already there, which meant that Troy didn't have to leave after all. She was worried he might have a row with his dad and not come back for the party. Now, Troy wasn't going anywhere.

Emily and Briony were the only ones left in the room. Briony watched Emily turn around, eyebrows raised. 'Now, don't tell me there's nothing going on between you two. That's the second time I've caught you in Troy's embrace.'

Briony rolled her eyes. Once again, she did not want to be reminded of that episode on the beach when Troy had thought he was saving her from drowning.

'What were you two doing here – or shouldn't I ask?'

'We were just watching the sunrise together, then we obviously fell asleep.' Briony was still shocked at how long they'd slept.

'Now I know what your excuse is – tired all the time,' Emily said, light-heartedly, but unless he's pregnant too—' she joked.

Briony's eyes went wide. She sat back down, and looked towards the door as she put a finger to her lips. 'Shush!'

Emily looked at her in surprise. 'You haven't told him yet?' She came over and sat down beside her.

'I was going to tell him, and then I fell asleep.'

'This sofa is so comfy. Little wonder you dozed off.'

'And then you guys showed up.'

'Don't blame me,' said Emily, clearly amused. 'You did say the Wolf Girls Club should meet up around half-past nine, and after a chit-chat, we'd have a private tour of your new abode …'

Briony didn't correct her, even though she knew it wasn't going to be her new abode, regardless of any full renovation plans she'd imagined. She reminded herself that none of the dreams she'd had were real.

Emily caught her expression. 'Did you write to Freddie?'

Briony nodded. 'Yes, and I even got a stamp.'

'So, you posted the letter explaining how you felt? He's not going to turn up here today – is he?'

Briony winced. 'Not exactly. I kind of lost the letter.' She wouldn't have wanted Freddie to turn up there, even if he had got that letter and read it. It was fortunate she'd lost it.

'You lost the letter?'

'Yes, and he doesn't know anything about the outbuilding or the party.' She picked up a cushion and studied it. 'Oh, bother.'

'What's the matter?'

Briony had just remembered that she hadn't emailed her mum during the week when she was working in the music shop as she'd intended. She made a mental note to do it the next week. She didn't think the extra couple of days over the weekend would really make much difference now.

'So, Troy really has no idea that you're—?'

Briony shook her head, although Emily's question had

reminded her that before they'd fallen asleep, Troy had said he had something important to tell her too. She still assumed it had something to do with the fact that this wasn't his real job, and that he was normally desk-bound.

'It really is something,' said Emily, admiring it the outbuilding. 'Troy did a fantastic job.'

'Yeah.' Briony started to wonder if what he had to tell her had nothing to do with his normal day job. She knew she had the furniture to pay for. Maybe that was it. She hoped not. Although she had insisted on withdrawing money from her savings and paying what she could, all along she had got the impression that he was subsidising the work. She hoped he wasn't going to ask for more money, because her savings had dwindled to next to nothing. She felt fortunate that Reggie had offered her a job at his music shop.

'So, when are you getting dressed?' Emily asked. 'Or have you decided to have a slumber party?'

Briony playfully threw the cushion at her, larking about.

Emily threw it back.

Willow appeared at the doorway with the two kittens, one in each hand. She squealed in delight, put the kittens down to explore, under Luna's watchful gaze, and came bounding over. Willow picked up a cushion.

'Oh, no,' said Emily, shielding her face.

Clarissa appeared too. 'We need more cushions!' After taking the kittens back to the house, out of harm's way, Clarissa reappeared with a small mountain of pillows and cushions. She dumped them on the sofa, rolled up her sleeves, and said, 'Let's get this party started!'

Willow stood on the sofa.

Briony joined her.

'Let the game commence!' Clarissa shouted out. 'Oh, one quick question. Briony, is it okay if my two kids come this afternoon? My dad is looking after them, and as he's coming to the party, and I can't get a sitter …' Clarissa trailed off.

'Of course they can!' exclaimed Briony, thumping her with a pillow. 'I forgot about your kids. Sorry, I should have invited them too.'

'Great!' Clarissa stood on the sofa too, and thumped Briony with the cushion. 'Oh, no. I forgot you're pregnant!'

'Don't be silly, that doesn't make me an invalid. I can still stand my ground in a pillow fight.'

'Fantastic!' Emily said. 'So can I!'

A few minutes later, they all collapsed on the sofa. Even Luna had joined in, a pillow in her jaws, getting a hang of the rules of the game – there were none. It was just a matter of thumping anyone and everyone.

Clarissa put the pillow she had in her hand behind her back, and sat back on the sofa. 'By the way, Briony, I'm glad it looks as though my dad is sorting your boat.'

'Well, he came along to look at it.'

'It's great that he took it, then. I hope he can get it repaired.'

'No, he didn't take it to the boatyard in the end. We discussed it, but I explained it belonged to my grandmother, and until she gets out of hospital and tells me what she'd like done with it, it has to be left as it is.' Briony wished that Peter had never turned up to look at the boat. She'd wasted his time. And she knew she should also have applied that logic to the outbuilding renovation project and left it well alone until her grandmother returned. Although Troy had done a fantastic job.

'That didn't stop you with the outbuilding,' commented Clarissa, as if reading her thoughts.

'Yeah, well, the outbuilding wasn't being taken away, stripped down, and possibly sold for firewood if I couldn't find the money to repair it. So your dad covered it with a tarpaulin. At least it's protected from the weather until my grandmother gets home.'

Clarissa said, 'Hmm. That is odd.'

'What is it?' Emily asked.

'The boat's gone,' said Willow.

Briony looked at her. 'What do you mean – *the boat's gone*?'

Emily and Clarissa exchanged a glance. 'Yep, it was the first thing we noticed when we turned up. The boat is no longer sitting on the sand under the lounge window.'

Briony dropped the cushion she was holding and raced to the door. She flung it open, rushed outside, and stopped. Even though she could see it wasn't there, she continued walking towards The Beach House. She stopped where the boat had stood. It was now just a patch of sunken sand in the shape of the hull of the boat.

Clarissa, Emily and Willow caught up with her.

Luna pawed the sand as if she understood there was something missing.

Clarissa said, 'If my dad didn't take it – then who did?'

Briony had an idea. She looked through the kitchen window and spotted Troy helping himself to party food.

Willow spotted him too. 'Troy is eating the food we left on the kitchen table until everyone arrives for the party!' She banged on the window. 'Stop that!'

Troy was just about to pop a sausage roll in his mouth. He

looked at Willow wide-eyed as she wagged her finger at him, hand on hip.

He looked at her sheepishly, and slowly put the sausage roll down.

Briony walked into the kitchen.

'Sorry, you caught me red-handed.'

'Never mind that – what did you do with the boat?'

Clarissa, Willow and Emily stepped into the kitchen too. He looked at each of them in turn. 'I'm sorry – what?'

'The boat outside.'

'Oh, right. Didn't that guy who came to look at it, Peter, take it away?'

'No, he covered it with a tarpaulin.'

'And then he took it away – right?'

Briony frowned at him. 'I know what you're up to, Troy. And it's not going to work this time.'

Troy looked at her innocently. 'Sorry, but I have absolutely no idea what you're getting at.'

'Is that what you wanted to talk to me about in the outbuilding this morning? Because I know you've renovated the outbuilding well below cost, so I couldn't possibly have you do the same for the boat too. I want you to bring it right back right now.'

It explained what he had been doing there so early. Someone had come along and helped him take the boat to the boatyard.

Troy held up both hands. 'I swear I know nothing about the boat.'

Briony still wasn't sure she believed him. 'Where's your dad – did he take the boat?'

'Of course not – why would he?'

Because he seems to have a sentimental attachment to it, thought Briony. But she didn't want to get into that, or bring up her mum.

Sebastian walked out of the lounge, one of the old leather-bound photo albums open in his hand. He stopped in the doorway. 'Sorry, I couldn't help overhearing something about the boat. I was wondering what had happened to the boat too.' He looked at Briony.

Willow came running up to her dad. He picked her up in his arms. 'What's that?' she asked.

'Oh, this – it's a photo album from years ago.'

'Can I see?'

Sebastian looked sheepishly at Briony. 'Sorry, I should have asked before looking at the photo album.'

Briony stared at Sebastian, who was affectionately holding his young daughter in his arms. Briony could tell he was a great dad. 'No, it's okay – look at it if you want to.' Briony caught Troy frowning at her.

Sebastian said, 'So, what do *you* think happened to the boat?'

Briony shrugged. 'I haven't the faintest idea.'

'It's a mystery,' commented Clarissa.

'We can find it,' said Willow. 'It will be like a Wolf Girls Club mission.'

'I like it,' said Emily, smiling.

'Me too,' Briony agreed although she didn't know how they'd go about finding it.

'A *secret* mission,' said Willow.

Sebastian looked at his daughter. 'Did you learn that word at school – *mission*?'

Willow shook her head.

'Something you're watching on TV about spies?'

Briony caught a look pass between Willow and Troy, and she saw Troy looking anxiously at his little sister. She knew they hadn't taken the boat, but something was going on. Were they hiding something else?

29

'I've been meaning to ask – what was all that about last weekend, when you invited Angel's parents in for dinner?'

It was Saturday morning. Lorna didn't know why Andrew was bringing last Sunday up now, almost a week later. 'It was nice to meet them, and I just wanted a friendly chat.'

'A friendly chat?' Andrew raised his eyebrows. 'Sounded more like a grilling to me.'

Lorna stood in their bedroom doorway, watching him pack. It brought to mind standing at her daughter's bedroom door, just over two weeks earlier, watching her pack for her trip.

Apart from the fact that she still hadn't heard from her daughter, Angel's parents had been on her mind for another reason – the way the couple interacted, joked, chatted together. She saw the way Angel's father, Trevor, looked at his wife; throwing her affectionate glances, touching her arm. She'd also seen the way Angel's mum looked adoringly at her husband across the dinner table whenever he spoke. Their feelings for each other after years of marriage were still apparent.

When Lorna caught Andrew glancing her way across the dinner table, although she could see he was enjoying the company and camaraderie of new friends, she didn't feel that he looked at her in the same affectionate, adoring way Trevor looked at his wife.

Of course, Andrew would often throw a smile her way, as she did with him, but it was the nuances, the subtleties of a look here, a knowing smile there, that were missing between them, whereas it was plain to see that Angel's parents were still very much in love.

Lorna had heard Andrew whistling a happy tune as he packed that morning. She'd been upstairs, putting some towels in the airing cupboard. His happy tune had drawn her to the bedroom doorway, where she now stood watching him. She was no stranger to his cheerful disposition whenever he was getting ready to go on a cruise for work. She leaned against the doorframe, folded her arms and stared at him.

She could tell that he must have felt her eyes boring into his back. He turned around. 'What is it?'

Lorna frowned. His happy tune and light-hearted disposition were getting on her nerves. They didn't normally, but it was different this time. She'd wanted to go with him in the past, it was true. But all the other times, Briony had still been at home, and consequently, Lorna had not made arrangements with work so that she could go with him.

This time she had, but during the past week, they'd spent hardly any time together. Lorna still hadn't found the right time to tell him she'd given up work – albeit temporarily – to have an adventure together, and spend some time getting to know one another again, *sans* Briony. This was a monumental change in their lives, their daughter leaving home for good, even though it was still playing on her mind that she hadn't heard from her.

Lorna left him to his packing and raced upstairs to the attic room while Andrew was busy. There was something she'd been meaning to do. She had planned to leave it until Andrew had gone, but what if Angel came back in the meantime? This was her only opportunity. It had to be now.

Lorna had the spare key to hand. She glanced down the stairs. Andrew was still whistling that familiar, *I'm off on another cruise*, irritatingly happy tune. He must still be in the middle of packing. She unlocked the door and stepped inside, quietly closing the door behind her.

She turned around and stared at the room. Although it was just the same old room, with the same furniture, lamps, and rugs, it didn't feel like Briony's room anymore. Her posters, books, various trophies and awards, knick-knacks and holiday souvenirs she'd brought back from her holidays staying with her grandpa in America – all the familiar things that had made the attic Briony's – were gone.

It reminded Lorna of the day her father had suddenly announced he was leaving Oxford University for a new position at Stanford University in America. She remembered the day he'd left, the room devoid of all his books, paperwork and detritus that made the old attic his own.

And now this room showed Lorna the stark reality that Briony had gone too – and she wasn't coming back.

Lorna hadn't been up to the room since Briony was packing to leave two weeks earlier. How could a fortnight seem like a lifetime? She missed her daughter terribly. But Briony hadn't just been packing for her trip. In the corner of the room were packing boxes. Lorna knelt and opened a flap of one of the boxes. Briony hadn't had time to seal them up. They contained all her things, ready for her move in with Freddie on her return.

Lorna lifted out an old school textbook, and one of the earliest trophy ribbons Briony had received for a science project when she was in high school. Lorna could feel tears in her eyes as she wondered where all the years had gone.

She carefully returned the items to the box and sat for a moment thinking back to what Andrew had said when she'd told him she wanted to contact the organisers of the expedition and check that Briony was okay. Lorna had come up to the attic to see if she could find the contact details. But she hadn't bothered to look for them. She realised that Andrew was right. He was always right. It was time to accept that her baby was an adult now, out in the world, making her own decisions.

And thinking of being an adult, and making her own decisions, Lorna stepped out of the room and closed the door. She remembered to lock it. A moment later, she'd joined Andrew in the bedroom, found her suitcase, and started packing.

Unsurprisingly, Andrew stopped what he was doing and looked at her in surprise. 'Why are you packing your suitcase?'

Lorna looked at him. She'd made a decision. She'd just checked that there was still availability on the cruise, pausing outside the bedroom door to Google the cruise on her phone before she stepped in the room. It turned out she'd get an excellent last-minute deal, including the flights, which meant she could join Andrew because there were loads of spaces still available. She was taking a leaf out of her daughter's book, making a decision for herself. She grinned. *Good times.* She had got to the last part of the booking process online. She would only have to press one more button after she'd told Andrew she was going with him.

'Aren't you going to tell me what's going on?'

Lorna threw a swim towel into her suitcase, still smiling. She wasn't sure whether they'd have one on board the cruise ship. She'd never been on a cruise before. Better to be safe than sorry.

She glanced at Andrew. She had thought of packing when he'd left, getting a taxi, and surprising him at the airport. Or even on the flight. Wouldn't that be something – seeing the look on his face when he saw her walking down the plane aisle? The trouble was she hadn't been abroad in an age and rather fancied some company on the way to the airport. Besides, it seemed such a waste, paying for two taxis.

'Oh, before I go,' he was still eyeing her suitcase, waiting for her to tell him what she was up to, 'here's this.' He got out a leaflet from his wallet.

Lorna had her hands in the wardrobe, looking for her summer dresses. She turned around. 'What's this?'

'I found the details of Briony's trip. It will save you sneaking up to the attic to try and find it.'

Lorna's face coloured. She hoped he hadn't caught her guilty look. Lorna cast the leaflet aside on the bed. 'Never mind that.'

He looked at her, surprised. 'But I thought you wanted to chase it up, get in contact with them, and check she's okay? I know I told you not to, but I guessed you'd do it anyway.'

Lorna smiled. 'I've changed my mind.'

'You have?'

'Yeah – you're right. I need to let her go.'

Andrew smiled. 'There, you see. I knew you'd come to your senses.'

Lorna's smile faltered. She tried not to take that as an insult. Andrew was always right. And it seemed he always had a way of making the point, and appearing to belittle her, although she was sure that wasn't his intention, and he was well-meaning.

'So, what's with the packing?' He nodded his head, indicating her suitcase.

She cast her thoughts about Andrew's rather condescending attitude towards her aside, and was about to utter the words, *I'm coming with you*, imagining his reaction when she told him, *You know the surprise I've been telling you about? Well, this is it.* But that thought was interrupted by the sound of her phone. She had a text.

She'd already played out the conversation in her mind, imagining what would happen when she told him she was going to accompany him on the cruise. She knew what his reaction would be: *This isn't going to work.* To which she'd reply, *Of course it is. I know you're working, but you must have some time off, surely. There are shore excursions I can go on. Perhaps some we can go on one together.*

'Aren't you going to look at that?' Andrew interrupted her thoughts.

Of course she was. That was why she hadn't said anything. Despite her seemingly blasé attitude, telling Andrew that she'd accepted Briony was off living her life, and that she'd let her go, it wasn't the case at all. Every time an email popped into her inbox, or she received a text or WhatsApp message, her first thought was Briony, and whether she'd finally got in touch.

This was no different. She quickly looked at her phone. 'Oh.'

'Everything all right?'

Lorna frowned. It wasn't from Briony. It was another one of those texts. She'd received the first text the previous Sunday, just before Angel's parents had turned up at their house and had ended up having dinner with them. Then she'd forgotten about it, which wasn't surprising. With Andrew's long hours, working in the orchestra in Oxford, their lives, and their relationship amounted, as usual, to ships passing in the night.

'And?' Andrew was busy carefully folding some starched white shirts into his suitcase.

Lorna sighed. She didn't want to talk about it. She'd got another text, a few days later, which she'd also ignored, just giving the unknown number a cursory glance. She'd assumed it had been sent to her phone by mistake. However it wasn't until the previous day, when she'd gone to delete them, and had actually opened the texts, that she'd realised her assumption was wrong. They *were* for her.

Now she had another one, along the same lines, asking her to get in touch.

Lorna sighed. 'It's from the hospital in Aldeburgh.'

'Hospital in Aldeburgh? Where's that?'

'On the Suffolk Coast. It's where my mother lives.'

Andrew stopped folding a shirt, and turned around. 'She's in hospital?'

Lorna stepped into the room. 'Yeah, apparently.'

'She wrote, didn't she? Saying she was going in for a routine op and wanting you to house-sit. That was weeks ago.'

So, the hospital got in touch now – why?'

'They wouldn't say. I don't suppose they can leave messages.'

'But they did leave you a message.'

'Of sorts.' Lorna glanced at her phone. 'There's no personal information. They just said I should get in touch.'

'She's put you down as the next of kin, then.'

'I guess. That was years ago, though.' She was staring at her phone when something occurred to her. Where had the hospital got her new mobile phone number from?

She looked up, about to share her thoughts, when Andrew said, 'You shouldn't have dismissed those texts.'

Lorna glared at him. She didn't want a lecture. But as usual, he was absolutely right. She looked at her phone. She had a bad feeling.

'Doesn't sound good to me, if the hospital is trying to get in touch with you.' Andrew turned around and continued packing.

Lorna frowned at his back. 'Aren't you going ask me if I'd like you to accompany me to the hospital?'

Andrew whirled around. He put his hands on his hips. 'You've been estranged from your mother all these years, not letting myself or Briony near her. Now she might be on her way out, you want me to give up this cruise and the money, drop everything, and come with you to see someone I don't even know?'

Lorna looked at the floor. He did have a point. Mind you, she'd be dropping everything too. She was going on the cruise with him – he just didn't know it yet.

Andrew sighed. 'Look, hopefully everything is going to be okay. Maybe they're getting in touch because she's had to stay in hospital longer as a result of some … complications, and they just need to inform the next of kin that's she's in for an extended stay.'

Lorna looked up. That sounded reasonable. It would mean she could still go on the cruise and choose to visit on her return. 'I've taken some time off work.'

'Excuse me?'

She looked at him askance. She'd been so surprised that he hadn't noticed she was no longer getting ready to leave for work.

She'd thought, sooner or later, that he'd ask, but he hadn't. Didn't that epitomise their relationship lately? He just didn't seem interested; his mind appeared elsewhere most of the time.

'Yeah, I've taken a sabbatical from work – a career break – until the New Year.'

Andrew stared at her. 'To spend time with your mother?'

'Of course not! I did it for us, to spend some time with you.'

Andrew furrowed his brow. 'I don't understand. Doing what?'

Lorna gaped at him. 'It's going to be my fortieth, I wanted to do something special – together. Like go away on a cruise with you.'

'What about your private music tuition?'

'I've put that on hold too. No more lessons until after Christmas. That's why I'm booking a last-minute cruise.'

'A last-minute cruise? Where?'

'To the Caribbean.' She grinned. 'I'm coming with you – surprise!'

30

'But … but you can't come with me. How many times have I told you that it's not a holiday?'

'Yes, I know.' Lorna mimicked him, when she added, '*I'm at work.*'

She stared at his expression. As she expected, he was looking dumbfounded. 'Well, say something, Andrew.'

'But what about us making decisions together? A big decision like taking a leave of absence from your job isn't something you should be deciding on your own.'

'Oh, I see, so it's all right for you to go making a big decision like signing up for work on cruise ships. It was meant to be a one-off to get us through a financial rocky patch a few years ago, but then it ended up that you went every single summer, and an autumn extended re-positional cruise too, when they came up.'

'But it's not like we were ever going on a summer holiday together. When you finished teaching at the end of the summer term, you then spent the holidays doing music lessons, most of the time.'

'I only did the music lessons, filling in during the summer, because you were away. And that meant because you were on cruise ships all the time, Briony and I spent our summer holiday with my dad instead.'

Lorna remembered there was no question of her and Briony joining him on a cruise because he'd always impressed on them that it wasn't a holiday, it was work. The inference was that it wouldn't be a family holiday, so there was no point them going. In hindsight, she realised that he'd positively discouraged them from going at every turn.

Looking back, it dawned on her that for years, they'd been leading separate lives. It was because the life they were leading appeared normal – just busy, like every family, she imagined, with little time to themselves. And yet, when she really thought about it, their marriage seemed to mirror her parents' relationship. As a child, she'd spent the summers at her grandparents' beach house, but her parents had rarely holidayed there together – it had mainly been just her and her mum.

As a professor lecturing at the university, her father should have had long holidays in which he could have spent six weeks in the summer at The Beach House with them. But he never had.

Lorna remembered asking her mum why her dad couldn't come too, on occasion, but all she'd said was that he had papers to write, research to do for his next publication, and summer courses to run for students.

Lorna had often thought, *Why couldn't he spend time with me instead?*

For the first time ever, Lorna wondered if her father had been having an affair. It would explain an awful lot – why they never really spent much time together as a family.

What if I got things all wrong, and it wasn't Mum who left Dad, and I blamed her for the break-up of their marriage?

'What is it?'

Lorna looked over at Andrew. He must have caught her expression. She shook her head, not feeling inclined to share her thoughts on her parents' marriage. Besides, it wasn't as though Andrew could share any insights. Lorna had met Andrew after her parents had split up.

'Maybe this works out for the best, Lorna, that you've taken time off from work. Whatever has gone on with you and your mother, maybe it's time to heal the rift, before it's too late.'

Lorna took a deep breath. That was not how she'd intended to spend the time she'd taken off work to celebrate her fortieth – with her mother. She wanted to spend it with Andrew, having new adventures, making new memories; not revisiting the past and opening up old wounds. But perhaps he was right. Perhaps it was time to lay the ghosts of the past – her relationship with her mother – to rest properly.

'I don't want you to have regrets for the sake of coming on a cruise, if something were to happen,' Andrew said sincerely.

Lorna looked at her phone. It had just occurred to her that she could phone the hospital straight away. They could tell her what was going on over the phone before she potentially wasted her time making a special trip to Suffolk. She could always catch up with her mother after the cruise if there was no emergency.

'I'm going to phone the hospital.'

Andrew frowned at her.

Lorna smiled when she got through almost immediately, stating her name and asking after her mother. Her smile faded. 'All right. When do you think that will be?' Lorna listened to the receptionist before she ended the call.

Andrew raised his eyebrows. 'Well – what did they say?'

'The receptionist couldn't give out any information on patients over the phone, and the nurses are doing their rounds at the moment. I'll have to wait for a call back, or call later this afternoon.' The trouble was that Andrew was leaving soon. She wanted to know what was going on straight away in case she could still go with him.

Andrew looked at her suitcase. 'There'll be other cruises, Lorna.'

'Does that mean I can go on the next one with you?'

The sound of the doorbell interrupted them. 'That'll be my taxi.'

Lorna watched Andrew zip up his suitcase. He looked at her suitcase. She followed his gaze. She could tell that it suited him perfectly that it looked as though she wouldn't be booking her cruise and would be going to Suffolk instead.

She still didn't get why he'd always discouraged her from joining him on the cruises. Yes, they wouldn't be able to spend the whole cruise together, but perhaps that wasn't a bad thing, considering how little time they spent together during their normal day-to-day lives. It might be too much if they were together the whole time. Perhaps, if they were, they'd discover they didn't much like each other's company.

Lorna frowned, wondering why that thought had popped into her head.

'As you're packed, you could always come with me in the taxi and get dropped off at the train station on the way.'

Lorna considered it for a moment. It was tempting. Taking a train would be more relaxing than driving. She'd have to quickly check the train times, but she imagined that she wouldn't have to pre-book a train ticket; she could just buy one at the station.

The problem was that she'd packed for a cruise in the Caribbean, not a trip to the East Coast of England, even though it had been an unusually warm October. However, that morning the weather had turned chilly, the temperature plummeting. Although it sounded as though it was going to turn out to be another warm day, the weather forecast had predicted that it would be the last of the beautifully sunny, mild weather before temperatures returned to normal for the time of year – meaning wet and cold.

Lorna glanced at her suitcase. She'd have to quickly sort through her suitcase, throw out her swimming costume, swim towel, and all the clothes she'd packed for the Caribbean, and then repack for the Suffolk Coast. The trouble was that she didn't want to. But what choice did she have? Unless the hospital phoned her back imminently, it would be too late to join Andrew on the cruise anyway.

A part of her just wanted to ignore the messages and pretend everything was okay. But after what Andrew had said, about seeing Blythe before it was too late, she didn't know how she'd go on a cruise and enjoy herself. She couldn't ignore her feeling that something was wrong.

She knew why Andrew had offered to share his taxi. He'd probably guessed that if she didn't go to Suffolk now, she might not go at all. Even so, the thought of getting into the taxi with him and not going to the airport would just make her feel worse. As it was, she'd have to cancel the cruise.

'No, you go ahead. I think I'd prefer to get a taxi separately, when I've gathered my thoughts.' *And repacked my suitcase, if I really am returning to Suffolk*, she thought.

'All right, sweetheart. You will go, though, won't you?'

Lorna didn't reply. She wasn't convinced she would, even though she was resigned to the fact that she wouldn't complete that cruise booking while she waited to hear from the hospital. *Then what will I do if I decide not to go to Suffolk, with no work, and no cruise to go on?* Use the time to plan another one for when her husband returned, and he had some time off before he rejoined the orchestra in Oxford in the spring. Or better still, just take off and have an adventure on her own.

Lorna hadn't been on her own since she was eighteen. She couldn't really imagine going on holiday alone. She thought of her daughter going all the way to the Galapagos Islands. Although technically she wasn't on her own, she was with a group – but even so, she'd applied, and flown out there by herself, not knowing any of the other people who'd be joining the research ship. Lorna was so proud of her. She thought, *If Briony can do it – then so can I.*

'I'll be back for Christmas.'

'So will I,' murmured Lorna. If she had to go and visit her mother, then so be it, but she wouldn't be spending the next six or seven weeks in Suffolk with her. No way!

Andrew stopped at the door. 'What did you say?'

Lorna had a thought. 'When I've visited my mum, I could fly out and join the cruise at one of the ports of call,' she said hopefully.

She silently cursed herself for sharing her thoughts. She could have done that as a surprise.

Andrew was already shaking his head at her idea. 'Sweetheart, let's plan a *proper* cruise, just you and me, nothing to do with my work.'

'Really?' It was the first time that he'd ever seriously

entertained the idea of them going on one together.

'Sure.'

Lorna frowned as he walked out of the bedroom, carrying his suitcase. She hoped he wasn't just saying that.

31

Lorna followed him downstairs. 'So, when you just said about booking another cruise, it wouldn't be one linked with your job then?'

'Oh, no, not at all. We could plan it together, a holiday, just you and me.' He put the suitcase down on the doormat. His violin was already by the door.

'Just you and me?' She looked at him. 'I don't understand what you mean. It would be just you and me if I'd joined you on this one.'

He suddenly looked flustered. 'Well, it wouldn't be. It would be you, me, and the quartet, obviously.'

'Oh, you socialise with them after work?'

Andrew shrugged. 'Well, I don't sit in my cabin all on my own, do I?'

Lorna had no idea what he did on the cruises because he never spoke about them. Why had it never occurred to her to ask what he did with his spare time? 'Oh, right – so you're, like, all good friends.'

'Well, of course. We have worked together as a quartet on cruise ships for years, darling. You know that.'

Lorna stared at him. Was this what it was all about – he didn't want her meeting his friends? Maybe he didn't want her to be a part of that life. Why was that? Was he embarrassed by her? She didn't see how that would be the case. Although she was turning forty this year, she had taken care of herself over the years – unlike her husband.

She was about to speak her mind when Andrew opened the front door to the taxi driver, who was standing outside, about to ring the doorbell.

'Well, I'd best be off. I'll see you in six weeks.' He leaned in and gave her a peck on the cheek.

'Do you need a hand with that, mate?' The taxi driver pointed at his suitcase.

'Ah, yes please.'

'And that?' The driver pointed at the violin case in Andrew's hands.

'Ah, no, I'll keep hold of that. It's precious cargo.'

The taxi driver raised his eyebrows. 'If you say so.'

Lorna started to close the front door. She didn't want to watch and wave Andrew off like she normally did. It was different this time. She didn't have work commitments. She wished she hadn't received the text messages. Regardless of what he did or didn't want, she'd be accompanying him in that taxi right now to the airport. In fact, after the conversation about his friends in the quartet, she would have been extremely interested to meet them.

She stared after her husband, thinking, *Perhaps I will go on one of Andrew's so-called work cruises, after all, and see what he really gets up to with his friends.*

As Lorna closed the front door, she heard the sound of a

mobile phone buzz with a text. It wasn't hers because it was in her hand. She put it down on the table in the hall. She looked up the stairs, then quickly opened the front door wide and caught Andrew just as he was awkwardly climbing in the taxi with the violin case in his hands.

'Andrew!' she called out. 'I think you've forgotten your mobile phone!'

'What?'

She stepped outside. 'Your mobile!' she called out again. 'I think you left it in the bedroom.'

'Oh right!' He struggled to get out of the taxi.

'No, don't bother coming in. I'll go fetch it!'

'No, please don't!' Andrew called out, still trying to get out of the back of the taxi with his violin case on his lap.

'Don't be stupid!' Lorna called back. 'Just give me a second!'

She ran upstairs, taking the stairs two at a time. She grabbed the mobile off the bed and caught sight of the leaflet Andrew had given her containing the details of Briony's research trip, which she'd made a point of discarding on the bed. She picked that up too.

As she walked down the stairs, her eyes on the leaflet, she caught sight of Andrew standing at the bottom of the stairs, looking up at her.

She frowned at him. 'I told you I'd fetch your phone. You didn't have to come back in the house. You could have waited in the taxi.'

'What are you doing?'

Lorna had been caught red-handed with the leaflet. *Briony is just busy – that's the reason she hasn't been in touch, having too much fun on her adventure.* Lorna had tried to convince herself. But still something didn't sit right. Maybe it was mother's intuition. And try as she might, that feeling just would not go away.

'You're going to phone that number, aren't you?'

'So what if I am!' Lorna replied defensively. It was too late to whip the leaflet behind her back.

'What happened to, and I quote, "*I need to let her go*" – hmm?'

Lorna eyed him.

Andrew slowly shook his head from side to side. 'It's my fault. I shouldn't have given you that leaflet. Just leave her be. She'll contact us when she's ready.'

'You don't know how it feels, Andrew. You're not—' Lorna stopped abruptly.

Andrew pursed his lips. 'Go on, finish the sentence. I'm not …'

Lorna stared at him as she slowly walked down the last three stairs. 'It's nothing.'

'What do you mean, it's nothing? I want you to finish that sentence … I'm not … go on.'

Lorna stopped in the hallway and dropped her gaze to the floor.

Andrew said, 'Let me finish that sentence for you – I don't know how it feels because I'm not a *real* parent, not a *real* dad.'

Lorna looked up. 'You knew what you were signing on for when we married, and we agreed we'd tell her the truth. But *you* didn't want that.'

'I'm her dad. Can you blame me for not wanting her to look at me any differently if she found out the truth?'

Lorna threw her hands in the air. 'Why do you think I've avoided my mum all these years? For you. Because you wouldn't tell Briony. And the last thing I wanted was for her to find out from my mother.'

'Oh, right. Put it at my door – your estrangement. I know there's more to it than that.'

Lorna remained silent.

'Besides, you went along with it, Lorna. You could have told Briony any time, but you didn't. And I know why. Because then Briony might want to know who her real father is, and you didn't want that either. It suited you to leave things as they were.' Andrew narrowed his eyes. 'Who is he?'

Lorna looked at him in surprise. 'Why are you asking me that now? You never wanted to know before.' She grimaced. 'I think you should go now.' She looked at his phone, and was about to hand it over, when she saw the text that had come through. She cocked her head to one side, and read it aloud, '*Can't wait to see you.*' Lorna threw him a questioning look.

'It's just one of the guys from the quartet.'

'Oh, really?' Lorna noticed the person had signed off with their name. 'Since when does a guy have a girl's name – Susie?'

Andrew looked at her nervously. 'It was just a figure of speech, you know. They're not all actually guys.'

'So I gather.'

They were interrupted by the taxi driver honking his horn and calling out, 'If you want to make your flight, we need to leave for the airport now.'

'Oh, right. Yes, better dash.'

Lorna stared after him. Any thoughts of joining him on that cruise – even if the hospital did get in touch now and it turned out her mother wasn't at death's door, and her visit could wait – had vanished the moment she'd read that text.

She stood at the door, watching Andrew get in the taxi. Just before the car took off, he looked out of the window. Their eyes locked. He didn't wave goodbye. Neither did she.

Lorna turned around, closed the front door, leaned her back against the door, and cupped a hand to her mouth in shock. *How long had it been going on – the affair with this woman called Susie?* It all made sense now, why he'd never wanted her and Briony to join him on a cruise. And why that one-off cruise had turned into two a year, and then several.

Was Susie married too? What was the plan? Were they going to continue meeting on the cruise ships – just continuing their affair? Or were they waiting for their kids to leave home – assuming this Susie was married and had children – and then drop the bombshell to their respective partners that they'd met someone else, and were leaving?

Lorna rushed into the kitchen, switched on her laptop, and Googled the quartet that was on the cruise ship. She wondered why she'd never done it before. She guessed she'd just been too busy with work and with raising her daughter. Now both were gone, and she had time on her hands to figure things out – like her relationship with Andrew.

She knew he loved her daughter. *But does he love me?* In the beginning, of course he had, otherwise why would he have stayed with her and married her when she'd told him, soon after they'd met at university, that she was pregnant with another man's child? She'd known even in the beginning that she'd never love him the way he did her. But he'd turned out to be all that she'd hoped for – a loving father and parent to her child. And a loving husband – in the beginning.

But they'd grown apart. She had to acknowledge that. They were going through the motions of being a married couple, a family, but Briony had been the glue that had held them together. Now that she was gone, what was left? A relationship, a marriage built on secrets.

A page appeared on her laptop with photos of the quartet and a brief bio of each musician. There were three men and one woman – Susan. She had thick, long blonde hair down to her shoulders, and bright blue eyes set in a round face. Even though the photo was just head and shoulders, she could tell that like Andrew, Susan carried some weight. But she looked like she carried it rather well. It suited her, as it did Andrew.

Lorna stared at her photo after reading the bio. She had been married since her early twenties. Now in her mid-forties, and recently divorced, she had two children at university and was looking forward to travelling extensively on round-the-word cruises, being off for months at a time.

Lorna sat back in her chair. So, that was the plan. When had he been planning to tell her that?

'I'm such a fool.'

While she'd been busy taking a leave of absence from her job, putting plans in place to do some travelling with Andrew, starting with a cruise, looking forward to surprising him with her plans for the year they turned forty, Andrew was several steps ahead of her, planning a new life on the ocean waves with Susan. Both had been biding their time until their commitments of raising children were finished and they were free to leave.

Lorna realised that all his talk, a moment earlier, about planning a *proper* cruise, *just you and me,* had been just that – *talk.* He would have said anything just so he could be on his way.

He doesn't love me anymore.

Lorna knew she should be sitting there, bawling her eyes out, but all she could think was that this was her mother's fault. *If she'd just let me stay at The Beach House with her, and raise my child there, I would never have met Andrew.*

Thinking of Briony, Lorna's eyes drifted to the leaflet containing the details of Briony's trip. All she wanted to do just then was speak to her daughter, hear her voice, and know she was okay.

Lorna closed the lid of her laptop. She didn't want to see Andrew or Susan's smiling faces staring back at her.

32

Lorna had just picked up her mobile phone, about to get in touch with the company running the trip her daughter was on, when she heard the doorbell ringing insistently and someone banging on the front door.

Andrew has come back to tell me he's sorry, he's not going on the cruise, and he and Susie are over!

Lorna rushed to the front door, wondering if that was what she really wanted. Would she want Andrew back after finding out about the affair, regardless of whether he gave her a grovelling apology and said it had been a mistake? How could an affair that had obviously gone on for that long be a mistake? It struck her that it wasn't just a fling. *They had plans.*

As she approached the front door, she realised it couldn't be Andrew – he had a key. She instantly recognised who it was – Freddie.

Her first thought was that he'd come round because Briony had been in touch. *Oh, wouldn't that be wonderful if, unlike Angel, he's going to sit with me, have a cuppa, and chat about Briony's trip?* It was just what she needed.

She opened the front door, smiling in anticipation, until she saw Freddie's face. 'Hi Freddie. Is everything all right?'

Unusually for Freddie, she didn't get a smile or even a hello. Instead, he barged in, looking about him. 'Where's Angel?'

'She's not in. She popped out. I think she'll be back soon.'

'I'll wait.' He started up the stairs.

'Her door is locked.'

Freddie whirled around. 'Well, do you have a key?'

'Um, yes.' Lorna didn't know whether she was doing the right thing, but she handed it to him.

He started back up the stairs.

'Would you like a cup of tea?' she asked, hoping he'd stop to chat.

He paused on the stairs and shook his head without turning around.

'Is everything all right?' She called after him again as he took the stairs two at a time. She'd noticed a letter in his hand. 'Is it about Briony?'

She heard the key in the lock and the door slam shut upstairs.

❖

Lorna was on the phone to the company that ran the research trip, on hold, waiting to speak to a representative. The music on the end of the line stopped. She heard a message asking her to continue to hold. She'd tried to contact Briony on her mobile phone, but it was either switched off or there was no signal. It just went straight to voicemail.

She heard a key in the front door. This time she didn't imagine it was Andrew. He'd be in the airport right now, probably sitting in the departure lounge, waiting to board his flight, looking forward to seeing Susie. She grimaced at the thought.

'Oh, goodness – it must be Angel.' Lorna leapt out of her seat and rushed to the front door. She'd handed Freddie the key to Angel's room. She hoped Angel wasn't angry or upset with her over that.

Lorna caught Angel in the hall, carrying an armful of Oxford University library books, before she walked up the stairs. Lorna lowered her mobile phone. 'Angel, I'm so sorry.'

'What is it?' Angel asked.

'Freddie turned up. He wanted to speak to you. He seemed … upset. So I gave him a key to your room.'

'You did what?'

'Sorry, he just seemed so desperate to speak to you. He said he wanted to wait. Upstairs.'

Angel looked at Lorna wide-eyed. 'Did he say what it was about?'

Lorna shook her head as she watched Angel dump her books on the sideboard by the door and start up the stairs.

'Would you like a cup of tea?' she asked, hoping she could pop upstairs with the tea as an excuse to find out what was going on.

Angel paused on the stairs and shook her head.

'Is everything all right?' she called after Angel as she took the stairs two at a time. 'Is it about Briony?' Lorna asked for the second time that morning.

She stood at the bottom of the stairs, heard the creak of the door as Angel opened it, and then heard Freddie's agitated voice – normally so polite and carefree – exclaim, 'Angel, do you know anything about this letter from Briony?'

'For goodness' sake, keep your voice down! Otherwise her mum will find out.'

The door slammed shut.

Find out what? Lorna wondered what on earth was going on. She slowly turned around, the phone to her ear, desperate to talk to someone about Briony's trip.

She silently berated herself for listening to Andrew instead of following her own gut instinct. Now she wished she'd got in touch sooner. Something was going on. It had been two weeks without any word. It sounded as though Freddie and Angel had received texts from Briony, and now Freddie had a letter, and she had a feeling it had something to do with her trip.

'Ah, hello. Thank god!' Lorna raced into the kitchen and closed the door so that she couldn't be overheard. She quickly explained what was going on: that her daughter had joined one of their organised trips two weeks earlier.

'What do you mean, you can't give out details about people on the trip? I'm talking about *my* daughter. Look, I haven't heard from her, and I just want to check she's okay.'

Lorna rolled her eyes at their reply. 'Yes, I know she's an adult, but it's the first time Briony has been away from home on her own, and I just need to find out about the trip, that there's been no … hitches.'

The young guy on the end of the phone appeared understanding. 'Can I just put you on hold for a moment?'

'Of course.' Lorna was just relieved he hadn't put the phone down. 'My daughter's name is Briony,' she repeated, hopeful he'd return with some news – good news, just to put her mind at rest, even if she couldn't actually speak to her daughter.

The wait seemed interminable.

Finally, he came back on the line. 'Can you hold just a moment longer? Sorry but there seems to be an anomaly.'

'A what?' But he was gone again, and that annoying music was blaring in her ear while she was on hold.

❖

Do you know about this?' Freddie paced back and forth in front of Angel. He stopped, hands on hips, to look at her.

Angel sat on the bed, eyeing him. 'Do I know about what?'

'This!' He pointed an irritated finger at the letter he'd thrust into her hands.

Angel shook her head. 'I don't want to read your personal mail, Freddie.'

'It's from Briony!' Freddie put both hands on the top of his head, and closed his eyes. 'This cannot be happening.'

Angel stared at him, wondering what the hell was in the letter. She knew all she had to do was read it to find out, but she was afraid to do that. She had already guessed that Briony had written to him to tell him she was pregnant. Now she had a dilemma. When was she going to own up that she already knew? The last thing she wanted to do was lose their friendship. But now she felt she had been put in the middle of a conflict between her two best friends. She had never wanted to take sides. That was the reason she'd fallen out with Briony before she'd left for Suffolk. Angel had wanted her to tell Freddie what was going on – she felt he deserved to know.

And now here he was, having received the news in a letter.

Angel breathed a sigh and slowly shook her head from side to side. Briony should have told him in person. The thing she didn't get, though, was why he was so upset about it.

Freddie opened his eyes and caught her shaking her head. 'You know something, don't you?'

Angel dropped her eyes to study her fingernails.

'She told you she's breaking up with me – didn't she?'

Angel looked up abruptly 'I'm sorry – what?'

'Did you know she was intending to go away and write me a letter?' Freddie studied her face. 'Oh! You didn't know either!'

Angel was lost for words. The absolute last thing she expected was that Briony would go away and decide to end it with Freddie. She'd had no inkling. What the hell had happened in Suffolk?

Freddie sat down on the bed next to her. 'I can't believe it.'

'Neither can I.'

Angel looked at the letter. 'May I read it?'

'That's why I gave it to you. Go right ahead.'

Angel started reading the letter, but she was almost immediately interrupted.

'Why does she want to start a new life in Suffolk? I mean – what's there?'

Angel replied, 'Her grandmother's house.'

'Yeah – so?'

'I joked with her that her grandmother might have written to her because she was intending to leave her The Beach House.'

'Yeah – so?' repeated Freddie. 'That's very nice, and all that, but why would she want to live there? Our lives are here, in Oxford.'

Angel read the short letter. There was no mention of anything else – just that she didn't see a future for them, and she wanted to stay living in Suffolk. Angel frowned. So, she still hadn't told him.

'There's something more, isn't there?' Freddie searched her face. 'Oh, no. She's met someone else. What has she told you since she's been away?'

'Nothing, honestly.'

He studied her intently. Angel looked away.

'But there is something else, isn't there?' Freddie suddenly started to cry.

'Oh, no, Freddie. Don't do that.' Angel turned to him, put her arms around his shoulders, drawing him close. He cried into her shoulder. 'What am I going to do?'

Angel drew back, put her hands gently on his cheeks and lifted his head, so their eyes met. 'You're going to get through this. We both are.' Angel suddenly felt like crying too. Like Freddie, she felt as though she'd lost her best friend. She might have joked about her inheriting a rather lovely beach house, but she'd thought that if that happened, Briony would be lucky, and would make it a lovely holiday home. She had not expected Briony to want to start a new life there. She had thought Briony would come back, and that they'd make up after falling out. Like Freddie, she was wondering what would she do without her.

Quite unexpectedly, Angel's tough exterior slipped completely, and she began to cry too.

'Oh, no, Angel, I shouldn't have come round and dumped all my problems on you. Now I've upset you.'

'Don't say that.' Angel shook her head. 'You're my best friend too, and I love you.'

Then something happened that neither had anticipated. Before Angel or Freddie knew what was happening, they kissed.

Freddie drew back first, leaving Angel sitting there, her eyes closed, wishing that moment, that kiss, was frozen in time and would last forever.

'I'm sorry, Angel. I don't know what came over me, I'm a

mess …' He flung his arms wide, and knocked over the lamp on the side-table. It smashed on the floor.

Angel touched his lips, the colour rising in her cheeks. 'Don't be sorry, Freddie. I'm not.'

❖

Lorna was still on hold when she thought she heard raised voices upstairs, and something smash on the floor. 'What is going on up there?' she wondered aloud. It sounded as though Freddie and Angel were having a fight.

She raced up the stairs and burst into the room to find Angel and Freddie sitting next to each other on the bed, Freddie's arm around Angel's shoulder. They turned their heads in her direction, looking surprised.

Lorna stood stock still, staring at them. She held up her hand before either of them could try to explain what they had been sitting there doing – Briony's two best friends. It was obvious. After all, where had that smudge of Angel's bright red lipstick on Freddie's lips come from?

For the second time that morning, Lorna put her hand to her mouth in shock. The whole world seemed to have gone to pot in one horrible morning. She closed her eyes for a moment, hoping the image of the two of them kissing would go away, but it didn't. When she opened her eyes, they were both still sitting there, looking as guilty as hell.

Freddie said, 'It's not what you think.'

Lorna ignored him and looked at Angel. 'So, this is why you've had a falling-out, you and Briony. Over Freddie!'

'How did you know we'd had a falling-out?'

Freddie turned to Angel. 'What's she talking about?'

Lorna walked out and slammed the door shut. She reopened it just as Freddie was saying, 'What did you two argue about?'

Lorna said, 'Angel, I want you to pack your things and leave my house – *now*!'

She heard Angel call her name as she thundered down the stairs. When she reached the bottom, she heard a voice on her mobile. She put it to her ear. 'Tell me it's good news,' she said, seething at the young man who had put her on hold for what seemed like an age.

He asked Lorna a question. 'Are you sure you have the right company?'

Lorna raised her eyebrows. *Is he serious?* 'Of course I have. I've got the details she left right here.' She headed towards the kitchen, where she'd left them on the table.

'And the date she joined the trip is correct?'

'Yes, I saw her pack her suitcase with my own eyes – I know when she left.'

Lorna was about to step into the kitchen when she heard someone thundering down the stairs. She could hear Angel's voice. 'Freddie, we can figure this out. For goodness' sake, don't ask her mum.'

'I need to see Briony about this letter.'

Lorna raised her eyebrows when she heard Freddie mention a letter. She was only half-listening to the young man on the end of the phone when he said, 'You weren't aware that your daughter withdrew from the trip?'

That got Lorna's attention. 'No, no you've got that wrong. There must be some mistake your end. She'd never do that. There's just no way she'd withdraw from a trip of a lifetime. It was all she could talk about …'

Lorna was just saying this as Freddie burst into the kitchen. He held up a letter, and said, 'Tell me where Briony's grandmother lives – exactly.'

Lorna, still on the phone, said, 'I'm sorry, what?'

Angel appeared behind him. She grabbed his arm in an attempt to pull him out of the kitchen and back in the hall. 'Freddie, Freddie, I need to tell you something.'

'What are you doing? Will you let go of my arm.'

'Freddie – she didn't tell her parents that—' Angel stopped short. 'Freddie, don't ask Lorna.'

'Ask me what?'

'What I said.' Freddie looked at her. 'Where is Briony's grandmother?'

'Why on earth do you want to know that?'

Freddie turned and looked at Angel.

Angel stepped forward, looked at her hands, avoiding eye contact and said in a small voice, 'Because that's where he'll find Briony.'

Lorna dropped the phone.

33

'Look, people are arriving for the party!' announced Emily.

'Already?' Briony glanced out of the kitchen window to see a line of people snaking their way up the beach towards The Beach House. She had invited everyone for lunch, expecting the beach party to go on into the afternoon, and hopefully the early evening when it got dark – weather-dependent. She was looking forward to switching on the string of pretty lanterns that Troy and Sebastian had helped set up, running from the outbuilding to The Beach House.

She checked the time. They were early. 'Where will they all sit?'

Briony, Emily and Clarissa, who had been in the kitchen putting the finishing touches to the party food, turned at the sound of the doorbell.

Sebastian popped his head in the kitchen. 'A van has turned up on the driveway. I think it's the company supplying the deckchairs.'

'Oh, thank goodness!' Briony raced to the front door and waved at the two guys in the van. As one of the men got out, she asked him to take the chairs around the side of the house and set them up on the beach. Briony raced through the house to the back door, wanting to be there to welcome her guests. They had all been advised to park in the small village car park by The Beach Café and walk from there, if they didn't mind. The parking was limited outside The Beach House, especially with Troy's truck there. And it was just as well they hadn't parked there, given the large van that had just turned up.

When Briony returned to the kitchen, Emily said, 'Have you got your phone ready?'

For a moment, Briony didn't know what she was talking about.

'You know, you said you were going to take lots of photos, and then print them off for a photo album to show your grandmother?'

Briony touched Emily's arm and smiled. She had forgotten. 'Oh, yes. Of course.' Briony and Emily stepped out of the kitchen and walked on to the beach.

The company were arranging the deckchairs in a large circle around a campfire that Troy had just lit.

Clarissa stepped outside too. 'Dad!' she waved. Peter was walking up the beach towards them, holding hands with her two children.

As soon as the children saw her, they let go of his hands and ran into her embrace. Briony smiled. Along with Peter, there was also a young man. She noticed Clarissa stop and tentatively smile at the young man before bringing her kids over to meet Briony.

Clarissa introduced her two very polite children – a boy and a girl.

'Who's the guy?' Briony asked.

'Oh, you mentioned that it was okay to bring a plus one.'

'Of course. But you didn't mention that you'd started dating someone.'

Clarissa smiled. 'It's true. I have.'

Briony watched her children run back to their grandfather and the young man. They each took one of the young man's hands, pulling him towards the deck chairs.

'Well, I'm pleased for you, Clarissa.' Briony stared at the children, thinking of her own situation. If Troy knew that she was pregnant, would he still want to be with her, and her child, as much as Clarissa's date did? He didn't seem to have a problem with Clarissa being a single mum. 'I must say, he seems really good around your children.'

'He should do – he's their dad.'

'Pardon me?' She stared at Clarissa. 'Is that your ex?'

'Yes. We've been dilly-dallying with a divorce, but neither of us would commit to sign the paperwork. We decided to make another go of it – well, I did. It's what he has been after for some time.'

'That's just wonderful. What was it that made your mind up to try again?'

Clarissa turned to Briony. 'You, to be honest.'

'Me?' Briony was taken aback. 'How so?'

'Well, you and Troy actually.'

Briony didn't understand.

Clarissa said, 'You two reminded me what it was like to be so young and in love. We were like you when we first met.'

'Like me?'

'Yes – you and Troy.'

'Me and Troy?'

'Now, don't try and deny it. Everyone sees the way you look

at each other. It just takes me back. I thought, why throw all that away? If it's still there, that spark, the love we had for each other, before the children – before responsibilities, and inevitably rows over money, reared their heads. The daily grind just got in the way. Now I realise that in the midst of taking care of the kids, and our jobs, and the roof over our heads, we forgot the most important thing we need to take care of.'

Briony asked, 'Which is?'

'Each other – of course. We neglected our relationship. At least, I did.' She put a hand on Briony's forearm. 'Don't let that happen to you guys.'

Briony stared at her. 'It's not that simple, Clarissa.'

'You're talking about the pregnancy.'

Briony nodded. 'Of course I am.'

'Well, make time for each other. I'll baby-sit.' She looked at the outbuilding. 'I bet you were both there last night, planning moving in. You'll need to finish off the plans, you know, for a mezzanine bedroom and shower room.' Clarissa wagged a finger when Briony opened her mouth. 'Don't deny it. We're friends. You can tell me anything, and my lips will be sealed – I promise.'

Briony grimaced. 'I need to tell you something, Clarrissa.'

'What is it?'

'Not here.' She took Clarissa's arm and led her towards the outbuilding, away from The Beach House, where Willow and Clarissa's children were headed for some party food.

Briony glanced at all the people arriving for the party, taking seats on the deckchairs around the fire. She recognised Thea, who wasn't with her father, Henry, but who had brought her partner, along with her nephew, who lived with them.

Emily and Joss had arrived, along with her mum, Cheryl,

and dad, Gerald, whom Briony had yet to be introduced to. Gerald knew Peter, and they struck up a conversation as they walked over to the barbecue that Sam had brought and set up on the beach. Sam and Sebastian were manning the barbecue, cooking sausages for hot dogs and burgers to have in buns.

Sebastian gave Briony a friendly little wave with the spatula as she passed by. Sam didn't, Briony noticed. She didn't really want him there, but he was Troy's work colleague, who had helped on the outbuilding, and she'd invited plenty of people she didn't know – partners, and friends of friends – so it wasn't like she had a choice regarding Sam. She could tell his frostiness towards her hadn't thawed since the day they'd first met.

Briony ignored him, and noticed that The Gossip Girls had arrived with Thea. Briony had known that Mabel and Marjorie would be there. They wouldn't miss a get-together and a chance to gossip about it afterwards. She noticed that Thea's partner had brought out two kitchen chairs for them. She hadn't thought about the fact that the deckchairs might not be suitable for everyone. She imagined that if the two elderly ladies did sit down in them, they'd struggle to get up.

Before she stepped into the outbuilding, she waved at Lili, who ran The Potting Shed. She had arrived with her partner and his two children, William and Maisie, whom she understood were from his previous relationships. She was so pleased they'd all come, and that Willow would have children to play with.

Looking at the blended families there –Thea bringing up her nephew, and Lili with her partner and his children – she realised that perhaps she was worrying out of hand about telling Troy that she was pregnant. Maybe he'd be okay with her *and* the baby. After all, Sebastian had taken on another man's child, and the mum hadn't even been around. *But Troy isn't Sebastian*, she reminded herself. And besides, when had she made up her mind that she was staying? That morning, when she'd fallen asleep with Troy on the sofa and had realised that her life would never be complete without him in it.

She glanced at Sebastian, who was flipping over a burger, before she stepped into the outbuilding. He looked up, caught her glancing his way again, and gave her a big smile and another friendly wave.

Clarissa saw that too. 'I know what you're going to tell me.'

Briony pulled her into the outbuilding and shut the door.

Clarissa exclaimed, 'It's Sebastian – isn't it?'

'What's Sebastian?' Briony didn't understand the question.

'You're going to tell me you've fallen for Troy's dad.'

Briony stared at her. 'Not fallen for him, no, but we get on so well; have done from the moment we'd first met.'

She hadn't told Clarissa that he was her mum's ex. And because Briony knew she looked so much like her mother – her mini-me – it was little wonder Sebastian was drawn to her. She didn't think about him all the time in the way she thought about Troy. But they had certainly hit it off immediately, especially over their shared passion for the ocean.

'He must be twice your age. Tell me it isn't true.' Clarissa studied her face.

Briony flopped down on the sofa. 'Oh, Clarissa, I'm so confused.'

'Oh, so this *is* about Sebastian.'

It wasn't at first, thought Briony, but now Clarissa had brought him up … 'I love chatting to Sebastian. I just feel a remarkable affinity with him.'

Clarissa sighed heavily.

'I can't help it, Clarissa.' She loved being in Troy's company, watching the sunrises together, always hoping that she could do that with him forever. But she couldn't deny she loved talking to Sebastian, spending time in his company, although she still didn't feel attracted to him. Even so, she looked at Clarissa, and said, 'What am I going to do?'

Clarissa turned to face her. 'Look, it's your hormones. I was a mess when I was pregnant with my two – didn't know whether I was coming or going.'

Despite everything, Briony managed a smile. 'I feel that way too. I mean I had written Freddie a letter, explaining how I felt—'

'About Troy and Sebastian?'

'Oh, no, not about them, about the fact that I see my life here now, on the Suffolk Coast.'

'And what will he think of you bringing up his child here?'

Briony bit her bottom lip.

Clarissa clasped her hands together. 'He still doesn't know?'

Briony shook her head from side to side.

'You didn't tell him in the letter?'

'Well, no. And that's the thing. I didn't send the letter telling him that it was over between us.'

'You didn't send it?'

Briony shook her head.

'Crumbs, I hope he hasn't got an invite to the party instead.'

Briony rolled her eyes. She'd had the same conversation with Emily. 'Would I do that? I mean, I know I'm all mixed up, but there's no way I'd let on about the party. I'm sure he wouldn't want to celebrate my decision to live here on the Suffolk Coast. And besides, I haven't told Troy either,' she said in a small voice, 'about me being pregnant.'

Clarissa stared at her.

'That's what I dragged you in here to tell you – that Troy doesn't know. I haven't told him yet.'

Clarissa took a deep breath, and rubbed her face with her hands. 'So, let me get this straight: your partner, Freddie, doesn't know about the baby, and you haven't told Troy you're pregnant either?'

Briony shook her head, staring at her fingernails, suddenly feeling embarrassed about the mess she'd made of everything.

'And you didn't send the letter.'

Briony didn't want to tell her that she'd lost it on the beach. Although she had put a stamp on it, she'd decided not to post it. The fact that she'd lost it was incidental. She had the rest of the book of stamps, and plenty of writing paper and envelopes in the old bureau upstairs in The Beach House. She could easily rewrite the letter.

Clarrisa took her hands. She said, 'Are you sure it's over between you and Freddie?'

'He's the father of my child.'

'That's not what I was asking, Briony. It's not a reason to stay with him. I can imagine that you love it here. You've met new friends. This place would be the perfect place to bring up a child, and I'm guessing your life with Freddie wouldn't be here, but back in Oxford.'

Briony didn't dispute that.

'So, the question I'm asking is: do you love Freddie? Because if you do, then you'd live with him in Timbuktu – if he asked you.'

Briony stared at her.

'And by the same reasoning, he'd find a way to move his life here, if he truly loved you, and it's what you really wanted.' Clarissa patted her hand affectionately. 'So, do you think not sending that letter was your subconscious telling you that you might still be in love with him, and don't really want to break it off until you've both worked things out?'

'I—'

Briony was interrupted by the outbuilding door opening.

'There you are! I've been looking for you all over.' Clarissa's ex stood in the doorway, smiling.

Clarissa bounced out of her seat. 'The guests are not meant to see inside the outbuilding until we cut the ribbon.' She shooed him outside.

'Oh, I got a sneak preview then.' He grinned before he closed the door.

Briony turned to Clarissa before they both stepped outside. 'I need to tell Troy the truth.'

'About the baby?'

Briony nodded.

Clarrisa squeezed her hand. 'That will be a start.'

But the start of what? thought Briony. If this was what it was like being pregnant, where she just felt so confused, and all over the place, then she never wanted to go through it again.

Briony opened the door and discovered that most of her guests had arrived. Someone had brought along a large music speaker, playing some songs from the playlist on their phone. *What we need*, thought Briony, *is some live music.* She had a bizarre thought; it was a shame her parents weren't there – her dad with his violin, and her mum playing the piano.

She looked around, belatedly realising that although everyone else seemed to be having a great time, she wasn't. How could she? They were lovely people who'd come, lots of new friends, and soon-to-be friends, but this just felt wrong. It wasn't the same without her family there too, her mum and dad, and especially her grandmother. And her best friends. She was thinking of Angel. But was she including Freddie too?

34

Briony glanced over at Clarissa, who was putting the red ribbon back across the door after they'd removed it to get inside. As she walked amongst the crowd, looking for Troy, friends congratulated her on the completion of the outbuilding and thanked her for inviting them to a wonderful beach party.

Briony remembered to take photos. There were a few people she didn't recognise who didn't appear to be with any of the people she'd invited. She imagined that they had wandered up the beach to see what the music and festivities were about. Briony invited them to help themselves to food and non-alcoholic drinks. They were there, and there was plenty of food, courtesy of the Wolf Girls Club, who had brought the party nibbles, and Sam and Sebastian, who had brought along all the barbecue food.

Briony glanced at her watch. It was now mid-afternoon. She was looking forward to the sun setting and the lanterns being lit. But first she needed to find Troy.

Up ahead, she spotted him standing with Sam, their backs to her. As she approached, she overheard Sam say to Troy, 'When are you going to tell her?'

'I don't want to.'

'What if she finds out?'

'Hey, Briony – how's things?'

Briony whirled around at the sound of a voice behind her. 'Ah, Peter. Are you enjoying the party?'

'I am. It's wonderful. You know it reminds me of those parties your great-grandparents used to throw right here at The Beach House.'

'You went to one of those?' Briony eyed Sam and Troy, who still had their backs to her, but she could no longer hear their conversation as they walked over to the barbecue stand.

'I did indeed. I wasn't really a guest, just a friend of a friend of Blythe's.'

'Oh really?' Briony raised her eyebrows. 'Did you know Fr—'

'Hey – where did the boat go?' Peter suddenly exclaimed.

Briony pursed her lips. 'So, I take it that it wasn't you who shifted it?'

Peter adamantly shook his head. 'Nope. I left it here with the tarpaulin over it.'

'Yes, that's what I said to Clarissa when she noticed it was gone.'

'So, where did it go?'

'It's a mystery, I'm afraid.' Briony's eyes roved over to where she'd last seen Troy. He wasn't with Sam at the barbecue. Glancing around, she spotted him walking into The Beach House. She turned to Peter. 'Excuse me, there's something I need to do.'

As Briony walked over to the kitchen door, smiling and nodding at the guests, she did notice that one person she'd invited was missing. So far, Reggie hadn't made an appearance. He'd promised he'd come. And he had said that her grandmother's piano was due for a tune.

Briony opened the kitchen door, expecting to see Troy helping himself to the party food. He wasn't in the kitchen or the lounge. She called out his name as she walked up the stairs, wondering if he'd gone to use the bathroom. At the top of the stairs, she noticed that the bathroom was free – the door was wide open.

She was about to make her way back down the stairs, thinking he must have gone out front to his van, when the door to the small bedroom where she slept opened. Troy walked out, looking surprised to see her at the top of the stairs.

'Ah, I came up to use the bathroom.' He looked flustered. 'Wrong room.'

Briony frowned. Anyone could see the bathroom at the top of the stairs, especially as the door was wide open. Perhaps he was trying to find her, and thought he'd see her amongst the crowd of people if he popped upstairs and looked out of the window.

She was about to ask him when she thought, *What does it matter?* She had something else on her mind. This was her chance, the only time she could speak to him today when they were alone.

'Look, Troy, things are not going to work out.'

'What are you talking about?'

Briony took a deep breath. 'You and me.'

'I don't understand.' Troy shook his head. 'How come?'

She looked through the open doorway of the small bedroom, with the view of the beach, the sea, and the renovated outbuilding. How had she thought she could stay there, with Troy? The fact that she'd kept her secret, had basically lied to him from the beginning, was probably going to sound the death knell for what might have been between them.

For the first time since she'd arrived, she wished she'd never overheard her mum and dad rowing about the letters that had come from her grandmother. She'd then never have found the letter in the bin, read it, and come here, and met Troy. And Sebastian. And lied to everyone. She'd be home right now, and Freddie and her parents would know she was pregnant.

She knew it was time to tell everyone the truth. Briony looked at Troy, and decided telling the truth started here.

She was just about to tell him she was pregnant when he said, 'Oh, I know what this is about.' He followed her gaze out of the window. 'I saw Sebastian waving at you.'

Briony looked at him, confused. 'So?'

Troy stepped towards her. 'Do I really have to spell it out?' He did it anyway. 'I've seen you two together, talking animatedly. Seriously, Briony, you do not want to get involved with Sebastian.'

'By *getting involved*, do you mean like a relationship?'

'Of course I to do. You do not want to go down that road. He's got a string of failed relationships behind him. Everyone leaves him, and some even leave him holding the baby.'

'You're talking about Willow.'

'Her mother left him when she found out. She returned to her high-flying job as an international buyer for a fashion chain. A child didn't really fit in with her career – she travels a lot to trade fairs and exhibitions abroad, so Sebastian is raising her. She visits Willow whenever she's back in England. I always know when she's been, because Willow has lots of new presents from her mother's travels around the world.'

Briony had always wondered about Willow's mother, but just then her focus was on Sebastian. 'Found out what?'

'That there were three people in their relationship. You'll find that out too, soon enough.'

Briony looked at him, perplexed.

'I'm convinced his heart belongs to another – god knows who, though.'

'The person who holds the key to his heart,' Briony mumbled under her breath.

'I'm sorry, what?'

Briony was thinking of the shell box. 'Oh, never mind. Look, I told you before, there's no reason for you to feel jealous of Sebastian. But there's something I want … need to tell you. Not about Sebastian,' she quickly added.

'Save it!' Troy headed back down the stairs, leaving her standing on the landing outside the bedroom door.

'Troy!'

She heard him open the front door. She rushed down the stairs, intending to stop him from leaving. She heard Troy exclaim, 'Oh, sorry, didn't see you there.' He stepped aside to let someone in, then closed the front door behind him.

At the bottom of the stairs, Briony came face to face with Reggie.

'Oh, Reggie, I'm so pleased you came.' She hugged him, with one eye on the door. 'Look, I must nip outside—'

'I'm not really here on a social visit.'

Briony was about to open the front door. She looked at Reggie. 'But you've come to my party …'

'I'm here to tune your grandmother's piano. It's long overdue, and I wanted to get it done for her before she comes home.'

Briony smiled at him. 'You're a good friend, Reggie. I'll be sure to tell her when I visit her next. At least stay for some party nibbles, or a burger from the barbecue. I'm afraid the party is non-alcoholic drinks only, though.' She was sure Reggie wouldn't mind.

'I'm not in the mood.'

'Oh, you soon will be. Just step out on to the beach. It's quite something. So many people came. It's a lovely atmosphere.'

Reggie looked her up and down. 'Well, if it's so lovely, what are you doing in here?'

Briony was used to Reggie's sarcasm. It was normally friendly, and well-meaning, but this time his tone was different, brittle. There was an edge to his voice.

He immediately dropped his eyes to the floor. 'Sorry, that was uncalled for.'

Briony touched his arm. 'Reggie, what's going on?'

He shook his head. 'You've got enough on your plate with your grandmother being ill. I can't burden you with this.'

Briony linked her arm in his. 'Oh, yes you can. What are friends for?' All these people she'd got to know had gone out of their way to help her out. Now, it was her turn.

35

'I can't believe we've done all this journey, virtually tail-gating her, and you lost her just as we turned into the village!'

Freddie glanced at Angel. 'It's not my fault a tractor pulled out in front of me. I couldn't even see her car in front of it, let alone get past the damn thing! Why couldn't she just tell us the address when I asked?'

Angel rolled her eyes. 'Oh, like she was going to do that, catching us in the attic, thinking you've been cheating on her daughter with me.'

Freddie rolled his eyes too. 'I'd forgotten about that!'

Angel looked at him. 'Really? Already?'

He glanced at her. 'No, actually. For some reason, I can't get that kiss out of my head.' He looked ahead at the road, saying to himself, 'I don't get why.'

Angel stared at him. For her part, she knew why she couldn't get it out of her mind. She'd been in love with him since the moment she'd set eyes on him, even though she'd thought she couldn't stand him – to begin with.

Angel got her phone out of her handbag.

Freddie glanced at her. 'What are you doing?'

Angel wanted to warn Briony that her mum was on her way. She'd sent several texts, but it didn't appear that Briony had read them. Perhaps mobile reception wasn't great at The Beach House, or she was too busy to read her texts. Angel looked at Freddie crossly. You didn't have to ask her mum where her mother's house is. It's called The Beach House, in Dunwich Heath.'

'But we don't know where that is – exactly. You don't know the address.'

'No, but we could have asked someone when we arrived in Dunwich Heath, instead of asking Lorna where her mother lives in Dunwich and giving the game away that it's where we were going to find Briony. You've lost Lorna's car anyway. I'm sure someone would give us directions in the village.'

'But what I don't understand, Angel, is why Briony never told her mum where she was. She looked so shocked when you told her.'

Angel nodded, not letting on that she had known all along not only that Briony had kept her whereabouts from her mum, but the reason she'd done so.

'She must have pretended she was still going on the trip to the Galapagos Islands. I don't get why.'

Angel stared out of the window, nervously biting a fingernail.

Freddie glanced at her again. 'You're quiet all of a sudden. What are you not telling me?'

❖

'Please, Reggie. I want to help.'

'I don't think you can help with this.'

'At least tell me what's going on.'

Reggie said, 'I got this letter.' He was about to hand it to

Briony when the phone rang. 'Is that your mobile? Aren't you going to answer it, Briony?'

'No, it isn't my mobile.' It was the house phone behind her in the hallway. 'I want to know what's up with you.'

'It might be important. Go on, answer the phone.' He looked forlornly at the letter in his hands. 'This problem isn't going away any time soon.'

Briony insisted that Reggie hand over the letter so she could read it as soon as she got off the phone.

'I'll wait in the kitchen.'

She eyed Reggie as she picked up the phone in the hall. 'Hello?' She listened to the stranger on the phone as she watched Reggie through the open doorway. He sat down at the kitchen table and stared at the plans for the outbuilding.

Luna immediately appeared by Reggie's side. Briony had had to keep her inside during the party. She knew Luna would love to make friends with all those people outside, but not everyone was a dog lover, and she didn't want Luna frightening people who had not met her yet because of her size and appearance.

Reggie gave her a friendly pat on the head. He smiled as he made a fuss of the dog.

Briony spoke down the phone. 'No, Blythe isn't here. This is her granddaughter. May I be of help?' Briony frowned. 'You're the firm who drew up the plans for the outbuilding?' Briony imagined that a firm of architects might have drawn up the plans. Troy hadn't mentioned they were his. What do you mean, *does my grandmother still want to go ahead?*

She listened as the person on the line said, 'We've been waiting to hear back from Blythe. We have some dates we can pencil her in to do the job.'

'You were going to do the work?' Briony didn't understand. 'But there's a guy who has been working from your plans already.'

'What guy?'

'What do you mean, *what guy?*' Briony glanced at Reggie, who was looking her way, raising his eyebrows.

Briony replied. 'Troy – of course.'

'There's no one by that name who works for us.'

'Ah.' Briony realised what had happened. Her grandmother had chosen to go with another company, the one Troy worked for, to renovate the outbuilding. Her grandmother obviously hadn't told them. That was awkward. 'Look, I'm sorry, but my grandmother chose to go with someone else, obviously.'

'Well, this is all rather odd.'

Briony winced. They would think that, seeing as they'd drawn up the plans and had assumed the job was in the bag. Briony apologised again because she didn't know what else to say. 'I have to go now.'

'I will have to speak to my manager regarding what will happen with her deposit money.'

Briony paused. 'Deposit money?'

'It's rather a surprise to hear she employed somebody else to do the work. You see, she said that she wanted us, and only us to do the job. She gave us a deposit as a retainer for our services, so the moment we had some free dates we could arrange with her to start. I'll speak to my manager when he comes back from holiday. We'll be in touch.'

'Okay,' Briony said in a small voice. She slowly replaced the phone and stared out of the kitchen window at the outbuilding. If her grandmother hadn't hired Troy, then what was he doing there? Briony recalled that when she'd discovered Troy on her grandmother's property, she'd just assumed he was there to do the job. If he wasn't, then why the hell had he agreed to do it?

'What is it, Briony?' Reggie asked. 'Who was that?'

'It was the company who drew up the plans for the outbuilding. Something isn't right.'

'How so?' Reggie asked.

Briony happened to glance at Reggie's letter, which she still had in her hand. 'What the hell …?' She took a closer look, just to be sure she wasn't mistaken. She stared at it, dumbfounded.

Reggie rose from his seat. 'What's wrong?'

Briony joined him in the kitchen. 'This letter – what's it about?'

Reggie breathed a huge sigh. 'I got it this morning. It's from a solicitor on behalf of the owner of the music shop. They've hiked the rent on the shop – massively. It's extortionate.' He rubbed his forehead in consternation.

Briony stared at him. 'Wait, why?'

'I asked myself the same question when I first opened the letter – why now?' He sighed in resignation. 'I guess that after all these years on a peppercorn rent, the shop felt like it had been forgotten, and it's come to the attention of some eagle-eyed accountant or something.'

'Oh, my goodness, don't excuse them for doing this. They must realise they'll put you out of business, hiking your rent like that!'

Reggie shrugged. 'Why would they care? It's business.'

'But is that even legal, to raise it so much all at once?' She looked at Reggie. 'Have you seen Joss about this?'

He shook his head. 'There are people with far worse troubles than me. I wouldn't want to take away Joss's time from someone else who needs his help.'

Briony was angry with him – didn't that just sum up his generation? Always thinking of others. She looked at the letter in her hand. 'This letter is from the same firm of solicitors behind the letters being sent to my grandmother. That's why I was shocked when I first saw it.'

'Are you sure?'

Briony nodded. 'Oh, yes. One hundred percent.'

Reggie looked at her in surprise. 'I don't understand … what is going on?'

'Either this is the biggest coincidence, or the person after The Beach House owns your shop.'

'You think they're after ousting me and getting their hands on Cobblers Yard too?'

Briony looked at Reggie thoughtfully. 'No, I don't think that's it.'

'What are you thinking?'

What Briony was thinking was far more disturbing. Joss's talk of grudges came to mind. She put her hand to her mouth in surprise. 'I think the person behind these letters found out Blythe's granddaughter is working for you, and decided to get back at anybody helping me.'

She swore, surprising Reggie. 'I am so sorry. You've got this because of me.'

'I don't see how that can be the case.'

Briony did. It made perfect sense. She explained, 'You said yourself that the owner seemed to have forgotten you, while rents in the area have gone up over time.'

Reggie sighed wistfully. 'Well, I suppose it had to catch up with me sooner or later.'

Briony held up the letter. 'But don't you see, Reggie? Everything was okay until I came along and started working for you.'

Briony and Reggie were standing in the kitchen, staring at one another as it all sank in, when they were interrupted.

'Briony?'

She turned around at the sound of Troy's voice, surprised he was still there. 'I thought you'd left?'

'No. I've been sitting outside in my van trying to figure out what to do.' He stepped forward, holding out his hand. 'Look, I want to work things out. I don't want to lose you, but there's something you should know. Something I need to tell you.'

Briony stared at him. She knew what this was about – the outbuilding. 'Not now, Troy. I need to find Joss.'

'Joss – why? What's going on?' Troy asked.

'Reggie has suddenly had his rent hiked.'

Troy looked at him. 'Why?'

'It's my fault.'

Troy turned to Briony. 'How can it be your fault?'

Reggie shook his head. 'It's not your fault, Briony.'

Behind them, the door opened, and Willow stepped into the kitchen. 'Troy, Daddy sent me to find you. He wants you to help at the barbecue.'

'Not now, Willow!'

Willow pursed her lips, stroked Luna, and retreated with Luna to the other end of the kitchen. She picked up a kitten and stood eyeing the adults as she held the kitten up to her face and stroked him.

'I wish Blythe was here now,' said Reggie. 'Perhaps she'd know what all this is about.'

Briony sighed. 'Me too.'

'How is she doing?' asked Reggie. 'Is she still in a coma?'

She nodded.

Troy said, 'Why didn't you tell me that your grandmother is in a coma?'

Briony turned to him, feeling guilty that she'd thought she couldn't trust him, or anyone, just because Joss had told her to keep Blythe's condition to herself in case it got back to whoever was behind the nasty solicitor's letters.

She looked at Troy. She could tell by his expression that he genuinely didn't know what was going on regarding Reggie and his rent hike.

'She had a stroke. I've been trying everything I can think of to make her wake up. I've even taken Luna into the hospital to visit her, but so far nothing has worked.' One thing she knew she hadn't tried was Blythe hearing her daughter's voice. Briony knew that was the last resort, and very soon she would have to contact her mum and tell her everything.

She was surprised the hospital hadn't been in touch with her mum; after all, she had given them Lorna's new mobile phone number. She'd been trying to prepare for the possibility that on one of her hospital visits, she'd find her mum there.

'Oh, Briony. I'm *so* sorry.'

She looked at Troy's face, full of concern, almost looking as though someone had died. 'Don't do that,' she said.

'I don't understand …'

'She's going to be fine, absolutely fine.' Briony swiftly turned to Reggie. 'Isn't she, Reggie?'

Reggie had also visited Blythe in hospital, bringing her flowers, and even playing a ditty on a violin. That hadn't worked.

She said it again, 'She's going to be fine – isn't she, Reggie?'

Reggie raised his eyebrows. 'Um, of course, of course.'

Briony ignored the look that passed between Reggie and Troy, getting the feeling that Reggie was just humouring her.

Briony changed the subject. 'We have to find Joss, tell him about the letter.'

'What letter?' asked Troy.

Briony really didn't want to get into all that right now. This wasn't the time. She passed the letter back to Reggie.

He held it up and told Troy, 'This letter is from the same firm of solicitors that have been sending letters to Briony's grandmother; whoever is behind these is after her house, her land. We think the same person or company who is behind the letters owns the shop; it can't be a coincidence.'

Briony rolled her eyes. She hadn't expected Reggie to tell Troy.

'Can I see it?'

Reggie handed it over.

'Troy, there isn't time to explain all this.' She watched Troy reading the letter, frowning. He looked up. 'What the hell!'

'Yeah, it's totally out of order,' commented Briony. 'Whoever they are, they must realise they'll put him out of business.'

'And out on the street,' added Reggie.

Briony and Troy turned to look at him in surprise.

'I live above the shop. It's my business *and* my home.'

It hadn't occurred to Briony that the shop was his home too. 'We must find Joss. Thank goodness he's at the party.'

36

Freddie said, 'Thank goodness we found Lorna! I mean, it's a lovely beach and all, but The Beach House can't literally be on the beach – can it? I hope she knows where she's going.'

'Of course she does.' Walking at a pace beside him, along the beach, Angel looked at Freddie, and added, 'Lucky that we stopped at the pub in the village, and the barman said to park at the beach car park and walk it.'

'Yeah, otherwise we wouldn't have found Lorna's car.'

'Or Lorna.' Angel pointed at Lorna, who was marching along a little way up the beach. 'We could catch up with her.'

Freddie shook his head. 'I don't think that's a good idea. We should hang back a bit, keep a little distance.'

Angel nodded. 'You're right.' They exchanged a knowing glance, aware that Lorna would not be happy to see either of them.

'Hey, look up ahead!' Freddie pointed.

'There's a lot of people.'

'I smell barbecue food.'

Angel glanced at Freddie. 'Me too. Is that a beach party?' She smiled. She was enjoying the walk along the beach, and the warm sunshine, but wished they were visiting under different circumstances.

She gave Freddie a sideways glance, wondering if she should tell him what was really going on with Briony – forewarn him. *But it's not my place to give away Briony's secret.* He had to hear it from Briony, Angel decided. Although she was afraid it would be the end of their friendship, the end of the possibility of something more, when he found out she'd known all along.

Angel didn't want to think about that. He'd know soon enough, if Briony was at The Beach House. Instead she said, 'They're lucky with the weather. Last of the Indian summer today, apparently.'

Freddie paused for a moment to look at her. 'Are you seriously talking about the weather right now?'

Angel shrugged. 'Just saying.'

They resumed walking, gaining on Lorna. 'Rather than talk about the weather, I'd like to talk about the elephant in the room,' said Freddie.

Angel knew what he was talking about – that kiss. 'I don't think now is the right time to talk about it.'

'I'm going to see Briony about this letter.'

'Yeah, that's my point. It's not the right time.'

'Well, it is – for me.'

Angel could feel his eyes on her as they walked along the beach.

He said, 'I'm confused.'

Angel wasn't – not at all, but she didn't let on. She said, 'It was just one kiss.'

'Yes, I know that!' Freddie sounded irritated. 'Didn't you feel something?'

Angel looked at the letter in Freddie's hand. 'I think you need to deal with that first.'

He looked at the letter too. 'Yeah, I guess so. It doesn't make sense. She seemed perfectly happy with me before she went away, then I get this completely out of the blue. And what's she doing here, anyway?'

Angel stared at Freddie, feeling uncomfortable.

Freddie continued, 'I know she said her grandmother had an op, and so I assumed she'd come here to look after her post-op. But now I've gone over that conversation in my mind, the one I had with Briony at the train station when I found out she wasn't going to the Galapagos Islands, I realise she didn't actually say much at all. I mean, it's a big deal that she gave up her trip to come here – right?'

Angel nodded.

'But something doesn't add up. For starters, why doesn't her mum know she's here?' Freddie paused. 'What is she doing here, really, Angel? I know you know something …'

Angel didn't dare look at Freddie; he'd already worked out in the car that there was something she wasn't telling him. Instead, she kept her eyes fixed dead ahead as they neared a crowd of people, some standing and chatting, others sitting in deckchairs. There were children running around, and two guys standing at a barbecue, flipping burgers.

'It *is* a beach party,' Angel said enthusiastically, forgetting for a brief moment the circumstances that had taken them there.

Two of the children were barefoot, throwing a ball to one another.

'Oh, look at that,' said Angel, grabbing Freddie's arm, so they both came to a halt. She pointed at a building. It looked quite stunning, with its floor-to-ceiling picture window looking out to sea. 'I wonder if they holiday-let the property. Wouldn't it be fantastic to spend a holiday here? If you two get married here, perhaps you could spend your honeymoon right here, in her grandmother's beach house.'

'Are you serious?' Freddie looked at the letter in his hand miserably. 'Somehow I doubt there's going to be a wedding any time soon.'

Unless it's ours. Angel raised her eyebrows wondering where that thought had come from – it had only been one kiss.

As they drew closer, she noticed another building – a white house with dormer windows in its roof. It looked like a chalet bungalow. She raised her eyebrows. 'So, there are *two* beach houses?'

Freddie replied, 'I guess the small one is like a summerhouse, or something.'

Angel came to a halt behind a row of deckchairs.

They both spotted Lorna making her way through the crowd of people, searching for her daughter.

Angel said, 'This is not going to end well.'

❖

Briony stepped outside and was immediately confronted by Emily and Clarissa. 'There you are!' Clarissa exclaimed.

'We were looking for you,' said Emily, taking her arm.

Briony said, 'I need to find Joss.'

'Yes, he's over there with the rest of the guests, waiting for you and Troy to cut the ribbon,' replied Emily.

Briony had forgotten all about that.

Clarissa took her other arm. 'Don't tell me you've forgotten about the ribbon-cutting ceremony!'

As she was led away from The Beach House, Briony glanced over her shoulder helplessly at Troy, who was following behind, holding Willow's hand.

Clarissa leaned in and whispered, 'Ah, you were with Troy. That explains a lot.'

Briony rolled her eyes. 'Look, I really need to speak to Joss.'

Emily said, 'Honestly, Briony, if it's about the letters, which I imagine it is, can't it wait until the party is over?'

Briony shook her head vehemently.

'All right, well, at least wait until after the ribbon-cutting ceremony.'

Clarissa and Emily deposited Briony outside the outbuilding door with the bright red ribbon taped to the door. Clarissa made sure Troy was standing beside her so that they were ready to cut the ribbon together.

'Now, you two stand real close,' said Clarissa, handing them a pair of scissors.

Briony looked at Clarissa in a deadpan manner. She could tell her friend was enjoying herself. She was probably a bit drunk too. Briony wasn't sure how – all there was to drink was lemonade and orange squash. *And any other drink that people have brought along to the party*, thought Briony. She'd noticed a large cooler beside the barbecue and imagined there were a few beers inside.

Briony stood awkwardly, very close to Troy.

Emily noticed Willow was about to step aside. 'No, it's all right sweetheart, why don't you stay right there, next to Troy, and you can officiate—'

'Um, what she means,' said Clarissa, 'is that you can check they cut the ribbon.'

When they were all in position, Clarissa passed the scissors to Briony, and placed Troy's hand on hers, so they cut the ribbon together. Clarissa got everyone to gather round for the opening ceremony.

Briony heard Troy whisper, 'I need to speak to you after the ceremony.'

She nodded, although she wasn't focused on Troy, but the large group of people gathered around them. She was feeling self-conscious. She glanced at Emily and Clarissa, wishing one of them could do the honours instead, wondering who had come up with this ridiculous idea. She couldn't wait for the ribbon-cutting ceremony to be over.

Clarissa and Emily opened the ceremony by introducing their new friend, Briony, and saying how much they had been enjoying meeting up, along with Willow and Luna, as part of the Wolf Girls Club.

'Now, without any further ado,' said Emily, smiling, 'I'll hand you over to the lovely couple, Briony and Troy, to cut the—'

'What the hell is going on here?'

People looked about them in surprise, wondering who had shouted out, rudely interrupting proceedings.

Briony stood stock still, her eyes wide, thinking, *No it can't be. I must have imagined my mother's voice*. Then the crowd in front of her parted to let someone through.

Briony dropped the scissors. 'Oh, god – what are you doing here?'

'What am *I* doing here?' Lorna said, hands on hips. 'What are *you* doing here?'

'That's what I want to know!' said Freddie.

Briony felt her knees buckle when she caught sight of him

and Angel. They walked up behind Lorna and joined her at the front of the hushed crowd.

Briony's eyes darted from her mum, to Angel, and finally to Freddie, who was not staring at her, but at Troy.

Troy said, 'You've got no right, barging in like this, and ruining—'

'What have you done?' Lorna asked, ignoring Troy.

Troy mistakenly thought Lorna was talking about the outbuilding. 'She's had it renovated – what does it look like? Excuse me, but who are you?'

'I'm her mother.'

Briony shifted her shocked gaze from her mum to Freddie, who was still staring at Troy, as was Angel.

Freddie pointed at Troy. 'So, this is why you sent the letter?'

Briony looked at Freddie, confused. 'I don't understand … what letter?'

'This letter!' He held it up.

Briony gasped when she saw it. 'I never sent that!'

'Oh, so that's why it's in an envelope with your handwriting, addressed to me, with a first-class stamp on it.'

Briony fell silent, still in shock that they were right there, standing in front of her. And Freddie had received her letter in the post. Some blooming good Samaritan must have found it and posted it.

Worse still, there was a large crowd of people standing there, in hushed silence, clearly not sure what to make of it all.

Neither was Briony. She could feel her face flush bright red. She didn't know where to look, or what to say. She stole a glance at her mum, who after her initial outburst, just looked too shocked at finding her there to say anything more.

Troy said, 'Will someone please tell me what's going on?' He pointed at Freddie. 'And who are you?'

Briony wanted a chasm to open up beneath her feet and swallow her whole.

Freddie stepped forward. 'So, she hasn't told you about me. I'm her fiancé, whom she dumped in a letter!'

Troy looked at him, bemused. 'I'm sorry – what?' He turned to Briony. 'You were engaged to be married?'

Briony didn't want to answer that question. She stole a glance at Angel, wondering whether she'd told Freddie and her mum the reason she was there rather than on the research trip.

Freddie looked up at the outbuilding. 'Looks like a nice pad. Was the plan to move in here with him?'

Troy turned to Briony. 'Really, that was the plan?'

'I … I don't know!'

'With the baby?' blurted Angel. She immediately slapped a hand to her mouth, shocked that she had said that out loud.

'Baby?' said Freddie, Troy and Lorna all at once, the three of them turning to look at Briony.

She looked at each one of them in turn while Angel kept saying, 'I'm sorry,' over and over, until Briony couldn't stand it any longer. She stamped her foot. 'All right – I'm pregnant! There – my secret is out! That's why I decided not to go to the Galapagos Islands, and come here instead, to see my grandmother. But that didn't exactly work out! She's in hospital, in a coma, after a stroke! But then I met lots of wonderful people, and a wonderful person in particular,' she stole a furtive glance at Troy, 'and all I wanted to do was stay here with my baby.'

'Is it mine?' Freddie asked in a hushed whisper.

'Yes – it's yours, Freddie!'

Troy grabbed Willow's hand. 'Come on – we're leaving!'

'I don't want to go!'

'The party is over, Willow.'

Briony turned to the door, clawed at the stupid ribbon adorning it, and felt for the door handle. Her eyes were so full of tears that she could barely see. She launched herself inside and slammed the door shut behind her.

Leaning her back against the door, she heard Troy's angry voice shout out, 'The party is over everyone – go home!'

Briony stood there in floods of tears, thinking that it well and truly was.

37

'Your secretary said I'd find you here.' Richard said, looking at his employer as though he'd gone mad. 'What are you doing here? You never come down here.'

'Well, I am here today, clearly.'

Richard frowned. 'Clearly.' He looked up at the vaulted wooden ceiling. The old boathouse had seen better days. It was cold and damp; far too cold for his old bones. Richard had arthritis. Mind you, he never complained, otherwise his employer would tell him to retire. He should have done so a few years earlier, but he'd always said that he'd only retire when his employer did.

They both turned at the sound of a chain grating. Two young men were pulling on a lever, hauling an old boat up to look at the hull.

'What is that?'

'It's a boat, Richard.'

'I can see that. But what's it doing here? It's in a bit of a state.'

'Yes, that's why I'm having it repaired.'

'Why? You could just buy a new one.'

'Yes, I could. But it wouldn't be the same.'

'No, it wouldn't. It would be better.' Richard looked at his employer. 'Frank, I don't understand …'

'And you won't. Now, what is so urgent that you came all the way down here instead of waiting for me to return to the house?'

Richard cast a glance back towards the house. He'd never walked this far down the extensive gardens of his employer's ten-bedroomed detached house, to the jetty on the shore, and the old, rarely used boathouse. 'We've heard from your … acquaintance.'

Frank rolled his eyes. 'You mean my spy. Let's say it like it is – shall we?'

'Alright then, your spy in the village. You know he told you that a young woman arrived and was asking directions to The Beach House?'

'Yes, yes. That was over a fortnight ago.'

'Well, I don't know if it's of any consequence, but he heard from the woman who runs the pet shop that she's been in there buying pet food.'

Frank turned around and gaped at Richard. 'You walked all the way down here to tell me that?'

'Well, no.'

'Then what is it?'

'She mentioned that she's got a part-time job in the music shop, in Aldeburgh, helping out a guy called Reggie.'

Frank narrowed his eyes. 'You mean Reggie is helping her out? I know all about that, already.'

'You mean from your other spies?'

Frank didn't answer that. Instead, he said, 'I'm sorting it,' and flicked his hand at his long-time personal assistant, dismissing him.

Richard wasn't ready to go. 'Sorting it – how?'

'You'll see.'

Richard was about to leave when Frank said, 'Don't tell them about this.'

'About the boat?'

Frank nodded.

Richard rolled his eyes. 'Tell who?' It would be helpful if he knew who Frank was talking about.

'My other spies, of course. Who do you think?'

Richard pursed his lips, swallowing a sarcastic retort. He cocked his head to one side, staring at the boat. 'Has this got something to do with The Beach House?'

'None of your business.'

'Your business is my business – remember?'

'This is personal.'

'So, it *is* about The Beach House.' Richard sighed. 'After all these years, you're not going to give up, are you?'

'I said that one day I'd own The Beach House, and I will, I swear.'

Richard stepped closer to the boat. On the corner of the hull he could just make out the name of the boat, even though there were a couple of letters missing. Richard arched his eyebrows in consternation. 'Oh, dear god – it's that sailing boat, isn't it? The one you used to take Blythe out in. Where did you get it?'

Frank wouldn't look him in the eye.

'You stole it – didn't you? Are you going to repair it, and give it back?'

Richard's questions were just being met with a cold, blank stare.

'Look, she's dug her heels in. No amount of money you

offer is going to change her mind and make her sell.'

'So, why doesn't she just answer the letters and tell me that?'

'Maybe because she doesn't know who's behind them. Perhaps if you stopped hiding behind the solicitor—' Richard stopped abruptly when something occurred to him. 'You're afraid of rejection again.'

'I am not!'

Richard was no fool. And he knew Frank like he'd know his own brother – if he'd had one. 'Why can't you just let The Beach House go?'

In the stony silence, Richard remembered what Frank had once told him. 'It's because the people who had it built were—'

'The making of me – that's right, Richard.'

'But not in a good way,' Richard muttered under his breath. Sometimes, he wondered how Frank's life might have turned out if Blythe hadn't rejected him.

Before he worked for Frank, they'd been childhood friends, and had grown up in Aldeburgh together. After Frank had left the Navy, he'd set up his property business, and had contacted his trusted friend, Richard, who had subsequently worked with him all over the world. This was the last place Richard had expected his employer to return to. The problem was that the move came with its own set of problems – personal problems. Down the coast was The Beach House, still haunting him.

Richard believed that sometimes it wasn't wise to revisit the past, and certainly not to return and put down roots again, but he also understood Frank's motivations for returning there. He wanted to prepare his grandson to take over the business when the time came.

So, three years earlier, when Troy had finished his A-Levels and was about to embark on a university degree, Frank had reappeared, bought a massive ten-bedroomed detached house overlooking the sea, with its very own boathouse and home office, and encouraged his only grandson to forget university and start as an apprentice in his business – much to the disappointment of Troy's father, Sebastian. Fortunately, his grandson, although not biologically related to him, loved the business; lived for it. Would do anything for it. Perhaps that, thought Richard, had not turned out to be a good thing.

And now, there they all were, and because Frank just couldn't escape his past, he'd dragged his grandchildren into it too.

Richard couldn't help himself. 'I really don't agree with all this.'

Frank raised his eyebrows. 'The boat was just rotting there.'

'I am not talking about the boat. Whatever grievance you had with her and her parents, you need to let it go.'

'I've offered a generous price for the house.'

'I bet you have. But when will you accept that she won't sell?'

'I want it.'

'You've wanted a lot of things, over the years, Frank. And as soon you've got them, you've cast them aside.'

'This is different.'

'What will you do with it, if she does give in and sell?'

'I think you know the answer to that. I'll enjoy burning the place to the ground.'

Richard stared at him. A terrible thought entered his head, and he voiced it without thinking. 'Why don't you do it anyway, and be done with it?'

Frank turned from the boat and stared at Richard, who assumed he would rebuke him for that remark. Instead, he coolly said, 'That has crossed my mind, but then her insurance would only rebuild the darn thing. No, the answer is I must own it first.'

'And what if she just refuses, and that's that?'

'Oh, I'm already on the case.'

Richard frowned. 'The case of the missing deeds?'

'Exactly! My solicitor thinks the property has never been registered with the Land Registry. It's possible that there are no deeds, which proves her parents just built the place on land that wasn't theirs. That obnoxious couple, thinking they could have anything they wanted, thinking they were above anybody else.'

Richard stared at him, thinking that the description of Blythe's late parents sounded just like Frank. Richard slowly shook his head, not at all surprised that Frank couldn't see that. He didn't bother enlightening him. Instead, he thought, *What does it matter, after all these years?* He knew what it was really all about. 'I thought, that after all this time, you would have got over her.'

Frank held his hand up. 'Not another word, Richard.'

Richard stole a glance at the boat, sighed, and walked out.

'Tell me when my other spies arrive, please,' Frank called after him.

Richard cast a glance over his shoulder and caught the two workmen in the boathouse exchanging a nervous glance. They knew better than to comment, or repeat anything of what they'd heard. Their employer paid a very generous wage, but that also paid for their silence – all Frank's employees knew that, even Richard.

Richard was making his way back to the house when he stopped abruptly. He looked at the paperwork in his hands. 'Oh, bother.' He'd got into that conversation over the boat, and The Beach House, and had just plain forgotten the reason he'd walked down to the boathouse in the first place. He turned on his heel. 'Maybe I should retire. I'm getting too long in the tooth for all this.'

'You're back!' said Frank in surprise. 'What is it now? You are getting rather tiresome.'

'About this …' Richard showed him some paperwork. 'I saw it on your secretary's desk.'

'Nothing gets past you, Richard.'

'I should hope not. I've been doing this job long enough.'

'So, what's the problem?'

Richard glanced at the workmen. He whispered, 'This is … delicate. I'd rather we discussed it up at the house.'

Frank heaved a sigh. 'All right.' He glanced at the two men. 'Can it be fixed?'

'Yes, with the right equipment. We might need to enlist the help of someone we know at the boatyard in Southwold with a lot of experience.'

'Can he be … discreet?'

Both young men nodded. 'With the right … remuneration, anyone can be discreet.'

Frank grinned. 'Isn't that the truth? I'll double your commission, and that of your colleague, if you can get the boat fixed ASAP.'

'Consider it done, Frank.'

'Good lad.'

Richard knew Frank didn't bat an eyelid at his employees addressing him by his first name. That was how he liked it. Although he was their boss, and a very, very wealthy man, he was still Frank, the boy who'd grown up in a little flat above a music shop in a place called Cobblers Yard; there weren't, and never would be, any airs and graces. All he expected from his employees was that they worked hard, very hard, as he had done all his life, and they would be remunerated accordingly.

Frank turned to Richard. He smiled. 'Let's go back up to the house.'

They walked through the gardens together, following the path up the gentle slope to the grand Georgian-style red-brick property. It had a large conservatory, which Frank had recently added on the back. The gardens, as always, were pristinely manicured by a full-time gardener.

Richard winced at the sound of a cement mixer ruining the peace and tranquillity. Workmen were building yet another extension; this time on the side of the house. The noise rather ruined the ambience. Richard rolled his eyes. He wasn't surprised that Frank was building another extension – that was him all over; never, ever satisfied with anything he did or had. Always chasing the next thing.

He'd said to Frank once, some time after his wife had died young, that he needed to find someone else – fall in love again. Then perhaps his priorities would shift from another extension, or work of art, or expensive car. Frank hadn't spoken to him for a week after he'd said that. Richard had made a mental note never to bring it up again.

And now he was fixated on something else – The Beach House.

Richard followed Frank through the house, up the impossibly grand, wide staircase to his study, passing the secretary sitting in an anteroom outside his home office.

Frank walked over to his ornate desk and sat down on the large leather chair. He leaned forward, hands together on the desk, and said, 'Right, what's this about?'

Richard took a seat opposite him and put some paperwork on his desk. 'I notice you've put up the rent on this place. I thought you'd got rid of that years ago?'

'I thought that nothing ever got past you?'

Richard caught the playful smile on Frank's lips. He ignored the comment. 'Well, I'm wondering why you still own it.'

'Call me sentimental.'

'Really? That's the last thing I'd call you.'

It was only because he'd been working for Frank since the beginning that he got away with his sarcasm and cheek. No one else would dare to speak to Frank that way. They might call him by his first name, but he was still their boss, and the person who held their livelihood in his hands.

Richard imagined that if they were in the outbuilding having this conversation, the two workmen would momentarily pause what they were doing to stare at him, probably thinking he'd be out of a job by the end of the day.

Frank sat back in his chair. 'It's just a normal rise in a market rent. Should have done it years ago.'

Richard stared at him. Now he knew why he had missed this shop – the shop Frank had inherited years earlier – on their books, and it had gone under the radar. It was because the rent hadn't been changed in years, decades. It was now tantamount to a peppercorn rent.

'It's time the place became a sensible, profitable business.'

'You're saying it's not profitable?' Richard frowned. 'It wouldn't surprise me if that's been the case for quite some time. It's not as though they get a lot of passing trade in Cobblers Yard, so I imagine it's rather word of mouth. But I happened to pop into the lovely old bookshop in Cobblers Yard for a novel just the other day, and got chatting to a friendly old lady sitting on the sofa having a cup of coffee. Now, what was her name?' mused Richard.

'Oh, never mind that. What is your point, Richard?'

'Well, I gleaned – from what she told me about the number of customers she's seen going in and out of the music shop over the past fortnight – that the shop's fortunes have rather changed. I bet the turnover is quite impressive.'

Frank rubbed his chin. 'You think so?'

Richard nodded. 'I wouldn't know exactly what that turnover is. I don't have access to Reggie's accounts, obviously. But as I said, I imagine he is rather pleased with the sudden change in his fortunes.'

Frank smiled. 'Even more reason to put up the rent, then.'

Richard frowned. 'That's not what I was getting at. This is an extortionate rise.'

'It's the going rate, though.'

'But to raise it like this, all in one go …' Richard trailed off, hoping he was making his point. It was unfair and unjust. He said as much. 'I know that with your money, you've lost all sense of proportion as to what money means for ordinary folk, but you'll put him out of business, for sure.'

Frank rounded on Richard. 'Would you like to find out what it's like to be put out of this business? Because I can arrange it.'

Through the open doorway, Richard caught the secretary looking up, open-mouthed, probably relieved it wasn't her sitting in his chair, getting an earful.

Richard got up, walked over, and closed the door. He imagined the secretary was probably feeling guilty that she'd let him have the paperwork he'd happened to see on her desk.

Richard turned around. 'How long have we known each other?' They both knew that it was a rhetorical question. 'I'm too long in the tooth to listen to your diatribe, Frank.'

'Then perhaps it *is* time to let you go.'

'I wish you would. I'm looking forward to that comfortable retirement you promised me.'

Richard was calling his bluff. Although he had invested wisely in a good pension, and had savings, he still needed the job. His wife had warned him not to commit to putting their three lovely grandchildren through an expensive private school, but Richard had insisted. Of course, there was the possibility he'd get ill, and he knew he would inevitably get old and eventually die – he was getting on in years – but he had insurance policies for that. What he hadn't counted on was the possibility he might lose his job.

He had never pictured a time when he wouldn't want to work for his best friend. But that time seemed to have come. Going after a little old lady's home just because he bore a grudge; getting his own grandchildren to spy for him – Frank could be unscrupulous in business. This was a side of his friend that Richard didn't much like.

He'd advised Frank that this move back to Suffolk would be a mistake – but had he listened? It was the first time that Frank had not taken his advice. And it was the first time that Richard had considered throwing in the towel – except that he couldn't retire. Not now. The grandchildren were all settled into their schools and relishing the opportunities that their expensive fee-paying privileged education was providing.

Richard slunk out of the room, wishing he'd listened to his

wife and not committed to those expensive school fees.

He started down the stairs and was surprised to see Troy slowly walking up the stairs towards him, his face like thunder. He'd thought Troy was meant to be going to a party. Richard passed him on the stairs, barely acknowledging Troy. He knew he was behaving out of character, but he had a lot on his mind. Besides, he knew what Troy was doing there. Richard had already passed the other spy sitting with the secretary, eating sweeties while she waited to see her grandpa. Despite the sweeties, Willow did not look happy either.

38

'What's up with Richard?'

Frank beckoned his eldest grandchild into the inner sanctum. 'Just a dose of reality.'

'Huh?'

'Oh, he just found out what happens if you question my decisions.'

Troy stared at him. 'You didn't fire him – did you?'

'No, of course not. We both know we'd be lost without him. Now, what have you got for me today, my favourite grandson?'

'Your *only* grandson.'

'Which is why you are going to own all this one day when I retire.'

'You'll never retire.'

'Never say never. I might surprise you.'

'That'll be the day,' quipped Troy.

Frank looked at his grandson, and chuckled. 'I heard that. You know me too well. I'll have to be six feet under, I'm afraid, before you can get your hands on my empire. In the meantime, I expect you to do what I say.'

'Tell me something I don't know,' said Troy miserably.

'You know, I was going to say the exact same thing. What have you got for me today?' he asked again. 'I was beginning to think you'd reneged on our arrangement and defected to the other side.'

'What made you think that?'

'Hmm, now let me see. Perhaps the fact that you've been avoiding me.'

Troy remained silent.

'Ah, you thought about it. But something happened.' He pointed at Troy in the awkward silence. 'Women – they break your heart. That's what they're put on this earth to do.'

Troy did not want to talk about women, and one woman in particular. Instead, he said glumly, 'What's so important about The Beach House, anyway?'

'That's none of your business.'

'Your business is my business – remember?'

Frank shook his head, thinking about Richard.

Troy noticed. 'What?'

'Nothing.'

Troy frowned at his grandfather. 'Talking of business, I thought you were giving me a promotion to a more senior position?'

'I was. I will. When you've upheld your end of the bargain. But let me remind you that this isn't business. This is personal.'

Troy sighed. 'Look, I wasn't avoiding you.'

Frank sat back in his chair and raised his eyebrows – he didn't look convinced.

'I was staying at Coastguard Cottage with Willow, like I promised Dad. You know he doesn't want Willow staying here with me while he's away working.'

'You mean, he doesn't want her staying here with *me*.'

Troy didn't want to get into that. 'Well, now he's back.'

'Sebastian is back? He didn't tell me.'

Troy gave him a look that said, *Are you surprised?*

'He's okay, then? I wish he'd come and work for me, or just accept some money so he doesn't have to do that dangerous job.'

'Me too. But you know he won't take any of your money.'

'What would persuade him to give it up, do you think?'

They'd had this conversation many times. Troy frowned at the thought of his dad having all those cosy conversations with Briony. Why did they get on so well? He'd overheard them talking about the ocean. Perhaps she'd persuade him to give it up.

'Have you brought Willow to see me too?'

Troy frowned. 'Yes.'

'Good.' He leaned forward in his seat. 'Now, are you done with working on that outbuilding?'

'I'm done there. I'm not going back.'

'Thank the lord. Honestly, I didn't know what you were playing at – do you? It started off simple enough. All I asked you to do was go and scope out The Beach House. Just have a look. Not start renovating an outbuilding on the property. What were you thinking?'

'Yeah, well it ended up to your advantage, didn't it?' Troy recalled the rather heated conversation when Frank had found out what his grandson was doing.

He'd surprised Troy when he'd said, *I want to pull down The Beach House, not renovate it.* To which Troy had replied, *I'm not renovating it, I'm doing the outbuilding. And why do you want to pull down a perfectly sound house? Are you after building a different property on the land?*

His grandfather had refused to give away his intentions. Troy had told him it wasn't his fault that he'd ended up with a renovation project. He hadn't expected anyone to catch sight of him out there, looking at the property. There had been no car parked out front when he'd turned up. Troy had said, *It wasn't my fault the granddaughter was there.*

She's got a granddaughter? was his grandfather's response.

That was when Troy had told him that Briony had got it into her head that he was there to renovate the outbuilding.

His grandfather had said, *But you didn't have to go through with it.*

And he'd replied, *But I wanted to.*

Troy recalled that conversation almost verbatim, because that was when his grandfather had said, *Why? Just because she's a girl, and I bet by the look on your face, a pretty one at that? What have I told you about the first rule of business?*

It's not personal, Troy had replied.

He frowned at the thought that it certainly wasn't personal anymore – not after what he'd heard at the party.

'You've got something for me?' His grandfather reminded him why he was there.

Troy said, 'Now you'll thank me for doing up the outbuilding. It's how I found this …' Troy slapped a dog-eared manila A4 envelope down on his desk.

He remembered the last conversation with his grandfather, there in his study. Troy had stormed out, wishing he'd never agreed to spy for him after what he had asked of him. Troy remembered shouting, 'Are you seriously asking me to go in the house and search through the owner's things when she isn't there?'

'Yeah – why not?'

'Why not?' Troy had looked at him thinking, *Is he for real?* 'Do I have to answer that question?'

'Look, you'll need to use the lavatory, won't you?' his grandfather had replied. 'And you'll be there on your own at some point.'

'Yes, and yes. She left me with a key,' Troy had responded.

'So, I don't see the problem.'

Troy frowned, recalling that conversation. It was the first time he understood why his father avoided his grandfather. Why hadn't he seen it before? His grandfather could be unscrupulous. Troy sighed. And now he was too.

He slapped the envelope down on his desk. 'There, you've got what you wanted.'

Frank frowned. 'What's this?'

'The deeds, of course.'

Frank gingerly took the envelope, and looked up at his grandson. 'Are you sure?'

'Yep. I had a cursory glance. They're the deeds alright. At least, I hope so. I didn't have time to check it thoroughly. There were loads of people at the party. I didn't want anyone to catch me.'

He didn't want to think about Briony catching him walking out of the second bedroom in The Beach House, when he'd come up with some lame excuse to explain what he was doing there rather than tell her the truth – he'd found the deeds in a secret compartment in the old bureau. He had intended to tell Briony where they were. Then he'd thought he'd give them to Briony as a surprise – his grandfather, and that stupid bargain he'd struck to get a more senior position, be damned.

Then he'd caught her and Sebastian exchanging smiles and

waves at the party, and had got madly jealous again, taking the deeds out to his van, full of indecision as to whether he should hand them over to his grandfather after all.

But as he'd sat in his van and cooled off, he'd had a change of heart. That was, until Freddie had turned up.

'Loads of people – you say?' Frank interrupted his thoughts.

'Yeah, it's a party to celebrate the grand opening of the outbuilding.'

'Why aren't you there, then? You renovated it.'

Troy rubbed his forehead. 'I don't want to talk about it.'

Frank sat back in his chair. His expression softened. 'You like her, don't you?'

'Who?'

'Who? The granddaughter.'

'I did. Until I found out she had someone else all along.'

Frank leaned forward and cupped his hands together on his desk, as if in prayer. 'Ah, the family curse.'

'What are you talking about?'

'First me, then your father. We've all had our hearts broken by a girl. I thought that as we are not blood-related, you might escape it. But clearly not.'

Troy stared at his grandfather. 'So, all this …' he glanced at the deeds, 'the reason you want that property is over a girl? A woman?'

Frank didn't answer. Instead, he opened the envelope and carefully slipped out a single sheet of paper. He was about to read it when he was interrupted by someone knocking on the study door, and a little girl's voice shouting out, 'Grandpa! Are you and Troy finished yet?'

'Just a minute sweetheart.'

Troy glanced at the single sheet of paper on the desk. 'So, what's written on the deeds?'

Frank picked up the piece of paper. 'Aha! So this is the reason that she wouldn't answer the letters, or let on that she had the deeds.'

'What is it?'

Frank looked up. 'A mystery solved. Or perhaps another one unearthed.'

'I'm sorry – what?'

Frank slowly shook his head from side to side. 'Who would have thought? All these years, she's been living there, keeping a secret.'

'What do you mean?' asked Troy.

'The Beach House. Turns out that all along, it has belonged to someone else.'

Troy was about to ask him what he meant by that when they were interrupted by Willow again, knocking on the door, and calling out, 'Grandpa! Can I come in now?'

Frank tucked the deeds back in the envelope with an enormous grin on his face, and called out, 'Yes, sweetheart, you can come in now.'

Willow thrust open the door, and ran into the arms of her grandpa. He'd turned in his swivel chair, in anticipation of getting his usual greeting from his sweet little granddaughter, jumping on his lap, and putting her little arms around his neck. He always got a kiss on the cheek for his troubles too.

'How goes the mission, sweetheart?'

'The mission?' Troy looked at his sister in surprise. 'Are you spying for Grandpa?'

Willow eyed her brother, dropping her gaze as though she'd

done something wrong.

Troy slowly sat down in a chair opposite them. 'What did he promise you?' Troy was guessing that it wasn't another senior position in Grandpa's company.

Grandpa bounced Willow up and down on his knee and smiled. 'Now, remember, getting your very own pet relies on the success of the mission. Nothing comes free in life, Willow. Everything is hard-earned. Now, what have you got for me?'

Willow pursed her lips. 'But I made a promise!'

Frank said, 'How's that?'

'I'm in the Wolf Girls Club. We're not meant to tell.'

Troy stifled a smile, feeling so proud of his little sister for not giving in to their grandpa. So, he wasn't the only one who'd met Briony and then had second thoughts about following through. He'd nearly reneged on his grandpa's stupid spy game himself because he'd met Briony and fallen in love. Troy raised his eyebrows. His grandpa was right: he'd fallen in love, and she'd broken his heart.

Frank studied his granddaughter. 'You know, sometimes we have to think of the greater good.'

Troy caught Willow's confused expression and sighed. 'What Grandpa means is that sometimes you have to give up something in order to gain something … bigger.' Troy frowned. That perhaps wasn't quite the definition he was looking for, but explaining it to a five-year-old wasn't exactly easy.

'Yes, that's exactly what I mean. Now, you have to choose. Which is more important – family, that's me, your grandpa – or your friends?'

'Frank!' Troy stood up. 'Really?'

'What? It's just a question.' Frank turned to Willow. 'Now,

how about it? Are you going to tell me the Wolf Girls Club secrets? There's a sweet little kitten waiting for you, if you do. Maybe even two?'

'I want Tom and Jerry.'

'Ah, the little foster kittens you told me about. Well, consider them yours.'

'Oh, Grandpa.' Grandpa got another kiss and a big hug. 'You're the best.'

'I know.'

Troy scowled at him.

'Now, what is it you want to tell me?'

Troy decided he might as well stay and hear what she had to say. Perhaps there would be something that cropped up in the Wolf Girls Club that explained why Briony hadn't told him about her fiancé or the baby.

Troy sat there listening to his little sister. It turned out there wasn't anything about Briony, it was just about Briony's grandmother, Blythe, asleep in hospital and wouldn't wake up. Troy didn't bother correcting her or mentioning that she was in a coma. Even so, he noticed Frank's happy demeanour slip when he heard that. He must have realised it was a euphemism.

'Well, thank you for that report, Willow. I shall mull it over.'

Troy caught his grandfather's expression, his voice sounded strained. Something was up.

'What about my kittens?'

'Of course. Troy will go and fetch them.'

'I will not! I'm not going back there.'

'Oh, but you will, if you want me to uphold my end of the bargain too.'

Troy frowned. 'Thanks, Willow,' he said sarcastically.

Five-year-old Willow didn't get the sarcasm. She climbed off her grandpa's knee, and ran over to Troy. 'You're the best.'

Troy hugged her tight and lifted her on to his lap. 'Frank, are you all right?' Were there tears in his eyes?

'Are you upset because I told you about the lady in hospital, Grandpa?'

Frank suddenly swivelled in his chair to face the wall, his back to them. 'Please leave me.'

Troy stared at the back of his chair. This was most unlike his grandfather He looked at Willow. She'd noticed too. He didn't want to worry her, so he said, 'Come on, let's leave Grandpa in peace. You know what a busy man he is.'

'Troy, are you going to take me to get my kittens now?'

Troy sighed heavily as they approached the door. As they stepped out of the room, he heard Frank's strained voice on the speaker phone to his secretary. 'Tell me when the visiting hours are at the hospital.'

39

Briony heard someone knocking at the outbuilding door. Startled, she shouted out, 'Go away!'

'Briony – it's me. I am *so* sorry.'

Sitting on the sofa, feeling sorry for herself, Briony shook her head. 'It's not your fault, Angel. How could it be? I should have told them in the first place. At least it's out there now.'

She hoped her mum wasn't standing on the other side of the that door with Angel. 'Where's my mum?' she called out. She wasn't sure she wanted to talk to her right now. In fact, she knew she didn't.

'She's talking to some guy.'

'Sebastian,' breathed Briony.

'Who?'

'Never mind.' Briony said, 'And Freddie? Is he … with you?'

'He's sitting on the beach at the water's edge. He said he wanted to be alone.'

Briony wasn't surprised. Not only had he got her letter, in which she had effectively dumped him, but he now had to digest the most unexpected of news; on the day he had learned they were breaking up, he had also learned he was going to be a dad.

How terrible that when this should have been the best of news, something to celebrate, it understandably wasn't.

Briony started to cry. 'I've made such a mess of things, Angel. For everyone.'

'Can I come in?' Angel asked tentatively.

Briony wiped the tears from her eyes, got up and walked over to the door. She opened it. But as soon as she saw her best friend, she dissolved into tears again.

Angel closed the door and embraced her. 'Oh, Briony. I've missed you so much. I hated that we parted on bad terms.'

'Oh, Angel, me too. Me too.'

They sat down on the sofa together, holding hands. 'This is really something,' commented Angel, looking around.

'My grandmother had drawn up plans to have the outbuilding renovated. The furniture was my idea. I wanted to add a mezzanine level with a bedroom and en suite too. I didn't do that, obviously. I wanted to wait and get permission from my grandmother first.'

'Look, I'm so sorry to hear about your grandmother.'

'I hoped she'd wake up. I knew I'd have to contact my mum. I felt like time was running out. It's just as well she's here. If my grandmother doesn't wake up soon …' Briony trailed off, not wanting to think about the inevitable – she wasn't going to get better. It was time she faced that fact, just as she'd have to face her mum and Freddie.

'I did it for her, as a surprise. I got it into my head that I could live here, with the baby. I knew Freddie wouldn't leave Oxford.' If he wasn't prepared to move there, even if it meant commuting for work, and she didn't want to return to Oxford, what did that say about their relationship?

She turned to Angel. 'I knew it wasn't just about that; it was about our relationship. That's why I wrote that letter. Then I got cold feet and didn't post it. I was thinking that I needed to put my baby first, not myself.'

'You shouldn't stay with someone just for the sake of your baby. That's just wrong, Briony. Your child will grow up the midst of an unhappy marriage. That wouldn't be good for you or the baby. But then I guess you knew that, because you ended up posting the letter.'

'Actually, I didn't. I lost the letter. Some so-called good Samaritan must have found it and posted it. I've got that person to thank for this.'

Angel took her hand. 'Look, call it fate or serendipity, but perhaps it was meant to be. I saw you with that guy, Troy. You love him, don't you?'

'Oh, Angel, I've tried to hold my feelings back.'

'Because you're pregnant with Freddie's child?'

'Yes.'

'Troy didn't know, did he?'

It wasn't really a question. Briony realised that Angel and everyone else had seen Troy's reaction. 'There just didn't seem to be a right time to tell him. All along, I was sitting on the fence, thinking that I should go back to Freddie – for the baby's sake, because it was the right thing to do.'

'The right thing for whom?'

Briony shrugged.

They both sat, looking through the floor-to-ceiling window at a young man sitting on the beach at the water's edge, his back to them.

Briony stared at Freddie. 'Will he be okay – do you think?'

'Will you?' Angel asked.

Briony turned to face Angel. 'I'm sorry, but it's always been all about me, hasn't it?' Briony wondered if that came from being an only child, doted on by her parents.

Angel didn't object to that statement, and Briony didn't expect her too. 'Tell me, how's it been living in the attic at my parents? Has everything been okay?'

'It was fine – until Lorna told me to leave.'

'Seriously? I'm not having that.' Briony stood up. 'It's not your fault I made a mess of things, and you kept my secret because I told you to.'

Angel took her hand and gave it a gentle tug for her to sit back down. 'That wasn't the reason she asked me to leave.'

'What happened?'

'We kissed.'

Briony furrowed her brow. 'I'm sorry – what?'

'Freddie and me. This morning. He'd been waiting for me in the attic, with the letter. He'd arrived while I was out. He thought I knew about the letter, knew that you were splitting up from him. Of course I had no clue. I was consoling him and – it just happened. It was my fault. You can't blame Freddie. I've fancied him so badly, for so long, and I just took advantage.' Angel looked at her hands. 'Now you know *my* secret.'

'You're in love with Freddie.'

Angel looked up. 'I swear it was just one stupid kiss. Your mum happened to walk in and see us, and of course she jumped to conclusions and thought we had been carrying on behind your back, and that was why you and I had had a falling-out.' She paused. 'Are you mad at me?'

'Of course not. How could I be? No one can help who they

fall in love with.'

'Like you and Troy.'

Briony sighed. 'Yes, like me and Troy.' She stood up.

'Where are you going?'

'To tell my mum that it was one big misunderstanding – you and Freddie. That she'd misread the situation. She has to take you back.'

'You don't have to do that, Briony.'

'But I do. I promised you my room, and I'm going to sort it out.'

'No, you really don't have to do that. You see, I'm moving in with Freddie, as a flatmate, while I sort out somewhere else to live. We talked about it on the way here.'

Briony sat down and placed her hand on Angel's arm. 'It's all right, you know. No more secrets. You have my blessing.'

Angel furrowed her brow. 'Your blessing? I don't understand.'

She shifted her attention to the window overlooking the beach, and Freddie still sitting alone by the water's edge. 'I know Freddie is going to be okay, and do you know how?'

Angel shook her head.

'Because he has you. And I know you love him, Angel. You always have. I see it now.'

'But it was only one kiss! We're not—'

'But you will be. I just know it!' Briony leaned over and hugged her.

Now, it was Angel's turn to cry into her shoulder. 'Oh, if only you're right.'

'I am – trust me.'

Angel said, 'You'll be going back to your old attic room, I imagine.'

Briony shook her head. 'I don't think so. There's no going back.'

'Where will you go? Will you stay here?'

Briony thought of Troy. How could she, knowing what she'd done, what she'd kept from him? What if she saw him in the village? Just imagining it was enough to make her feel she had to leave the place. She'd been sitting on her own in the outbuilding, figuring out what she was going to do. She said, 'I've already got plans.'

'Will you tell me?'

'I will. Just not right now. I need to think. I have unfinished business here.'

'You mean that guy – Troy?'

'No, not Troy.' Briony felt bad for abandoning Reggie, but she would have to swallow her pride and phone Joss. She wanted to make sure he'd get in touch with Reggie to try and sort out his letter and the extortionate rent rise.

She didn't know what would happen about her grandmother's place and those letters she'd received, but her mum was there now, so that problem was in her hands.

Briony resolved to make one last visit to her grandmother in the hope that she might wake up. She knew in her heart that it wasn't going to happen, and wished the thought hadn't crossed her mind that it might be the last time she saw her grandmother alive. At least she could hold her hand and tell her that she loved her before she departed.

'You're not leaving tonight, are you?' Angel asked.

'No, I'm going to stay here tonight, and pack my things in the morning.' Briony was just thankful she'd bought a comfortable sofa for the outbuilding. And there were throws, and cushions. She wasn't going to think about what she'd do if she needed the loo in the night. She'd have to sneak into The Beach House. In the morning, she intended to head off to the hospital, and then she would leave for good.

Briony glanced around the outbuilding. With her mum there, there was no way she was going to stay in the house. She imagined that her mum was probably going to stay the night. Briony wanted to stay as far away as possible. She did not want or need the third degree from her mum just then, or to be told what a disappointment she'd turned out to be.

She'd have to face the music in the morning, though, when she'd need to return to the house to pack her things and have breakfast before she left.

'Angel, I wish you could stay here too, but there's only this couch. You could stay in the house. I have a key, and there's a spare bedroom.' Briony wasn't convinced that her mum would let Angel stay, though.

'I'd love to, but Freddie booked two rooms at the pub in the village.'

'You stopped off at the pub? Did my mum book a room there too?' she asked hopefully.

Angel shook her head. 'I'm afraid not. We didn't travel down together, obviously, as she was still mad at us. We were following her, then lost her, so we had to stop in the village and ask directions at the pub. The barman directed us to the beachside car park near a café.'

Briony smiled. 'Yes, the barman did the same when my taxi driver asked for directions too.'

Angel said, 'So we spotted her car, and followed her. The car park was pretty full, though – we were lucky to get a space.'

'Yes, because of the party.' Briony winced, thinking of the people at the party and how it had ended so abruptly on such a sour, embarrassing note. She didn't know how she could look those people in the eye ever again. It was another reason to leave.

Briony wondered why her mum hadn't parked in the driveway outside the house. She said as much.

'There's a driveway?'

Briony nodded.

'The barman didn't mention that.'

'Yeah, I know.'

'Maybe he wasn't aware,' commented Angel.

'Or maybe he just likes to make things awkward for out-of-towners.'

'Wouldn't be unheard-of in a small place such as this, I guess.'

'Still doesn't explain why my mum parked at the beach car park and walked, though.'

'Perhaps she just wanted to have some thinking time before she saw you.'

Briony looked at Angel. 'I think you're right. She must have been pretty mad when she found out I'd lied and was here in Suffolk all along.'

Angel looked at her for a long moment. 'I wouldn't say mad. She looked … anxious. Scared, even. Do you think it might have something to do with your grandmother? After all, she didn't want you to come here. She did bin the letter your grandmother sent you. And I'll tell you another thing …'

'What is it?'

'I'm sorry to tell you this, but I saw the relief that swept over you mum's face when you said your grandmother was in a coma.'

40

Briony woke up with a start. She'd finally slept through the night again, as she had for the first few nights after her arrival on the Suffolk Coast. It was the sound of the alarm on her mobile phone that had woken her up. She'd thought as she'd settled down that she'd wake up freezing at some point; she was, after all, sleeping on the couch in the outbuilding in her clothes under a throw. But she found that she wasn't cold at all; she was so warm and toasty under a thick duvet that she didn't want to get up.

Briony sat up with a start and looked at the duvet. 'What the …?' She hadn't fetched a duvet from The Beach House the previous night, nor a pillow. She hadn't wanted to bump into her mum – or Sebastian – in The Beach House. She still did not want the third degree from her mum about what she'd done, lying about the trip and about her pregnancy. And she really did not want to discover that Sebastian had stayed the night too. She didn't even want to think about that possibility.

So where had the duvet come from?

She remembered saying goodnight to Angel and watching her fetch Freddie and walk with him back in the direction of the car park, on their way to the pub, where they'd booked rooms.

Freddie had looked towards the outbuilding, but if he had wanted to talk to her about what would happen next, with the baby, Angel had dissuaded him. Briony had told her to. She wasn't ready to have that conversation, and she imagined that with Freddie still absorbing the news that he was going to be a father, he wasn't ready either for the practicalities of what was going to happen now they were no longer together.

Briony stood up and wrapped the duvet around her as she walked over to the little kitchen to flick the kettle on. She switched on an electric heater. The weather had changed. There was no mistaking the season now; as dawn approached, rain pelted the window. The sea looked rough; it was going to be a grey, overcast day.

'What a difference a day makes,' said Briony miserably. *Was it really just this time yesterday that I was snuggled up with Troy, watching the sunrise with him, looking forward to a perfect day with my friends and a party to celebrate the completion of the outbuilding?*

She cringed at the thought of what had happened with the arrival of her mum, Angel and Freddie. Little had she known that, as she was preparing for the party, they had been on their way, making the journey by car from Oxford. If their intention had been to embarrass her, their timing couldn't have been better. *Serves me right for lying to them all.*

Briony slumped down on the sofa with a cup of tea. She wouldn't be sitting for long. The reason she'd set the alarm was not so she could watch the sunrise – it would have been a complete waste of time that morning anyway, with the thick mass of dark grey clouds. She'd set the alarm to sneak into The Beach House, and hopefully pack up her stuff, without waking her mum.

The previous night, her mum had knocked on the outbuilding door, asking her to open up so they could speak. Briony had told her to go away. It wasn't her mum's fault – well, not all of it. Briony should have just told her that the Galapagos Islands trip was off. But she hadn't. And that had come back to bite her. Although she still wouldn't have told her where she was going instead – to her grandmother's. Not after her mum had had the cheek to bin that letter addressed to her from her grandmother.

She finished her tea, stood up and folded the duvet. She knew where it had come from. Troy had left a spare set of keys to the new outbuilding on the kitchen counter. Her mum must have crept in later with a duvet and pillow, and some provisions, when she was fast asleep, stocking the kitchen cupboard with teabags and sugar. Briony had found a fresh pint of milk in the fridge. There was even a box of cereal – the opened one she'd been eating in the mornings in the house.

Briony put her mug down on the glass coffee table and looked at the piece of notepaper she'd found by the kettle. She read the brief note from her mum.

Sweetheart,

I'm not angry with you, if that's what you're worried about. Not at all. Please come up to the house when you wake. I left you some breakfast cereal, but I'd love to have breakfast together. We have a lot to talk about. I love you. Mum x

Briony sat down and stared at the note. She'd had a plan. Now she didn't know what to do. She could feel her eyes growing heavy. It was so early. Perhaps there was no harm in having an extra half-hour's doze under the cosy duvet before she made up her mind about what she was going to do.

❖

Briony woke with a start at the sound of a text. She reached for her phone and saw the time. So much for her plan to steal into The Beach House before her mum woke up, pack her stuff and leave. Unless her mum was having a lie-in too, that plan was out of the window.

She read the text. It was Angel, asking if she was okay, and hoping she was still fine with the fact that she and Freddie would be heading back to Oxford. It was Sunday, they had work tomorrow, and she was moving her stuff into the spare room at Freddie's flat. She added that Freddie wasn't ready to speak to Briony.

Briony wasn't surprised. She imagined he was still processing it all. the break-up, the baby, seeing her with Troy. She was still processing it all herself.

She replied to Angel, thankful that they weren't returning to The Beach House but were going home instead. Briony still had the note from her mum; she'd fallen asleep with it in her hand. She had things to deal with before she left Suffolk, and then she'd phone Freddie when she was ready – and find out if he wanted to speak to her about the baby, or have anything to do with it, now they weren't together.

'If I hadn't written that letter …' Briony frowned at the thought that without it having been posted to him, they wouldn't have all turned up at the party. Her face coloured at the thought that Freddie had seen her with Troy and had assumed she'd been cheating on him. Although it wasn't true, there was no point telling Freddie. Something Troy had said came to her mind, about his father. About Sebastian's heart belonging to another. *My mother*, thought Briony.

'And now my heart belongs to another.' She wished she'd never met Troy, and fallen in love. 'Oh, I've made such a mess of things,' Briony said again, aware that she sounded like a broken record. She looked at the note, and cried, 'I need my mum!'

She fled from the outbuilding and raced up the beach. All evidence of the beach party yesterday – the deckchairs, the barbecue, the fire – had gone; all apart from the string of lanterns, still flickering, lighting the way from the outbuilding to The Beach House in the gloom of the grey, overcast day. In any other circumstances, the pretty row of lanterns would have lifted Briony's spirits – but not today.

She stepped into the kitchen and glanced at the sleeping kittens. Their water and food bowls beside their bed were empty.

'Mum!' she called out. She heard something and then saw Luna and Wilbur emerge from the lounge, both bounding up to her as though she'd been gone for years. 'Oh, sweethearts. Did you think I'd left you? I wouldn't do that – not in a million years.'

Tears started rolling down her face at the thought that she'd forgotten all about her grandmother's dog, and the two little rescue kittens, along with her own little foster fail, Wilbur. 'I am so sorry! I forgot about you.'

It took a good few minutes for both exuberant dogs to calm down. 'Mum!' she called out again. She raced up the stairs, the two dogs following behind. Her pace slowed when something horrible occurred to her – what if her mum was having a lie-in – with Sebastian?

She shook her head. Her mum wouldn't do that – would she?

Cheat on Dad? Besides, Lorna and Sebastian – that had been many years earlier. But what of the passage of time – would that have changed their feelings if it was true love?

Briony suddenly thought of her grandmother and Frank, and those love letters. If they met today, over half a century later, would their love have dimmed with the passage of time, or would it be as strong as ever?

'Mum?' Briony called out in a small voice. She tentatively pushed open the door to the double bedroom, expecting to find her mum and Sebastian fast asleep, entwined in each other's arms.

Briony breathed a sigh of relief when she discovered her imagination had run away with her. Sebastian wasn't there. Neither was her mum. The bed was made. But her mum *had* stayed the night there. Her overnight bag was on the floor, and her silk pyjamas were neatly folded on a pillow.

Briony had a quick look around, checking the small bedroom, where the duvet and pillow were missing. In the bathroom, apart from her mum's toiletries, there was no evidence she could see that anyone other than her mum had stayed the night.

Briony turned around to find Wilbur and Luna standing patiently on the landing, looking up at her. 'What am I going to do with you? I can't stay here.'

She remembered the note from her mum. *Perhaps I can stay here until Blythe comes home*, she thought. She frowned. Would her mum want her to? She suddenly recalled what Angel had said – *I saw the relief that swept over you mum's face when you said your grandmother was in a coma.*

She's come here to take me home to Oxford, Briony realised.

Briony walked into the spare bedroom and began packing her suitcase. *She won't let me stay here, not when she returns to Oxford;*

not if there's any possibility that Blythe will wake up and tell me the big secret – whatever it is that Mum doesn't want me to know.

Whatever it was, Briony would rather not know. She had enough problems and complications in her life as it was.

She realised it was for the best that her mum wasn't in the house after all. 'I can't go back to Oxford,' she said aloud. She didn't know how to face her dad and his look of disappointment when he found out she'd lied to them. Perhaps he was off on one of those cruises. The trouble was that she didn't want to get in touch with him and find out, otherwise some awkward questions would ensue regarding the Galapagos Islands trip.

She continued packing. There was one place she could go. She closed the suitcase, grabbed her bag, and turned around. The two dogs were ganging up on her with their droopy ears and sad puppy-dog expressions. Wilbur whined as he padded over and sniffed her suitcase. Luna cocked her head to one side, listening to Briony's voice as she said, 'I don't know what I'm going to do with you all. You can't come with me.'

Briony deposited her case and bag downstairs in the hall. Wilbur and Luna followed her into the kitchen and watched her open the back door. They ran outside, straight to the back of the outbuilding, to do their business. Briony sighed and returned to the hall. She picked up the phone, took a deep breath and dialled Emily's number.

When Emily answered the phone, for a moment Briony didn't know what to say. She was so embarrassed about the previous day and was feeling heartbroken that she was having to make this call.

'Briony – is that you?'

'Yes,' Briony said in a small voice.

'Oh, I'm so pleased you rang. I was worried about you.'

'I didn't think you'd want to hear from me.'

'Why on earth not?'

'Because of what happened at the party.'

'Listen, Briony, no family is perfect. We've all got out problems, our little secrets hidden away in closets.'

'But mine came out of the closet in front of everyone – big time!'

'Well, I'm glad it did. Well, I'm not glad that it happened in front of everyone, that was a bit … unfortunate, the timing of their arrival. But I think it's for the best that your secret is out. Secrets fester, and in the end they just cause harm.'

Briony wondered what secrets her mum and grandmother had been keeping from her – and what harm they might do, after all these years.

'I'd love to see you. Can I come over? We can have a Wolf Girls Club meeting,' Emily said hopefully.

'I was thinking of coming to you, actually.'

'Perfect. Shall we say this afternoon? We can have lunch together.'

Briony winced. 'It isn't really a social visit. Look, I need you to do something for me.'

'Anything name it. What are friends for?'

Briony looked down at the two dogs, who were back, sitting either side of her legs. She was trying her best not to look at them. They were sticking close, sensing that something was up.

She heard a mewing and saw the two kittens appear at the kitchen door. She instantly thought of Willow, who she knew would love to have the kittens. But she knew that she couldn't just hand them over to her without discussing it with her father first. And that was another problem. She did not want to see Sebastian or anybody else who'd been at the party and witnessed the terribly embarrassing incident.

She didn't think her mum would look after them if she left them at the house. She hadn't that morning – that was obvious. Neither Luna nor Wilbur had been fed, and their water hadn't been changed. The kittens had been given no food or water either, and their litter tray hadn't been cleaned out.

And the dogs hadn't been let out, otherwise she was sure the sound of them sniffing and whining outside the outbuilding, realising she was in there, would have woken her up.

Briony felt a lump in her throat over what she was going to say next. 'I need you to take Luna, Wilbur and the kittens back.'

She waited for what seemed like an age before Emily replied. 'You're leaving?'

'I think so – yes.'

'Oh, Briony, don't run away because of what happened yesterday at the party. I know you must have been so embarrassed, but we're a lovely bunch of people. Honestly, nobody is going to hold it against you – I swear.'

'It's not about the party.'

'It's Troy, isn't it?'

Briony fell silent. She didn't feel like she could stay there. Her grandmother was still in hospital, and things weren't looking good. Who knew what would happen to The Beach House and the outbuilding if she didn't return? There were just too many variables, and Briony needed to make a decision about her future. Besides, even if it turned out that she could stay on there, what would be the point if she wasn't with Troy? Every sunrise would be like a stab to the heart without him by her side. Every sunrise would just remind her of what could have been.

Emily said softly, 'Joss seemed to get on well with Troy. Would you like him to speak to Troy for you, explain—'

'No, Emily. Thank you. But no.'

'I'll miss the Wolf Girls Club.'

Briony sighed. 'Me too.' She looked down at the two beautiful dogs she loved, and the little kittens pouncing on her shoe, and felt sick with grief that she had to give them all up. Give all this up.

'Don't worry about the pets, Briony. Of course I'll take them. Is your grandmother still … not well?'

'Probably. I'm going to see her before I leave.' It occurred to her that perhaps her mum had rushed out that morning to see Blythe in hospital, deciding to feed and water the cats and dogs on her return. She hoped that was the case. But even so, she wanted to know she'd left them with someone she could trust. She didn't trust her mum. She'd kept her grandmother from her, and her past with Sebastian, along with a side of her Briony had never known – her love of the beach and the sea, diving; all the sorts of things she'd discouraged Briony from pursuing over the years.

She looked about her and thought of her grandmother in hospital. She was convinced that was where her mum would be. She'd see her there before she left.

'I'll come and pick them up later this afternoon. I don't normally work at my practice on Sunday, but I've got an emergency appointment this morning, I'm afraid.'

Briony still had the keys to Blythe's car in her coat pocket. She recalled that her mum had driven up in her own car separately from Freddie and Angel.

'I'm going to visit the hospital now, but I'll come back and wait for you here.'

'Good, good. But you do realise that when I come, I'm going to do my very best to persuade you to stay.'

Briony managed a smile.

'I might bring reinforcements too.'

'Clarissa?'

'Oh, yes. That reminds me. She's going to get in touch with you. She found out—'

'Look, can you tell Clarissa, thanks for looking into the solicitor's letters, but my mum is here now. I'm sure she'll get to the bottom of what's going on.'

'All right, Briony. But she'll want to pop along in any case just to see you before you leave. I'd bring Joss along, but he's opened his doors today, because this time of year, at the start of the run-up to Christmas, there are so many people with all sorts of money worries.'

Briony raised her eyebrows. She'd forgotten about Reggie. 'Oh, Emily, you've reminded me about Reggie.'

'Reggie?'

'Yes, he got some bad news. He received one of those solicitor's letters. I think it's from whoever is after my grandmother's house.'

'They want his house too?'

'His business. *And* his home.'

'The music shop in Cobblers Yard?'

'Yes. They've hiked his business rent all of a sudden, like massively. It'll put him out of business. And out on the street. He lives there too. They must realise that. I think they've done it on purpose. I don't think he'll go and see Joss, though.'

'Why not? I'm sure Joss could help.'

'Yes, that's what I thought. But Reggie insisted there were people far worse off than him, so he didn't want to take up Joss's time with his problems. I promised I'd get in touch myself and see if there's something Joss can do.'

'Briony, I'll be sure to tell him. It doesn't sound as though Reggie will go over and see Joss, so I'll be sure to ask Joss to pay him a visit instead.'

'Oh, would you?' Briony asked, relieved. She'd have felt awful, just leaving without mentioning Reggie's predicament to Joss. As it was, she was walking out of her job in the shop – that was bad enough. She looked again at the sweet cats and dogs by her feet and felt a lump in her throat at all the people and animals she was letting down.

'You really don't have to leave, Briony. Come stay with us.'

'At your vet's practice?'

'It's a hotel too.'

'For cats and dogs.'

'Yes, but we've got more than enough room to put you up.'

'That is so kind of you, Emily.'

'You're not going to come and stay with us, are you?'

She'd lost Troy. Whatever happened – whatever her mum told her, or didn't tell her, about what had gone on between her and Blythe, and the reason Briony had never been to The Beach House before – what did it matter? The life she'd thought she might have had there, with Troy, was over.

'The offer is always open, if you change your mind.'

'Thank you, Emily. You've been a good friend.'

'I'll see you this afternoon, Briony.'

'Yes, see you then.'

41

Briony walked along the corridor, taking deep breaths. When she'd parked in the hospital car park, she'd spotted her mum's car. She was there too. Briony was aware that she could have waited at The Beach House for her return, but she had a feeling she should see her grandmother straight away, because she imagined that once Emily had picked up the pets that afternoon, she wouldn't be able to bear spending a second longer in The Beach House. And she'd be so tearful that she really wouldn't be in any fit state to pay her grandmother a visit.

As Briony approached the nursing station, she saw a lot of nurses moving to and fro. She was just thinking that there was a lot more activity than usual, when a nurse spotted her. 'Briony!'

That was when she knew. It was her grandmother. She swallowed. Something had happened. She felt her knees go weak.

As the nurse approached, Briony said, 'I'm too late – aren't I?'

The nurse put an arm around her shoulders.

Briony was about to burst into tears when the most beautiful singing voice, a man's voice, almost operatic, stopped her.

The nurse said, 'It's a miracle.'

Briony looked at her. 'What are you talking about?'

'Oh, you haven't heard the news – she's awake! Your grandmother has awoken from her coma. And apart from some weakness down her left side, she's doing fine.'

The news was so unexpected, when Briony had been starting to prepare herself for the worst, that she was having a hard time taking it in. 'Are you sure?'

'Oh, yes. It's a blooming miracle – that's what it is!'

Briony frowned. It wasn't a miracle. Briony had already guessed how it had come about.

'It's my mum, isn't it? Lorna. The sound of her voice woke her up.' She knew she should have contacted her mum sooner.

'No, it was some guy.'

'Some guy?'

'*That* guy – listen.'

Briony looked towards the ward. 'The person singing?'

'Yes, to your grandmother. He said he was an old, dear friend. He has the most beautiful voice I've ever heard. I asked him if he was a professional singer. You'd think so, with that voice. Brought me to tears, and a lot of the staff and patients too.'

Briony swallowed. 'Who is he?'

'Said his name is Frank.'

As the singing stopped, Briony found a tissue and wiped her cheeks, which were wet with tears. 'It's Frank!' She took the nurse's hands in hers and did a little happy dance right there in the middle of the hospital corridor. 'I don't believe it – he came back!' Briony hugged the nurse and ran into the ward, heading for her grandmother's private room. She couldn't wait to meet him, along with her grandmother.

She was about to step into the room when her phone buzzed with a text. Briony wanted to ignore it. But what if it was Troy?

She paused and reached for her phone. It wasn't Troy, but Clarissa. She was about to put her phone away, and read it later, when a word in text caught her eye – *Frank*.

Briony stepped to one side of the door. She could hear two voices she didn't recognise; it was Frank and her grandmother, talking, saying how much they'd missed one another. She knew her mum was there too; she'd caught a fleeting glimpse of her, sitting by Blythe's bedside, holding her hand, although her mum hadn't caught sight of her as she'd looked in.

Briony also caught a fleeting glance of the tall, slim, older gentleman standing by her grandmother's bedside, dressed in a pale cream linen suit. He had his back to the door, so Briony could only see him from behind.

Briony stood on the other side of the door, out of sight, and read the text just as she heard Frank say, 'Well, I'll leave you for now, so you can talk with your daughter. I'm sure you've got a lot of catching up to do.'

'As have you and I. You'll come back – won't you, Frank?'

'Of course I will, Blythe. But in the meantime, I have your letters to keep me company.'

Briony put her hand to her mouth in shock when she read Clarissa's text about Frank.

42

Briony was sitting in her grandmother's car in the hospital car park when she saw the tall gentleman in the cream linen suit, Frank, stride out of the hospital entrance. He paused for a moment to put on a Panama hat. He had thick, silvery-grey hair and watchful blue eyes. She noticed he had a neat stack of letters in his hand – the ones she imagined Blythe had written to him, that he'd never received until now.

Briony didn't know why she ducked down in the car as he stood in the hospital entrance, looking about him. He didn't know her. It wouldn't matter if he'd caught sight of her waiting in the car. He had no idea she was, and that she intended to follow him home.

Briony put her phone down. She'd rushed back to the car to call Clarissa. The nurse who had given her the good news had noticed her short visit, and Briony had made an excuse, saying that something had come up and that she'd have to see her grandmother later.

Something had come up alright. Something she couldn't believe was true.

She'd phoned Clarissa the moment she'd got back to the car.

She'd had to. The text she'd received about Frank couldn't be right.

Clarissa had answered immediately, and had talked at length about what she'd discovered. She'd done some digging around but initially had not found Frank. Then she'd turned her sights on the solicitor's letters. She had been disappointed that she couldn't shed light on those either, and her dad had noticed that something was up. So she'd happened to mention to him that she was trying to find Blythe's long-lost friend from years ago. She didn't have a lot to go on, only that his name was Frank Cribbins, and he'd grown up in the music shop in Cobblers Yard, Aldeburgh.

Clarissa had no idea why it hadn't crossed her mind to ask her dad. Peter had worked all his life in the boatyard, and she knew, from what Briony had been told by The Gossip Girls, that Frank had joined the Navy and gone to sea.

Would he have worked in the boatyard as a young man? Would that have given him the idea to join the Navy? It was a leap, but sometimes that's what investigative journalism was, looking at something from all angles, and investigating possibilities, no matter how tenuous.

And so it had turned out that the answers Clarissa was looking for were a lot closer to home than she'd realised. Unbelievably, her father had known Frank. They'd known each other as young lads, and had worked together in the boatyard, Frank doing extra hours around helping his father in the music shop in Cobblers Yard.

Peter recalled that Frank had been saving money for when he asked Blythe for her hand in marriage. But that was not to be. He'd told Peter once that he knew her parents looked down on him. They were middle-class, with money, and The Beach House – where he'd met Blythe when the boatyard had delivered their new boat – was their holiday home.

Then one day, Peter had learned that all Frank's plans were in tatters. He believed Blythe didn't love him the way he did her. She didn't respond to his letters. Then he heard she wasn't returning for the summer that year, but was spending it travelling abroad on a grand European tour.

He left the boatyard, joined the Navy, and that was the last Peter had heard from him.

At first, Briony had been relieved to hear all this. But what Clarissa had still to explain was why on earth she thought Frank, the guy who'd loved Briony's grandmother, was the person who was also after Blythe's home.

'Oh, no!' Briony had exclaimed when Clarissa had told her that. She'd asked Clarissa if she was sure she had the facts right. It just did not make sense – not until Clarissa told her that her father had bumped into him soon after he'd returned to Suffolk a few years earlier.

Frank was unrecognisable. If he hadn't introduced himself, Peter would not have imagined that the young lad who'd left to join the Navy could turn into such a distinguished-looking gentleman. If appearances were anything to go by, Peter's immediate impression was that Frank seemed to have become quite wealthy in the intervening years – for a start, he drove a Bentley. That wasn't all that had changed. Frank's broad East Anglian accent had gone; he spoke with a clipped English accent, as though he'd had elocution lessons, even though it turned out he'd lived abroad for years, sending his son, Sebastian, to boarding school in Suffolk.

He'd even given Peter his card, in case he wanted to buy a property. That was how he'd made his money, apparently. Of course, Clarissa had Googled Frank's company. The sorts of homes his company built, great sprawling mansions, were completely beyond Peter's means. Her dad had commented that Frank appeared to have lost all sense of proportion; lost touch with how ordinary folk lived. Peter would have had to win the lottery to afford one of those properties.

Listening to all this on the phone, Briony still hadn't understood what it had to do with the solicitor's letters. Or perhaps she just didn't want to make the connection. Clarissa made it for her. Still bitter, all those decades later, about Blythe's apparent rebuff, when Frank had finally returned to Suffolk – having made good on the promise to himself that he'd become the person that nobody, not even Blythe or her parents, would ever look down on again – he'd resolved get hold of The Beach House by whatever means possible.

Briony had asked Clarissa if that was what he'd told her dad.

'Of course not,' she'd replied, 'not all of it, at any rate.' He'd said enough, though, that when Clarissa had chatted to her father, and they had shared what they both knew, it wasn't much of a leap to come to the obvious conclusion: he'd been driven by revenge, pure and simple.

It had sounded to Peter as though Frank's move back to Suffolk had just opened up a festering emotional wound, and the only way he'd thought he could heal it was to get his hands on The Beach House.

'But he must have known Blythe was living there,' Briony had said, shocked that after all those decades, Frank still harboured such ill-feeling towards Blythe and her late parents.

'His heart was broken.'

'He's still in love with her,' they'd both concluded before ending the call.

And now, as Briony watched the old man getting into his Bentley, she thought, *I'm still going to have it out with him, because he put her in that hospital.* She recalled finding one of those solicitor's letters open in Blythe's car. She'd had a stroke right there in the hospital car park because of it – Briony was convinced of it.

Briony's expression clouded. She said out loud, watching him cross the hospital car park, 'Don't you think you're getting away with it! If you still love her, you have to tell her the truth – it was you.'

Briony had her fingers on the car key, ready to switch on the ignition and get going as soon as he passed her in his great big Bentley. As soon as the green Bentley passed slowly by, Briony turned the key in the ignition. Nothing.

'No, no, no! Don't die on me now!'

She tried again. Still nothing.

She slapped the steering wheel angrily, then tried once again. The engine started. 'Thank goodness!'

Briony wasn't thanking her lucky stars for long. She had to stop abruptly for someone backing out of a parking space in front of her. By the time she turned into the high street, the Bentley was nowhere to be seen. 'For god's sake!' Briony slapped the steering wheel again in frustration. She pulled over to the kerb.

Briony frantically rang Clarissa back. She said, 'Tell me you know where he lives.'

'Who?'

'Frank – of course. I was going to follow him, but I lost him.'

'What do you mean – follow him? You don't know who he is, what he is capable of. Actually, scratch that, you do know who he is, and what he's capable of.'

Briony raised her eyebrows. So she did know where he lived. 'Clarissa, just give me the address!'

After another argument, Clarissa relented. 'At least let me come with you.'

'There isn't time.' Briony had to be back at The Beach House that afternoon for when Emily arrived to collect the kittens and dogs. She didn't want to think about that right now – the heart-rending moment when she'd have to hand them all back. However, her grandmother was alive and well; that meant she'd hand Luna over to Emily just for a little while until her grandmother was well enough to return home and look after her.

She had no doubt that the playful kittens would find loving homes, although Willow would be so upset about that. She knew the little girl really wanted to keep them for herself.

But it was Wilbur, the little sausage dog, who had been given up by his elderly owner, and who'd had no luck finding a home before she'd come along, that bothered her the most. *I could take Wilbur back with me if I went home to Oxford.* But it wasn't Briony's plan to return to Oxford.

Briony tried to focus on one problem at a time. First, she would deal with Frank. Somehow, he'd found out that Blythe was in hospital. Briony drove along, following Clarissa's directions, which she'd had to commit to memory because her phone map just wasn't playing ball. She wondered how Frank had found out. When it came to her grandmother's whereabouts, she'd taken Joss's advice and had told very few people. The only people who knew were Joss, Reggie, Troy, and the Wolf Girls Club. So how on earth had Frank found out?

She scowled as she turned into the driveway of a large new mock-Georgian house, thinking that if Frank had assumed he could just turn up and make like everything was okay, and sweep under the carpet what he'd done, or what he intended to do, taking Blythe's property, then he could think again.

The gardens leading up to the massive house were manicured and impressive. She was lucky that the wrought-iron gates were still open. After making a couple of wrong turns, and getting lost, she'd finally arrived.

She didn't see the Bentley, but then she saw that the driveway led to a triple garage and imagined he'd parked the car in there.

Briony parked, stepped out of the car, and walked past the fountain in the middle of the driveway to the front door. Clarissa was right: she didn't know this man. And she was there on her own. Clarissa would have been on her way – she wasn't at work, as it was Sunday – but Briony had insisted she wanted to go on her own. Now she was there, though, she wondered if it was a mistake.

She rang the doorbell before she could change her mind.

43

Briony stepped back in surprise when the door opened. 'Willow? What are you doing here?' *Had Clarissa given her the wrong address?*

'This is Grandpa's house.'

Briony stared at her. 'Your … grandpa?'

'Yes. I'm not allowed to answer the front door, but I saw you from the window. Have you come to see me? I miss you.' She opened the door wide. 'Come on.' She beckoned Briony inside. 'Let's play!'

'Um, yeah … sure.' Briony tentatively stepped inside. 'Can I see your grandpa first?'

Willow, who had been skipping down the grand entrance hallway, stopped and whirled around. 'Why?'

'There's something I want to speak to him about.'

'Grandpa went to the hospital when I told him about the lady.'

'The lady?'

Willow looked at the floor. 'I broke the Wolf Girls Club code.'

'Broke the Wolf Girls Club code? Whatever do you mean?'

Willow's chin was on her chest, although she did glance at

Briony sheepishly. 'We're not meant to talk about what we say in the Wolf Girls Club, but I told Grandpa.'

Briony walked down the hallway towards her. 'Told Grandpa what?'

'About the lady – your grandma in hospital.'

Briony stared at her for a long moment, realising something. She knelt down in front of her and gently lifted her chin. 'Don't be sorry. There's nothing to be sorry about. You see, if it wasn't for you, she wouldn't be getting better.'

Willow said, 'How come?'

'She was in hospital, very unwell. Nobody could wake her up. I tried. Luna tried. My mum tried too, I expect. But it was your grandpa. When he visited, he woke her up, and now she's going to be okay.'

Willow smiled her beautiful little smile, and then quite unexpectedly threw her arms around Briony, saying, 'I'm so happy.'

Willow drew back. 'But how did Grandpa wake her up? Did he give her a good shake, like this …' Willow took Briony by the shoulders and gave a surprisingly rough shake for someone so small.

Briony managed a smile. 'No, no, nothing like that.'

'Then how?'

'Ah, it was so easy. My grandmother loves music. She plays the piano, and taught music too …' Briony had also tried playing Blythe some music on her phone, thinking the sound of some classical music – she'd also tried jazz, on Reggie's advice – might bring her round. But it hadn't.

Willow frowned. 'But my grandpa doesn't play an instrument. At least, I don't think so.'

'No, it wasn't that. He woke her up with his beautiful singing voice.'

'Grandpa sings?' Willow said in surprise.

Briony nodded, guessing that it was a part of himself he'd kept hidden.

'I want to speak to your grandpa.'

'You want to say thank you for helping your grandma.'

Briony bit her lip, and said, 'Um, yes. Of course.' She cast her gaze around the expansive hallway and glanced up at the rather grand staircase rising to the first floor. 'Can you tell me where he is?'

Willow shrugged.

'I thought your grandpa came home?' Briony didn't mention she'd tried to follow him.

'I don't know.'

Briony guessed that in a place this size, it was easy to miss someone coming and going.

'I know! I'll ask.' Willow skipped down the hallway. Briony tentatively followed her up the first flight of stairs to a room at the back of the house. The door was open. Willow stepped inside while Briony hung back by the door, out of sight.

Her eyes went wide when she heard Willow say, 'Troy, where's Grandpa?' Briony froze to the spot, wondering why it hadn't occurred to her that if Frank was Willow's grandfather, then he was Troy's too. And that Troy might be there. He had said he lived with his grandfather; he'd obviously brought Willow over to see him.

Briony heard Troy reply, 'He came back, then said something about the boat, then went out again.'

'Richard, where's Frank?'

Richard? Briony mouthed, surprised there was someone else in the room with Troy. She heard an unfamiliar voice reply, 'He said he had to transport a boat. He's doing that now. But I don't know where he's taking it.'

'What boat?' asked Troy.

'The one he had fixed up. I was surprised they got it repaired so blooming quickly. I'm not sure how they did it. The boat looked in quite a bad state, but then I guess they were remunerated very well to work overtime to get it repaired.'

Briony immediately thought of her grandmother's missing boat. She stepped to one side, appearing in the doorway just as Troy was rising from his seat behind a rather nice mahogany desk, placed by a window that overlooked the back garden. From where she was standing, she thought she could just make out what appeared to be a boathouse at the end of a beautifully lawned garden leading down to the shoreline. It appeared that Frank's rather lovely sprawling grounds backed on to an estuary.

Troy had his back to her. As he rose from his seat, Richard saw her standing in the doorway. 'Oh, I say, who are you? I didn't know we had a visitor.'

Troy whirled around as soon as Willow said, 'This is my friend, Briony. I'm in her Wolf Girls Club.'

Richard said, 'I'm sorry – what club?'

Before Willow could reply, or Troy, who was standing there gaping at Briony, could find his voice, Richard added, 'We only have visitors to the office by appointment.'

Willow stamped her foot. 'Richard, Briony does not need an appointment. She's my friend.'

Troy finally found his voice. 'What on earth are you doing here?'

Briony looked him up and down and folded her arms. She was just as taken aback to see him as he was her. It wasn't just his presence, though, that surprised her. He looked different, confident – where he belonged.

He was dressed in formal, smart-casual attire, a blue blazer with a crisp white shirt underneath, and blue chinos. She'd never seen him in anything other than ripped jeans and a t-shirt.

She remembered overhearing Sebastian saying to Troy that he'd never worked a day in his life – not *real* work, and how she'd assumed he was usually desk-based. Now she fully understood what he'd meant. This was where Troy worked; for his grandfather's business – for Frank.

Had Troy been working for his grandfather when she'd first met him outside The Beach House? She'd assumed he was there to scope out the job on the outbuilding. But had she got it all wrong? Had he been there about The Beach House, spying for his grandfather?

The penny dropped immediately when she recalled the phone call from the company who'd drawn up the plans for the outbuilding. They didn't know who Troy was when she'd mentioned who was doing the work – and she expected that if she asked her grandmother, she'd have no clue who he was either.

She stared at him angrily. She had so many questions, but the first question that came out of her mouth was, 'Why didn't you tell me that Frank took my grandmother's boat?'

Richard turned to Troy. 'You know her?'

Troy's focus was on Briony. 'Why didn't you tell me – about Freddie and … and …?'

Briony saw his gaze drift down to her mid-section. He couldn't even say the word. She frowned at him. 'Really – is that all you've got to say?' She looked about her. 'I guess I'm not the only person with secrets. I know what's been going on here.'

'If you do,' Richard butted in, 'would you mind telling me, because I'm—'

'And what do you think is going on here?' Troy said coolly.

'I'll tell you exactly what's going on,' Briony said to him, also ignoring Richard, who clearly worked for Troy and his grandfather. 'You're a spy.'

Troy stepped forward. He looked at her as though she'd lost the plot. 'I'm sorry – what did you say?'

'How could I have been so stupid?' Briony tapped her forehead. 'It all makes sense now.'

'What does?'

'I met you on the beach and assumed that you were there about my grandmother's plans for the outbuilding. But you'd never even seen those plans, had you? Not until I showed them to you.'

Troy avoided eye contact.

'I got a call from the company who drew up the plans and were meant to be doing the work. They'd never even heard of you. You weren't there to work on the outbuilding. You don't do the *real* work …'

She could tell by his expression that he knew what she was talking about.

'You were spying on my grandmother's house for your grandfather – for Frank.'

Richard interrupted. 'What did he promise you, in return?'

Briony's mouth dropped open. So it wasn't her imagination. It was true.

Troy turned around and glared at Richard. 'Do you mind?'

He gestured at the door. 'This is a private conversation.'

Richard raised his eyebrows. 'If you're asking me to leave the room, I will not. Anything that concerns Frank's business is *my* business.'

'Well, that's the thing,' Troy replied. 'It's personal, although what his obsession with that house is, god only knows.'

'So, it *is* true! You *were* sent there to spy,' said Briony. She wanted to hear it from him. A confession. An apology, even.

Briony folded her arms, waiting for an explanation.

Troy breathed a sigh. 'All right, yes. It's true. That's how it started. I was never meant to doing any work on the outbuilding. But then I met you, and I wanted to be around you, get to know you, and I didn't want to leave. You kind of assumed I was there to renovate the outbuilding – and one thing led to another, so that's what I did.'

'So, that's why you haven't been around the office, these past weeks,' commented Richard. 'I knew something was going on.'

'Why were you dressed like a labourer that day,' Briony asked, sceptical.

'I was doing Sam a favour, helping him out on a site because his mate was ill. It was an absolute one-off, that day when I turned up at The Beach House.'

'Spying on me,' said Briony.

'I had no idea you'd be there.'

'On my grandmother, then.'

Richard turned to Troy. 'So, that's where you've been. Frank wouldn't tell me where you were.'

That reminded Briony. She turned to Troy. 'It's my grandmother's – isn't it? The boat.'

'Your grandmother's?' Richard butted in again.

Briony turned to Richard. 'Yes, her name is Blythe. She's someone Troy's grandfather knew a long time ago. And I believe Frank stole her boat.' As well as being after her house.

Troy cut in. 'The boat had been beached for years, probably decades. I reckon it wasn't repairable, otherwise Peter would have taken it to the boatyard there and then. So he didn't steal anything, just a heap of firewood – if we're talking about the same boat, which I doubt we are, actually.'

Richard looked at Troy. 'You're wrong. It *was* Blythe's boat. And it must have been repairable,' Richard countered.

'And now he's taken it somewhere,' said Briony, eyeing Richard. 'What I want to know is – where?'

Richard said, 'So do I. None of this makes sense,' he said to himself, shaking his head. He had been thinking about it. 'Frank wanted to raze The Beach House to the ground, so why did he want to repair her old boat? For sentimental reasons – that's all I can surmise; because the stupid fool is still in love with her.'

When the room fell silent, Richard, who had been staring out of the window, looked up and realised he'd spoken out loud. 'Oh,' he mumbled.

Briony stared at Richard. So he knew Frank had been after The Beach House too, and what his intentions were.

Troy turned to Richard. 'What are you talking about – razing it to the ground? He just wants to buy the property. He's offered stupid money for it.'

Briony stamped her foot. 'So, you knew all along he was after my grandmother's house – her home!'

'He didn't tell you his intentions, though,' said Richard, still speaking to Troy.

Troy avoided Briony's angry gaze as he replied, 'Well, no. I assumed he might want to build something bigger and better in its place.'

'Not at all.' Richard shook his head sadly. 'You see, he had his heart broken by Blythe many, many years ago.'

Troy nodded. 'So, it is true. I asked him if all this over the property was because of a girl, a woman from his past.'

Richard nodded too. 'Yes, it's true … and he never got over it.'

Troy's gaze shifted to Briony.

Richard added, 'I knew it was a mistake when he returned to Suffolk. I warned him not to return. Nothing good ever comes from dredging up the past – that's my take.'

Something horrible suddenly dawned on Briony. 'I know where he took the boat!'

Willow had been standing by the doorway, quietly listening to the conversation. 'So do I.'

Everyone turned at the sound of Willow's voice. Briony had forgotten she'd been standing there the whole time.

Troy said, 'Where?'

'Isn't it obvious?' said Willow, sounding far older than her years. 'He's taken the boat back to where he found it. To The Beach House.'

Richard said, 'That doesn't make sense.'

Briony stared at him. 'I think it does. You see, it turns out Blythe wrote to Frank, but he never got her letters. Her parents hid them, rather than posting them. I found them. And now Frank has them. He knows the truth. She really did love him.'

Briony thought of all those romance novels her grandmother clearly loved lining the bookshelves in her lounge, and felt that all these years later, despite the passage of time,

Blythe was still in love with Frank. And he was in love with her. She guessed he was, otherwise why would The Beach House still bother him so?

'Oh, no,' said Richard. 'I bet he's intending to take the boat out by himself. He hasn't sailed for years, to my knowledge, the crazy old fool.'

Troy said, 'We'd better go – right now!'

'Go where?' Richard asked.

'To The Beach House, of course.'

Richard, Troy, and Briony ran down the stairs and out of the door. Troy ran around the side of the garage. A moment later, he reappeared in a car. He drew alongside Briony.

'This is your car? What happened to the old pick-up?'

'That was Sam's. I was borrowing it. Jump in.'

'No, thanks.' Briony did not want to ride in his two-seater sports car. Besides, she didn't want to leave her grandmother's little car there. She looked up at the house, not intending to return there ever again.

She caught Troy looking at her, disappointed. What did he expect? That everything would be all right now? Well, it wasn't. Not a bit of it. In fact, it was worse, much worse than she could ever have imagined. But it wasn't about Troy spying, and lying about who he really was – that wasn't great, but then Briony had been guilty of not being truthful about her circumstances.

What was worse was what might happen next – Frank had found out, after all these years, that Blythe had really loved him. He might be thinking that he'd caused her stroke, sending all those nasty letters. He obviously wasn't thinking straight if he really was taking a boat out sailing on his own; especially as, according to Richard, he hadn't sailed for years. Briony looked up at the sky. Large, dark clouds were gathering. And the wind was picking up. What if he got into trouble all alone out at sea?

'Bring diving gear!' Richard shouted at Troy over the noise of the sports car engine. He was glancing up at the sky too. 'I don't like the look of the weather coming in.'

'Diving gear – why?'

'They used to go out in that boat – him and Blythe, during the summers when she was there on holiday with her parents.' Richard suddenly tapped his temple. 'I remember now. The last year he saw her, he called it a summer to remember.'

'Oh, god. So, you definitely think he's taken the boat out alone?' Troy had his phone to hand in a millisecond. 'Dad – you've got to come to The Beach House. Bring diving gear! Yes, that's what I said.'

Briony raced to her car. She'd left it unlocked. She got straight into the car and discovered Willow in the passenger seat. 'Oh, Willow. You can't come. You've got to stay here, at the house, in case, um, your grandpa comes back.' *He might do that,* thought Briony. *He might have just gone to drop the boat off at The Beach House, and return to see Blythe, not do something really stupid and go sailing in it, especially with a storm on the way.*

So, why in her heart did she think that was not the case?

Willow didn't budge.

Whatever happened at The Beach House, and she hoped it wouldn't be bad, Willow couldn't come.

Troy pulled up alongside her car and shouted out, 'Sebastian is on his way, with the gear.' He caught sight of Willow. 'Willow – go back in the house.'

'I'm five. You can't leave me home alone,' shouted Willow through the open window.

'You're nearly six!' Troy shouted back.

Briony rolled her eyes.

Troy looked at Richard. 'Where's Rachel?'

'Day off.' It was Sunday, so Rachel, Frank's secretary, wasn't there.

'Get out of the car, Richard.'

'No, not a chance. I've known your grandpa nearly all my life. He's my best friend, like a brother to me. I'm coming.'

Troy looked over at Briony.

'Don't expect me to stay here either, Troy.' Briony sighed as she started the engine. 'I'll hang back, though, until I know things are … okay.'

Troy closed his eyes momentarily in relief. 'What can I do to make things up to you?'

Briony rolled her eyes. 'Are you seriously asking me this right now? We have to get to The Beach House!'

Sitting next to Troy in the car, Richard butted in, 'For goodness' sake, Troy, let's sort out your grandpa's love life first, shall we?'

Briony followed Troy in his car. She soon lost sight of him as he sped up, leaving her grandmother's little car with its one-litre engine behind.

'Won't it go any faster?' Willow asked.

'I'm afraid not.' Briony thought that perhaps it was just as well. 'I think we should look in on the kittens first,' Briony suggested, thinking she could leave Willow in the kitchen with the kittens while she went outside on to the beach.

That was if The Beach House wasn't a pile of embers.

Briony put her foot down. She knew why that horrible thought had crossed her mind. It was because of what Richard had said, about Frank's intention to raze The Beach House to the ground. Even so, that was not what Briony thought was going on. Frank had the letters from Blythe. Surely, he wouldn't do that now.

'Is Grandpa going to be okay?' Willow asked.

Briony looked at her, not surprised, after what she'd heard, that she realised something was up.

Briony slapped a reassuring smile on her face. 'Of course, he is. He's just delivering my grandmother's boat – that's all.'

'But why is everyone looking so worried?'

'I'm not looking worried, am I?' Briony's fake grin belied her true feelings. For Willow and Troy's sake – and Blythe's, not to mention her own for her part in Frank discovering those letters – she was praying that Frank was not doing something really risky and stupid at that moment.

44

Briony left Willow in the house, in charge of two kittens and two dogs. She knew she shouldn't leave a child unsupervised with dogs, but she really didn't have a choice. Although Luna and Wilbur were friendly, she left them in the kitchen, shut the door, and gave Willow strict instructions to stay in the lounge with the kittens until she returned.

When she was satisfied Willow had listened, and promised to do as she was told, Briony raced down to the beach, feeling relieved that the wind had dropped and it looked as though the storm clouds were dissipating. She could see Troy, Richard and Sebastian standing at the water's edge. She'd heard another car arrive on the driveway outside the house, and guessed it had been Sebastian.

The only person who wasn't on the beach was Frank. The boat was nowhere to be seen either. Briony hoped that perhaps he'd taken the boat somewhere to sell it and make a nice profit. But now that he'd reunited with Blythe, she couldn't imagine him doing that.

As Briony rushed towards the water's edge, she imagined that Frank must have had help from the people who had fixed up the boat, if he had indeed taken it there. Frank's green Bentley wasn't parked outside The Beach House as she'd expected. Maybe he'd launched the boat from the beach car park.

That probably explained why Richard, Troy and Sebastian were looking down the beach, in the direction of the car park, perhaps hoping, like Briony, that they'd discover he was just taking a gentle walk along the beach to clear his head. Maybe they'd rushed to The Beach House for nothing.

As Sebastian turned to greet her, Briony attention was drawn to something bobbing on the water in the distance. She pointed. 'What's that?'

Troy, Richard and Sebastian turned as Briony asked, 'Is that my grandmother's boat?' If it was, then they'd been looking in the wrong direction.

Richard had a pair of binoculars.

'Oh, heavens!' Richard exclaimed as he looked through the binoculars. 'I think the boat is adrift.'

Sebastian said, 'Richard, let me see.'

All three of them watched Sebastian raise the binoculars to take a look. 'Oh, no.' He lowered the binoculars. 'I've got to get out there.'

'What is it?' asked Troy.

Sebastian passed him the binoculars.

Troy looked out to sea. 'Oh, no!' He lowered the binoculars. 'Dad – the boat is too far out for you to swim to it, even if you brought your wetsuit.'

'I did bring my wetsuit. I'm wearing it. I'm going to attempt it.'

Briony said, 'What's going on?'

Troy looked at her. 'No time to explain.'

Briony grabbed his arm. 'Explain!'

'There's no one aboard.' Troy looked through the binoculars again. 'I think Grandpa took the boat out, and by the look of those waves, he fell overboard.'

Troy handed the binoculars back to Richard as Sebastian started to wade into the water, leaving the tracksuit he'd been wearing over his wetsuit on the beach, where he'd hastily stripped it off.

'Sebastian – wait!' Richard yelled out.

Sebastian had been about to dive under a wave and start swimming towards the boat. He turned around and shouted out, 'What now?'

'I see him.'

Everyone turned to look at the boat in the distance.

'Are you sure?' Sebastian shouted back.

Richard passed the binoculars to Troy. 'I see him too!'

Squinting, Briony now saw a shape in the boat. 'There's someone in the boat!' Briony shouted excitedly. It had to be Frank.

Briony breathed the biggest sigh of relief. She wanted Frank to feel remorse for sending those letters; of course she did. But she didn't want anything to happen to him, depriving him and Blythe of the chance to get to know each other and fall in love all over again. All she had wanted was a confession. But now all she wanted was for Frank to return safely to shore.

Sebastian, still standing in the surf, shouted out, 'Is it definitely him?'

Troy called out, 'Yes, Dad, it's definitely Grandpa, and it looks as though he's making his way back to shore. Look – the sail has gone up.'

Briony saw that too, even though she didn't have the binoculars.

Satisfied, Sebastian returned to shore.

Now that the drama was nearly over, Briony confronted Sebastian with a question that had been on her mind ever since her mum had turned up at The Beach House. She knew it was most definitely not the right moment, but she couldn't help herself. She needed to know. 'Is my mum leaving my dad for you?'

Troy overheard. He looked at Sebastian. 'What's going on?'

Briony looked at Sebastian too and thought, *If he isn't going to tell Troy, then I am*. 'Troy, you once said you were convinced Sebastian's heart belonged to another, but you didn't know who. Well, I thought it might be my mum, but I wasn't a hundred percent sure.' It all made sense; Sebastian's shock when he saw Lorna's daughter, because she looked just like her mum. The shell box that Willow had found, which belonged to her dad, with the key to The Beach House and the wolf necklace inside. And the little bracelet Briony had found accidentally in a secret compartment in her mother's identical shell box, inscribed with the words, *A Summer to Remember*. She looked Sebastian in the eye, and said, 'Well, now I *am* sure.'

Sebastian eyed her a long moment. 'We will talk, I promise. But there's something you need to know.'

Briony looked at him expectantly. It sounded just like what her grandmother had written in that letter. She folded her arms. 'Well …?'

'You need to talk to your mother.'

Briony scoffed, 'She's the last person I want to speak to right now.'

'Is that because you're pregnant, and you didn't tell her?' Troy asked.

Sebastian was picking up his track suit and shaking the sand out of it, when he stopped. 'Oh, I didn't congratulate you – about the baby.'

Briony did not want to be reminded about that embarrassing party and her pregnancy being revealed to everybody present.

Sebastian smiled at her fondly. 'It's such wonderful news, Briony – truly wonderful.'

Briony thought, *At least someone thinks so.* She'd caught Troy's grimace. That seemed to answer her question of whether Troy would want to raise someone else's child.

Sebastian surprised her by stepping forward and enveloping her in a hug.

Troy fixed his frown on his father. 'Can you let her go now, please?' Troy grabbed her hand, and took her to one side, still frowning at his father.

'Um, sorry,' Sebastian apologised to Briony. 'I've made your clothes wet.'

'It's all right.' What wasn't, though, was that he hadn't answered her question about his relationship with her mum. She realised she had no choice but to ask Lorna.

Sebastian said, 'I'm going into the house to change out of my wetsuit. But first I want to give my dad a piece of my mind.'

They all turned to look out to sea. The boat with the single occupant was heading to shore.

Troy still had hold of Briony's hand. He leaned in and whispered, 'I love you, Briony.'

Briony turned to look at him, wide-eyed.

'Say something, Briony.'

I love you too, she wanted to say, but instead, she said, 'We need to talk about—'

His eyes roved to her tummy. 'I know.'

Richard exclaimed, 'Here he comes!'

Sebastian joined Richard and Troy to help pull the boat to shore. They held it fast as Frank, in a black wetsuit, climbed out of the boat on to the beach.

Sebastian lifted off. 'Did you go diving? I thought you were just sailing the boat! What the hell is wrong with you? You know you don't go diving alone, especially when you haven't dived for years!'

Troy, Briony and Richard stood behind Sebastian as they all waited for an explanation.

Frank shrugged. 'I needed to clear my head, Sebastian.'

'You – what?'

'I just told you – I needed to clear my head. I've got a lot on my mind.'

'Why didn't you just go for a walk, like ordinary, *sane* people do?' Troy asked.

'Because of these?' He reached in the boat and took out a wad of letters in a plastic wallet. He sighed. 'She loved me. All along she loved me, and I never knew.'

Sebastian looked at the letters. 'Who are you talking about?'

Richard stepped forward. 'Blythe.'

Sebastian turned towards The Beach House. 'Blythe? Lorna's mum?'

Frank nodded. He looked at the boat. 'I wanted to go out and read them alone, then go for a dive, like I used to. You're right; it was a pretty stupid thing to do. I'm sorry.'

Sebastian folded his arms indignantly. 'And so you should be.

You scared me, all of us, taking the boat out like that. We thought you'd drowned. Where did you get it from, anyway?'

Richard raised his eyebrows at Frank. 'Shall I tell them about your spy in the village? That's who told you about the boat, isn't it? Because I know for a fact Troy didn't.'

Frank breathed a heavy sigh. 'All right, Richard.' Frank glanced at the boat. 'The barman at the pub—'

'Your spy.'

Frank threw Richard a look of annoyance. 'Yes, Richard, thanks for pointing that out,' he said sarcastically. 'My spy in the village heard about the boat from Peter, a guy I knew years ago who used to work at the boatyard. He'd popped in there for a pint, apparently, and happened to mention that he was in the village to see if a boat beached outside a property could be repaired.'

Sebastian looked at the boat. 'Are you saying this is the boat that Phoebe, Lorna and I used to go out in? Because it doesn't look like it is. Not at all.'

On closer inspection, although the boat had been in a bit of a state when it was beached in front of her grandmother's house, and Briony had imagined it would look quite different when restored, she didn't think it looked like the same boat either.

Frank said, 'It's not her boat.'

'Oh, my god. What did you do with it?' Sebastian asked.

Frank sighed. 'I wanted it repaired ASAP. I told them I'd pay whatever it took. However, because of the condition the boat was in, they had to take it to the boatyard in Southwold; said it could take up to six months to do a proper refit, the hull, the sails, the onboard motor; everything needed replacing. I'm used to getting what I want, when I want it. But this time …'

Richard shook his head. 'I'm not surprised. How did you think they could possibly get it repaired in one day? Anybody could see that wasn't going to happen – except you, Frank.'

Richard held up his hands before Frank responded. 'I know, I know, with the right amount of money, miracles can happen, which is what I had considered, but even I was surprised when I assumed it was Blythe's boat you'd sailed here after I'd seen it in your boathouse.'

Sebastian said, 'So, where did this boat come from?'

'I bought it.'

'Today – just like that?'

'Yeah – why not? I noticed it for sale in the boatyard where they'd taken Blythe's. They launched it for me from Walberswick and I sailed here.'

They all stared at the rather impressive little sailboat. Up close, there was no mistaking it for her grandmother's old boat.

Frank turned to Sebastian. 'I know why you reacted the way you did, Sebastian.'

'Are you saying I overreacted?'

'You were afraid that what happened to Phoebe would happen to me.'

Briony stared at them. She glanced at Troy's pained expression, realising they were talking about his mother. She said, 'Phoebe – drowned?'

Frank replied, 'She went diving alone.'

'It wouldn't have happened if I'd been there,' said Sebastian miserably.

'But you weren't to know,' said Frank, 'that she'd do something irresponsible and go diving alone.'

'I still blame myself. I thought Lorna did too, until I

discovered, when I met her again just recently, that Phoebe had asked her to go too. It led to the biggest misunderstanding, because I assumed Lorna blamed me, when all along she'd blamed herself for Phoebe's death, and consequently stayed away.'

Briony stared at the boat, wondering if there was more to her mother trying to put her off her love of the ocean, over the years, than just her past with Sebastian. Perhaps after what had happened to Phoebe, she was afraid her daughter would learn to dive and would drown, like her friend.

'You were so close, the three of you,' commented Frank, especially you and Phoebe. I thought that out of Lorna and Phoebe, it would have been Phoebe you got together with. After all, you were both from the same very well-off background, and at the same school, although you were boarding, and Phoebe was a day pupil. Whereas Lorna was the outsider, just spending her holidays here in Suffolk.'

Briony listened to all this with interest. This was her mum they were talking about. She realised that maybe Lorna couldn't face returning to The Beach House – not only because of her parents' break-up, and because of Sebastian, but because of the tragedy that had befallen their best friend Phoebe. But it sounded as though it really was not of their making. For whatever reason, neither of them had turned up to dive with Phoebe that day. But Frank was right: it wasn't their fault she had chosen to go out alone.

Frank continued, 'When you told me she'd had a baby at seventeen by her then boyfriend, I then realised it wasn't Phoebe, but Lorna, Blythe's daughter, that you were smitten with.'

Sebastian said, 'The day neither of us turned up, we … we knew we should be with Phoebe, but we didn't bring it up because … because we were together.'

Briony stared at Sebastian, catching his pained expression.

'In hindsight, I should have known she'd do something … stupid. Her boyfriend, the father of her child, had just dumped her, and she wanted … needed to go out and just dive, to get away from her cares.'

Briony stepped in. 'But you were only teenagers. How were you to know the repercussions?'

Frank looked at Briony and nodded in agreement. He turned to his son. 'I'm sorry, Sebastian.'

'And so you should be – going out alone, scaring the hell out of us, out of me.'

'No, I'm not talking about that. I'm talking about the phone call.'

Sebastian shook his head. 'Phone call? What are you talking about?'

'Lorna phoned to speak to you when she returned to Oxford.'

'Yes, I'm aware of that now. When she came back here, in search of her daughter, and we met up again after all these years, she told me she'd phoned, and recalled that you answered the phone and told her you'd pass on the message. I was surprised – I didn't recall that. But then so much went on that summer with Lorna's grandparents passing away, and then discovering Lorna and I were together when … when …' Sebastian paused. 'I wasn't in a good place, having just lost Phoebe. I don't remember.'

Frank pulled the hood down from his wetsuit, his wet hair plastered to his face. 'I wanted you to break it off with Lorna. I thought she'd break your heart, just like Blythe had broken mine.'

Sebastian stared at him. 'What did you do?'

Frank grimaced. 'I'm sorry, son, but I never passed on her message for you to phone her back. She wanted to speak to you. There was something important she wanted to tell you, apparently.'

'What was it?' Briony interrupted.

Frank shrugged. 'I have no idea.' He turned to Sebastian.

Sebastian shook his head. 'All these years, I thought she'd cut off contact with me, and didn't want to see me anymore.'

Frank sat down on the beach and stared out to sea. 'You were so young, only eighteen, still just a boy. I thought I knew what was best for you. I assumed you'd move on, and meet someone else. But I should have known …'

Troy looked at his father. Sebastian had fallen silent, so he asked, 'Known what?'

Frank looked around at Troy. 'That Lorna was the love of his life.'

Briony felt Troy's hand close around hers.

Frank took a step towards his son. 'Can you forgive me, Sebby? When I went to see Blythe at the hospital, and Lorna was there, I … I couldn't look her daughter in the eye. I was so overcome with guilt. I had to leave.'

Briony stared at Frank before turning her attention to Sebastian. His reaction to finding this out said it all – he was still in love with her mum. The question was: was her mum still in love with him?

Frank suddenly looked puzzled. 'Now you know what *I* was doing here. What are *you* all doing here?'

Troy said, 'Looking for you. We were worried about you.'.

Frank fixed his gaze on Briony. 'By the way – who are you?'

'She's my girl.'

Briony turned to look at Troy as she felt his arm slide around her waist.

Frank stared at her. 'So, you're the girl who stole my grandson's heart.'

'Yes, this is Blythe's granddaughter.'

'Ah, I see the resemblance. You take after your mother's side, for sure.' He stepped forward and pointed at her. 'Don't betray him, and break his heart – I mean it.'

'I … I …'

'She won't,' Troy said.

Briony turned to Troy. 'But—'

Troy put a finger to her lips, and whispered, 'I think we're both even on the lying by omission front, don't you?' He cocked his head at his grandfather.

Briony knew immediately what he was talking about – spying for his grandfather. She shifted her attention from Frank to Sebastian. 'I'd better go.'

'Go – where?' Troy asked.

'I have some unfinished business.'

'With your mum?'

'Yes. And my grandmother.' There was something her grandmother had wanted to tell her. She couldn't wait to meet her – and find out. She just wished something that Angel had said hadn't suddenly come to mind – *I saw the relief that swept over you mum's face when you said your grandmother was in a coma.*

45

'Here, before you go.' Troy put an envelope in Briony's hands. He looked over at his grandfather. 'This doesn't belong to you. I wish … I wish I'd never been your spy.'

Briony looked at the envelope. 'What's this?'

'It's the deeds to The Beach House. I found them.'

'How … when?'

'When you found me upstairs during the party, remember? I'm ashamed to admit it, but I was searching high and low for the deeds, as per my grandfather's instructions.'

Briony threw Frank a filthy look. How could she tell her grandmother that he was behind all this? How could *he* tell her? Now she knew why he had been reading those letters on that boat, and going for a dive. He had been figuring out how he was going to tell her himself – without losing her again. That wasn't Briony's problem.

She turned to Troy. 'Are you saying they were in The Beach House all along? I looked myself, and never found them.'

'They were in the old bureau you'd brought in from the outbuilding.'

'They couldn't have been. I looked in there too.'

'But you didn't find the secret compartment.'

Secret compartment? Briony mouthed.

Troy nodded. 'I've been such a fool. I was going to give them to you, save them for after we'd cut the ribbon, during the party. Then I saw Sebastian waving at you through the window, got mad, rushed downstairs, and stashed the deeds in the glove compartment.'

'You came back in the house,' Briony recalled.

'Yes, I sat in the truck, calmed down, and realised as usual I was just overreacting, so I thought I'd give them to you after the party, as a surprise.'

'Then Freddie turned up.'

Troy nodded. He didn't need to say anything more. They both understood what had happened.

'Can you forgive me?'

Frank stepped forward. Briony noticed. She held up her hand, and said, 'Don't. Say. A word!'

Frank surprised everyone by shutting his mouth.

Briony smiled at Troy. 'You know I can.'

Richard looked at Frank. In all the years he'd know him, Frank had only ever let one person talk to him that way, and it wasn't himself or Frank's late wife. It was Blythe. He peered at Briony, a young woman Frank had only just met, and thought, *What makes her so special?* Perhaps it was the fact that she reminded him of Blythe.

Richard's lip curled into a smile. This was just what Troy needed. If he didn't know how to stand up to his formidable grandfather, then here was a young woman, someone he was going to spend the rest of his life with, who would teach him how – it was a match made in heaven. He slapped his knee. What were the chances that Troy would fall in love with Blythe's granddaughter?

Briony glanced at Richard, wondering what he was looking so pleased about. She then turned her attention to Frank. She'd shut him up because she didn't need him telling her that she must forgive Troy. She could tell Frank was used to giving the orders, getting his own way. Briony looked at the man she loved and decided that things were going to change.

Troy took her hand. 'You will come back – won't you?'

She offered him a reassuring smile. 'Of course I will. But Troy, will you do something for me?'

'Anything – just name it.'

'Will you look after my grandmother's dog, Luna?'

Sebastian overheard. He stepped forward. 'I'll do it.'

'No, I'll look after her dog,' said Frank.

Briony eyed Frank. Perhaps that wasn't a bad idea – Luna might help break the ice when he told Blythe the truth. 'You have to take her with you to the hospital. My grandmother will love to see her. But Luna is also a therapy dog in training.'

'Ah,' said Richard, 'she needs to earn her stripes.'

Briony looked at him quizzically. She had no clue what that meant, but Frank was nodding, and so was Sebastian. She shrugged. 'Well, yeah I guess.' Briony added, 'You need to take her to visit the people on the ward where Grandma has a side room. Oh and the children's ward.'

She caught the look on Frank's face, and smiled a knowing smile. Frank had to come down from his ivory tower and meet some ordinary people in the community for a change – families with sick children going through a tough time. Maybe he'd learn a bit of humility along the way.

That thought gave her another idea. 'Oh, and Luna has other rounds too.'

'What – more therapy?' Frank raised his eyebrows.

'Of sorts. You have to take Luna to see Joss.'

'Who?'

Troy said, 'He is quite a guy. I like him. He's a lawyer who volunteers his time helping people in the community sort out their problems.'

'For free?'

Nobody bothered to dignify that question with an answer, although Sebastian said sarcastically, 'That's why they call it *volunteering*, Dad.'

'Why would he do … that—' Frank stopped short when he caught everyone staring at him.

Sebastian shook his head at his dad. 'I'm going up to the house to change.' He scooped up his tracksuit from the sand.

Troy rolled his eyes at his grandpa and said what everyone else was thinking. 'Because helping others is just the right thing to do. I should not have to spell that out. Perhaps Luna here will give you some lessons in humility.'

Briony grinned at Troy. So did Richard.

Briony thought, *He's taken the words right out of my mouth.*

Troy turned to Briony. 'Sorry, but I don't understand why you can't take her with you if you're going to see them in the hospital?' He halted. 'Oh, god – you're not planning on coming back – are you?'

Briony squeezed his hand. 'I told you – I *am* coming back. Just not immediately.'

He raised his eyebrows.

'I have some … unfinished business in Oxford.'

He whispered, 'Freddie?'

She nodded.

She glanced at Frank. 'It's agreed, then. You'll take Luna. And do what I said.'

Frank stared at her. 'All right, yes. It's agreed.'

Frank caught Richard grinning. 'What's got into you – grinning like a Chesire cat?'

Richard's eyes roved to Briony.

Troy said, 'Wait, what about Wilbur, your foster fail? And the kittens? You're not taking them with you – are you?'

Briony looked at him. She knew she'd arranged with Emily to take all the animals back, although she couldn't imagine handing any of them over, most especially her sweet little sausage dog.

'I'll take him,' Troy said quickly. 'I'll take Wilbur.'

'All right. But I'll be back for him.'

Troy grinned. 'I know. I'm counting on it.'

Briony smiled. She knew what his game was. If he took her dog, he knew it was guaranteed she'd be back.

Luna came running down the beach, straight up to Troy.

'Hey girl!'

'What is that?' said Frank, his eyes wide, taking a step back.

'That is Luna,' said Briony, realising Sebastian must have let the dog out when he went to change. For some reason, she thought it might have been Frank who'd secretly given her grandmother the puppy, although thinking about it, she couldn't imagine why he'd do such a thing. She guessed it might remain a mystery unless Blythe told her where Luna had come from.

'What about the kittens? Can I have them?'

Briony whirled around at the sound of Willow's voice behind

her 'Willow, sweetheart, what are you doing out here? I thought you were looking after them in the house?'

'I wanted to come and see Grandpa. I was worried.'

'There was nothing to be worried about,' said Frank reassuringly. 'And by the way – do you know you're my favourite granddaughter?'

'I'm you're *only* granddaughter,' said Willow, rolling her eyes, looking as though she'd heard it all before.

Briony was smiling at that comment when she saw that Sebastian had joined them again, now dressed in his tracksuit.

Willow looked at her grandpa. 'You promised I could have the kittens.'

Grandpa looked nervously at his granddaughter. 'Willow, why don't we have his conversation in private.'

'You promised that if I was your spy, and told you everything that happened at The Beach House, then I could have them.'

Everyone turned around and looked at Frank.

Sebastian rounded on his father. 'Really? A five-year-old child. What on earth are you teaching her?' He looked at Troy and mumbled, 'And that's the reason I wanted her kept away from his influence.'

Troy lowered his eyes. 'Sorry, Dad.'

Frank lowered his eyes too, and said, 'I'm a bad person, aren't I?'

Everyone said, 'Yes!' in unison, apart from Willow. 'No, you're not. I love you, Grandpa.'

Grandpa knelt down and gave her a hug.

'Ugh, you're all wet, Grandpa. Where are your normal clothes?'

'Right there!' Frank pointed at the boat. 'Now, let's go and find those kittens, shall we? And then Grandpa can get out of this wetsuit.' He picked up a carrier bag containing his clothes out of the boat, and paused in front of Briony. 'Is it okay if she has the kittens?'

Briony said, 'I think you need to ask her dad – don't you?' She turned around and looked at Sebastian. So did Frank. Before he had a chance to ask, Willow was begging her dad, 'Please? Please can I have them?'

Of course, Sebastian said yes.

How could he not? thought Briony.

Frank looked at his granddaughter, before settling his gaze on his son. 'You won't … keep her from me, will you? I promise to mend my ways.'

'No more spying, Grandpa,' said Willow, frowning at him.

Frank crossed his heart. 'I promise, no more spying.'

Sebastian sighed. 'Go on, then, take your grandfather and show him your kittens.'

Briony had been holding her breath, hoping Sebastian would forgive Frank.

Frank took Willow's hand. As he passed Troy, he paused, and put an affectionate hand on his grandson's shoulder. Briony saw Frank looking her way. She heard him whisper, 'You've found a good 'un, Troy, like Blythe.'

Frank glanced at The Beach House. 'I should have confronted Blythe's parents, then I'd have probably found out the truth – that she still loved me. But I didn't. Like the fool I was, I ran away to sea, and then resolved to earn a lot of money, and prove I was worth as much her parents. I know they looked down on me, thought I wasn't good enough for their daughter. I had no idea she did not feel the same way. I thought it had rubbed off on her.' He sighed. 'All these years, and who would have thought it – I didn't have to prove a thing.'

'Come on, Grandpa! Stop talking! I want to show you my kittens.'

Frank managed to get one more sentence in before Willow dragged him away. 'Whatever you do, don't let her go. Follow her, follow her to the ends of the earth, if you have to. Don't end up like myself, or Sebastian.'

Sebastian also put a hand on Troy's shoulder and gave him an affectionate squeeze before following Frank and Willow to The Beach House.

Briony watched them before turning to Troy. 'I will be back, I promise.'

Troy smiled. 'I know. And do you know how I know?'

Briony knew all right. 'Because I love you, Troy.'

Richard stood there, awkwardly. 'Well, I guess I'm done here.'

'I'll meet you back at Frank's house,' said Troy.

Richard shook his head as he gazed at the little boat, imagining Frank spending many happy hours taking Blythe sailing again. Little wonder he'd left it there, probably anticipating that very thing. 'I have a feeling Frank will no longer require my services.'

Troy's expression clouded. 'He's not going to fire you, is he, for telling us about the boat?'

'No.'

'Oh, you're retiring?'

Richard shook his head. 'Not me, no.'

Troy looked at him quizzically as Richard's gaze turned from the boat towards The Beach House. 'Now your grandfather has found Blythe, his priorities are going to change.' He turned to Troy. 'Are you ready to step up and head the company?'

'Are you serious?'

'Oh, yes.'

'I'll need you, Richard. I hope you're not going to retire if my grandpa goes.'

Richard grinned. 'I think there's still some mileage in the old engine yet – if you really want me to stay on, that is.'

'Of course I do!' Troy frowned. 'But I might not be here myself.'

Richard knitted his brow. 'Where are *you* going?'

Troy turned to look at Briony, who was standing with her back to them, looking out to sea.

Richard smiled. 'Oh, I understand. Perhaps I'll see you later today up at the house. Or perhaps not.' He walked over and gave Troy a hug before he took his leave.

Briony turned around. She'd heard the conversation. As she watched Richard walk to The Beach House, probably to catch a lift with Sebastian, Willow and Frank when they all left, she said, 'I'm going to the hospital to see my grandmother.'

'Wherever you're going, Briony, I want to come with you.'

'I know.' Briony took his hands in hers. 'But I need to do this on my own. You understand – don't you?'

'Of course. Then you're straight off to Oxford to … sort things out?'

Briony looked over at The Beach House. She wasn't just going to Oxford to see Freddie. If her mum and Sebastian were getting back together, then someone had to break the devastating news to her dad. But that was up to her mum to do – wasn't it? She still couldn't believe her mum would do that, break up with her dad after all these years together. But then, if it had turned out she'd been unhappily married all this time to the wrong person – Freddie came to mind – then could she really blame her?

Briony looked at the envelope Troy had given her. At least one thing had been cleared up. She had the deeds to her grandmother's home in her hands.

'Have you looked at the name on the deeds?'

Briony shook her head. 'I haven't even opened the envelope.' She looked up. 'That's a peculiar question – why do you ask? Have *you*?'

He shook his head. 'No, I haven't opened the envelope either – but Frank has.'

'And?'

Troy shrugged. 'I don't know, but something's going on, because he said something really odd.'

'Oh yeah – what did he say?'

'He said that all these years, your grandmother has lived here keeping a secret.'

'What do you mean?' Briony asked.

'That's exactly what I asked him.'

Briony waited for an explanation.

'He just said that it turns out The Beach House has belonged to someone else all along.'

Briony said, 'What are you talking about?'

'I guess someone else's name must be on those deeds.'

They both looked at the envelope in her hands and then turned to look at The Beach House.

Troy said, 'At least it explains one thing.'

'What's that?'

'Why your grandmother hid the deeds.'

46

Briony paused outside the door to her grandmother's hospital room, trying to summon the courage to face her mum. She had a feeling of déjà vu. She'd been down this road before, just that morning, hanging back, listening to Frank and her grandmother talking before she followed him home. Now it was her mum and grandmother chatting.

Just step inside the room, rather than hide behind the door this time, she admonished herself. *But I don't want to interrupt them.* Although she didn't want to eavesdrop again, she would rather not walk in on them when they were deep in conversation – not when she hoped that after all those years of estrangement, they would finally put the past behind them.

Briony hung back, listening, waiting for the right moment to make her presence known.

'I'm so sorry, Lorna – about everything.'

'I know, Mum.' There was a pause. 'I met Sebastian again.'

'You did?'

'Just yesterday. I told him that all those years ago I tried to get in touch with him, but he never returned my call.'

Blythe said, 'I'm so sorry, Lorna. I don't know why that was.'

Briony did. She'd heard Frank confess to Sebastian that he hadn't passed on her message, believing Lorna would break his heart in the way he had assumed Blythe had broken his. Frank had thought he was protecting his son.

'I have to confess, though, that I was pleased he hadn't got in touch with you, Lorna. I knew that Sebastian was Frank's son. Frank had broken my heart many years earlier – or so I thought. Stupidly, all I could think was, *Like father, like son*. I didn't want you to go through the heartbreak that I had.'

'But don't you see, Mum? I was heartbroken when I thought he hadn't called back, and he'd broken it off.'

'I know that now. I am so sorry, darling. So awfully sorry.'

Briony wiped away a tear. How terribly, terribly sad that what her great-grandparents had done – keeping Frank and Blythe apart, apparently believing he wasn't good enough for their daughter – had haunted future generations.

Not me, though, thought Briony.

'It wasn't just because you and Dad broke up, and I blamed you, that I stayed away.'

'It was because you thought Sebastian had broken up with you?'

'Yes, we had … plans. But it was more than that.'

'It was about Phoebe, wasn't it?' said Blythe.

There was a long silence, during which Briony stood by the door, full of indecision. Should she go? Come back later? If she stepped in now, they might think she'd been eavesdropping. And they'd be right. But she didn't want to leave, especially now the conversation had turned to Troy's mum.

Lorna replied, 'Yes, I always blamed myself for what happened that day, and thought the reason Sebastian didn't return my call was because he blamed me too. But when I met him yesterday, I discovered my message had never been passed on all those years ago, and it had been a big misunderstanding.' She paused. 'I know why we blamed ourselves and thought we blamed each other. Because we were together that day, instead of with Phoebe.'

'You can't blame yourself, Lorna. You were young and in love.'

'And I'd just lost my grandparents. The last thing I wanted to do was go diving on that occasion.'

Briony listened as she looked around the ward. Fortunately, all the patients in the room were either dozing in their chairs or were occupied with visitors of their own – otherwise she wouldn't have been surprised if one or two of them asked where Luna was, giving away the fact that she was there, listening to her mum and grandmother in the side room.

Briony was about to leave, deciding to come back a bit later, when she heard her grandmother say, 'There's something I need to tell you, Lorna.'

'What is it?'

'I have a confession to make.'

Briony looked at the deeds in her hand. She heard her grandmother say, 'It's about The Beach House.'

'I guessed as much,' said Lorna. 'You're leaving The Beach House to Briony – aren't you?'

'No, that's your prerogative.'

'I'm sorry? Oh, right. You're leaving it to me now?'

'No, it was already left to you, by your great-grandparents. When they died. In their will.'

Briony looked at the deeds in her hand. There was her

mum's name, her maiden name, in black and white. Unbeknown to her mum, she'd owned it since she was eighteen. Briony had already looked at the deeds before she'd arrived at the hospital. She slipped the precious piece of paper back in the envelope.

'I'm sorry – what did you say?' Lorna asked.

'You loved the ocean, the beach, and you loved that holiday home. Your grandparents knew that. And they assumed I was happy in Oxford with Edwin. So, they left you The Beach House.'

There was another long, drawn-out silence. Briony anticipated that her mum would ask Blythe why she'd kept that from her for all these years. But what did it matter now? Besides, it was obvious; Blythe hadn't been happy in her marriage. She hadn't been in love with Edwin. All along, she'd been in love with Frank.

Briony realised that when Blythe's parents died, The Beach House would have come into its own as somewhere she could live if she left Edwin. But it came with one glaring drawback which Blythe had managed to keep a secret the day they died – The Beach House, where she'd lived all those years, did not belong to her.

After looking at the deeds, Briony had hoped her grandmother would tell her mum the truth. She imagined that was what Blythe had written to them both about. She was giving it back. Perhaps she hoped that, if all went well with her operation, Lorna would let her carry on living there. And then her granddaughter would inherit it one day.

Briony was just pondering it all when she overheard her grandmother say, 'We both put on a good show of it, you know, for my parents' sake. For society's sake.'

'What are you talking about, Mum?'

Blythe continued, 'But then Edwin met someone, and we couldn't keep up the pretence anymore. I had to leave. I had nowhere to go – don't you see? But there was The Beach House—'

'What do you mean – Edwin met someone?'

'Oh, that relationship didn't last. But we both knew it was the end of ours.'

Briony stared into space. So, her grandparents had had a marriage of convenience, both in love with other people.

'I never knew,' Lorna finally said.

Another silence followed in which Briony imagined her mum was trying to process that revelation.

'That last summer we spent at The Beach House together was a summer to remember for all the wrong reasons,' said Blythe.

'I know. Grandpa and Grandma died that summer,' said Lorna. 'They'd had a good innings, though, the two of them. They always seemed so in love, right until the end.'

'It's true. That's why they went, one after the other. They'd always said they couldn't imagine life without each other, and wished they could go together. Well, they almost got their wish,' commented Blythe.

'The last summer I was here, I turned eighteen. I was in love – with Sebastian.'

Blythe said, 'It was the summer you became a woman.'

'Yes, it was a summer to remember all right. The summer I became pregnant with my beautiful girl.'

Briony stood stock still. Her mum had been in love with Sebastian, *and* she'd fallen pregnant that summer. Briony frowned. That wasn't right. She must have become pregnant a month later.

When she started university and met … my dad.

Oh, my god, Briony mouthed behind the door. If what her mum had said was true, that meant—

'Does Sebastian know – about Briony? Have you told him?'

'Of course I have.'

Briony put her hand to her mouth in shock. She then recalled something Sebastian had said on the beach. He'd said, *We will talk, I promise. But there's something you need to know.*

She remembered looking at him expectantly, waiting for him to tell her what that was. But all he'd said was, *You need to talk to your mother.*

Now, her impulse was to flee the hospital; she didn't want to hear any more of this. But she found herself rooted to the spot, listening to her mum continue.

'When we met up and talked for the first time since we lost Phoebe, we realised that at least something good – no, something amazing – came out of that last day Sebastian and I spent together.'

'You're talking about Briony.'

'Yes. I know we weren't there for Phoebe, but I think we're both starting to come to terms with that. We can't change what happened.'

Blythe said, 'And who's to say it wasn't the first time she'd taken a risk and dived alone?'

'Yes, I had thought of that possibility.'

Blythe added, 'Perhaps if things had played out differently that day, and you'd all met up like you usually did …'

Briony was listening intently, suddenly feeling frustrated that her grandmother had trailed off.

'I know what you're saying, Mum. I thought about that

myself many times, over the years. I might never have had my Briony.'

The room fell silent for a moment.

'Oh, Mum. I needed that house, all those years ago. I wanted to raise my daughter there.'

'And I wanted you here.'

'You did?'

'Of course I did. What mother wouldn't? But it was your father who persuaded me to … lie about the will, which I didn't really have to, not overtly; it was just assumed that my parents had left The Beach House to me. He wanted to make sure you stayed with him in Oxford.'

'Why?'

'He said I'd be ruining your future if you stayed here rather than taking up your place at Oxford.'

'Ruining my future by staying here with Sebastian? The love of my life, and the father of my child?'

Briony shook her head slowly, still finding it hard to accept. *Sebastian is my father? It can't be true – it just can't.*

'We thought … Edwin thought Sebastian wasn't good enough for you, and he believed you were too young to decide what you wanted, even though I'd put it to him that we should let you decide whether you wanted to come here and live with me. I knew I was being selfish; it was what I wanted – three generations, you, me and my grandchild living in The Beach House. But he said you were only eighteen, and he knew what was best for his own daughter. I recall that he said, *What does an eighteen-year-old know of love?*'

What does a fifteen-year-old know of love? thought Briony. *Oh Grandma – you and grandad repeated history.*

'But that wasn't your decision to make,' said Lorna. 'Like it wasn't Grandma and Grandpa's decision to make about you and Frank.'

'I know,' Blythe said, barely above a whisper. She paused before adding, 'But you met Andrew and got your degree, and had a nice life in Oxford.'

'But at what cost, Mum? And do you know how much I tried to dissuade Briony from her love of the ocean, just because I couldn't stand going to the beach? It just reminded me of what could have been, if only you'd been different.'

'If only Edwin had been different,' Blythe corrected her.

'But you could have said no and told him that I was going to live with you.'

'Edwin was very persuasive. You have to understand, Lorna. I'd grown up doing as I was told, by my parents, and then by my husband. And I truly thought I was doing right by you, putting you first, putting aside my own feelings of how much I wanted you here with me, how much I wanted my grandchild here, with me, because Edwin told me that if I didn't, I'd just hold you back.'

Briony heard her grandmother sigh heavily.

'I've been such a fool, Lorna. How was I to know the repercussions of going along with Edwin's plan – that I'd lose you, and my grandchild? I had no clue that you would cut me out of your lives. You know how many times I tried to reach out to you, over the years, and to Briony, sending her birthday and Christmas cards? But I respected your wishes. All along, Edwin said it was a sacrifice I had to make for you to have a better life, in Oxford, with Andrew. He sent me photos, and we communicated over the years, about you, about Briony.'

'This is mad! Why didn't you tell me all this – that it wasn't your idea, but Dad's?'

Blythe paused for a moment. 'He believed that if you didn't go to university, find yourself, you'd regret it, and you might come to resent your child for holding you back.'

'Never!' Lorna exclaimed.

'But you'll never know, will you? Because you *did* go up to Oxford.'

Briony looked down at her tummy. Was that what would happen to her if she didn't do her master's? She'd already given up that Galapagos Islands trip. In the future, would she come to resent her child for all those lost opportunities?

'But Andrew wasn't the man I loved, truly loved. I'd have given all that up, the house, the degree, just to bring her up here, with you.'

'No, you mean with Sebastian.'

Lorna fell silent.

Blythe said, 'I couldn't go back to Edwin, and give up The Beach House, but I didn't have it in my heart to tell you that it was Edwin who had broken our marriage vows. You were always such a daddy's girl, and you had enough going on in your life back then. I didn't want you to fall out with Edwin too.'

'But I … I couldn't forgive you for not letting me stay here.'

'Can you forgive me now – for everything?'

'Yes, yes I can, Mum. I guess I do feel fortunate that, under the circumstances, I met Andrew, who has been a doting father.'

'Yes, I heard.'

'We argued, just recently, before I came. I wanted to tell Briony, years ago. It had always been the plan that she'd grow up knowing that Andrew wasn't her biological father. But Andrew loved her so much, he said it would break his heart if she found out he wasn't her dad. I realised that I couldn't do that to him. You know, I wanted to bring her here, to see you, but I couldn't risk breaking Andrew's heart if you told Briony the truth.'

'And perhaps,' said Blythe, 'there's another reason you stayed away. You couldn't risk breaking your own heart all over again, if your daughter wanted to find Sebastian.'

Briony stood there, tears rolling down her face. She didn't know whether she was angry with her parents for not telling her, but she knew she was hurt, more than anything else, that everyone else seemed to know the big secret.

'What now, Lorna? You can't keep this a secret anymore.'

'I know.'

Briony willed herself to step into the room. It would be the perfect time to show her face and tell them what she'd overheard. But she just couldn't.

The room fell silent. Then her mum whispered, 'I think we stayed together for Briony's sake. I found out this morning that Andrew has met someone else.'

Briony's eyebrows shot up. She didn't know how much more of this she could take.

'Oh, Lorna. When?'

'I think it's been going on for some time. The cruises.'

'Cruises?'

'Yeah, he goes on cruises to earn money playing in a quartet. He left for a cruise yesterday. It's someone in the quartet.'

Briony's mouth dropped open. Her dad wasn't her dad, and now she was finding out he was having an affair. Suddenly, she felt she didn't know him; she didn't know either of her parents. The two people in the world she thought she could trust, whom she assumed she knew better than anyone, were not who she thought they were; it felt like her whole life was all a lie.

Before Blythe could respond, Briony heard her mum say, 'I think Briony has met someone else too. I want to tell her not to make the same mistake – to say: if you are in love with this new man in your life, don't stay with Freddie for the sake of your baby. You'll be unhappy. You'll live to regret it.'

'Oh, Lorna. Is that what's happened to you?'

'Andrew and I, we were happy, in the beginning. Of course I could never love him the way I loved Sebastian, but we shared good times raising Briony. I'd say we were happy, once upon a time, but—'

'You knew something was missing?' ventured Blythe.

'Yes. Always did.'

There was a pause before Lorna said, 'Why did you write to Briony, after all these years, when I'd told you to stop sending the birthday cards and Christmas cards?'

'I was going into hospital. It was only a minor operation, but you know, going under general anaesthesia is not without risks. I had to sign a waiver, and then I realised if it turned out it was my time, I couldn't go with things left … unresolved.'

'Well, there's no fear of that now, Mum.'

Briony was surprised to hear them both laugh out loud. When the laughter subsided, she heard her mum say, 'You know, my girl is going to have a little one of her own.'

Briony's eyebrows shot up. What was her mum saying?

'A little one of her own? She's going to have a baby?'

'Yes, you're going to be a great-grandmother.'

'Oh, Lorna, it's such exciting news.'

'Yes, isn't it! I can't believe my baby is having a baby. I'm so excited too, to be a grandmother.'

Briony could feel relief sweeping over her.

'You are – even though you're so young to be a grandmother?'

'Of course. Life does have a habit of not going to plan, Mum. I know that more than anybody.'

'So, do I,' Blythe agreed.

'But just because the timing may be a bit … off,' continued Lorna, 'that doesn't mean there's any less reason to celebrate.'

'But I thought she wanted to go back to university and become a marine biologist?'

'You know about that?' said Lorna.

'Edwin told me.'

Lorna said, 'My daughter is very resourceful. Knowing her, she'll have the baby, and still do her course, and even go to the Galapagos Islands.'

'The Galapagos Islands?'

'Yes, she should have been there right now.'

'Oh, is it because I asked her to come that she gave that up?'

'No, I think she needed somewhere to go, and someone to speak to, when she found out she was pregnant.'

'So, she came here, to me?'

'Yes, Mum. I just wish she hadn't felt she couldn't come to me.'

'Why didn't she, do you think?'

Briony listened, wondering what her mum would say to that.

'Because I think she felt I would have been disappointed in her, repeating the same mistake, getting pregnant so young.'

'But it's not a mistake. A baby is never a mistake. And she's not quite so young. Not like you were.'

'Yes, that's what I'm dying to tell her, if she'll just give me a chance. She didn't have to run away and deal with this all on her own.'

'Well, she's not on her own now,' said Blythe. 'She has you and me.'

Her face wet with tears, Briony held her breath and stole a glance into the room – although she was still not ready to face either of them quite yet. She caught her mum, who was sitting by Blythe's bedside with her back to the door, take Blythe's hand, and squeeze it tight. She said, 'Yes, she does.'

'Where is she? I want to meet her. She left me flowers, you know, and a card to say that she's been visiting me almost every day, and that a surprise awaits me when I return home to The Beach House.'

Briony heard her mum sigh heavily. 'I'm afraid she's locked herself in the outbuilding. I crept in using the spare key and left her a little note last night, along with a duvet, pillow, and some provisions. But she stayed in there all night. I hope she comes to talk to me today.'

'The outbuilding! She can't stay in there!'

'Oh, dear. I think I've ruined her surprise. It was her surprise for you, for when you get better and return home. She's had it done up, you know, exactly to the plans you left on the kitchen table.'

'She has? Oh, my goodness! I can't believe she did that. She sounds so wonderful. I really can't wait to meet her. We've got so much catching up to do.' Blythe paused.

Briony knew that this would be the perfect cue for her to make an appearance. She wiped the tears from her cheeks.

'Talking of catching up,' said Blythe, 'Don't take my word for all this. I think it's time you spoke to your father.'

'I speak to him all the time.'

'Of that I have no doubt.'

'But I still wish you'd told me all this – why you wouldn't let me come and stay at The Beach House, with you, instead of leaving me to believe, all these years, that it was all your decision.'

'Oh, Lorna, your father is your idol. I was afraid that if I told you, then I'd end up telling you … something else about your father. The reason we parted ways, and I had to leave him. I've kept his secret for far too long.'

'You're talking about his affair?'

'Well, it's more than that. It's so silly, to me at any rate, to almost everyone, I expect, but he's just been so afraid you'd look at him … differently … if you knew.'

'Knew what?'

'It's not for me to say what he should have told you about himself years ago, but if he does summon the courage, it will explain everything.'

Briony stood staring at the door. That was exactly what she needed right now: someone to explain everything. Her impulse to take flight had returned. She did not want to talk to her mother and grandmother just then, who had kept a humongous secret from her all her life. What she needed was to see her grandfather, and for him to explain everything.

47

'Ah, feels like old times – doesn't it?' Edwin placed her suitcase down on the single bed in the spare bedroom. 'I remember when you used to come and stay. It seems like a lifetime ago.' He smiled. 'Once you started university, and met Freddie, it was understandable that you'd be busy – too busy to visit your old grandpa.'

She glanced at him. He winked – *just kidding!*

'So, I have to say I was quite surprised when you phoned out of the blue to say you wanted to catch the next flight here. What happened? I thought you were in the Galapagos Islands?'

Briony turned around and eyed him. He was standing in the bedroom doorway of his university-owned rental home.

When she'd phoned him at the airport to say that she was getting the next flight over, if he could buy her a plane ticket, because she was short of cash, he'd sounded surprised that she wasn't on her research trip. But she could tell he was keen to see her, and was going along with her simple explanation – that she'd decided not to go. He hadn't pressed her for a reason, probably not wanting to put her off with a bout of twenty questions about her cancelled trip, and lack of money, before she arrived.

She was intending to tell him what was going on, but she expected something in return – the truth, and the whole truth, about Blythe and their relationship, and Sebastian – everything, along with the answer to another question; did her dad really know she wasn't his biological daughter?

She wanted, needed, to be sure what she'd overheard was all true, and that she wasn't imagining it all. And the one person she still trusted was him – even though it sounded as though he had a secret too.

Albert brought in a tea tray with cups of tea and English scones that he'd baked. As she took a scone, and looked at him – her grandfather's lodger who'd lived with him for years, ever since he'd moved to Stanford – all the pieces finally fell into place. Why hadn't she seen it before? Why hadn't her mum? Busy in their own lives, they'd never stopped to look, *really* look.

'So, what's this all about?' Edwin asked, 'You, here.'

'I've got something to ask you.'

'You flew all the way here to ask me a question?'

Briony watched Albert pop a scone on Edwin's plate too, his hand brushing Edwin's shoulder before he left the room.

Briony called out, 'Albert, why don't you stay for tea too?'

He turned around at the door. 'Oh, I couldn't possibly. You've come here to talk to Edwin about family affairs.'

'Yes, that's right. That's why you should join us too.'

Albert hesitated. 'I don't understand …'

Briony shook her head and smiled. 'But I do. I should have known. All along, since I was little coming here for holidays, it was staring me in the face, but I just didn't see it – until now.'

Albert exchanged a glance with Edwin, and said to her, 'Darling, I have no idea what you're talking about.'

Briony pointed at the seat on the sofa next to Edwin. 'Come, sit down.'

Albert shrugged nonchalantly. 'Well, if you insist, but I still don't know what this is all about.'

'Well, you're in good company,' commented Edwin.

Briony watched him take a seat, looking uncomfortable.

Edwin asked, 'What *is* this all about, Briony?'

She stared at the couple before her. They'd hidden their relationship well. Briony smiled at them. She realised she'd done a lot of growing up in the past two weeks, finding out she was pregnant, and leaving home on her own for the Suffolk Coast. She'd changed. She'd found herself, and along the way she'd discovered that her family members were not exactly who she'd thought they were. But she could forgive them that – how could she not? They were only human with their flaws, their secrets, and their fears. She looked at her grandfather and wished he hadn't been afraid, all these years, of telling them all the truth.

Briony leaned forward in her seat. 'Tell me about my grandmother, about Blythe. I've seen the photos you sent her over the years of me and mum.'

Edwin was out of his seat in an instant. 'You've been to see Blythe! She told you, didn't she? Blythe told you about … about us.' He exchanged a glance with Albert.

Albert reached up and took his hand. 'Sit down, you old fool, and stop getting so worked up. I guess she knows now, and there's nothing you can do about it.'

'Is that why you sent her all those photos over the years, of me and mum? An unspoken agreement that if you kept your side of the bargain – keeping her updated with our lives – she'd keep your secret?'

'All right, yes. It *was* kind of an unspoken agreement.'

Briony sat chewing her fingernail. 'Oh, Grandpa. Albert is right, you are an old fool. You didn't have to hide who you are from us.'

Albert said, 'See, I told you.'

'I'm just so happy you're not alone, and you have Albert in your life.'

The three of them sat quietly for a moment, drinking tea. Edwin wiped tears from his eyes, realising that the years he'd spent hiding his relationship with Albert, for no reason other than his own fears, were over. They were both right: he'd been a silly old fool.

Edwin put his teacup down, and asked, 'Why did you go and see her, Briony? How did you even know where she was?'

'Because she wrote me a letter, and asked me to go. She said there was something she needed to give to me.'

'What was that?'

'The truth – I guess. I haven't spoken with her yet. She was in hospital.'

'Is she all right?'

Briony caught the genuine concern in his voice. 'Yes, she's going to be okay. Mum is with her now.'

'Your mother is there with her?' he said in surprise. 'Have they patched things up?'

'I think so – yes. You shouldn't have done it, though.'

Albert turned to Edwin. 'What did you do?'

Edwin turned to Briony. 'How much do you know?'

'Everything!' But she still wanted to hear it from him. She wasn't sure why – perhaps hearing it from the one person in her life, besides her parents, whom she trusted implicitly, would make it seem real – Lorna's relationship with Sebastian, and the fact that they'd been kept apart. Besides, this was the only place she'd been able to think of going to clear her head and take on board what she'd found out.

On the flight, when she'd settled into her seat, and had finally had some time to finally think about things – after first rushing back to The Beach House to pack, and organise a taxi to Heathrow, and a flight to Stanford – something had suddenly dawned on her about Troy. Although they weren't related – Sebastian had adopted Troy and wasn't his biological parent – it did make them step-siblings. What did that mean for their relationship? Should it mean anything? She hadn't spoken to Troy yet, although he had texted, checking she was okay, asking whether she had given the deeds to her mum, and when he could expect her back from Oxford.

That had been just before she'd caught her flight. She hadn't answered him. Not yet. Not when she'd suddenly realised that Sebastian wasn't all they shared; Frank was her biological grandfather. He and his late wife were her paternal grandparents; not Andrew's parents, with whom she'd never been that close.

And then it had dawned on her that there was someone else she and Troy shared. Willow – Sebastian's other biological child. *I have a sibling, a half-sister!* She couldn't wait to tell her. She guessed that little Willow would be so happy to find out she had a big sister.

But what would Troy make of finding out that Sebastian was her father? At least it explained one thing – why she was drawn to Sebastian, and why they had hit it off so quickly, and had so much in common, with their shared love of the sea.

The time she'd spent on the flight, thinking, had raised more questions than it had provided answers.

Briony put her hands together, looked at Edwin, and said, 'Well?'

Albert turned in his seat to face him. 'Edwin?'

Edwin breathed a heavy sigh. 'I should never have married Blythe, obviously. I always knew I … I could never really love a woman, not in that way.'

Briony looked at her grandad in surprise. She was expecting him to talk about her mum and Sebastian's relationship – not his own.

'When I started work as a professor at Oxford, her parents, who knew mine – both worked in academia themselves – brought Blythe, who'd just come back with them from a European tour that summer, to meet me. We hit it off, as potential friends might, but that wasn't what the meeting was about. Her parents were keen for she and I to tie the knot. So we did. I sensed she'd had her heart broken, as had I. In a way, we needed each other; were both fragile from breakups, and somehow our friendship was railroaded into marriage.'

Albert said, 'You had your heart broken?'

'He wasn't the first. And wouldn't be the last, before you came along.'

'So, she didn't know – at first?' Albert asked.

'I thought I could quash those feelings by marrying Blythe, but it was not to be. I had an affair. It didn't last long, but I couldn't hide who I was from her any longer, even though I didn't want to lose her. She was … still is … my best friend.'

Briony understood. At the time they'd met, Blythe must have been broken-hearted, thinking Frank didn't love her, and so she'd married Edwin. The marriage hadn't been right for her either.

Edwin continued, 'A few years later, after we divorced, I met someone else. It was a bit of a scandal, I suppose. At least from my perspective, as a professor falling for a student.'

Briony understood. 'The university doesn't allow personal relationships between staff and students.'

'Oh, that was long before those new rules. But even so, I felt I had to leave, get away.'

'I remember,' said Briony. She'd been nine. 'It all seemed so sudden. You'd been at the university for years, and suddenly, for what appeared to be no reason, you were leaving and moving to America.'

'That's right. But lucky me – if I hadn't made that decision, I would never have met Albert.' He took Albert's hand and squeezed it tight. Edwin suddenly looked worried. 'Does your mother know?'

'Grandad, did you really think she'd look at you any differently? She, like me, would have loved to know you weren't alone. Blythe was waiting for you to tell her yourself.'

'But you both knew I had Albert.'

'We thought he was your lodger. It's not the same as knowing you were in a long-term relationship, and had someone who obviously loves you dearly.'

'I really have been such a fool, haven't I?'

Briony frowned. 'Yes, in more ways than one. Let's talk about Sebastian.'

Albert said, 'Sebastian?'

Briony looked at Albert. She realised there were things he didn't know about her family. 'Sebastian is my real … biological father.'

Edwin looked at her, shocked. 'I thought, after all those

years of keeping you in the dark about it … that you'd never find out.'

So, that answered Briony's question – he'd known all along too that Sebastian was her father.

'Oh, right. But Lorna married Andrew.' Albert looked at Edwin as if to say, *That's right – isn't it?*

Edwin looked uncomfortable. Briony could tell he didn't want to talk about it. 'Grandad?'

'Yes, all right. You mother and Sebastian used to meet at The Beach House in the summer. I thought they were just friends until …'

'Until she got pregnant.'

'Yes.' Edwin lowered his eyes. 'Sebastian wasn't academic. He loved the ocean, surfing, diving. I could just see that if she stayed there, living in The Beach House, she'd be sucked into a life that …'

'Wasn't you?' said Albert.

Edwin looked at his hands. 'I made a mistake. I thought, *my daughter can't be in love with him. He's not right for her.* But how was I to know who was right for her? I didn't know what love truly was until I met you, Albert.'

Albert smiled at Edwin.

Edwin continued, 'That summer, when I thought I'd fallen in love with this student – it was an infatuation – and Blythe found out, it knocked her for six. The timing couldn't have been worse. She'd lost both her parents that summer, one after the other. But I'm afraid that worse was to come. Blythe discovered that they'd left The Beach House to their only grandchild. Lorna was eighteen, she could do with it as she pleased, live there, bring up her child – you – with Sebastian.'

Edwin slowly shook his head from side to side. 'I did not want that. I thought I knew what was best for her. Blythe could no longer live a lie, with me. So, we hatched a plan, or rather I did, for Blythe to go and live in The Beach House. It was what we both needed, to separate – and what I wanted; for Lorna to stay with me, in Oxford. Lorna would never find out The Beach House belonged to her. I told Blythe to hide the deeds. We both knew that Lorna would get the house eventually, just not … straight away.'

'You lied to your own daughter?' Albert said.

'Yes, about a lot of things, obviously – about The Beach House. And … about me and the real reason Blythe and I couldn't stay together.'

The room fell silent.

Briony stared at her grandfather. 'I could have had a different life, with my mum and Sebastian, growing up in that house.'

'Yes, and Blythe could have known you instead of just second-hand through me and those photos I sent of you. How was I to know Lorna would cut her out of her life – and yours?'

'But you still didn't tell my mum anything.'

Edwin studied his hands intently. 'No, because I didn't want to rock the boat. She'd met Andrew soon after starting university, and he was the most loving dad and dutiful husband that any father could have wanted for their daughter.'

Briony frowned.

'What is it?'

'I think my mum and dad, they stayed together all these years because of me. My dad … he's met someone else.' Briony paused. 'He knew, all along, didn't he?'

'Yes. Your mum told Andrew. I didn't want her to, in case

they split up. She said that he was in love with her, but she wasn't going to trick him and let him believe you were his. *Two wrongs don't make a right*, that's what she said.'

Edwin looked up at Briony. 'I thought she was happy in her life with Andrew, and she'd mend bridges with Blythe, eventually – which she has.'

'Only because I—' Briony stopped short.

'Because you …?'

'The reason why I didn't go to the Galapagos Islands, why I ran away to Suffolk, was because I found out I'm pregnant.'

'You're pregnant?' Edwin slowly stood up. 'Really? Are you sure?'

Briony threw her grandfather a deadpan look.

'Oh, how wonderful! I'm going to be a great-grandpapa.' He walked over and held out his arms.

Briony stood up and walked into his embrace. She hugged Edwin. And then stepped towards Albert. 'I hope you don't mind being a great-grandpapa too.'

Albert burst into tears, stood up and gave her a hug too.

When they all stood back, looking at one another, Edwin said, 'But how can you ever forgive me?'

'I can. I have. You see, Grandpa, I hope you don't mind me saying this, but I'm not going to repeat the same mistakes that you and Grandma – and my mum and dad – made. I'm not staying in a relationship just for convenience, or for my child.'

Edwin sat down. 'You're leaving Freddie, aren't you?'

'I have to. I've met the love of my life. Do you understand?'

Edwin glanced at Albert. 'Of course I do. Who is he?'

Briony thought what a small world it was. Years earlier, her mum had fallen in love with Frank's son. It wasn't just Edwin who had wanted to keep Lorna and Sebastian apart, but Frank too, believing that Lorna would break his son's heart, just as Blythe had apparently done to him.

'It wasn't just your fault, all of this, Grandad. Speak to Blythe about her parents – and Frank.'

Edwin looked at her blankly. 'Frank– who is Frank?'

As Briony suspected, Blythe had never told him about the young man she'd thought had broken her heart. The mess had gone down the generations, but it was stopping with her. Nobody, certainly not her parents, was going to interfere with her life, and the person she hoped she was destined to be with.

'I'm sure Blythe will tell you one day soon.'

Edwin nodded. He asked, 'Who is he – the young man you're going to marry?'

'Going to marry?' Briony stared at her grandfather, her lips suddenly parting in a huge grin. 'Yes, I suppose I am.'

Edwin was still looking at her, waiting.

'His name is Troy. I'll tell you all about him when you meet him.' Briony had decided that just then, Edwin had enough to take in without her telling him that she'd quite randomly fallen in love with Sebastian's adopted son. And how it had turned out that her paternal grandfather was her grandmother's true love.

Albert said, 'Life has a funny way of leading us to where we're meant to be.'

'And to whom we're meant to be with,' added Edwin.

Briony grinned. 'Yes, I suppose it does.' It hadn't been planned, obviously, having Freddie's baby, and marrying someone else, but then again, what family wasn't without its complications? She rested her hand on her tummy and thought of the future. There would be no more secrets in her family.

48

'You can't keep him, you know,' said Briony, throwing them a wry smile.

Briony had been watching the new grandparents, who were looking adoringly at their grandchild. They were all gathered outside on the beach. She glanced back at The Beach House. She imagined it must feel to her mum and Sebastian as though they had turned back the clock, being there together. It was how it might have been for them years earlier if things had turned out differently.

But Briony knew that if things *had* been different, her mum wouldn't have met Andrew, and she wouldn't have been raised by her wonderful dad, and met Freddie, and had her beautiful son, Sky.

She looked over at Angel. As her best friend had said, fate or serendipity had stepped in – in the form of her great-grandparents who hadn't wanted their daughter to marry a local boy, a shopkeeper's son. It was snobbery of the highest order.

That one event, keeping Blythe and Frank apart, had led them all, rightly or wrongly, to where they were today; had shaped the trajectory of all their lives. No one could turn back the clock. And Briony was glad of it.

Briony smiled at her parents as they held their grandchild. She walked over and stood beside them. 'Now, remember, it won't be long, and I'll be off on the Galapagos Islands trip, and then as soon as I return, you two will have to hand him over.'

Lorna and Sebastian managed to tear their eyes away from their grandson long enough to say, 'We know.'

Briony knew that her son would be raised by a wonderful dad, Troy, but unlike her own upbringing, Sky would know his father, Freddie, too.

'He's such a bonny baby,' commented Blythe.

Briony looked down at her grandmother, who was sitting in a deck chair, drinking a cup of tea.

Frank came over and put a protective hand on her grandmother's shoulder.

Briony exchanged a smile with the grandfather she was still getting to know. She glanced at her grandmother. It hadn't been all plain sailing for Blythe and Frank since they'd got back together. Blythe had handed over the keys to The Beach House, along with the deeds, to Lorna, who had promptly handed them to Briony. Briony had spent the remainder of her pregnancy in Oxford, studying for her master's. Her grandfather had decided to retire and had returned to live there with Albert. Briony smiled. It was where Edwin belonged. Albert had settled in well in Oxford. And it was lovely living with them.

She'd felt so lucky to get accepted straight onto a course the previous autumn, even though she had some catching up to do as lectures had already started. But the timing had fitted perfectly with her plans. She'd known that soon after the baby was born, once she'd finished the course in the summer, she would be returning to Suffolk to raise her child in The Beach House – that was non-negotiable.

The problem was Blythe. She just couldn't settle in Frank's large house.

All those bells and whistles, all that extravagance – it just wasn't her. And it wasn't Frank either. He'd proved himself to a dead couple – Blythe's parents. What Frank hadn't realised was that no amount of money would have elevated him in her parents' eyes because no amount of wealth would have changed where Frank had come from – he was the son of a shopkeeper in Cobblers Yard. That's what Blythe had told Briony during their long conversations since their first meeting all those months earlier when she'd returned from her impromptu trip to see Edwin.

Blythe had told her granddaughter what she'd said to Frank. *Could you divide the house in half, or perhaps a quarter, to make it more homely, like a little cottage?*

Of course, he couldn't do that, but as Troy had once commented, if you loved someone that much, you'd follow them anywhere to live, or up sticks and move into a little bungalow on the fringes of the town, if it made them happy.

Blythe couldn't find the little cottage she'd pictured – there were none for sale. She turned down Frank's offer to build her one. They found a little bungalow for sale, within walking distance of The Beach House, so they could visit their grandchildren and great-grandchild as often as they wished. It was just the ticket. It was, Briony realised, the place they might well have bought and retired to, if they'd been married all along.

Briony was so pleased with Frank's decision, and Troy's, to no longer live and work at Frank's old property. Frank had handed over that big house, and boathouse, to Sebastian. Not to live in; Sebastian and Lorna didn't want that. Sebastian had decided that the house, together with the boathouse, were going to be used for the benefit of the local community and schools as an outdoor activity centre, where children could grow in confidence. Sebastian would teach them sailing, canoeing and diving.

Briony would volunteer in her spare time, teaching children about North Sea marine life and ecology. It perfectly suited the new job that she would be starting after she returned from the Galapagos Islands. She'd landed a role working in North Sea marine conservation for a Suffolk wildlife charity. Going away for two months, leaving her baby and Troy, and the beautiful Suffolk Coast, was going to be the hardest thing she'd ever done, but everyone, friends and family, had persuaded her to take up her place this time.

She'd been reticent to reapply, but Troy had encouraged her, saying that if she did get a place on the research trip, it was meant to be. And she had. She had been lucky to get chosen – but this time it wasn't because someone had dropped out. And it wouldn't be long before she returned to live with Troy and Sky at The Beach House, and start her new job.

Lorna said, 'It's been a lovely wedding.'

Sebastian agreed. 'If I were to get married, I'd like to get married on this beach.'

Briony saw him raising his eyebrows at Lorna as if to say, *Would you?*

Edwin and Albert nodded enthusiastically, making Briony smile. She imagined this might catch on. At this rate, she'd have to turn The Beach House into a wedding venue.

Willow said, 'Oh yes. I want to get married on the beach.'

Briony smiled down at her sister. She was standing behind Willow, a protective arm across her chest, holding her close.

Briony recalled her mum saying that although Willow looked like Sebastian, her personality and her mannerisms reminded Lorna of Briony as a little girl. Briony got the impression that her mum was going to enjoy raising Willow with Sebastian.

Briony had had long, meaningful conversations with her grandmother, and especially with her mum, over the past few months. She'd learned that her mum and Sebastian had exchanged the shell boxes that summer, years earlier – the summer when her grandparents had passed away. Among the mementos were two keys. They had been going to write to one another, and had agreed to meet at The Beach House in the autumn; her mum had been planning to buy a train ticket and meet Sebastian there, and do something stupid-crazy – get married. Then they'd planned to figure out afterwards how she could still attend Oxford if she got a place.

Sebastian had never received her letters, and she'd never received his – Briony already knew this. But it shouldn't have stopped Sebastian getting a train to Oxford and calling on her to find out what was going on. Or stopped Lorna taking a train to Suffolk. But when Lorna had discovered she was pregnant, and had received no word back from her letters, she'd believed she had her answer – their plan to elope and marry was over.

Soon after, with the help of his father, Frank, Sebastian had taken on the responsibility of fostering Phoebe's child, Troy. He wanted to stay in Suffolk, in Troy's life, even though he'd have to wait until he was twenty-one to formally adopt him.

And then Sebastian had heard that Lorna had got a place at

Oxford University. Blythe had told someone in the village. A pint in the local pub, and village chatter, was how Sebastian had found out. And then he'd heard that she'd married a fellow Oxford University undergraduate.

Briony overheard her mum saying to Sebastian, 'I see you've been left holding the baby again.'

Her mum knew about Troy and the sacrifices Sebastian had made to raise Phoebe's child. She just wished he had known that she'd never once blamed him for what had happened to her.

Sebastian quipped, 'Holding our grandson just washes away all the years. I could be holding Troy.'

'Or Willow,' Lorna added.

'The wedding was amazing!' said Willow.

Briony smiled at her. She wasn't surprised that Willow was enthusiastic too, even though she didn't know the happy couple all that well. Willow had been a flower girl.

Willow looked up at Troy. 'When are *you* getting married?'

Troy put a finger to his lips, Briony noticed, silently shushing his sister. Briony understood. So did Troy. It wasn't their big day yet. They were hoping to keep Briony's proposal to Troy, and his acceptance, and the rings she'd bought them both – they were officially engaged – just between themselves for a little bit longer. They didn't want their news to overshadow the happy couple's big day.

They all turned to look at Freddie and Angel, who were standing by the door to the outbuilding, holding a pair of scissors in their hands, about to cut the red ribbon adorning the door.

Troy, standing behind Briony, whispered in her ear, 'Talk about déjà vu.'

Briony smile faltered at that comment. She turned around and whispered back. 'Except this time, it's not you and me standing there.'

'Thank god!' replied Troy. 'Let's hope no one comes up and interrupts proceedings like last time.'

'And embarrasses the happy couple, about to cut the ribbon,' Briony said. She exchanged a knowing smile with Troy, who added, 'Well at least we know your mother won't be turning up, asking what's going on. She agreed to the new renovations.'

'Only because you did such a fantastic job the first time around. She didn't hesitate at all in going ahead with my ideas for the outbuilding. But only on the proviso that you rolled up your sleeves and did it yourself.'

'You mean did some *real* work!'

Briony caught Sebastian smiling. He must have overheard. He winked at the in-joke.

She smiled affectionately at her new dad.

Troy was smiling too. 'I wanted to do it myself. We discussed those extra renovations months ago.'

'Even though you wouldn't be doing the work we discussed months ago so that I could live there.'

'Yes, because I knew that after completing your master's, you'd return to The Beach House.' He paused. 'How are Albert and Edwin doing now?'

'They've taken on a lodger since I left – another student who is doing a PhD, I think. Although my grandfather found it a bit strange, when he'd lived in the attic for so long, being back living in the main house.'

'But the house is his again now.'

'Yes, things have gone full circle,' commented Briony. She

smiled warmly at Edwin and Albert, who were standing together, both with wine glasses to hand, looking as though they were really enjoying themselves. They raised their glasses in her direction. She raised hers. Briony added, 'I think they got used to me being around, so they're going to visit often, and stay in the guesthouse.'

Troy nodded. 'Now he's retired, they could come down to the Suffolk Coast as often as they like.'

Briony smiled. It was true.

Her maternal grandfather wasn't the only one who'd retired. Frank had too, surprising no one with his plan to spend all his time with Blythe, and enjoying a few new hobbies.

There would also be some voluntary work thrown in; Briony had persuaded Frank to go and work for Reggie in the music shop in Cobblers Yard, in a voluntary capacity – he wouldn't be paid. It would be an interesting experience for him, working for someone else, after so many years as the boss of his own company. He'd attempted to give the music shop to Briony, saying she could the charge a peppercorn rent if she wanted. Briony wouldn't hear of it. She'd insisted that if he was giving it to her, she wanted him to give it to Reggie instead. After all, he was the one who had been working there, and looking after the place, for so many years. Besides it was his home, and as Briony had told Frank, it could be his penance for being a mean old man and upping poor Reggie's rent extortionately.

And so Reggie's business, and home, were now secure, and he had a part-time volunteer too, whom he didn't have to pay one penny piece to work for him. Briony was over the moon to hear that Reggie had forgiven Frank, and that they'd become firm friends.

It didn't take much persuading for Frank to return to the music shop, even though he did have to eat humble pie. Frank's father had always wanted him to take over the shop. Even though things hadn't turned out exactly as his father might have envisaged, Frank had told Briony that he knew his father would be so happy if he could see him now, keeping the old music shop, and his legacy, alive. It was the reason Frank had not sold the music shop years earlier. He said he was a sentimental old fool, and glad of it.

He'd told Briony that in the beginning, after he'd left the Navy, when he'd inherited the music shop and had just set up his property business, the shop had been a fallback – something small where he could live and just about earn a living if his budding property empire went south. But in his heart – and he had never been able to explain it – he'd always thought, despite his success, that one day he'd be back. He just hadn't expected it to be quite like this – as a volunteer working for somebody else – although he couldn't have been happier with the arrangement.

As with the house he'd passed to his son, and the blessing he'd given to his grandson, Troy, to change the business model to his own vision, Frank knew that with the music shop, it was time to give something back – quite literally.

It was his singing though, his gift, that Briony, Blythe, Lorna, and The Gossip Girls – who had been so happy to meet him again after all those years – were having a hard time persuading him to use. He abjectly refused to apply for a place on one of the talent shows on television. He did not want to be a celebrity, even if it meant the world could hear his beautiful singing voice.

Blythe had told him, *You'd be bringing joy to so many people.* But he wouldn't budge on the issue.

The Gossip Girls had suggested something closer to home, something less in the television spotlight. They'd heard of a little old rundown theatre by the sea that had recently closed. It was a lovely place, but there was a rumour that if it didn't find a buyer soon, and prove profitable, an unscrupulous developer was going to swoop in, buy it, and demolish it.

Mabel had said to Frank, only semi-jokingly, *That wasn't you – was it?* To which he'd replied, *What would I want with an old, rundown theatre?*

It wasn't Frank who was after the place, and he had no idea who it was.

Briony eyed Frank. She had him in her sights. She'd been trying to persuade him to consider investing in the old theatre. But he knew her game. Next, she'd be after him appearing on stage in the shows. Briony frowned, recalling her conversation with him. And he'd told them that Troy had all the money – he now ran the company – and that Sebastian owned the house. He'd said, *If you're that interested, ask them. They hold the purse strings now.*

Lorna and Sebastian weren't interested just then – understandably they didn't have time to take on a rundown theatre. They had a grandchild to look after for the next couple of months. Although they were hoping, with Briony around for part of the summer, that they'd also have some time to themselves.

Briony had an inkling what they were after doing. She glanced at the sailboat, bobbing on the water. She'd overheard Sebastian and her mum talking, making plans to relive some of their youth – and rekindling another one of her mother's lost loves – diving for wrecks off the Suffolk Coast.

Briony's thoughts returned to her grandfather, and the old theatre that was waiting for a miracle to happen – for someone to come along and revive its fortunes before it was too late.

Troy didn't have time for that either – he had a business to run.

The Gossip Girls said they'd get involved if Troy bought it. But as he'd pointed out, they were octogenarians, and they had a charity shop to run. It would take more than them, and the help of some of their friends, to make a theatre profitable.

So, Briony had shelved that idea – for the time being, hoping that the little theatre did not go under offer or end up swallowed up and spat out by a large corporation before she found time to consider other options – meaning trying to twist Frank's arm to get involved. She knew he must have some money tucked away somewhere.

In the meantime, she had found a choir in the local church that was after a tenor. She hadn't told him yet. Could he be persuaded now he had so much time on his hands after handing over the company reins to Troy?

Thinking of Troy, Briony recalled that at first, months earlier, he had refused to take over Frank's company, insisting that he was going to stay with Briony in Oxford while she completed her masters.

Briony wouldn't have minded, but she wanted Troy to get on with realising his vision of the company, and she knew that in his heart it was where he belonged.

While she had been in Oxford, they had seen each other most weekends. It had meant that Troy had been able to start straight away with his vision for the property development company he'd taken over from his grandfather. He wanted to build ecologically sustainable, affordable homes for local people; homes that didn't damage the beauty of the Suffolk coastal environment. The work was already underway.

They hadn't had a problem with their long-distance relationship for those few months before Sky was born. They both knew they would be together for the rest of their lives following her studies and her research trip, so what was a few short months? And now there they were, in the summer, with just the research trip on the horizon before Briony moved to Suffolk permanently.

Briony was so happy that Freddie and Angel had arranged their wedding so that she could attend before she set off.

Troy had completed the work on the outbuilding before Freddie and Angel's wedding so that they could spend their honeymoon there. Briony knew that it was going to be lovely for them, spending their honeymoon in the guesthouse, if a little unorthodox; Freddie was going to spend some time getting to know his son and being a hands-on dad for a bit while Briony was away on her trip. It was what Angel wanted too.

Briony took Troy's hand as someone shouted out, 'Drum roll!'

Freddie and Angel prepared to cut the ribbon.

'You did such a lovely job of redesigning and renovating the outbuilding.' Briony squeezed Troy's hand.

'I missed our sunrises together, though,' said Troy wistfully.

Briony grinned, looking over at The Beach House. 'Well, we will be making up for that very soon.'

Troy grinned too. 'I can't wait. He took her arm in his. 'Have you decided who's going to walk you down the aisle, or more specifically, along the beach, at our wedding?'

'My dad – of course.'

'Sebastian? It's going to be weird having my dad walk you down the aisle.'

Briony shook her head. 'No, he's your dad. I mean *my* dad.' She looked over at Andrew, who was there with his new partner, Susan. Except she wasn't new; they'd been together some time.

Troy looked at Briony quizzically. 'You mean Andrew?'

'Of course, Andrew. He'd be devastated if I didn't choose him. And besides, I'd be devastated if he didn't walk me down the aisle. He's my dad. Do you understand?'

'Of course I do. Like Sebastian is my dad.'

She hugged his arm tight. Drew him close to her. 'I can't wait until our big day.'

'I know. Neither can I, but I'm glad we planned it for the autumn, after you get back. It will be significant – a year to the day since we first met. I just hope it will be beach weather, like last October.'

'Me too. I've made sure my dad has put the date in his diary so that he and his partner don't disappear on a cruise.'

'They look very much in love,' Troy said. 'I hope you don't mind me saying.'

Briony looked over at her dad, standing with the love of his life. Briony cast a glance over at her mum and Sebastian. 'They stayed together all those years for me, Troy.'

'Your mum and Andrew?'

'Yes. When I found out, I realised I didn't want that to be Freddie's and my story.'

'It couldn't have been, could it?' Troy observed.

'No, you're right.' She thought about what would have happened if she had gone on her research trip the previous autumn, as she'd planned. With her out of the picture, she thought her two best friends would have got together. Fate had a way of bringing people together – eventually. She looked at Freddie and Angel. 'It was just meant to be.'

'Like you and me,' said Troy, smiling.

'Oh, yes, Troy – like you and me.'

'Wish you weren't going on that research trip,' mumbled Troy.

'I know.' Briony didn't know how to be apart from Troy and Sky for eight weeks. It would not be the same as the last few months when they'd seen each other often. But there was Skype, and if their separation got too much, she could always fly home. But she *was* going. Everyone knew that. Like her master's, and the new job she had lined up, it was just something she had to do.

Her parents knew the plan; once Freddie and Angel returned to Oxford after their honeymoon, Troy would be moving into the guesthouse and getting to know both his new stepson and his new stepmum. Lorna had resigned from her teaching position in Oxford and let go of her music lessons, taking over Blythe's music students there on the Suffolk Coast.

Troy said, 'I hope your parents are going to be okay giving up The Beach House, and Sky, on your return.'

'Oh, they'll have to be.' Although Briony knew they wouldn't be giving up Sky completely; with her new job in marine conservation, and Troy's property business, her mum and Sky's great-grandparents were all going to be very hands-on. They'd have to be.

She looked at Troy. 'Thinking of our new home, I think Sebastian has plans for him and Mum.'

'Really? You know something, don't you?'

'I do.'

49

Sebastian stared at the baby in his arms. 'My only regret is that we'll only have him with us while Briony goes on her trip, and when she returns, she'll move here with her own little family.'

Lorna sighed. 'I feel the same way too.'

'We could plan to go on a cruise together, in the autumn – if that would make you feel better.'

Lorna shook her head.

'Briony told me you'd always wanted to go on one.'

'Not anymore.'

'What changed your mind?' As soon as he'd uttered those words, his eyes darted Andrew's way, and his lips formed into a great big *oh*. 'Sorry, that was a stupid question.'

'Not at all.' Her eyes drifted to Andrew too. 'He's not the reason I changed my mind about the cruise.'

'Briony said you wanted an adventure.'

Lorna looked at Sky, and then at Sebastian. 'I think my adventure is just beginning.'

Sebastian grinned.

She drew close, staring down at the baby in his arms. 'I've got everything I'll ever want right here, on this beach, with you.

It's just …'

'You don't want to leave The Beach House either – do you?'

'Don't you dare say anything to Briony.'

He smiled. 'Cross my heart.'

'I'm not going to repeat Blythe's mistakes. The transfer of the deeds into her name is already in hand.'

'Yes, I know. You're using my father's solicitors to do the transfer, aren't you?'

'Yes. Ironic, isn't it, considering—'

'We won't talk about that, if you don't mind.'

'No, we won't. All is forgiven.' She paused. 'It's just that this place … I've got some wonderful memories here, of you and me, when we were young.'

'That summer to remember?'

'Yes, when we were last together.'

'I know. Here, take Sky for a moment, will you?'

'You won't get him back in a hurry,' she joked, carefully holding the baby's head as she cradled him in the crook of her arm.

'I have something for you.' Sebastian bent down and whispered something in Willow's ear.

Willow grinned and ran into The Beach House. She returned and stood in front of Lorna with something behind her back.

'What have you got there, sweetheart?'

Luna ran up the beach towards Willow and stood sniffing what was in her hand. Willow made a big show of taking it out from behind her back. 'Surprise!'

'Hey – I recognise that!' Lorna looked at Sebastian in surprise. 'You kept it all these years?'

'Oh yes.'

'I kept mine too.'

'I found I couldn't bear to look at it, though,' said Sebastian. 'I'm afraid it just reminded me of a life that might have been – a life with you. So I put it away. Willow found it.'

'Yes, Briony found mine when she was around Willow's age, but I still couldn't bring myself to part with it.'

'Me neither.'

Lorna had to reluctantly hand Sky back to Sebastian. She took the shell box.

'Look inside,' Sebastian prompted.

Lorna opened the shell box. She looked over and caught Briony smiling. She had a feeling there was a little conspiracy going on.

Lorna looked inside the box and got out the wolf necklace. 'Hey, this used to be in my box!' She glanced at Sebastian. That's when she noticed there was a pendant on a chain hanging around his neck. It must have been tucked out of sight in his shirt.

He said, 'Troy had mine. I asked for it back.'

Lorna put it on.

'What's this?' She'd found something else in the shell box. 'It doesn't look like the key to The Beach House that I gave you.'

'It isn't. It's the key to our future together.'

'Huh?'

'I finally had some money off dad. He's passed the business to Troy, but insisted on giving me a lump sum in shares, which I cashed in. I decided this time I could not refuse.'

Lorna smiled. She knew what that money meant. 'No more deep-sat diving? I heard all about it from Willow.'

'No more deep-sat diving. I'm staying right here, with you and Willow. And my daughter, son and grandchild.'

'We'll have to get a place – you and me, once Troy and Briony move into The Beach House for good.'

'Yes.'

'It will have to be close. I need to see Sky every single day.'

'Me too.' Sebastian grinned. 'I've got that covered.'

Lorna narrowed her eyes. 'What do you mean, you've got that covered? What are you up to?'

He pointed. 'Up the beach there. That wouldn't be a bad spot, would it?'

'For what – a house?' Lorna brightened. 'Not at all. Then we'd be practically next-door neighbours.' She frowned. 'But someone's already building a white clapboard beach house in the perfect spot.'

'Yep.'

He held up an identical key.

She looked at the keys, then at the clapboard house. 'No way! It's ours?'

'Oh yes. We'll make lots of memories there. There'll be lots of summers, just like this one, to remember.'

Lorna looked at Sebastian. 'Hold that thought – I'll be right back.'

Briony was talking to Angel and Freddie before they stepped into the outbuilding, ready for their honeymoon, when her mum came marching towards her and took her hand. 'Come on.'

Briony looked at her quizzically. 'Where are we going?'

'Not far.'

On the way, she collected Blythe too. 'Where are we going?' she asked as they helped her out of the deckchair.

'You'll see.'

Briony shrugged at her grandmother. She had no idea what it

was all about either. The three of them walked, hand in hand, Blythe in the centre, Lorna and Briony either side, down to the water's edge. Behind them, the summer sun was setting.

They stood together, staring out to sea. 'It's a beautiful sunset,' commented Briony enjoying the cloudless sky ablaze in red and pink hues as the sun set behind the house. 'Almost as amazing as the sunrises here.'

The three women watched the sky turn a beautiful shade of pink until Lorna broke the silence. 'I'm loving this summer, Mum, with you and Frank, Troy, Briony, Sebastian and the baby.'

Blythe turned around and glanced at The Beach House. 'It's felt like old times, when your grandparents were alive, Lorna, and the house was full of people and laughter, and they used to have parties on the beach. Do you remember?'

Lorna nodded. 'Of course I remember.'

Briony noticed her grandmother frown for a moment. She asked her, 'You still have fond memories of those times, even now you know your parents were responsible for keeping you and Frank apart?'

'I do. Yes. I realise that they thought they were doing right by me, keeping us apart, and encouraging me to 'marry well,' as they put it.'

There was a pause. Lorna turned to her mum. 'Where did you get that funny-looking dog, Luna? I've been meaning to ask.'

'Is that what you brought me down to the water's edge for, to ask that question?'

'No, of course not. I just wanted a moment with my mum and daughter, just the three of us together, to savour this beautiful sunset.' She paused. 'But I'd still like to know about the dog.'

Briony laughed. She wanted to know too. Ever since she'd discovered her grandmother had a wolfdog, she had been wondering the same thing. Emily had asked Blythe once, but she'd been evasive, even though she did have all the paperwork, so the breeder was legitimate.

Briony glanced at her mum. 'Luna is a wolfdog.'

'Yes, I know. And I know something else – it's not exactly the sort of thing I imagine you go to a breeder to buy. Not like Wilbur.'

Briony looked about her, but she guessed where Wilbur was, back on his favourite sofa in The Beach House. He'd settled well into the attic room in Oxford over the past few months, getting on with the change of scenery, but his heart, like Briony's, belonged in Suffolk.

Out of the corner of her eye, Briony saw Luna heading towards them. Luna stood in front of them at the water's edge, looking out to sea.

Blythe turned to her daughter, reaching up to touch the wolf necklace around Lorna's neck. 'You're wearing it again.'

Briony looked at the necklace too. She smiled. Sebastian had given her the shell box with the necklace, that Briony had given to him to pass on to her mum, and the keys to their new home. They were going to be neighbours.

'Has it got something to do with this necklace – you getting a wolfdog puppy?'

'No, not at all. That's just a coincidence.'

'Oh, okay.'

Blythe stared at her dog and sighed. 'You know, it was the silliest thing. Your father always worried I was lonely at The Beach House, living here on my own.'

Briony glanced at her mum, who also knew that after the divorce, her parents had remained friends – or co-conspirators, as Lorna had light-heartedly called them – with Edwin keeping Blythe updated about her daughter and granddaughter in exchange for her keeping his secret; unnecessary as his secrecy had turned out to be.

Blythe continued, 'Over the years, he hoped I'd meet someone, like he'd met Albert. So, when I didn't, eventually he did the stupidest thing and bought me a puppy, sending it over from America, with the paperwork and everything.'

Lorna and Briony gaped at her. 'Grandad sent you a wolfdog puppy, from America?'

Blythe rolled her eyes. 'Of course he hadn't actually seen the puppies. He'd chatted to a guy on the phone who had just the thing, apparently.'

'A wolfdog puppy?'

'No, a Welsh corgi puppy.'

Briony exchanged a glance with her mum. She had to ask, 'How on earth did he get that so wrong?'

'The young man's American accent, I imagine. Apparently, he spoke really fast.'

'Oh, my goodness! Only Dad could make a mistake like that.' Lorna cupped her hand over her mouth.

Briony looked at her mum and could tell she was trying to stifle a laugh.

'So, he had the puppy shipped unseen to me, and of course I fell in love with her instantly.'

Briony and Lorna burst out laughing. Lorna said, 'Dad can be so silly sometimes. At least his heart was in the right place.'

Blythe turned serious. 'Not always. Lorna. Can you really put the past behind you, and forgive the mistakes your father and I made? I just worry, now you're back for good, that you'll start to have resentments about what might have been if … if …'

Briony looked at her mum and held her breath. Although her mum and grandmother were no longer estranged, her grandmother did have a point – all those years her mum and Sebastian could have been together, those lost years, were because of them.

Lorna put an arm around her mum's shoulders. 'Of course I can. This isn't about the past anymore. This is about the future.'

They both turned to look at Briony.

Briony grinned, guessing they were talking about her and her baby. She held her grandmother's hand.

Lorna turned to her mum. 'Well, I guess we'd better head back to The Beach House. The wedding reception will be starting any minute, once the happy couple have changed.'

'You mean the beach party,' Briony corrected her. She looked down the beach, in the direction of the car park, and saw people carrying lanterns, making their way along the beach. They were all her friends – the people from the local community nearby, and in Aldeburgh and Cobblers Yard; people whom, with Freddie and Angel's agreement, she'd invited to a beach party. She'd also promised them all that the party wouldn't be cut short this time.

Briony's attention was drawn to the newly renovated guesthouse just as Freddie and Angel stepped outside. She waved before turning her attention back to her grandmother and mum. They weren't looking Freddie and Angel's way. She knew who had caught their attention – Sebastian, who was holding the newest member of their blended family.

Blythe still had hold of Briony's hand. She took Lorna's hand in the other and said, 'We're making new memories, the three of us.' She held their hands tight.

They each shared her sentiments when she said, 'This has truly been a summer to remember.'

The Sunrise Coast Series continues in

The Little Theatre by the Sea

Paperback and Kindle eBook available soon from Amazon

If you enjoyed *A Summer to Remember*, I would be grateful if you would leave a review on Amazon.

For further details about the author and her novels, visit the author's website.

www.elisedarcy.com

Printed in Dunstable, United Kingdom

72956885R00255